Publisher: Rutgers University
Executive Editor: J.T. Barbarese
Senior Contributing Editor: M.M.M. Hayes
Senior Advisory Editor: Howard Marchitello
Senior Associate Editors: Lisa Zeidner, Lauren Grodstein, Jayne Anne Phillips.
Managing Editor: Zac Roesch
Editorial Assistants: Matt Charles, Jonathan Deane, Timika Elliot, Peter Gambino, Barry Graham, Therese Halscheid, Jay McKean, Amy O'Hearn, Scott Oliver.
Founding Editors: Pam Painter, Tom Bracken, F.R. Katz, Thalia Selz, and Delores Weinberg.

StoryQuarterly, founded in 1975, is an independent magazine of short fiction published by Rutgers University in Camden, New Jersey. We welcome submissions year round only through our submissions portal, which is available at http://storyquarterly.camden.rutgers.edu/. We no longer accept hardcopy or surface-mailed submissions. Any opinions expressed in this magazine are not necessarily the opinions of the staff. For subscriptions, please visit us online. For all other correspondence, email the editors at story.quarterly@camden.rutgers.edu.

StoryQuarterly
Department of English
311 North Fifth Street
Rutgers University
Camden, NJ 08102

Book design and cover design by Zac Roesch
Website by Denise Avayou

Rutgers University - Camden

StoryQuarterly

From the Senior Contributing Editor

Swimming Upstream
M. M. M. Hayes

Reading thousands of submissions, as most literary publications that accept submissions online now do, we see larger movements in what's being written and thought about, and our instincts have been honed afresh. The number of workshops and MFA programs nationally has lifted the quality of writing. Most of what we see is very well crafted, sometimes glittering. The bar has been raised for the quality of the writing, which means that the level of reading too has been raised. Hallelujah. But what then distinguishes the story that hooks and holds us?

More and more, we read rough criticism about *subject matter*. An excellent southern editor says bluntly, "No one is writing about anything important. It's all the same." He even says to his readers, "For Christ's sake, write something we may want to read." Elif Batuman, in a recent *London Review of Books*, says American writing in particular is writing in a Knowledge Vacuum—of the masters: Dickens, Shakespeare, Cervantes, even Proust, Joyce—or even History, Geography, Climate, and religious or secular background and thinking.

Batuman also attacks foreign or "victimization" stories that abound as writers try to stand out, be exotic, or perhaps out of a shame at being American and not devastated by war, famine, pestilence or conquest, or White, or affluent enough to be able to afford writing time.

I hate to say I agree but mostly I do. Reading thousands of stories a month, an editor sees the same overly familiar coming-of-age story; relationship/marriage story; the death of a loved one story; and yes, the growing up victimized by parents and/or schoolmates story. Nothing happens. Again and again, the story stays in the mind of a narrator, usually a first person narrator. After too many of these, set nowhere, a reader needs to open a window for fresh air. Lots of writers are "getting it right," but it's becoming a template that spins its own cocoon and doesn't let in the outside world—which exists everywhere, wanted or not. But I'm not just bitching about the state of current writing. What I see are missed opportunities. A writer doesn't need to be born in lower Tasmania of Lapland to be exotic, or more importantly, *unfamiliar*. These qualities are all around us, but we're not seeing them in fiction. Batuman feels that we're seeing better non-fiction than fiction now because the non-fiction writer is forced to write from knowledge; the reader learns something. Fair point, but anything the non-fiction writer uses is also there for the fiction writer. Why not?

I spend a lot of each summer in the West's high country, and one year, I returned to the Midwest quickly and opened a car door to notice the August scream of locusts in a thick stand of trees. After the light air of the mountains, the Midwest's rich, moist air fell on me like a heavy blanket that nourished the bright green breadbasket of our country for over a million square miles. I could no longer see the Big Sky between the branches—all those darn trees. I noticed what I always knew: that the Midwest if a natural *forest*. Weeds that pop up and are hard to pull out will turn into wild oak trees. The whole region lies on a mesh of thickly knotted roots. And where is some silence? Lay in bed at night and listen: clocks, hum of electricity, the refrigerator going on or off, the house creaking, maybe the little scratching of a mouse or chipmunk in the wall, airplanes, cars nearby, the distant blat of a commuter train. You can't find silence if you try.

W. D. Wetherell told a group once, "Write everything as if your reader lived in China." If readers lived in China, how many of them would guess any of these things about the Midwest, or any other region, from current fiction? The same is true of stories set in cities, where at best you might get a street name and a Starbucks or a bar. Hemingway could set a city by looking at the mirror behind the bartender and noticing a few details that brush-stroked the whole tone of the room.

Dinosaurs, then Indians, then religious refugees from Europe, then came the "tired, the poor, the huddled masses." This is a collage of regions heavy with narrative. It's in every single thing one picks up—rocks, broken springs, Ipods—a history. Little of this ever appears about any region. This knowledge affects the politics, religion and work lives of the people, what they actually think about, but how often do you see such inner life?

Knowledge doesn't need to be from Shakespeare, Proust, and Dickens, although certainly there's plenty there. The European approach, until recently, was to study Chemistry, Psychology, and Engineering, not creative writing. Then the writer wrote from life knowledge. Putting together knowledge with fine writing seems a reasonable idea.

Viewpoint: I haven't read a good book in the last two or three years that didn't use multiple viewpoints. Yet when I suggested better and multiple use of viewpoints in a lecture recently, someone commented that viewpoint "shifts" brought out the "police" in workshops. Police. Wow. Is conformity an objective? When did more than one viewpoint become a "shift"? Annie Proulx can put five or six viewpoints in a single paragraph and the reader is always absolutely clear who is thinking what (see *Shipping News*). Clarity would seem to be a better bottom line.

A first-person viewpoint is easier to write, but Proust talked of viewpoints as prisms on a sphere, and he used these slices like strobe lights to illuminate the dark corners of the ordinary, which, in his hands, became the exotic— *something floating in a cup of tea*. Reams are now written about the role of memory, but Proust conjured it with a time shift in viewpoint.

This summer, millions read the three Swedish books by Stieg Larsson, *Girl with the Dragon Tattoo*, and sequels. They weren't as well written as submissions we see, at least the

English translations weren't, and they are genre fiction, but after 2000 pages, you had traveled to Sweden, tromped about the Arctic Circle, soaked in Swedish culture and bad coffee, and sorted out convoluted plotting while bad guys crept up on you in the dark around isolated permafrost cabins. This totally foiled everyday-ness. And those taciturn Swedes did have inner lives, albeit secular ones.

Poet Ted Kooser said in The Writers' Chronicle, "If you want people to read more poetry, write books people want to read." So what do people want to read? Five million or so viewers watched the finale of the Kardashian Sisters reality show. What glues people to these careening bauble/women—clothes, cars, the glut of the things? Too easy. Pay attention. What is it about celebrity that obsesses our own culture? Yeah or nay, it's the competition. Study what worked, take what is useable, and go on. Shakespeare stooped to steal.

The audience for genre fiction or the Kardashian sisters is neither less than bright, nor poorly educated. In my extended family, I have a Ph.D. who regularly makes lists of women who have broken the glass ceiling, and she says about any fiction at all, "Why would I want to come home and read something trying to manipulate me? I get that at work. I get that when I come home to my children." It pays to listen to this.

I once sent a group of high school teachers home to read Carver's "The Cathedral." The next day a couple of them claimed they couldn't read it because they hated the narrator: This blind man, an old friend of my wife's, he was on his way to spend the night. Look what they missed by standing publicly on the "right side" of disliking a bigot. Weren't they judging him the same way he judged the blind man? Look at the incredible trip they missed, the trip taken by this man who couldn't distance himself enough from "this blind man," and came to "see" the cathedral in a way he never could have before.

Kooser said in the same Writers' Chronicle article, "I look for marvelous under every stone on the road. To show my readers something remarkable about an ordinary, ubiquitous thing is part of my calling as a writer." I vote for Kooser. That sounds about right to me, and not because the subject matter is Nothing, but because he finds in it Something.

On Denise Gess's Trespasses
Paul Lisicky

A writer works on a novel for years. She wakes up with it, she goes to bed with it. She loves it like a person, tenderly, even if that person is recalcitrant, a bit of a shithead, with ideas of his own of where he'd like to go. The writer gives up so much to tend to this person. He won't answer her phone calls when she needs him, won't bring her a cup of green tea when she has strep throat. But he'll be there when she has seventeen comp essays to grade that night. Or he'll sit beside her on her bed twenty minutes before her family's about to come across the river for a holiday dinner. She's grateful for those times, though. Her life has meaning in those times, all of her wanting alchemized into order, drama, beauty.

Not that those times are enough. The novel must be shared, as a holiday dinner must be shared: simple as that. It's not alive if it ends up on a hard drive on some outdated computer in the back of a garage. But the sharing part is hard. What if she's done everything she could to make that sharing happen? She's written a good book, of course. And all the editors like it, but never enough to buy it. Well, what do you do but blame yourself and decide to write the damn thing all over again? Over and over and over again, and even give it a different name: *Second Love*. But how do you write it over again when your head is already onto the next thing, and new things are tugging at your coat, not the least of which is a terminal illness, which must be taken care of with all the tenderness of a novel.

This is the story of Denise Gess's third novel, *Trespasses*, a lovely book that should have found its way into the world while she was alive, but didn't because of external reasons: bad timing, a distracted agent, a greedy publishing industry.

This is what we have of it: the opening chapter, originally published in the *North American Review* back in 1990. In these pages, we meet Rosalie Rucci, who's content with Lenny, her husband of many years, who has a secret life, a life that will undo the orderly, comfortable retirement they've been working toward. So much happens in these pages: we see Rosalie's dedication to routine, we see Rosalie's shock, and then the heat of confrontation, where Rosalie probably learns that she has more ferocity and commitment than she knew.

One thing that shines in these pages is Denise's refusal to categorize these characters. I think a less generous writer would be prone to patronizing Lenny and Rosalie, to seeing them through some restricting blue collar lens, as if their struggles would somehow be related to the fact that they didn't have much money, that they weren't educated at Princeton, and didn't spend their summers on Nantucket or The Vineyard. She writes about these characters as John Cheever would write about his own, with elegance, detachment, and a little wit. They might as well be from Greenwich not Somerdale, New Jersey, and in doing that, she does a political thing but doesn't wave a sign about it. She makes it all look easy: the language, the confrontation, the unexpected urge toward possibility. She writes with the grace of a singer who's sure of her phrasing and never needs to push too hard.

Denise Gess
1952 - 2009

Coda: Talking to Denise
William Lutz

The third novel began tentatively. The voice of a female character spoke often to Denise, but it wasn't clear what her story was. Other characters joined her, each voice adding to the confusion. Suddenly, a man appeared and joined the narrative. Still, Denise wasn't sure where they were taking her. The story changed, sometimes radically, even as characters and voices changed. The manuscript grew but reached what Denise said was a dead end. So she started over, trying to figure out who these people were and what were they trying to tell her.

And so it went. Denise wrote almost every night. That's when she was happiest, when the writing went well. There was a rhythm to our life, a rhythm based on writing and the worlds and people that writing created and in which Denise lived part of her life. Every morning, she would emerge from her little writing house in our back yard. Sometimes the news was good: "Jack really opened up to me last night. The words just flowed." Sometimes her people abandoned her: "It's all crap. It isn't going any place. I don't know what he was saying." Why were they doing this to her, she asked and poured another cup of coffee.

We did not measure time by the usual metrics. Hours meant little, and days of the week were vague markers of some necessary human activities. Shopping, paying bills, laundry were addressed only after paying due attention to the call of the writing house. The passion she had for and poured into her writing was the same passion she had for life and for people, all kinds of people. She loved and cared for all the characters in her writing just as much as she cared for all the people in her life. Which is why she could be so devastated when her characters let her down.

The novel was not going well and it hadn't been going well for a while. She spoke little during our morning coffee, and I knew not to ask or say anything. She suffered alone in that dark area that only writers know. The most she would say is that it wasn't going anywhere, it just wasn't working, it just didn't make sense. How could they do this to her? I made another pot of coffee.

Sometimes she asked for my help, bombarding me with questions. What did I think Jack should do? Did I think the house burning down was believable? I had no answers and offered none. I became an expert in the indefinite reply, a few words unarticulated in a voice that trailed into silence. She wasn't listening anyway. She stared out the window at her writing house and sipped her coffee. She would have to go back there, to that little house, to those people who weren't talking. She would have to face the terror of the blank page and the silence of her people.

Then, one morning, she mentioned that someone new had spoken to her, someone who was barely a minor character in the novel. She was surprised but fascinated by this voice. During the next days, the voice grew strong and clear. Rosalie emerged and she was followed by Lenny. They were telling Denise a whole new story. Gone were all the previous characters and their world. Now, there was Rosalie and Lenny and their family. They spoke so much Denise couldn't quiet them if she wanted to. As if by magic she knew these people, knew everything about them, their life together, their family. She could tell me what they were like as teenagers, how they met, every detail of their thirty-eight year marriage. So real were these people I expected to have them come to our house for dinner. To Denise, they were as real as I was, and she knew them as well as she knew me.

Over morning coffee during the next few months, I came to know these characters and their lives. I marveled at the creative process as I watched a writer give birth to real people with real experiences in the pages of her third novel. Or was it her fourth novel? Because Denise left a manuscript of another novel, an unfinished novel, because they had stopped talking to her. Now, that novel can never be completed because those characters have no one to talk to, no one to whom they can tell their story. Denise isn't here to listen to them, and without her, there is no one to give them life and tell their story. There is only the empty writing house, the blank page, and the silence.

Trespasses
Denise Gess

There were several people at the cosmetic counter when the saleslady curtly held our Rosalie Rucci's MasterCard and told her that it had been rejected.

The saleslady's voice was shrill and she snapped her wrist twice, card in hand before Rosalie could take it from her. "I haven't used this in almost a year," Rosalie said, but the woman had already pushed her purchases—a bottle of liquid foundation and a mascara—off to the side,

"You'll have to talk to Credit."

Rosalie glanced at the woman standing beside her, hoping for sympathy, but the woman averted her eyes, and in that instant, Rosalie felt her confusion turn into humiliation. Clearly, the saleslady and this other customer had already defined her as a deadbeat, or careless, or simply stupid for not knowing there was a problem with her card. She backed away from the counter that glittered with silver and gold-capped bottles, sleek black compacts, and hourglass flasks of expensive perfumes, but she told the saleslady, "I'll be back for those," and pointed to the makeup.

It was a sweltering Saturday afternoon, mid-August, and the shopping mall was crowded. Rosalie disliked the malls and still preferred unrestrained, city-street shopping, but years of living in the suburbs had made driving into the city seem an extraordinary inconvenience. There was something insistent about mall shopping that rattled her, and whenever her daughters dragged her out with them, she noticed that they moved from store to store with grace and determination and left the mall, swinging packages, grinning as if they'd just been released from a funhouse. They had credit cards in their own names, not the names of their husbands. The card

Rosalie had with her that day was in her husband's name:
Mr. Leonard Rucci. Her daughters often teased her about
this, but she told them, "If your father has to see the bill, it'll
keep me from going haywire and buying out the store." And
they would roll their eyes at her because they'd never known
their mother to go "haywire."

Rosalie was pretty in a plain way, with broad high
cheekbones and smooth olive skin. She wore a simple, pinkish
lipstick and some powder on her face, and her clothes too
were simple and tasteful, chosen always to hide the girth
of her hips. She was fifty-eight years old, and in the past,
year she'd been giving a lot of thought to doing things
differently in her life. She had signed up for an aerobics
class two evenings a week, and although Lenny disapproved
and grumbled about it, she took a part-time job in a card
store three days a week. There was a small bookstore in the
shopping plaza where she worked, and while she'd never
been much of a reader, now sometimes on her lunch hour
she would wander in to page through books and magazines.
She read articles about "empty nesters" and the second half
of long marriages. She even flipped through the pages of
a book about sex in middle age and was surprised at the
ink illustrations of sexual positions. The drawings were
meant to be realistic renderings of older bodies—men with
slight paunches, and thinning hair; women with rounded
bellies from childbearing and soft upper arms, less than firm
breasts. In all of the drawings, the expressions on the faces
of the men and women were just short of shock. There were
positions she and Lenny had never tried, or been aware of
in their thirty-eight year marriage, and her lack of sexual
technique made her feel slightly naive and dowdy. One day,
holding the book shyly to her chest, she made it halfway to
the checkout counter, then changed her mind and returned
it to the shelf. But many nights while Lenny lay snoring
loudly beside her, she wondered if she should go back and
purchase it after all. Other than these brief misgivings about
whether she and Lenny were behaving as older marrieds

should, Rosalie felt their life together was a pleasant one. On weekends, they had dinner with friends, or went our to the movies, or drove to Atlantic City to see a show at the casinos. It wasn't a jet set life by any means, but she was happy with it right now, however, as she stepped onto the escalator and made her way to the credit department. She was stupefied by the embarrassing scene that had taken place at the register. Lenny usually dealt with the business of credit and taxes, mortgages and car payments, and it was unlike him to forget to pay a bill. She pushed down the tide of suspicion that the problem might be more serious. Lately, he'd come home from his mail route so tired he would fall asleep in the chair before the evening news. When she questioned him about it, he said, "Nothing's wrong—except that I'm old." But twice in the past week, she woke from a sound sleep to find him staring out into the night from the bedroom window. Now, she wondered if he was sick and keeping it from her, so sick that he'd gotten sloppy with the bills.

The credit department was on the second floor, and Rosalie was relieved to find it bustling, too. Apparently she was not alone in this. When it was her turn, she stepped up to the high Formica counter and slid her card across to the customer relations expert. "The cosmetic department sent me," she explained. "The computer downstairs rejected it."

The young woman behind the counter smiled and took the card. "We'll just check it out here." She turned away and moved to her computer. Rosalie watched the amber figures and lists appear on the screen, watched the woman's fingers flying over the keyboard, the pause she took when the screen flashed something new, the frown on her face. She held a finger up and said, "Just want to double check." Then began the process again. Finally, the woman made a quick phone call and spoke in low tones that Rosalie couldn't distinguish, then she handed Rosalie the card. "I'm sorry," she said, "but that card is $200 over the permitted limit and it's a month overdue."

Rosalie laughed. "Now I know there's a mistake. We

didn't buy anything costing that much. I haven't even seen a bill for anything."

The young woman shrugged. "Well, you'd better call your bank. Talk to them. The computer shows a total of $8,200 and your limit is $8,000."

For several seconds Rosalie was speechless then she was shouting. "Eight thousand two hundred? It's impossible!"

"I'm sorry," the woman said.

As Rosalie walked away from the counter, she swallowed hard and the taste was sour. She had to pass the furniture department on her way to the "Down" escalator and felt so light-headed she plopped into one of the plush chairs in the middle of a living room display. At first, everything was a blur, a collision of colors and sounds she couldn't assimilate, but once she caught her breath, she remembered that they'd been talking about a new living room suite too, some papering and painting. She lifted the price tag that was hanging off the arm of the chair. Seven hundred dollars. Then she leaned forward to read the tag on the coffee table. Fifteen hundred dollars. She looked all around the decorator room and mentally listed the objects in it, estimating the price when a salesman touched her shoulder. "May I help you?" he asked.

She stood up waving her hand in the air. "How much would a room like this cost?"

He quickly withdrew a mini-calculator from his breast pocket and said, "Well, why don't we add it up and see."

But Rosalie stopped him, "I really want just a rough idea."

He squinted his eyes and strolled through the room then turned to her when he reached the sofa table. "You want me to consider the—accoutrement—in this rough idea?"

"Yes. Please."

He pressed his lips together, took one more glance around and said, "About twelve grand, if you go with the A fabric list. Ten grand for B. Fifteen grand if you throw in the fireplace mantel."

Rosalie considered his estimate. "What might I get for

$8200?"

He seemed to realize that he wasn't really going to make a sale with her, then he raised one eyebrow and sighed, a bit rudely, she thought. She felt guilty at first that she was taking up his time until she remembered what Lenny always said when people in the service professions were rude: "Hey, he's not taking me out to the movies."

She had only one more question for him, and she walked over to where he stood to ask it, "Has anyone ever come in and bought a whole room as—as a surprise?"

"You mean a gift?"

Rosalie nodded.

"I guess so, but—people usually don't tell me those things."

"No, I suppose they don't," she said.

"Is that it then? Is that all you wanted?"

Actually, what she wanted was to ask him if an average-sized, thin, 60 year old man with dark hair and a slow deliberate way of talking, dressed as a mailman, had come in and bought a room from them then charged it to his credit card. "Yes. That's all I wanted."

Instead of dropping by to visit either of her daughters as she sometimes did when she was out on a Saturday and near their neighborhoods, Rosalie went directly home, and she was surprised when she turned into the cul de sac to see Lenny's mail truck backing down the driveway. Her car and his truck were parallel to each other as he pulled out to make way for her to pull in, and through her open window she said, "It's four o'clock. What are you doing with the truck? You should have been home an hour ago."

"Overtime. Just a few more stops, be home by five-thirty."

"Wait till I tell you what happened at the store—"

"Roe, an hour and a half. I've got to go."

He put the truck in gear and revved the engine as she called out, "I couldn't buy a thing with that damn MasterCard."

She thought she saw him lurch, she thought she saw his

entire face fold in, but it was hot, so hot that the air seemed a blurry screen, and he pulled away leaving her with nothing to do but park the car and go inside the house.

At nine o'clock that evening, after the dinner had dried up from so many reheatings, after she'd called the post office at least twenty times and got no answer, after she'd called both of her daughters and half a dozen friends and no one could tell her where he was, she heard the back door open. She walked quickly from the den out to the dim kitchen where the only light was the one under the stove hood. At first, she almost started to cry she was so glad to see him alive, but after that initial rush, anger shoved its way up so forcefully it was like an electrical jolt to her skin. The central air unit kicked on, a dull hum, while Lenny stood near the door with his shoulders hunched forward, his shirt ringed with sweat under the arms. He looked like a man who'd spent the day running without water or rest.

"What is it?" she said. She'd only seen him look this way when Lolly was a baby and the doctor thought she might have spinal meningitis and when Vivian was in that awful car accident the night of her junior prom and whoever called to inform them didn't know if she was dead or alive and when he had to tell her that her mother had already died just as she was about to leave for the hospital. Each time, he'd been the one to bear the bad news first, the one to carry the burden of the telling.

He didn't move from the doorway, seemed in fact to be cowering near it He held his hands out, palms up. "Roe, I don't know how—"

"What on earth is wrong?"

Suddenly he broke down, started sobbing, and she rushed to him to put her arms around him. Through his weeping, he was saying a stream of things she couldn't understand. She managed to guide him to a kitchen chair, and she pulled out a chair for herself, drawing it up near his, holding his hand, waiting for him to catch his breath and speak.

"I've been losing some money," he said with a huge sigh.

Still she wasn't sure what he meant.

"Out of your pockets? Like, on the street?"

It was something like that, he said. In the beginning just football pools and baseball pools at work, regular stuff, he said. A few times on his day off, he'd gone to the track with some of the men from work because he liked horses, he said, and Rosalie found this information astonishing. They had no pictures of horses in their home; he never *talked* about horses; they'd never gone horseback riding, not ever.

"You bet on them."

And he smiled—inappropriately, she thought, after such a storm of tears. "Yes. I know, you see. I was on a streak. That's how 1 bought you the emerald ring last Christmas and the pearls for Mothers Day," he said, and his eyes lit up as if she should have been pleased with this part of his confession. "Then on those casino trips, I was winning. I was winning big, so I had to start betting bigger. To keep up with myself, you know? So, so I borrowed a thousand or two on the MasterCard, and I won most of it back and it was all working out, but I don't know what happened. I used up some money from the credit union, and 1 had to put it back, so 1 borrowed more from the MasterCard and—" His voice cracked and he dropped his head into his hands. "My God, Rucci," he said, referring to her as they referred to each other on occasion, by their last name, as if they were one person. "I never wanted you to know. I was going to clear it up."

Rosalie's cheeks burned; her head was pounding. She squeezed her eyes shut, felt her mouth open, but couldn't make her tongue or lips work.

He let his hands fall away from his face. "I can fix everything."

She pressed her fingers into her thighs till is hurt. She was wearing culottes and when she opened her eyes again, there were bright red indentations in her skin. The whole day was flashing by her: that hideous saleswoman, the credit department and the room full of luscious opulent furniture, her own foolishness at thinking he'd charged a new living room suite as a surprise. She thought of all the afternoons he said he was working late, the nights in Atlantic City when he'd been quiet riding home in the car and claimed it was "just the excitement of the evening," the haggard, dark look that sometimes swept across his face out of nowhere.

"We've been married thirty-eight years," she said.

"I'm so sorry. I didn't mean for you in find out—"

"I'm sure you didn't." She recalled some of those movies they'd seen together, movies with alcoholics and gamblers and drug addicts and love addicts in them; it startled her that what he was saying to her now sounded like make-believe.

"I was going to tell you, Roe, after I cleared everything up, cleared up the debt—"

"Lied more, you mean. Lied some more—"

"No!" he insisted. "No! Cleared it all up."

She slammed her open palm on the tabletop, and he flinched.

"How much money? What money?"

He shook his head, pulled out a hanky and wiped his sweaty forehead, and she could see him calculating how much further he should go, how much more of the truth he should divulge.

He mumbled, "The credit union. The savings account. The MasterCard. The IRA."

A wail escaped and she wasn't even sure it was her own until she felt her throat pinch. She leaned up from her seat, her head near his head, feeling like a senile old woman. "Who are you?" she whispered.

"Roe," he said, reaching out for her hand, but she pulled it away and flopped back into the chair. She rubbed the tabletop.

"We have grandchildren. We have daughters we could have helped out if they needed it. We've spent our whole lives sacrificing so that now, now, we could have some freedom, and you do this. 1 don't understand." Her eyes flashed at him. "Make me understand, you bastard!"

More than her shouting, it was the word "bastard" that seemed to jolt him. In all their time together, neither one of them had ever uttered anything more profane than hell or damns in an argument

"I was doing it for us," he said.

"For us to do what? To end up on the street?"

He shrugged and the shrug enraged her so much she thought she'd punch him. "To give you things you didn't have before."

She stood up, her arms at her sides, then, as soon as she was standing, felt she couldn't hold herself up much longer, so she simply sat down the way she'd had to sit in the showroom earlier, wondering what things he could have wanted so desperately that he would wipe out close to $50,000 to get them for her. She looked down at the emerald on her right hand; it was ugly now, a grotesque green nugget. She heard Lenny stirring in the chair. "Have you," she began as steadily as she could, "have you used your paychecks too?"

He didn't answer right away; she wasn't surprised when he said, "A few."

"And you just made sure you saw the credit card bill, right? You just didn't deliver the mail to us."

"Yes."

She nodded her head. "You left that card on the dresser by accident today and when you realized you didn't have it, you came back to get it."

"Yes."

She looked up. He could have been a Black man or an Indian or Chinese, so little did he look like her Lenny. "1 want you to go now."

"What?"

"I want you to go, but first I want you to give me your car keys because you can't have she car."

His eyes widened. "Where—where do you want me to go without a car?"

"Walk. You're a mailman—you're used to walking."

He began to cry again, begging her to forgive him, to help him, insisting that it was for her, but she held her hand up as if stopping traffic. "Please—just leave now."

"What are you going to do?"

"I'm not sure." She extended her hand, waiting until she felt the keys drop into it, and she closed her fingers around them. She didn't watch him go; she just waited for the sound of his footsteps, the sound of the door opening and closing.

In the hour or so that must have passed after he left, Rosalie sat at the kitchen table. When had they stopped being the Lenny and Rosalie Rucci she thought they were? How was it that she couldn't see this coming? She rubbed her neck, it ached so. She thought about the sex book and berated herself for not buying it. Maybe that was the problem. They'd never had sex on the staircase or on the beach or standing in the shower. He liked the horses because they reminded him of sex, and the excitement of winning reminded him of sex, and she'd been too blind to see it. Then she remembered all the times she'd told him she wanted a sable coat, She wanted one in the way many women want one, a wish but certainly not a necessity. No, it wasn't only me. There have been two of us, all these years, two of us. She tried to pinpoint a cause for this sudden reckless behavior, but neither of them had ever been reckless—not with each other or with their family.

For a while, she considered calling her oldest daughter, and then she considered calling Vivian. Vivian was a college professor. She taught literature and surely she might know of a character, a story or a book, that could shed some light on this. But she couldn't manage to pick up the phone, and she discovered that she was perspiring despite the central air.

She hoisted herself up out of the chair, her body like lead, and walked slowly to the sink where she turned on the faucet. She splashed cold water on her face then held her wrists under the faucet, letting the icy water run, feeling the chill shoot up her arms, After a few minutes, she dried her wrists and face with a fresh dishtowel, then finger-combed her hair, using the kitchen window as a mirror. Studying her faint image in the window, she realized that she hadn't gone back to the cosmetic counter for her new make-up; this made her even angrier. All those years she hadn't indulged herself and now, even if she wanted to, she and Lenny were on their way to the poorhouse—or worse, to prison. It was entirely possible that he'd gotten involved with mobsters or loan sharks; it was entirely possible they were hiding out in the Syringa bushes with clubs and guns and brass knuckles and whatever else they used when they wanted to let someone know they were unhappy with a payment plan. At that moment, she wanted new make-up. She knew it was too late to go back to the mall, but the mini-mart was open till twelve, and they carried a basic make-up line at cut-rate prices. She turned away from the sink and picked her leather purse from the back of a chair where it had been hanging since she returned home that afternoon. She grabbed her keys from the table and left.

There was a narrow cement walk along the side of the house leading to the inclined driveway, and she walked gingerly, her eyes darting about for signs of Lenny, the mobsters, or the FBI. When she reached the car, she thought she heard something moving or breathing close by but decided that in her present emotional state she was letting her imagination get the best of her.

"Go ahead, back out."

Because the night was so incredibly still and dark—the street lamps burned out like matches—because there was nothing to illuminate Lenny's belt buckle or the shiny chrome of the fender. Rosalie thought she imagined the resigned voice that floated up from the driveway. She jangled her keys once, a signal, and heard Lenny sneeze. Sure enough, when she followed the direction of the sound, she found him lying on the ground, in line with the heavy back tires. He was on his side, his knees drawn up as if he had a stomach cramp of a charley horse, some expected run-of-the-mill pain people made no effort to conceal, not even from strangers. A cricket trilled.

"What are you waiting for?" he asked.

She couldn't believe her eyes or ears, couldn't believe

that this absurd day could get any more absurd, "Lenny, get up from there."

"I don't think so," he said in a voice thick with effort. Rosalie squeezed the keys till they dug into her hands. She'd had just about enough thwarting for one day.

"I'm going to buy make-up. The make-up I wanted this afternoon, the make-up I couldn't buy because of you and your crazy idea that you're some kind of Jimmy the Greek. I need mascara—not a fur coat, not an emerald ring—and I need it now."

He didn't budge, nor did he say anything

"Do you want me to run you over?"

"Like an ant," he said, "What the hell?"

She surprised herself when after a short pause she said, "Fine."

With that she yanked the car door open arid slid inside. The vinyl was coal against the backs of her thighs, the odor in the car was pungent where stale, stubbed-out cigarettes in the open ashtray mingled with the lemon scented cardboard air freshener that hung front the rear view mirror. She sat for a minute or so, seething: waiting for him to get up and appear at one of the windows to put an end to this, but when he didn't, she put the key in the ignition. Before she turned the key, before she pressed her foot on the accelerator, she felt completely capable of backing down the driveway, of feeling the car meet resistance like backing out over a cement stump, like backing out over the curb. She could claim anything, after all that: after an argument, she decided to take a drive to calm her nerves, it was dark and she was upset and how was she ever supposed to think that her husband was lying beneath the tires like a stupid cat seeking shelter wherever he could find it? Or no, no argument at all, just that it was a hot summer evening and she wanted air, she wanted to drive along an uncluttered highway, windows rolled down and feel air beating back her hair, whipping across her face.

She turned the key, pressed her foot down on the pedal, listening to the engine's choked rumble. She smelled gas, exhaust, and glanced up to see plumes of it swirling up from the rear. She shifted into reverse, her foot still on the brake. Then slowly, she let her foot rise off the pedal and felt the car roll back just a fraction of an inch, astonished that she would go this far before she jammed the shift lever into park again. She sat there shaking, tears stinging her face, the car idling loudly for several seconds before she cut the engine.

The night was silent and unchanged; no voices called to her to stop—not Lenny's, not God's. The scars had not been altered and no neighbor's living room light flicked on to see what was the matter at this late hour in their suburban cul de sac. This potential murder would go unnoticed and misunderstood. Only Lenny, who would have been mangled in front of his own house, could have come to her defense, could have said, "I deserved it. I asked for it."

She pushed the door open and looked down, toward the back tires where Lenny's sneakered foot was jutting out. He moved it, scraping its edge along the asphalt until she could see that he was shoving himself away from the tires, that indeed, he was moving away from the car. She had no idea which direction he might take or even whether he would stand up, but before she could tell if she'd actually hurt him, she heard his voice, gravelly, broken. One word, "Rucci," he said.

The name, like a hypnotic suggestion, triggered something in her and, without thinking, she dropped down on all fours, the surface of the rough drive abrasive against the flesh of her bare knees, the palms of her hands. Her shoulder and hip brushed against the hot metal of the car, and it must have seemed as incomprehensible to him as to her when she discovered that in the dark, close to the earth, they were crawling toward each other.

Contents May Have Shifted
Nicole Pearce

In the car, they didn't speak, and because each was lost in thought, no one saw what happened. It was Saturday morning and Paul Allen had wanted to go for a drive, the old-fashioned kind with no destination. He envisioned them in a convertible. Judith would be beside him, a chiffon scarf flapping up and away from her neck like the tail of a kite. The twins would be in back, battered by the wind but nonetheless squinting and smiling into the sun. They would take their time, heading east into the light. They wouldn't stop until they got hungry.

The problem was instead of a scarf, Judith was wearing her tight-lipped expression, and instead of a convertible, they were in a gray Lexus sedan, recently detailed and reeking of chemicals. When the girls climbed in—arms crossed, frowning—they kicked the back of the seats, leaving charcoal footprints. On the Interstate, cars rocketed past them in a steady stream, generating in their wake an enormous, unnerving drone. As Paul Allen slowed to exit, he cut off an enormous eighteen-wheeler, and the squeal of the truck braking was reminiscent of a human wail. Paul Allen was relieved when they turned onto a peaceful country road.

Twenty minutes later Bitsy tapped his shoulder. "Hey, Dad, who's the kid?"

Paul Allen looked at the rearview and almost swerved into a tree. Judith, straining against the seatbelt, said, "What are you doing?" And then, glancing back, "Oh my God!"

Paul Allen straightened the wheel. "Where did he come from?"

"I'm not sure," Bitsy said.

"He's hogging all the room!" Ann backed her shoulders

against the door.

Between the girls sat a boy of nine or ten. His mouth hung open and his hands were folded in his lap. A fringe of red hair fell across his pasty forehead, and a wide space separated his front teeth.

Paul Allen peeked again at the mirror. *Well, well, well.* He was not as surprised as he might have been.

The road dipped. A low hedge began to follow them on either side. It was the sort of precise fall morning where every ocher and auburn leaf stood out in stark relief. Trees bowed in the wind, casting dappled shadows onto the road, and the cool air carried the scent of wood smoke. Inside the car, it was stuffy and warm, and Paul Allen had fallen into the buzzy state of daydreams.

He had always been a sensible man, a man rooted in and satisfied by the ordinary. But since his father died the year before, he often found himself drifting off, veering toward the layer of existence he now believed hovered beyond his own. In the months following his father's death, he'd been drawn to the sore void of his absence like someone testing a strained muscle, flexing and jabbing it, seeking reassurance in the pain. At times, in search of connection, he meditated or fasted. He'd begun to explore the space/time continuum. Humans, as three-dimensional beings, perceived time only as a result of memory. If we had zero memory, Paul Allen thought, we could not detect time. Any given object—a molecule, a planet, a person—begins when that object comes into existence and ends when that object ceases to exist in that form. Paul Allen wasn't some crazy dumbbell. He knew his father was dead. But if all objects existed in all dimensions, as he had begun to suspect, it was possible his father continued to exist at a different point in time.

"Hello?" Judith snapped at his temple like a mosquito. "Do you think maybe we should do something?"

Paul Allen slowed the car. The hedges prevented him from pulling over. The road was hilly and he didn't want to stop completely for fear of being rear-ended.

"I'm sorry, son." He addressed the mirror. "We don't usually give rides to hitchhikers. Did you get in at the stop near I-360?"

The boy remained silent.

"Can I drop you home? Is it far?"

"It's not far."

After more silence, it was clear the boy was finished explaining. Paul Allen wasn't sure what to do next. He'd skipped breakfast and his stomach rumbled. The chemical smell—ammonia-like, maybe the K-2 they used to clean the leather—had grown stronger in the closed space. He cracked his window and when the wind rushed in, it sounded like a thousand flags waving.

"Dad!" Ann said. "It's freezing!"

He rolled it back up. Next to him, irritation radiated off Judith like body heat. He said, "Let me find a place to turn around."

He knew his wife thought he was a dumbbell. It didn't help that the factory—his father-in-law's factory—had become nothing more than a lowly distribution point for computers streaming in from China, where they were now assembled. Paul's responsibilities as plant coordinator—never, he had to admit, significant—had dwindled even more over the last few years. His primary task was overseeing the shipping crates when they arrived at Port Arthur. From there, they were taken to the factory where they were opened, sorted, and shipped by truck to purchasers throughout the country. Other than keeping track of what went where, his job—with the help of two other employees who doubled as drivers— was to affix labels on the individual boxes, white stickers with bold black letters that said, "Caution While Opening." As if after journeying across a continent and then an ocean, people would expect to find that nothing had shifted inside.

"There's no place to pull over." Judith arched her neck over the dash. He'd been amazed he'd been able to drag her away from the television long enough to get her in the car. She said, "God, this hedge is like a fucking tunnel."

He knew better than to say anything. The emptiness in his stomach had given way to a dull, burning sensation. They crested a hill and he kept his eyes on the curve of the horizon. A curve, extended indefinitely, becomes a circle, or better yet, a sphere. But a sphere, looked at microscopically, appears as a level surface, which was why primitive people perceived the earth to be flat. This gave Paul Allen hope. Like these primitives, he thought, we simply did not know enough. We had not yet grasped the fourth dimension, the dimension of time.

In the rearview, the boy caught Paul Allen's eye. The boy nodded and said, "There's so much we don't understand."

"Could I *please*," Ann ground out, "have a little more *room*."

Trapped in the middle, the boy had no place to go. "I'm not doing anything wrong." He turned and glared at Ann. His skin glowed as if it were lit from beneath. "And I didn't *do* anything wrong, either."

"Just leave him alone," Bitsy said.

Ann turned and faced the window. She could feel the heat in her face. If she were Bitsy, she would at least know enough to have people start calling her Elizabeth. Even Liz would be an improvement. Bitsy! Like a baby! Like the spider going up the water spout. Bitsy's chest was flat as a cracker while in the last year, Ann's had ballooned until she no longer fit into her t-shirts. Bitsy hadn't even gotten her period yet. How could they be twins when her sister was so immature?

The car had slowed considerably, and when they passed through a long stretch of shade, Ann could see her reflection in the window. She tugged on her hair, fanning the strands against her shoulder. She felt sore, down there, and the pain was searing and liquid. She'd been flashing hot and cold all day. When she thought about yesterday—what else could she think about?—she told herself she felt grown up. But the truth was any hint of satisfaction had become fused in her mind to embarrassment and confusion.

It was before lunch and she'd been at her locker. The hallway was emptying and the din of people talking at once, some of them laughing and calling out to one another, had gradually diminished. She was hurrying to science class, the single bag of potato chips she'd had for lunch making her sick to her stomach. They were having a pop quiz and Mary McCormick, the girl she usually copied, was absent. She'd pulled out her textbook and folder when Dana Kahn and Kimmie Crossman approached.

Dana was on the tennis team, and because she was the oldest of four and both of her parents worked, she already had a hardship driver's license. Kimmie was thin and pretty like a mermaid, with round eyes that popped away from her face. She was "going with" a senior named Mark. Dana and Kimmie were well liked but under the radar of *the* most popular. Ann had been trying to get in with them since the beginning of school.

"Hey." Kimmie leaned against a locker. "We're cutting history."

Dana glanced up and down the hallway. "Wanna skip?"

The parking lot in back was a wide expanse of pavement in view of the cafeteria and the eastern wing of the school. It wouldn't be easy to get into Dana's car without being spotted. But instead of hopping into the jeep as Ann had expected, they continued through the parking lot toward the field house and the football stadium behind it. As they made their way, Kimmie explained that she and her boyfriend had had a fight and she wanted to do something to piss him off. Her idea was to steal all the jock straps from the varsity football team, string them together like a banner, and hang them across the gym entrance.

"They're all out on the field at practice," Kimmie was saying. The girls had rounded the field house and could no longer see the school. In the distance, Ann heard the coach's whistle and the answering drone of the boys responding to drill commands.

"Why don't you do it yourself?" Ann said. "He's your

boyfriend. It's your fight."

They were standing close together. She'd noticed that Kimmie tugged at her eyelashes when she got nervous, and now they were almost gone, leaving her with a vacant expression.

"I can't get caught." Kimmie made a show of looking over her shoulder. "I've already had detention like three times, and it isn't even Homecoming."

Ann wasn't dumb enough to think they weren't using her. But it was only a prank, and if she managed to pull it off like it was no big deal, she figured there was a decent chance Kimmie and Dana would start hanging out with her. She was lonely. She wasn't like Bitsy, who'd found her clique the first week of school, a group of girls who didn't care what they wore or bother to pluck their eyebrows, brainiacs who would make the Honor Society by the time they were sophomores. Ann knew she wasn't smart. If you asked her outright, she would say, "I don't know anything." In fifth grade, she'd finally taught herself not to print her letters backwards, but occasionally, she still wrote a "b" when she meant to put down a "d." Teachers complained that she was spacey and couldn't keep track of time. In algebra, she pretended she had inverted the equations on purpose. Over the years, she'd found ways to cover up her stupidity, but at times, it was simply exhausting.

"They keep their extras on the shelves in their lockers." Kimmie opened the door. "We'll be right here, on lookout."

Inside, the field house was one big room. Free weights and Nautilus equipment occupied the front half. Toward the back in an open tiled area, a row of shower heads poked out of the wall. Next to that were lockers and a storage area where the boys hung their gear. Opposite the door Ann had entered was a closed door that was painted green and white, the school colors, and Ann assumed it was another entrance. Her stomach quivered. The room was as hot as an attic and smelled of dirty socks. She hurried over the concrete floor to the lockers and opened them one by one. She'd shoved three jock straps into her backpack when the green door opened and Kimmie's boyfriend, Mark, emerged.

Except for a thin white towel tucked about his waist, he was naked. He was trying to wrap an Ace bandage around his wrist and forearm. When he paused to tighten it with his teeth, he glanced up and saw her. He let go of the binding and said, "I know you."

Ann's mouth went dry. Whatever bravado she'd been faking vanished. Later, when she thought back to this moment, she told herself she was mostly worried about getting in trouble. But alone with Mark, his chest gleaming with sweat, his arms and legs roped with muscle, every thought was fleeting.

"You're that chick who follows Kimmie around." Mark sauntered toward her. Ann stepped backwards.

"The one with the big tits."

"I gotta go." Ann's throat was tight and the words came out in a croak. Behind Mark, through the open door, she saw a cabinet filled with bottles of rubbing alcohol and a waist-high table like the kind doctors use to examine people.

He said, "Did you follow me in here?"

"My friends—Kimmie—she's waiting."

"It's cool." Mark's eyes were slits.

She didn't see him lunge. He grabbed her by the shoulders, pressing his torso into face. She pushed at him, trying to breathe. His skin was smooth, slightly damp. He shoved both hands up inside her shirt. She knocked into someone's football equipment, and a pair of shoulder pads clattered to the floor. He'd gotten under her bra and was squeezing her breasts hard. When he pinched one of her nipples, Ann let out a little cry.

"You like that?"

She was terrified. The towel around his waist had fallen to the floor, and she could feel his penis stabbing her hip. He reached over, unfastened the snap on her jeans, and pushed her pants down. Ann felt a hook in the wall jab her in the back. Mark was panting against her neck. Before she could think, he had in one steady motion jammed two fingers inside her. She gasped. Mark moaned. A second later a sticky wetness covered her stomach.

He straightened and pushed the hair away from his face. "God, you were great. Kimmie would never let me do that."

Now, as they drove past a field dotted with pumpkins, she thought again about what Mark had said. Not, *it* was great, or *that* was great. *You* were great. What did he mean? Did she cause what happened? Would he tell Kimmie? After Ann had collected herself and gone outside, both Kimmie and Dana were gone.

The car smelled weird and Ann felt sick to her stomach. They crested a hill and she had the sensation of being aloft. She imagined herself suspended in the air, wavering on the hilltop, where it would be just as possible to fall backward as forward.

Next to her the redheaded boy's mouth had widened into a feline grin. She glared at him and shivered.

"Mom, give me your sweater."

"I'm sorry." Judith's voice was high and melodic. "What did you say?"

"I said. Give. Me. Your. Sweater."

"Puh-puh …"

"Please!"

Judith untied the sweater from around her neck. These girls and their attitudes! She was a failure as a mother. She was a failure as a wife, too, but that was mostly Paul Allen's fault. When she passed the garment over the seat, she paused to give the boy a good once-over. He was wearing a white t-shirt with a cartoon globe on it and some sort of slogan underneath. She didn't quite process what it said because she was speculating about whether a pair of males would have been easier to raise. The boy was self-possessed and quiet, but there was something peculiar about him. His eyes were the green of artificial grass, the pupils diamond-shaped. He stared straight at her without blinking. She turned and faced forward. Oh, God, what did he want from her?

Paul Allen had sped up again but there was still no turnoff in the immediate distance. What was with the fucking hedge? It was making her claustrophobic. She gazed at the sun, low in the sky, a clean-edged face with no features. They had forecast rain. Those fucking weather people. What did they call themselves? *Meteorologists.* Judith hated it, *hated it,* when the top story on the news was about the weather. Like you couldn't look out the fucking window and see for yourself that snow covered the ground, that wind and rain were whipping the trees like saplings.

She wished it *were* raining. Maybe then she wouldn't be trapped in the car with two moody teenagers and Mr. Paul, Loser. Taking a ride in the country—one more thing she didn't want to do. Her day was filled with them: driving the girls to chess club and the math tutor, folding the laundry, trying to remember that they were out of toilet paper and light bulbs, going to the Safeway to buy the toilet paper and light bulbs, unloading the dishwasher, doing it all again the next day. The only time people noticed her was when something went wrong. When *she* forgot it was picture day at school, when *she* neglected to go to the bookstore for Paul Allen's special order, *Physical Relativity: Space-Time Structure from a Dynamical Perspective.* (What was *that* about?) *Chomp, chomp, chomp.* She was a giant cookie. They were eating away. Soon she would be nothing but crumbs.

Next to her, Paul Allen sighed. Exhaling was his new thing. For months, he'd had his head in the clouds—or up his ass, depending on one's viewpoint. She had to beg her father on a daily basis not to fire him. Well, that wouldn't be an issue much longer. They were closing the plant at Port Arthur, selling what was left of the facility to a Taiwanese toy manufacturer. Her father—he was the reason they had the Lexus, the four bedrooms in Pineywood—he'd have to find something else for Paul Allen to do. Could there be a more sappy, less ambitious person? She'd come to accept her utter lack of love for him, but the lack of respect was doing her in.

The woman on Oprah Winfrey—what did they call her? A "life coach"—said if you were planning a change, the first thing you had to do was to imagine yourself at the happiest point in your life. This would help define what it was that made you happy to begin with, and from there, you would know how to move forward to a positive future. But when Judith thought about her past, all she could envision was her mother in her bed at home, an IV dripping into her arm, the smell of sickness and decay mingling with the dust motes floating through the crack of the drawn curtains. In her memory, the room appeared through a broad lens, curved at the edges, everything filtered by a pale red light. She was fifteen when her mother died, and she'd gone straight from taking care of her to taking care of the house and her little brother and sister, remembering they were out of toilet paper and light bulbs, then going to the market to buy them.

It was impossible to remember the happiest point in her life because she hadn't yet lived it, and according to Oprah Winfrey, until she'd lived it, she couldn't move forward.

Judith opened the air vent but it did little to alleviate the stringent smell of whatever it was they had used to clean the car. There was an inconsistent pressure on her back, and she said to the windshield, "Bitsy, stop kicking the seat."

Bitsy dropped her feet. From the corner of her eye, she watched the boy stretch his arms in front of himself and yawn. Wouldn't it be fun to have a little brother! She wouldn't lord her seniority over him like some people. Ann was only eight minutes older, but the way she acted, you'd think it was eight years. She was obsessed with her breasts and dumb stuff like reality television. Whenever Bitsy said anything remotely intellectual, Ann's response was, "You think too much."

The boy had been holding his hands in his lap, but now he rested one palm on the seat next to his thigh. Bitsy placed hers alongside it until their pinkies almost touched. When had he gotten into the car?

For most of the beginning of the ride, Bitsy had been engrossed in recreating her dream from the night before. In it, she'd been standing on the deck of an immense boat. It pitched and weaved; the sky was the color of a gun. Bitsy was part of a group of people who had been taken prisoner. The country was involved in some kind of war, and though Bitsy in her dream wasn't surprised by what was going on, she didn't know the details, either. Her captors were friendly, like the other prisoners, and at times, she got the two sets of strangers mixed up. Everyone stood on the deck of the boat, and it was clear they were waiting for something. On the horizon over the bow, a cloud went up, and they knew it was bad, it was a bomb, but they still hoped it wasn't the most horrible kind. It wasn't gray like the one in the movie *The Enola Gay*. It was pitch black. Finally—it could have been minutes or hours or days, it was dream time, so Bitsy didn't know—the right part of the cloud turned into a funnel, and it rose high into the sky. The bottom exploded, reverberating dull and ominous in the distance, and a moment later, waves hit the side of the boat, causing their legs to sway. But the cloud hadn't mushroomed—that was the important thing— and the mood of dread on the ship changed to one of collective relief.

Bitsy yanked the seatbelt away from her chest. The air in the car reminded her of the bathroom after her mother cleaned it with Clorox. It stung her throat. She shared the bath with Ann but had her own bedroom. She thought about asking the boy if he liked to read. Lining her bookshelves were titles like *The End of Nature* and *Annals of the Former World*. She'd tried something by Sartre but got spooked and quit halfway through. She had enough to worry about with global warming, the possibility of getting shot during a school massacre, and terrorists. Earlier in the week, she'd watched a PBS documentary about hijackings. They showed a plane crashing off the coast of an island in the Indian Ocean. It was near a resort and people on the beach were swimming out to help. One survivor said, "I stayed completely calm. I knew in this sort of hijacking, one rarely died." Bitsy thought, *well, no one was likely to think that now!* You couldn't board a plane without practically taking your clothes off. It seemed the nation was at war all over the world. Someone you didn't even know could pulverize your country's biggest buildings in your country's biggest city, and even if the government had a clue, they didn't know what to do about it. No place was safe.

Sometimes Bitsy longed for the sweet plastic smell of her old Barbie dolls. She wanted her Grandpa George, who died last year, to come back and play tea party all afternoon like he used to long after everyone else had lost patience. She thought about the little cupboard he'd made her—with his own hands—three shelves, painted red. He'd stuck decals shaped like giant daisies to the outside. It was her first memory.

The boy had been watching her. He said, "In a time like this, at a time like this, peace doesn't seem possible." He nodded and shut his eyes. "But thinking makes it so."

A pleasant warmth spread over Bitsy's chest. He was like a little orphan straight out of Oliver Twist. There was a forlorn quality to him. Forlorn but lovable. She reached over and grasped his hand.

Paul Allen turned onto a dirt road. "Okay, finally. Here we go."

In the car, they didn't speak, and because each was lost in thought, no one saw what happened. Bitsy, focused on memories of her grandfather, was filled with tranquility. The road was rocky and rutted and she pretended that she and her grandfather were horseback riding—they had never done this but she was in her mind and in her mind, she could do anything—and her grandfather reached out and she felt his hand, which, like the boy's, was as warm and dry as parchment paper.

On the other side of the car, Ann felt the bumps, too, but

she couldn't see where they were going because tears fogged her vision and ran in slow rivulets down her face. She'd seen the movies in health class, the sperm swimming fast and furious, and she knew that one of Mark's had probably swum down her stomach and gotten up inside her, and now she had to deal with that, and she didn't know what to do, and she didn't feel grown up at all.

Judith was contemplating how she was going to tell Paul Allen about the factory and for the first time, felt no delight about doing this. She gazed out the window at a telephone pole, thinking what was it doing way out here on a dirt road, and soon it would be obsolete anyway. She realized that on the little boy's shirt, underneath the cartoon globe, it had said, *save it, save yourself,* and she wondered if it was a sign that if she didn't seek at least a sliver of freedom, she would die.

At first Paul Allen was thinking about the factory, too. He was envisioning the rows of labels, *Caution—Caution—Caution,* and pondering how such a mantra, over time, could affect a man. Then he deliberately turned his thoughts to a day a few years before when he'd gone fishing with his father. They'd stood together, warm in their waders, casting their rods with gentle flicks of their wrists. The river curved like a snake. Sun glittered on the water's surface, turning it to shards of glass. The sky! There was no way to describe it. Cool as mint, frosty at the edges, purple-blue like an iris. As they jostled along the road, trailing a cloud of dirt, Paul Allen realized he was no longer hungry. His head felt light and tingly, as if electricity were running through every tiny capillary. Ahead, a cliff, but no need to worry, the world wasn't flat, it was round, curved like the fourth dimension, and besides, look at the blue of that sky! My God, he had just been thinking about it, and now there it was. The exact sky! Paul Allen bore down on the gas. The Lexus immediately picked up speed. Their heads bounced in unison. They came to the edge of the earth, and as they flew over the side, the four of them had, for the first time all morning, perhaps for the first time ever, the same thought at the same time.

The Dog Dies
Bethany Reece

1. *The Afterlife*

No one blamed the girl. She explained what had happened and the family accepted that it was just one of those things, like accidentally pouring a guppy down the drain or having your bike stolen.

When his owners took advantage of the seemingly endless summer to go on a long overdue second honeymoon (thumbing it around Europe to prove how old they hadn't gotten), their aging retriever went on hunger strike and began to suffer sleepless nights and red-eyed daytime moping on the second floor landing. His downy fur fast became like tangled yellow angora because no one had stopped to explain the situation or even say goodbye. *Two weeks is all. Fourteen days. Twenty-eight bowls of food and at least as many walks. Good-bye.* On the fourth morning with twenty-one meals to go, the house sitter returned from a jaunt to the farmer's market with an armload of tomatoes and an art student's phone number written on the back of her hand to discover the old dog lukewarm and stiffening under the bedspread in the master bedroom, bloody vomit already cooling in the narrow, shady sliver of tile between the toilet and the shower (a place where the owners knew and would later explain their dog had always preferred to vomit, a preference they hypothesized arose from his well-developed dog-sense of wrong-doing; he felt guilty, always guilty, and seemed to have identified that spot in the bathroom as someplace dark and inconspicuous, the way people do sometimes, curling inside themselves to be alone with the corrosive pain of some unbearable secret failing). Because he had so stubbornly turned his nose up at his Elderly Canine Kibble, the girl had, the previous night, coaxed him into polishing off a Whopper, and though he had only reluctantly nibbled and licked her pickle-scented fingers, she had dared to hope that all he needed was a little special attention, and she invited him to join her in an evening of Lifetime movie reruns, lying on a giant couch brimming with throw-pillows, his head burrowed into her lap like he couldn't get close enough to the idea of being loved and wanted, hoping that that kind of reassurance might be the start of a turnaround. She had even sought out movies featuring dogs like *Lassie*, and *Milo & Otis*.

Now she petted the cadaver's head affectionately but couldn't deny that death renders a body unrecognizable. "You *know*," she thought at the dead dog, eyes closed as if asleep, "it didn't have to be this way. You used to be the sum of parts, and now you're just parts and parts and no sum of anything. How sad. How weird. You don't flick your ear when I scratch the same spot long enough to get annoying. How bizarre. You've gone and turned into something unyielding and indifferent."

She had no way to contact the owners, and the neighbors whom she'd been instructed to call in case of an emergency were not answering their cell phones. She eventually found a listing for biological waste disposal only to be told by a man with blocked nasal passages and lazy diction that the crematorium didn't pick up dogs. People, yes, but not dogs. The girl tried to explain how she was a stranger to the city, didn't have a car, didn't know anyone who could help, was at a loss, but the operator muttered something about a bad line on his end and hung up. The girl searched through every closet in the house and eventually located a dusty retriever-sized, hard-backed rolling suitcase. Inside, she arranged the still-pliable dog, padded a few places with towels to prevent shifting, and before noon, had dragged the cadaver to the subway—she hadn't even cash for a cab—and boarded the southbound train. Several passengers peered curiously at the girl struggling under the weight of her luggage, among them a tall, pale man wearing a black hooded windbreaker who, without waiting for her to ask, rose from his seat and helped her to hoist the suitcase into the car. When inside, he took a seat beside her, pulled a Mars bar from his jacket, and offered her the bigger half. The girl said thanks but she wasn't hungry. She kept one hand on the suitcase while the train was moving—afraid it would fall over on the turns, which didn't seem right.

"That mother's heavy," the pale man said, eyeballing the case. "Mind if I ask what's in there?"

"No, I don't mind," the girl said, pulling out her subway map.

He waited expectantly, regarding her with interest, but she didn't say anything. "So," he said. "What's in the suitcase?"

"Computer parts."

"That so?" He nodded, contemplative. "Delivery girl. I see. Where are you getting off?"

"A little past downtown." She looked again at the subway map. Many of the stops were circled in different colors with little near-illegible scribbles to explain what was what. Whenever she found a place she wanted to go she circled it on the subway map and wrote a note about it. Now she pointed to a stop double-circled in pencil. "Green Street."

"That's a great stop," the man said. His eyes glistened so pale they resembled little copper coins. "There's an arboretum near there. A garden. It's beautiful and open and free to everyone, always, day and night. There's a rose garden with a koi pond and a vineyard hothouse where they grow wine grapes year-round. There are more winding paths running up the hillside than you could ever put on a map and more different sorts of trees than anyone ever knew existed. A lot of people like to walk their dogs there."

"Sounds like heaven," she said, liking him. "Are we far away?"

"Yes. Very."

The lights in the car flickered as they rattled through a tunnel, and the conductor applied the brakes as he pronounced an unintelligible announcement about the next stop over the intercom. You just had to know where you were and where you were going on this subway system. The man again offered the girl food, this time salted peanuts, and again, she declined. She really wasn't hungry, she said, really. The man asked her if she needed help with her suitcase.

"You mean it? Well, yeah," the girl said, thrilled. The few other figures on the car remained indifferent. Soon a few of them started moving, slinging the handles of bags over their arms, grabbing the rails, getting ready to disembark.

Steadying himself with one hand on the pole, the man stood—he was so tall that when standing, he towered high above her—and said "Let me see how heavy that thing really is." He grabbed the handle and tested the weight. He lifted the suitcase as though it was nothing—like it was no heavier than a book bag—and when the train doors opened, he re-gripped the suitcase like he was hoisting up a girl about her waist, spun around, leapt out the train doors, and ran, suitcase hugged close, disappearing into a swarm of boarding passengers shoving, as always, to get on.

2. Motive

One of the training exercises in the Peruvian guerilla army—a so-called bravery test—involves tying a camp dog—usually a mongrel pet belonging to the soldiers—spread-eagle, torso upright and exposed, between two vertical poles and letting the bare-chested commandos-in-training take turns sprinting at the howling animal, slashing and stabbing repeatedly at it with knives until it dies, sometimes hours later. The animal can only move its head. When the dog is finally dead, the soldiers eat its heart and drink its blood.

International observers have been primarily unnerved by the lack of a commercial motive.

3. Knock on Wood

The family liked to cook and their kitchen was nearly as well-equipped as a small restaurant with open cabinets and a raw maple counter regularly rubbed down with olive oil; the dad always made a point of keeping their knives and cleavers well-sharpened. In an adjoining room, the dinner table was lit by a low, overhanging stained-glass fixture, and as the last daylight leaked through pale yellow drapes, they could hear the distant sound of heavy traffic subsiding, the public buses more infrequent as the off-peak period began.

The table was fully set. There was cubed ice fresh in the water glasses, bread in the basket, utensils arranged. The mom and nine-year-old son were already seated. They nibbled on a baguette while they waited.

"What did you learn in school today?" the mom asked.

The kid sliced for himself a huge daub of butter which he slowly spread over a thick slice of bread. "We talked about anthropogenic environmental disasters."

The mom said nothing. She didn't prompt her son with questions the way she might normally have, but he elaborated anyway.

"That means stuff like global warming, Chernobyl …"

There was a rapping, deep and wooden, from the center of the dining room. The son stopped talking and frowned at his mom; after a few moments, the rapping stopped.

A giant cast-iron pot burbled softly on the stove, smelling of carrots, celery, onion, potato, entrails. The severed head of a Shih Tzu, still wearing a lacy yellow bow meant to keep its silky rust-colored hair out of its eyes, rested on a transparent glass platter beside the stove. Much of the blood had drained onto the plate, and the skin around the ears, where the fur was thin, looked quite pale. Every so often the dog head licked its lips and blinked, watching the dad move efficiently about the kitchen.

Occasionally its ears would rotate, hearing something of interest in the other room.

"Did you know there's plutonium in everything?" the son explained to his mother, moving his elbow to make room when his dad brought the platter with the head and set it on the table. The platter was placed to the side of the boy, facing the center of the table, just as though it was one of the diners. "My teacher told us that the governor has just signed a contract for a nuclear power plant here, too. She said it might not be a bad thing, if it doesn't explode."

More hard-knuckled rapping from under the table, louder now.

"Honey, would you stop that?" the dad said sharply.

The mom looked up. "Stop what?" The rapping kept on.

The dad frowned. Momentarily, the rapping subsided and the oven timer beeped.

"I guess I'm done cooking," said the dog head, looking at the oven.

"I hope it's tender," the dad said, doffing mitts and peeking inside the oven. It emitted a burst of steam. "This looks beautiful," he called over to the table. "You guys are going to love this."

He brought a large, covered casserole dish and set it in the center of the table. The head watched with interest as he removed the cover, revealing a crouched, crispy body underneath many slices of orange and baked to a glorious golden brown. The embedded thermometer had popped.

"Who wants a thigh?" the dad asked and started serving.

"Oh, me!" the son said. He always took the thigh; his mother waited until her husband got around to cutting into the breast. In addition to the orange slices, the dad had puréed some fresh cranberry sauce for dipping the meat in.

"Do I taste good?" the head asked.

"You're very muscular," the mom said, chewing. Tilting her head, she looked thoughtful, contemplative. "Kind of stringy."

"Sorry," said the head.

"At least you can't taste any adrenaline," the dad said, addressing the mom. "I chopped her head off too fast. She didn't have a chance to get upset. Isn't that right, girl?"

"Yes, it was fast," the head agreed. "I didn't know what was going on."

"There's some rosemary flavor, too," said the mom.

The dad got excited. "So you can taste that? Good." Finished with his first serving, he cut off the left foreleg and put it on his plate. "It was an experiment. Can you taste the lime?"

"Oh," the head said, "That's why you started putting rosemary and lime in my food. I was wondering."

The son got up and when he returned he was carrying a green bone-shaped biscuit.

"Can I give her this?" he asked.

"No," his dad said. "Don't be silly. We already put her stomach in the stew."

The mom daubed her mouth with her napkin; the knocking resumed, this time sufficient to rattle the dishes. Everyone looked at her and even the dog head rolled its eyes. Mom always did this.

"Mom, you're going to break the table or something."

The dad shook his head, frustrated, and stood and took his plate with him to the sink.

The kid looked at his mom; she was disassembling the paper napkin in her lap. He also glanced at the dog head, its eyes focused on the strips of meat still clinging to the small canine rib cage in the center of the table. They had eaten most of it; the rest was leftovers.

"Can you help me clear the table?" mom asked finally, pushing back her chair.

"Sure," the son said, jumping up. The first thing he picked up was the dish with the head. He scratched the head affectionately behind the ears. The bead-black eyes regarded the boy keenly.

"Mom?"

"Yeah?"

"Are we done with this?"

She nodded. With his fork, the son scraped the head

into the trash where it would lie blinking, a bit of broken eggshell slicing uncomfortably into one ear, nose pressed up against a moist and molding banana peel. It took the dog's eyes a long time to adjust to the deep dark in the trashcan, and the voices and movements of the family as they cleared the dishes had a strange muffled echoing quality.

4. Fear of Goodbyes

The dog was a mud-brown mutt with coarse hair and triangle ears, nervous and asocial on account of having been locked inside his crate for entire days in his late puppy-hood; he belonged to a reclusive man who made his living selling baby dolls over the internet. Today, the man was moving about the house in a state of agitation, checking lists of orders and addresses, boxing and labeling shipments and putting them in a pile near the front door. At some point, he encountered a mis-manufactured doll—it was missing its glass eyes—and tossed it into a corner of the room where the dog retrieved it, carrying it gently in his mouth to his crate. There, he groomed it affectionately with his tongue as his owner paced about, ignoring him.

The dog had caught a stomach parasite six months earlier after drinking stagnant water pooled in the back yard and had been trying to conceal the constant pain from the man, although it had gotten bad enough that now the pain shot through his body every time he moved. He wasn't eating. He still tried to act like things were normal.

His terminal stomach cramps started soon after lunch. The dog bit his long tongue and tried to follow his owner about the house until finally, with a little convulsion, his body stopped and a blue translucent spirit emerged from the carcass and kept right on going, following his owner about the house while the man continued arranging and packing doll shipments. At some point though, the soul glanced over his blue shoulder and saw his body just lying there, detached. He barked at the body and growled at it, then cautiously crept up to his corpse and sniffed, nudging it with his nose as if to say, "Wake up."

The owner looked over. With one blue front paw, the dog soul pointed to his body and whimpered. *I died.* His attitude was clear.

"Stop crying," the owner snapped. "You're the one who quit eating. What did you expect?" The dog soul sniffled. "Stop feeling sorry for yourself," the owner said. "I mean it. Shut up!"

The dog soul skulked under the kitchen table the way he had done when his owner yelled at him, this time dragging his own carcass by the nape of the neck, as though he expected to find comfort amidst the wooden chair legs. He curled up in a tight ball, fetal position, embracing his body like a doll. Every time his owner moved closer to him, the dog pulled farther under the table and curled tighter into his body, whimpering louder.

"Why are you afraid of me? I'm not hurting you. Why are you under the table?" The dog soul drew himself more tightly under the table, in shambles. He curled into his still warm body, putting his nose into fur wet with urine—apparently he'd wet himself when he died—trying to take comfort in his body's corporality. He had died miserably and in pain.

He was still here.

The owner squatted down and slapped the dog soul's face.

"That doesn't hurt," the man said. He slapped the dog soul's blue, translucent face again, loud enough to resonate. "Why are you acting like I'm hitting you?"

After a time the owner started crying silently. He left and locked himself in his room. The dog soul lay curled in a ball for what seemed like hours, but eventually, he dragged his poor limp sack of bones back to his crate by the scruff of the neck. The inside of the crate was rank with the stale, sweet bodily odor of fear. So many times the dog had been locked in this crate, left bored, forgotten. By now it was routine, and he so expected it that that at last he had come need it, the way a foot painfully swollen is still a needed appendage. Here, ensconced in the crate with his doll—which actually provided more comfort than he had felt since his death—he began to think of ways to cut the body up and sew it back together in such a way as to construct from the carcass a suit for himself, and so find a way to carry on.

5. Strongest Dog

She looks like the over-muscled god of canines or somebody's idea of a joke. Even the top of her head is ripped; when you scratch behind her ear, instead of feeling bone, it feels like touching her solid, undulating thigh. Every part of her body is chiseled, contoured muscles like ropes woven and knotted underneath her short, wiry fur coat. Zeusette.

"They're called bully whippets," the owner explains to a visiting reporter, one of many. "There aren't a whole lot of them." He doesn't mention that she somnambulates, heads east. Waking up, she seems to remember something, returns to the farm.

Strongest Dog in the World, read the headlines. Obviously. Just look at her. She could rescue ten children in the time it takes Lassie to save one. Stories circulate about the wild boar she killed last month. It may have been a bear. She's heavy enough to break down a door by ramming it with her shoulder. She lives on a farm in Wyoming, not a ten minute drive west of the unmarked, prefab buildings where grown-ups with science kits breed research and anomalies. She's not a police dog or enlisted for the USSR special services—calculated scare-mongering, bloggers contend.

These days, the dogs in the unmarked laboratory are smoking. There are two floors devoted to cancer research. New orifices have been cut into their throats, the perfect size and shape for holding a tobacco cigarette. In addition to smoke, the air is thick with ammonia, burning their eyes.

The dogs are limp, unexercised, containerized in stereotaxic chairs for weeks, completely immobile, and as the smoked-out dogs die off, new ones are brought up from the nursery.

Even the dogs know that they are being used. Most of them live their whole lives within one or two floors of where they were born. Even knowing nothing else, they notice the permanent stale odor wafting through the iron bars of their cages, permanently seeped into the concrete, and with no basis for comparison, they suffer the weakness of their own bodies.

6. *Housebroken*

The father had spent his childhood reading comics underneath his aunt's plastic-covered couch, hiding, always kept indoors to observe the Sabbath, but now, he lived in a house furnished with real antiques and sleek copper pans, and he didn't believe in God. He no longer owned any comic books, though he knew, deep within, that someday he would end up underneath a couch, wedged in, alone and permanently stuck, and that when this happened, he would die. His death would be slow and he crossed his fingers that when it happened, there would be something worth watching on TV. Until then, he went through his days feeling like an imposter, a placeholder in someone else's life. Even so, he wasn't unhappy.

Today he was in an upstairs bedroom helping his son with his math assignments, trying to conceal the embarrassing fact that he had no idea what he was talking about, thinking all the while that his wife was far better at this sort of thing, more patient at explaining. His son, meanwhile, made no secret of how much he hated school in general, and while he and his son were bonding over their dislike of the whole math situation, they heard the family hound start barking in the living room, not half-heartedly like she did when there was a rabbit on the lawn or a kid riding past on a tricycle, but loud and desperate, like she actually thought it was necessary to alert them of something.

"I'll be right back," the father told his son, handing him the eraser, this one full of teeth-marks. The father peered out the bedroom door down the flight of stairs. The stairwell coiled and he could see nothing of the room below. The dog's barking had given way to whining.

Their dog was an Afghan. When they had decided to get a dog, his wife had insisted that the Afghan was the supermodel of canines, and he knew that she believed, silently and unshakably, that owners and dogs all sooner or later come to resemble one another. Theirs was blonde in color and temperament.

"Hold on, Dad," his son said. "I'm not comfortable with number seven."

"Which?"

"Out-of-control speeding trains."

"I'm not very fond of that one linking water contamination and deforestation, myself," the father said. "Get started without me. I'll be back in a minute."

The father was in his socks and sweats, and he hadn't been outside all day. His knee was acting up but he was still in denial about needing knee surgery. He felt vulnerable. He slipped down a few steps and at the foot of the stairs, he found himself locking eyes with a woman standing in the middle of his living room. She was a stranger with long hair, flitty eyes, maybe a junkie. There were no cars parked round back, so she had probably thought the house empty. She was standing over the dog, bent slightly at the waist, hand stretched out, palm up. The dog was eating out of her open palm, making a soft crunching, snapping noise, like chewing a dog treat or the bones of a small animal. *Who would break into a house just to feed an animal to a strange dog?*

"Stop," the man said. She looked up. She was wearing his leather bomber jacket, one of the few things in his closet these days that didn't feel like a costume.

"Sit," he said. "Just ... sit down."

"I'm not a dog," said the housebreaker.

"What are you doing here?"

"What are *you* doing here?" the woman said.

She suddenly turned and bolted out the back door, which he now saw was wide open. He hesitated, then took off after her. He hobbled in stocking feet and lost her when she leapt the fence, turning her body sideways like someone well-practiced at fence vaulting. He stood by the fence, watching her disappear far down the street, a cacophony of neighborhood dogs barking after her, and then, defeated, came back inside. He paused on the threshold to peel off his mud-soaked socks, feeling oddly resentful of the lovely cream-colored carpet he had just bought for the living room, feeling the absurdity of having grown into a life where things as irrelevant as carpets wanted minding.

Inside, he found his son and the dog. The dog had crawled almost completely under their high-legged Victorian-style divan and lay there limp and motionless. His son tried to pull her out, grasping her two front paws so hard his knuckles were white, leaning backward with all of his weight. Heavier than the boy, the dog was unresponsive. The father was not encouraged by the way his Afghan's red tongue dangled, mouth agape, and her half-open eyes rolled up, showing only the whites. He knew then that the boy would wear out, give up, and grow up knowing that people who steal jackets can be dangerous. For now, the boy still tugged away at the dog, pausing every few moments to rest and pat her head tenderly and say encouraging things like "good girl," and "I love you," and "get up."

The Cowboy
Adam Peterson

My father ordered my cowboy boots on the day I was born, but it was twenty-three years and nine months before I put them, still warm, upon my feet. This is how things are with cowboy boots.

On the day my father scratched his signature onto the order form and had my mother paste the carbon copy into my baby book, a telegram arrived at an aluminum trailer balancing on cinderblocks some 2,000 miles away from where I cried. A man balled the greasy paper in barbwire-scarred hands and took a bottle of beer from an ice chest. He dried his hands between his retriever's ears. The screen door slapped closed behind him when he entered the trailer.

"Mother," he said. "It's time."

His wife punched out a cigarette and fished two glasses out of the dirties piled in the sink. She sudsed them up and dried them with her dress as the man opened the beer with the countertop and his palm. Each of the two glasses he poured were three-quarters head. They toasted the future.

Dirt blew against the windows. The dog howled. The moon rose.

Nine months later, The Cowboy was born while I took my first tentative steps on pigeon-toed feet. They couldn't raise the doctor, so the veterinarian delivered The Cowboy in the trailer of his conception. When the veterinarian slapped his bottom, The Cowboy kicked him in the nose with a tiny boot. The boots were black like hell. Neither light not dust could stick to them. The Cowboy kicked just to watch them throw sun around the trailer.

From the beginning, we were so very different. As his mother strapped The Cowboy to her chest for the barn raising, I had my first Chinese lesson. My parents hoped I'd pick it up while my language acquisition faculty was sharp, seeking, indiscriminate. The bored tutor read me a romance novel. To this day, I know the Chinese for 'strong hands,' but the rest has left me along with so many other indulgences.

By seven, The Cowboy dug his black boots into the stirrups of his pony to go with his father as he rode the fence. At home, his mother cored apples for a pie. There was talk of the world beyond the scattered fields he tended with his father, but he didn't know what the words meant. Airplane. Park. Lawyer. He told his father he did not understand these words. His father only spit tobacco juice onto the dust and looked sadly at his son's feet. That night, his parents showed him the crinkled order form.

"But pa?" The Cowboy quivered.

"This is how things are with disappointment. And with fathers."

My father didn't tell me, not yet. Instead he told me about mortgages. I learned the word lien. I added it to a notebook I kept with such words. Lien. Estoppel. Patrimony.

At nine, the dam broke and the reservoir came pouring over the scorched hills and knocked the trailer on its side. The Cowboy's mother hit her head on her mother's mother's sowing machine, and she went, as the reverend said, to where angels sing. The Cowboy did not cry because his father did not cry. This is how The Cowboy learned about love.

I learned about love when I learned about The Cowboy. My father looked at a pair of untied sneakers I wore as I left for college and said, "I have a surprise for you." He told me everything.

I knew even then I loved The Cowboy.

But it wasn't time for us to meet. The Cowboy had to grow into a man which he became slowly, first with sips of his father's whiskey after the old man fell asleep, then by fighting older boys behind the church. The Cowboy bled then scarred. He allowed himself the vanity to wear starched t-shirts tucked into his blue jeans.

When he found his father face down in the field, The Cowboy buried his face in his father's flannel shirt. The Cowboy dug the hole as the sun set purple over the trailer. He washed his dishes. He drank his whiskey. That night he slept in the room that had been his parents' for the first time. He was 18.

But everything he saw was not his. The boots itched beauty, and even in the night, he could see them at the bottom of his parents' bed and knew why he was and how he would end.

We were drawing closer. I could not forgive my father for the harvest to come, so I told him I never wanted to speak to him again. This his how things are with sons.

When he was twenty-two, The Cowboy met a girl at the county fair. They shared a swinging Ferris wheel bench together underneath a night of stars made dim by fireworks. He took her hand into his but couldn't think of anything to say. She wore a ribbon she'd won for her rhubarb crisp. He felt its silk and then kissed her cheek.

They were walking home from the fairground when she said, "Your boots are so black it's like you're walking on the night itself."

He said thank you, tipped his cap, started his truck, drove her home.

The crops rose and rose and rose again until the day we'd been fated to meet. We were both men, men with size 11 feet. I clutched the receipt in my hand as I drove my rented Cadillac through a dusty field. The trailer looked like a coin God had dropped as it flashed on the horizon. No dog barked. The dog had been dead for years, buried with a cross of sticks near the tombstones of The Cowboy's parents.

He came out to meet me. I tried hard not to look at his feet, but I couldn't help it. The boots drew the eye fierce. The Cowboy tipped his cap and drawled, "I dreamt of you."

I said, "I dreamt we'd go for a walk."

We walked by a creek which he pronounced so it rhymed with trick. We climbed a hill and there The Cowboy fell to his knees. I began to cry. He did not.

"Please, mister," he said, "I reckon we can figure some other way to live."

I reached in my jacket for the revolver and aimed the barrel at his bolo tie. He had blue eyes which wouldn't betray him while mine would not focus. I had never seen such a sun. The shine from the boots could have lit the world themselves.

"I'm sorry," I said. "You know how things are."

The Cowboy took off his hat and held it over his heart.

After, when I stopped for a drink to steady my shaking hands, the waitress looked me up and down and said, "I knew someone with boots like those. Do you like 'em?"

I told her I loved them, but I had paid too much.

Health Nuts
John Oliver Hodges

Tough men stop come lunch to gobble our spud salads:
Mutinous Mustard and Mad Mayonnaise. Construction
workers, plumbers, they stop for a dose of Lunacy Noodles
with Vegetable Sauce, say, or Brainy Burgers with Doodle
Sticks. Maybe they're in the mood for some Touched Tofu?
Some Cracked Cookies or Moonstruck Minestrone? We've
been at it three years, a family-run funhouse, everybody
snappy. When our daughters get off the bus, they help us till
closing. We're adored, the charmed cheese. Vitamins, snacks,
we stock them in prettified rows and dish out the best chow
south of the Georgia line. We have a jukebox to play Loony
Tunes off your quarters. We're good for a dose of hilarity.
We give people cud to chew—that's organic cud, friend—and
shit to shoot. My how we Chattahoocheeans love to gossip,
to storytell.

Take yesterday. Now this is typical: Jeanne, the skinny
chickadee from Floor One comes in orders a order of Booby
Balls—that's our term for falafel smothered in our special
tahini concoction. Jeanne was initially hospitalized through
the power of her momma, Bakeracted and branded the
drooling fool. Girl was too much of a slut's what we gather,
chafed her momma's refined sensibilities. That's what started
it, only Jeanne was a model crazo. She made it down to Floor
Zero quickity split, but like many of our patients, once they're
given the all-clear, it's vacation time's all it is. Soon they're
back for some new little crime of smallness. Poor Jeanne, she'd
been away less than a month before she up and escaped her
Tallahassee halfway house, got bonkers in a crackhouse. As
we get it through the trickle-down, Jeanne started smoking
boric acid when the crack run out. That's what made her

Kooky with a capital K. Whereas before, she'd only been, now forgive me for saying this, but Slutty with a capital S, or to put it another way, an insult to her momma. Now she was unalterably changed forever for the worst, like way down deep in the DNA jungle of her girl's private soul, daffy, as they say, no lie.

So Jeanne comes in yester's prelunch, her pleasantly plump homegirl in tow. Dee preps Jeanne's Booby Balls at which this intimate-made Abe is proffered. Dee just looks at it, him, the dangle of his eyes in Jeanne's been-there-done-that fingers quite lovely still despite having rid life's cruel tides. "It's wet," Dee says. "Why's it to be wet?"

"I peed on it," Jeanne giggles, and Jeanne's homegirl giggles.

Dee pulls back the Booby Ball plate, sets it on the counter behind her. That's when Jeanne starts wailing out like a heartsick hound over she wants her Booby Balls. Everybody is looking at her, soaking up the details for the telling of a good tale on it later to whoever is willing to listen.

There's another customer in line, an older dude with a nose I've not seen the like of. It's a screwball nose, a S-nose, call it a snose over that it first goes one way then the other, makes you to think of a snake when you look at him. He is waiting to get his own order. "What's the deal?" says he.

"She pissed on her money," says Dee. "I ain't taking it. She's got to give me some dry money. Would you take a five dollar bill had pee all over it?"

"I'll wash it!" Jeanne shrieks. Jeanne's homegirl flops out her tongue and Jeanne rubs old Abe back and forth over the girl's taste buds, as if that will remedy the situation here. With tears in her eyes, Jeanne tries handing the bill back to Dee, who says, "I don't take no wet bills, baby."

That's when Mr. Snose, our Good Samaritan, offers to pay for Jeanne. She's a good-looking gal, Jeanne, a chickadee in all the right places. That's part of it, the why of how she ended up back here where her momma first put her, Bakeracted and branded the drooling fool. Once free, all male no-goods—there's an endless supply of those—wanted a piece of her to chew on. I can't say I blame them. Like I say, Jeanne has got it going on in the body department. But Jeanne, poor gal, she likely thought she had not a thing to lose in the world. She give it up to whoever wanted a bite, have at it. When your All means nothing to the One whose All means All to you, you become worse than worthless, odious unto yourself. I understand that mental frame.

Take back in the day, this of the time those goosers, my peers, took live girls damward to learn the smooching business. That would be about the tenth grade, the eleventh grade, and the twelfth grade. All those grades passed me by like opened windows flapping gloriously, but I could not hear them, could not see them. I missed out on the fun stuff guys do as they grow up to be men of this world. I was like how I imagine Jeanne was before she knew she wanted to get high, a nothing human being who suppressed the desperate wanting. What I wanted, only, was for Momma to be happy. For that, I hid things from myself. I appeared healthy and happy, and I might even have believed that I was. The difference between Jeanne and I was many a man saw her, admired her, wanted quite clearly to partake of the livid wet thing her skin concealed, and with some effort, did so. Jeanne, I can be jealous of her in my times of weak nostalgia. Me, I was invisible those years of no return, daddyless, without a girl's crush, unwanted by all. What I knew of the gleaming windows were sharp flashes that burned me in my sleep.

Yet who is the wiser today?

Hell, I'm in foods!

It is me, against the boys who defiled the temples of their prey, who shines most happily and with a general bearing of peace and ease. By my own opinion, I would say so. It is me to live the happier of lives now. It's not so strange. Jeanne's window got bricked over, slam-dunked in her face. The many boys of yore now-drugged-out or drunked up, the plumbers and the concrete pourers, their windows too got slam-dunked. You go hopping through open windows it's bound to happen. In my sizeable emptiness refocused, I've had to face things, "get over it," as I've heard so many say of the daily life dramas. My small-peaness, as I now understand it, was akin to a boulder I stood in the way of as it rolled over me. How else could I unburden myself? I stood in its way, the guilt roped about the shame not the least sigh giver, that tandem high-roller of serious dung. One need not wonder much as to the color of mine eyes.

Now, I was born in the Florida panhandle in a place made famous by a sprawling institution. My momma nursed there, "cared" for the crazoes, fed them drugs, and strapped them down in their beds when they got out of hand. She told me stories of it when arriving home from work, a real complainer, my momma, and tough, strong. My daddy, she always told me, had been a criminally insane patient, and there was a good chance I would grow up to be her charge. "Rat can't run from rat," she said. "All rat does is hide, like you're doing right now. When his rat's blood finds you, I'll commit you." It scared me. "You're crazy!" she screamed if, say, all I did was opinionate. It didn't matter what the opinion was. All opinions coming from me were out of the picture, her picture. My punishment more often than not was a physical thing, like push-ups and sit-ups. My momma was big on calisthenics and all things healthy. "Run around the block ten times," she'd say, or, "Drop down and give me forty." Other times when my crime was more severe, if I, say, made a facial expression of self-assurance, she'd suddenly pretend like I was more trouble than I was worth, like she'd tried everything, had done all she could for the rat that I was, but the time had come to send the rat to the devil. I'd be left alone to do as I pleased, which you'd think I would have liked, but I didn't. I felt slimy, guilty, rejected, worthless. She wouldn't acknowledge me in any way till I started begging. That little boy of twelve, I see him, I feel him, he breaks. The last drop of self-love he took it upon himself to try and stow away in secret is thrown out—that is his gift to her, laid sorrowfully at her slender feet—and she stares down at him contemptuously, her arms crossed, waiting for him to try and hug her leg so she can kick him away. No, she will not consider absorbing him back into her loving fold till he says the magic words, till he delivers everything, all. "Stop mumbling!" she says. "I can't hear you." And the little boy declares it loudly: "I am a rat, Momma!" The special words have been spoken. What follows, the seal on the deal, the act, the what it is that's got to be done for life to go back to normal, then happens, but I don't want to think about that now. What I want to do is focus on the good things.

Me, now. Jumping thirty years up to now, to my life as I live it today, you will see a happily married daddy of two towheaded girls of nine and eleven. They're the prettiest things you ever saw, just precious beyond belief. And my wife, oh what a beauty! My wife and I, throughout our fifteen years together, have worked hard in the pursuit of our dream. We have cut corners, denied ourselves the artificial pleasures that give people so much satisfaction in life: travel, education, things and more things: boats and guns and tools from Sears and rings. In fact, I've never worn a wedding ring, though I did buy one for Dee, got it for forty dollars at Cash City. Dee, like most women, and little girls too, I have found out, is a sucker for jewelry. But the two of us did some saving, Dee her money from secretarying at Chattahoochee Electric, and me, the money I saved, the bulk of it, came from years spent working for Harvey the Happy Plumber, everybody always asking me was I was Harvey, even though my name, you know, it was sewn into my shirts plain as day. We pooled our resources, Dee and I. We did what we needed to make our family life perfect. We purchased our dream, opening the first health food store and eatery ever to be opened up in Chattahoochee: Health Nuts.

The crazoes, those given passes to leave the nuthouse till curfew, visit us, bring us their Abes, Georges, and Andrews. They buy sandwiches and cartons of chocolate milk, them from Floor One, labeled harmless by the folks in charge over there, the psychiatrists who are greatly influenced by what the nurses tell them. If a nurse don't like you, you might as well hang your soul out to dry, buddy. They'll drug you and belittle you and lock you up, and they might even, like my momma did to some such inmates, run off with your seed! Lucky for me, that is one story about my mother that has not yet been circulated throughout our populace.

Only today, that man comes back in, the Good Samaritan with a screwball nose. He devours a Sanity Salad and washes it down with a medium Loco Cocoa. He returns to the counter, says, "Let me see Jim."

"What you want Jim for?" Dee says.

I am in the office doing paperwork, but I can hear.

The man clears his throat. "I'm his daddy."

Call it horror, what I felt then. Momma, she told me my rat's blood would find me one day. By that, I thought she meant that I would go crazy, not meet my goddamn daddy in the flesh!

Now, it was me to throw together the Sanity Salad for him to eat, hold the cheese. He hadn't struck me in any amazing way, like what you hear about on TV, how long lost relatives recognize each other in crowds of strangers without even thinking about it. He was just a man, quite ordinary but for the snose on his face, a snose that was caved in at the tip with pink and green veins crackling out of it like lava. Not that there aren't plenty of folks around here with messed-up noses, just this man's nose, his snose, was not of the local variety. My first impulse, after hearing him speak that craziness about him being my daddy, was to close the door and hide under the desk. I didn't want to mess with this. Whatever it was about, I wanted it to go away, only before I could motion for Dee not to speak to me, to pretend that I'd gone out the back door to get some scallions from the farmer's market, she spoke up. "Jim, there's a man out here says he's your dad."

I went out there and we looked into each other's eyes,

and I still didn't recognize him from did. I said, "You made it down to Floor One, that it? I don't recall seeing you before today."

"I was released years ago," the man said all soft in the voice, and he said, "Your ma sent me a letter before she died."

My heart was beating real fast but I played it cool. I said, "You're crazy, you know that?"

"I'm a hundred and fifty percent serious," he said. "You wanna see the letter? I'm shy, that's why I didn't catch up with you. I'm off the booze though."

What does a man say to that?

"When were you released? " I said. "What year?"

"That would be nineteen eighty," the man said.

That was twenty-five years ago.

"I'm sorry, son," he said.

I said, "I ain't your son, you crazy bum. Get outta my store fore I call the cops!"

"Jim," Dee said.

"I didn't mean to upset you," the man said, and I about to popped a brain cap. I picked up the closest thing at hand, the plate he'd done ate his Sanity Salad off, and made like I was to bust it over his most-bald head.

He focused his eyes down hard on me.

"I will!" I shouted, raising it up to slam.

"Jim!" Dee said.

I was walking at him. He backed up out of the store, and it's a good thing he got away, cause I don't know what I might would've done. My heart was beating so fast. My heart never beats like this, not no more it don't. I figured in my head right quicklike that he was released when I was twelve. Twelve, I thought, and busted apart like a damn baby. I felt sorry for my wife seeing me like this, but what could I do? This man had come in here and stuck a fork in my heart. All this gooey goo was flying out of my heart where the fork went in. The goo kept flying and flying and I hid myself and cried. I needed it out of my system before the girls came in. I didn't want them to see me upset. When I left the office I wore a smile. Poor Dee was glad to see me back to normal now, but she had a few questions.

*   *   *

I do see the dumb boy that I was, Lord have mercy. I'm eleven. I'm off the bus from school. I feed the rats in the large aquarium, then watch *General Hospital.* I do my homework. I read the instructions Momma has left me, what exercises to do, what record to listen to while I'm exercising, what chores to do before and after my shower, which is at five o'clock. Before showering, I clean the sinks, the toilets, the tiles in the kitchen, and the rug in the Peace Room. After showering, I begin dinner, putting the roast in the oven, if that's what's on the menu, or starting the soaked beans on the burner, whatever, making salads, peeling potatoes. When Momma gets home, I say, "Welcome home, Momma," and hug her, and kiss her once on the cheek, then return to the kitchen to check things, make sure all's in order, prepare our plates. By this time Momma has showered, and as we eat, she quizzes me on my day, and I ask her questions and she tells me about her job and we have a nice dinner. Then we watch TV, and I massage her feet, or maybe we play Scrabble. Sometimes we go in the back yard and play horseshoes or take a walk down to the river. When Momma says things to me that require a yes or no answer, I always follow it up with Momma. Yes, Momma, No, Momma, no variation, always Yes or No, Momma. I keep a straight face. Momma don't like no laughter. If I giggle or snicker, I have to do push-ups. Yes, Momma. She stands over me counting, and when I'm done, she's upset for the remainder of the day. I am afraid of her often, but mostly I want Momma to love me. I even, sometimes, as amazing as this sounds, giggle just to put myself in her brain. Momma knows when I do that. She has me run around the block ten times, rain or shine. Momma says I like to push her buttons. She says I try to get her goat and asks me please to respectfully stop messing with her.

Finally she reaches her limit. I have crossed the line so I cry out the magic words: "I am a rat, Momma!" I try to kiss Momma's hand after that, but she won't allow it. She pushes me away. She treats me mean. If we've already eaten, we wait until the next day to make things right, but if we haven't eaten yet, we do it now. Momma loads the rat trap with a piece of cheese. She lowers it into the aquarium. When a rat comes up for a nibble, down the bar slams, crushing its neck and making blood come out of its mouth. Mama pulls the struggling rat out of the aquarium and when it finally dies she pries open the trap and drops the rat onto a plate. She stabs the rat with a fork like you would a russet potato, this so that it doesn't explode while it cooks in the microwave. As the microwave hums, Momma heats up a can of cream of mushroom soup, without mixing in the milk. She pours this gravy over the rat, and I am not allowed to get up from the table until I have eaten the bulk of it, its legs, its tail, its eyeballs, all of its insides. The only things I don't have to eat are its bones and its teeth. Mama uses a nutcracker to bust open the head for me to eat out the brains. If I throw up while I am eating it, I have to eat that up too. When I'm finished, Momma says, "Now you're a good boy."

The world is home to a full variety of crazy folks, I know, but in Chattahoochee, we house five types: the Pigeons, the Nose-Pickers, the Seers, the Brainers and the Stovepipes. The Pigeons, they rock back and forth all day long on the benches jabbering. The Nose-Pickers pick their noses all day long or masturbate in front of people, not distinguishing the act from normal behavior. The Seers, as we call them, they see things that nobody else can see, like elephants walking down the sidewalk. The Brainers just seem like total geniuses but are in reality schizophrenic crackpots. The Stovepipes, last but not least, are the criminally dangerous ones, the incurable. Stovepipes are good at hiding their crazinesses. That's why we call them stovepipes, because when you look at a stovepipe what else can you see but a stovepipe? It is my opinion that Momma was a Stovepipe.

*   *   *

My daughters, God bless them, bounce into the store like two thin sticks of joyful butter. I lift them into the air, one by one, and hug them. Penelope is nine, Jurisprudence eleven. They are the loveliest little girls you ever laid eyes on, hands down. Good workers, too. After the hugs, I hand Jurisprudence the pricing gun. Penelope on the step ladder dices garlic cloves. "I'm going to go find that man," I tell Dee, my beloved, and she holds onto my arm tight.

She says, "Jim, you're not planning nothing, are you?"

"Course not," I say. "I just want to talk to him."

"Promise me you're not going to do anything to him. I still can't believe you lifted that plate up like that. What was going through my man's brain?"

"I promise," I say. I say, "If he really is my father, it's not his fault. I'm just something that Myrna stole from him."

"Jim, you're beginning to scare me."

"Don't worry your pretty little head," I tell Dee and kiss her and head through the doors into the sunshine raining down. Across the highway, the institution is lit up like a rectangle caterpillar. All them windows. All them crazy people with eyes that see. They look though their windows at the world out here. I wonder what the world looks like through their eyes. Does it have special colors that normal people like me can't see? Is the air swelled up with God's heartbeat? Can they see its pulse, hypersensitive as they are, the air shifting back and forth, grainy, pulling and blowing, blowing and shifting? That'd be enough to drive a man or woman crazy. My heart goes out to the people in that place. I cannot gaze at the institution without that my heart softens. What those poor bastards must go through every day of the week wins my sympathy.

I walk along Main Street, looking for my supposed daddy, thinking I bet he's gone down to the river. I walk that direction—it's the direction he turned when he left Health Nuts—and when I get there, sure enough, there he is, standing against the concrete edge of the dam, propped against it and looking over at the scenery, his back turned to me. Now he's got a backpack with him, and it's on the ground at his feet. He is smoking a cigar and has no idea that I am behind him. I say, "Daddy?" and he turns. "Son," he says. We look at each other a moment. He sees that I am not here to hurt him, so he holds out his arms. We embrace. After a moment we let each other go, and he says, "I was looking at that black snake, a water moccasin, I guess. Big ass sucker."

I look over at the sludge below. A huge cotton mouth lies over some sticks, but not so huge as to be extraordinary. "He's a fat one," I say.

"I sure would hate to get bit by him."

"You'd survive."

"Listen," he says.

I say, "I should apologize."

He says, "There was nobody to report her to."

"Don't worry," I say.

"I couldn't stop tripping. I checked myself in on my own."

"You were a seer?" I say.

"I reported her after I was out," my daddy says. "I know they got a file in there somewhere that says everything I said. All I wanted was to stop tripping, but when the trip eased off, I had all this other shit I was dealing with. Your ma was a complete crazy woman. I was at her disposal." My daddy's body trembles, jerks. He begins to cry a little and is sniffling, remembering those awful times.

"She was a very intelligent woman," I say.

"I'm not proud of it."

"She said you were a rat," I say. "She said that you killed an old lady and stole off with her ovaries. Is that true? Did you pour epoxy over them and try to make golf balls? She said you had it in mind to make a fortune off selling goveries."

"I saw dinosaurs. I was completely mad. I was living in prehistoric America. The shit I saw would knock your socks off, son, but Myrna, I'll give her this, she made me understand that I was delusional. She was a talented nurse. Other people I have told this story to say it's cool, that I should be happy to have fucked a—wait, I'm sorry, I don't mean to be talking bad about your ma or nothing, but I don't think she should have done that to me, not while I was restrained."

"I'm fine with it. Go ahead."

"She used the situation to cure me. She was a genius and a maniac both at the same time. I bet that's why you're a successful man," Daddy says and laughs, and I laugh.

"Did you love her?" I ask him.

"Fiercely."

"Don't that suck?"

"Enormous."

I grab my daddy in my arms and hug him tight. Then I begin the telling. I tell of his grandchildren Penelope and Jurisprudence, and of Dee, how I started that crazy health food store with what Dee and I saved up from doing so much plumbing and secretarying. The woman who'd stolen his seed, my mother, had had her boobs removed during that last year of her life. When she died, my wife and I became about as high on the hog as we could ever hope to be, having inherited all her savings. I even have a boat now, I tell my daddy, and his face brightens because he loves to fish. We got a steady flow of cash coming in, I tell him, and say that we have a shed in our backyard that could easily be turned into a little bedroom if he wants to stay with us.

"I wouldn't want to put you out," he says.

"It won't be any trouble at all," I say, and I say, "I need me somebody to watch football with on the weekends and somebody to babysit the girls now and then. You do love football, don't you?"

"Aw, shit yeah. Bobby Bowden has got it going on, baby."

"You love little girls?"

"Aw, shit yeah," Daddy says.

"Bobby is a great coach," I say and can just hardly believe

that I am standing here talking to my flesh-and-blood daddy about Bobby Bowden and the Florida State Seminoles.

"Listen," my daddy says, "I've been married twice since I knew your mother."

"I don't care about any of that," I say.

"I look like a bum, don't I?"

"Yes, you do," I say.

Daddy laughs. "Thanks for being honest," he says, and he says, "I've sort of been meaning to get me a new wife, you know what I'm saying? I've noticed there to be quite a few pretty gals in Chattahoochee."

"Oh, they're all crazy," I warn him.

"Only a crazy woman could love me," Daddy says.

*   *   *

Daddy moves in. He's here all the way from California, and I am touched. Daddy eats with us at the supper table, us the big happy family, and he works at the store with us and takes the girls on drives and is a great personality. A great many stories Daddy tells, and Dee loves him, loves even his snose, it has grown on us, and it seems absolute craziness that this man could ever have been declared a loony tune. His name is Dan. Dan Hornstein. I'm a Glover, based on Momma's, what they call, maiden's name. Dan Hornstein and Jim Glover, that's us. It is nice having him around, makes us feel more like a family. That's what happens with people. They get together, next thing you know they're taking delight in each other, just being a family. A real family. A perfect family. A real perfect family.

We are out on the water in my boat, fishing, just me and Daddy.

I tell Daddy that Momma told me that my rat's blood would find me one day, but in reality it found me long ago, I say. My heartfelt prayer, that she kick the bucket, it was answered. Momma sucked a nut down her windpipe and suffocated.

"Damn. What kind of nut was it?"

"I don't reckon I ever found out."

"Well," Daddy says, "I prayed the same thing against her. I bet lots of people prayed for Myrna to die, so don't take it to heart, Son. Me, I'm pretty sure I'm up for the chopping block myself. I got a cancer in my brain, I can feel it."

I think Daddy's bullshitting me, trying to manipulate me into feeling sympathy for him, into being more generous to him and more all-around lenient. Of late, he has been dating Crazy Jeanne from Floor One, who is part Nose-picker, part Pigeon, if you know what I mean. They have been spending time together in the shed in my backyard. I'm pretty sure that's against the rules of the institution and that Jeanne could get in trouble. I have expressed my disapproval to Daddy because Jeanne is one skinny chickadee who has had an awful time of it, just so many people have taken advantage of her—and besides, Jeanne, at least through my eyes, seems way too young for Daddy. Daddy says he just wants to protect her, that he likes her as a friend, that he would never dream of trying to impregnate her. He says they just play checkers together, and acts offended that I would suggest such a thing about his intentions. Really, I should be ashamed of my cynical mind always being at work, but I can't help it. When Daddy says this thing about a cancer on his brain, I play along with it, even though I have my suspicions, and tell him I'm sorry. He asks what for? I tell him I don't want him to die, that he's my true blood father and I'm so happy that he's come back into my life.

"I just want to be a good boy," I say, and finally confess what I've never told a body before, the secret, how Momma would feed me up the most disgusting dishes. It wasn't just rats, neither. I had to eat raw frogs and other creatures both vile and harmless: lizards, garden snakes. She once brought home a fresh dead infant bulldog, put it on a plate, stabbed it with a fork, microwaved it up, and poured butter sauce over it. That was the worst ever. It took me half the night to get it down. My favorite though, what I wished was the only thing Momma ever fed me, was a yellow butterfly. She fed it to me off the tip of her finger, and I'll never forget the way it grabbed the tip of my tongue with its legs, very gentle, as if it understood that this was not my idea. I love that butterfly still, whenever I think of it, and that is why, on our menu at Health Nuts, we have Butterfly Brains, which is a butterfly-shaped omelet filled with garlic and sweet corn.

"That is the most amazing story I ever heard," Daddy says and is looking at me like, Is it possible to eat a baby bulldog?

"I swear to God it's true," I say, and Daddy stands up, causing the boat to wobble. He wants to embrace, which is a thing we've been doing a lot of lately.

"You poor thing," Daddy says, and we are hugging out here in the middle of the lake. "I'm sorry I wasn't there for you, son," he says, and I believe him. We both shed a few tears and when we sit back down and cast our lines back out, I feel so much better, I do. In fact, I cannot remember ever feeling quite so good as this.

Later, we are in his shed. Instead of saying beer-thirty, like people do, Daddy says, "Peanut-thirty," and brings out the huge plastic screw-can of organic nuts he's got, all the nuts of the rainbow. He bought the damn thing from Sam's Warehouse in Tallahassee, using my card, of course, and we reach in and fill our guts with all the finely salted nuts. I think I see a pair of black panties shoved under Daddy's bed, but don't say a thing. Instead, I agree with him that all that salt on the nuts is a great thing. Dan says they might even put more salt on the nuts. I agree, like father like son. Dan though, he only eats the almonds from the mix. He says, "I'm screwing up the nut ratio," and we laugh. It's just so delicious and so tasty, what else can one say? I reach in, grab a handful and slosh them back and get to crunching. "Pure protein," Daddy says, and we crunch on, just the two of us, crunching the nuts.

Perfect Practice Makes Perfect
Mathew Goldberg

Horvitz lowered the boom on a Friday, one hundred and seventy-two months, three weeks, and twelve-point-four hours into my tenure at the D.C. Metropolitan Transit Authority. Horvitz, the head of Logistics, was my seventh manager at the MTA, and now, with me sitting across from him in his dark, windowless office, he smiled like the cat who ate the canary.

"Max," he said, "you had to know this was coming." He swiveled his chair and tapped a silver Cross pen against his desk in perfect 6/8 time.

"No," I said, my eyes fixed on the pen. "I don't know anything." I placed my hands under my thighs and did my visualization exercises, imagining the echo of a pebble tossed into a clear, mountain lake. "Is this about my work?"

"In a matter of speaking." Horvitz reached into a drawer and dropped a ream of paper onto the desk between us.

"Where'd you get that?"

Horvitz smiled broadly enough to show his teeth. "Anything one does on a company computer falls under corporate work product."

"So you've been spying on me."

"It's my job to know what you're doing."

"Your job." Horvitz was a baby—thirty-one to my fifty-four. My previous managers—St. Onge, Satz, and Hsu—valued the appearance of propriety as ninety-two percent of the job. I'd done the numbers, quantifying promotions and yearly cost of living adjustments against work hours, deliverables produced, and projects won. The data came from an imaginary project I had submitted to payroll, my own numbers too small a sample size, especially since in my fifteen-odd-years at the MTA, I had never stepped foot on a Metro train. I made it a point to arrive at the office pre-dawn with I-69 still swathed in darkness to provide what I thought was sufficient veneer for me to complete my treatise. The report on Horvitz desk was ten years in the making. I followed his eyes to the cover page—*VOWS: Variable Operational Win Shares and the Fallacy of "Team Chemistry."* The acronym itself had taken months to hone.

"Feel free to fill in an explanation."

I tried not to wring my hands. "I'm doing important work."

"I see that." Horvitz flipped through the report using his index finger and thumb, carefully detached, as if he could catch an infection by exposure to its pages. "What is this shit? Batting averages?"

"Actually, on-base percentage is a better assessment tool than batting average, especially when you consider runs created instead of runs-batted-in and take into account walks, sac flies, hits by pitch, etc."

The pen dropped and Horvitz brought his hand to his head. "Jesus, Max. We're a goddamn transit system not the New York fucking Yankees."

"It's going to change the game."

Horvitz leaned back in his chair. "Listen, Max. What you do with your free time is one thing—I play bass in my brother's band—but I pay you for fleet management, for relative fare prices, not," and here he struggled through some of the report's more abstruse phrasings, "Pythagorean winning percentages and defense efficiency ratios."

Of course he was right. But I had worked the numbers hard cloistered in my cubical and in the basement of my house—where I kept my desk even after Susan left—and when I compiled my programs, I saw men knocking dirt from their cleats, snapping towels at each other, passing chew from hand to hand, and I saw calculus. There was no such thing as an intangible; everything could be averaged. Through veteran-to-rookie performance ratios, relative salaries to team market share, contract-year multipliers, and win-shares of day-after aces, I could finally quantify what sabremetricians had always considered unquantifiable: the dugout and the locker room.

"I'm aware of your condition," Horvitz said. "So, of course, I vetted this with legal. They gave me the green light."

"What condition?"

"Don't start, Max. I'm tired." Horvitz pushed the report across the desk and wiped his hands in what I took to be a symbolic gesture. "Here. Take this back. But your laptop is MTA property."

"Wait," I said. "At least let me save it to disk." I saw Horvitz in the owner's box at Fenway, sipping chardonnay with Theo Epstein, my treatise in his hands.

"Can't do it." Horvitz picked up his pen. "Get some sleep, Max. You look like shit."

I wasn't sure what I said next—something about Horvitz colluding with the clandestine network of GMs who for years had been hacking into my computer, or maybe something about my power to crash every train in the MTA system—either way, it was enough for Horvitz to call security. Before the guards took me by the shoulders and shoved me through the Jackson Graham Building's wide lake of cubicles, I rushed to my desk and gathered my books— Bill James' abstracts and an arm-full of issues of *Baseball Prospectus*—along with the single existing hard copy of my treatise.

"I can't ride elevators," I told the guards. "I'm claustrophobic."

The guards looked at each other, then back at me. We were on the ninth floor, and the thought of standing in a four-by-four-by-ten foot metal square with two pituitary-cases made me want to rip out my fingernails.

"Don't make me do it," I said, clutching the bundle in my arms.

The guards both sighed. "It's that kind of day," one said

as we clomped down the stairwell, me in the lead, them a step behind. "The O's are throwing Cabrera tonight."

"He's gonna get shelled."

"It's not as bad you think," I said over my shoulder. "They're in Toronto, and Cabrera pitches 2.43 with cold hands."

"No shit?" The guards stopped mid-floor. "2.43?"

We discussed the Orioles the rest of the way down: the grandiose dementia of the Angelos family and their colossal ignorance in signing Miguel Tejada, Sammy Sosa, Albert Belle, Bobby Bonilla, and a slew of other high-priced, over-the-hill free-agents with atrocious defense efficiency ratios and equally egregious secondary averages.

"You should be a GM," the guards said at the bottom of the stairs.

"I know." I whispered, glancing up at the ceiling, "But they would never let that happen."

The guards shared another look and then unceremoniously slid my ID badge off from its chain around my neck. And then, despite any bonhomie engendered by our conversation in the stairwell, they maneuvered me into the revolving door and leveraged two sets of meaty hands to whirl its glass.

Disoriented, dropping magazines, I stumbled to my car. Though the Jackson Graham Building adjoined the Gallery Place/Chinatown station, I drove to work and parked in the garage across from MCI Center—twelve dollars a day a fair price to pay to avoid the dark, constricted bowels of mass transit. Even the parking garage was a little too much to handle; closed in spaces made my head feel like the arm-vise of Safeway's blood pressure machine. These days I went to games less and less. The Lamictal was supposed to help with this, but I'd been off the pills since Susan left, the past four months the most productive of my life. There was something to be said for the knuckle-cracking, elbow-throwing, manic kinetics of bipolarity—the best of times like blasting around the base path while an outfielder scrambled for the ball only to overthrow his cutoff man—it was the swell before the

storm. I arranged the treatise in the backseat of the car with
a handbook on either side, two magazines on top and three
on the bottom, the pages perfectly square. It wasn't until I
started the car when I realized I had absolutely no sense of
where to go.

My father had weaned me on Cal Ripkin Sr. and the
Oriole Way—*Perfect practice makes perfect!*—and when I sat
with him in the nosebleed section of Memorial Stadium, I
always kept score, balancing the program on both knees,
marking each diamond with deliberate hand. I still had the
program from Jim Palmer's first win—a relief effort against
the Yanks where Palmer whacked a two-run shot off Jim
Bouton. I had scored the at-bat with four perfectly vertical
lines. I was proud of this. Baseball *was* numbers, keeping
score as sacred a duty as reading the Midrash; there was an
ethic to marking the direction of every hit, to chronicling
every out, because, under perfectly drawn conditions—
where every coach at every level taught the game the same
way and where every fan and journalist understood every
level of the game's parts—we would have a fluid system
with replacement parts (players, media, and fans) that could
be substituted seamlessly into a big league club with little
or no adjustment. This was my vision.

As individuals, we were all disposable—players blew out
ACLs, were traded or retired; fans died, their paraphernalia
turning to kitsch after a club moved or changed its name
(the O's had been the St. Louis Browns, and before then,
the Milwaukee Brewers); pitching mounds, ball parks, and
strike zones shrank while biceps ballooned and records were
eclipsed—but the numbers, or rather, the numbers behind
the numbers were constant, proof of something larger and
more important than ourselves, something I wanted to be a
part of. Even in '86 (post-Robinson, Powell, and McNally)
when the team lost its first twenty-one straight games, I
opened the paper every morning to pick through anemic
averages with the same verve and attention I afforded Cal

Jr.'s 2,632nd game.

Keeping score, I cast fire from my hands, and after recoding a game's final out, the scorecard hugged to my chest, I felt like Moses carrying the commandments down from the mountain. Even as a child in the urinal lines, huddled among the sweaty masses, I imagined bell curves and standard deviations (not the schmaltz from *Field of Dreams*), and when my father, a survivor of Stalinist Russia, locked me in the hall closet for defacing the kitchen table with proofs suggesting Earl Weaver was holier than Abraham, I used baseball to quiet the mind and help me breathe. In the darkness, I ranked players by position, determining Joe Morgan to be the all-time best statistical second baseman despite the man's complete lack of faith in numbers. I imagined librarians living whole lives prostrate before the Dewey Decimal System, and I aspired to such devotion.

Susan, on the other hand, only had so much faith. She was staying with her friend Stephanie-the-lesbian in an Arlington townhouse a few blocks from the courthouse. After making two quick stops in Georgetown, I sped over the Key Bridge, parked in front of the house, and fed all my change to a meter. It was an overcast September afternoon, the sky bright as tin. A stray dog on the other side of the street ate flower bulbs from a front yard. When it saw me, it lifted its head and neighed like a horse, snorting cold air through its nose before it resumed its digging. Through an upstairs window someone was practicing the trumpet, ushering wobbly half notes up and down chromatic scales. I couldn't help but hum along. It sounded like a baseball organist trying to pump up the crowd for a late-inning rally. I tapped my foot. I'd stopped in a few stores on the way over, and now I held in one hand a bottle of Dom Pérignon, in the other a 24-pack of condoms.

When no one answered the doorbell, I tucked the champagne bottle under my arm and flipped through Stephanie's mail. One letter had my handwriting—it was addressed to Susan but I could not remember having written it. I tested the knob and found the door unlocked, the TV on. The TV faced a dark green sofa-loveseat set and broadcast an old episode of *The Facts of Life*. Susan joked that there were two versions of the facts of life, though I never knew if she meant the cast of the TV show or life in general. Last year at Stephanie's dinner party, I'd tried to enlist everyone in playing Milton Bradley's Game of Life right here on this living room floor. It was the original version (no money or pastel-colored station wagons) so I explained the rules: how one moved from infancy to happy old age, how the game used a teetotem instead of dice, how the squares represented vice or virtue, and how the game really had no end. "I don't know," Stephanie said, ashing her cigarette onto the game board. "It sounds a little too moralistic this close to Halloween."

Instead of playing the game, we passed a joint and watched *The Wizard of Oz* synchronized to *Dark Side of the Moon*. Both Susan and Stephanie wrote off the convergence to coincidence, but I knew about dynamic systems and the higher powers behind chaos theory. I also knew about conspiracy. That night, Stephanie had initiated her plan to steal Susan from me. She'd practically forced a cigarette down Susan's throat. Pot was one thing, an occasional thing, but Susan and I had both quit nicotine after grad school because in Susan's words, *it poured gasoline on the fire*.

"Come on," Stephanie said. "Smoking is the most fairly sure, fairly honorable method of suicide." She stole this from Kurt Vonnegut, but Susan didn't seem to care; she brought the cigarette to her lips, and in the light of the scented candle, she flashed Stephanie a mischievous glance. Since she quit smoking, Susan had put on weight, though she had never been as skinny as Stephanie, whose shoulder blades jutted out like a vestigial set of wings. Susan had a rounder face, biceps, and more meat around the hips. Maybe despite the lack of real-life, empirical evidence, it was true what they said, that opposites attract. I imagined a new square on the Checkered Game of Life—*wife seduced by dyke girlfriend, go back four spaces*—the equivalent of a catcher balking on an intentional walk. I bet Milty would have loved baseball (he'd only been alive for its nascent years). Along with Life, he invented croquet and the one-arm paper cutter, and sometimes when I gripped the paper cutter in the MTA's ninth floor copy room, I imagined shaking hands with the inventor, asking him about the forces behind life's more elusive rules.

Upstairs, the shower was running. I climbed the stairs, opened the door to the bathroom, and carefully balanced the champagne bottle on the sink before I found a seat on the closed lid of the toilet. From the ample curves of the shadow behind the curtain, I could tell it was Susan. In bed, statistics scrolling beneath my eyes, I liked to watch her sleep. She lay on her side and showed me her eyelids, her short hair touching the dimple on her chin. She hated that dimple even after I told her it was a sign of intelligence, that God, like an ethereal conveyor line supervisor, had stamped her chin with his thumb. Susan was an atheist, but when she slept, I saw proof of a higher design; her breathing was oddly metrical—arpeggio and hemiola—a code waiting to be cracked. I liked to imagine that in those small hours, she told me things she could not otherwise say—that she loved me, that she supported my work, and that in her sleep, her communal with the numerical world proved that God did not in fact play dice with the universe—that she and I were meant to be together.

We met in Ann Arbor while I was completing a PhD in agent-based modeling, she one in linguistics. We both attended a New Year's Eve party where based on a few conversations, Susan deduced the origins of every guest (not only where they grew up but the ethnicities of their grandparents). It was a neat trick and it worked for everyone but me. "There's something wrong with your speech," she said after a thoughtful drag of her cigarette. Later that night, the two of us alone in the spare bedroom, I told her how sometimes my words came too fast to speak. She kissed me mid-explanation.

I felt a similar jolt when water shifted from showerhead to faucet and Susan yanked open the shower curtain.

"Jesus Christ," she said, covering herself with the curtain.

"No. Just Max. And I've seen you naked before."

"Get out," she yelled. "What the hell are you doing?"

"It's okay," I said, uncorking the champagne, using both thumbs to rocket the cork off the ceiling. Bubbly foamed into my lap.

"I'm finished," I told her. "I'm free." I dropped down to my knees. "Now we can be together."

"Jesus, Max." She saw the condoms I'd arranged in three rows of eight on the bathroom floor. "You have to leave. Now."

"But we're celebrating." I thought back to New Year's Eve in Ann Arbor, the two of us making love under the pile of coats. "Here." I held up the champagne. "To us!"

"You're off your meds," Susan said. "I can hear it in your voice."

"Look," I said, "the way I figure it, it's the bottom of the ninth, there's a man on third, and I've still got two outs."

"I'm calling the cops."

"Baby, I've done the math—in five years we've had 12.5 fights, and that's quantifying a fight by the slamming of a door where a half a fight is a relatively strong but not too strong slam which gives us 4.8 fights a month which is only 1.2 a week. Even if you've switched teams, you can't ignore the numbers."

"I haven't switched teams." Susan lifted one foot from the water pooling in the tub. "I can't do this anymore. We both know where this goes."

"Hold on," I said. "What about chemistry?"

Susan dropped the curtain only to reach out and grab a towel from the rack above my head. "Chemistry's a myth. You've said so yourself."

"No. Wait. You're not hearing me." My voice was louder than I would have liked. To calm down I thought about rosin bags, bat tar, and the fat mesh of a catcher's mitt. A big inning was slipping away. "Listen to me," I said. "Listen to where I'm coming from."

"Come on, Max." Susan cinched the towel around her chest. "I never knew where you were coming from."

I should have predicted this. I should have applied VOWS to our marriage and found transferable stats for "locker room guys" like Jeff Conine and Kevin Millar. But Susan never cared about numbers. In the past, she'd recognized the *Walden*-like quality of my work, but now, as I quoted Thoreau, she pushed me down the stairs. She threw changeups at me, saying that even in seclusion, Thoreau had lived one mile from his mother. "She cooked for him. She cleaned. But maybe that's what you want. Not a wife, but a mother."

I protested—my mother only existed as a dim, disapproving memory—but I remembered how Susan used to bring me dinner when I worked late in the basement. *I should make a spreadsheet*, she said, *of how you never eat*. If we lived in a different era, if I were a novelist or a philosopher, she'd take me in her arms instead of forcing me out the door.

"Go home to your report," she said. "It better be worth it."

I had more to say, but the words wouldn't come, and I was at even more of a loss when I returned to the car, or rather, the empty space where my car had been. The parking meter flashed a cycloptic red eye, and only after copying down the towing company's Fairfax address did I realize what I had left in the backseat.

I already knew about loss—the tidy, yuppie Camden Yards replacing the beautifully dilapidated Memorial Stadium; the skinny, hairless arm of Jeffrey Maier manufacturing Derek Jeter's '97 playoff homerun; and Babe Ruth, Baltimore's proudest son, being sold in 1914 to the Red Sox on his way to becoming the Yankee juggernaut, a move which, considering the O's past decade of miserable, sub-500 seasons, might have cursed us after all.

Racing back to the house, I imagined Ralph Ellison—

Susan's favorite writer—standing outside his burning house and watching through the window as his second novel turned into kindling one page at a time. I stabbed at the bell and nearly broke my fist off on the door, but Susan wouldn't respond. I saw the three little pigs—Susan, Stephanie, and Horvitz—sitting in the living room, laughing, lighting my treatise with the ends of their cigarettes.

"I'll huff and I'll puff," I yelled. "I'll break it all down."

The stray dog stampeded down the block, and I no longer heard the trumpeter. The count was 0-2 and I was fouling off pitches. I didn't want to be the guy who made the last out, so when Susan finally slid a Metro card out from under the door, I rubbed the gooseflesh on my arms and resolved to swing away.

Even when funneled through the turnstiles, escalators, and tunnels of Camden Yards, I was promised a green expanse of field, a view into the open arena of certainty. I tried to imagine that view now, but a few feet down the escalator's steep, subterranean descent, I was back in my father's hall closet with only numbers in my head. The Fairfax station was seven stops from Courthouse, a distance of 10.51 miles, a travel time of 21 minutes, a fare of $2.35—no, $3.45 in rush-hour. Rush-hour! I moved as far right on the escalator steps as I could and let the hurried crowd jostle past. They struck me with satchels and umbrellas, and when they glared up at me, I imagined a vicious dog foaming at the mouth, tearing at the ground, fighting against its leash. The MTA escalators were the longest in the Western Hemisphere, and back over my shoulder through the entrance's shrinking maw, I saw the light of a dying star.

During our disaster of a honeymoon in New York City, I'd been too afraid to leave the hotel, so Susan had traveled alone up to the top of the Empire State Building. I was not proud of this, nor was I about to give up. The treatise meant a front-office job—even in the National League—which would finally prove to Susan the importance of my work.

I'd read about Grigory Perelman, the Russian mathematician who solved the Poincaré conjecture. He was a recluse who lived in St. Petersburg with his mother. He grew out his hair and fingernails and only left the house at night to see the opera where he sat in the last row and listened for harmonics. Instead of publishing the proof, he declined the Fields Medal and posted the solution on-line. *If the proof is correct,* he said, *then no other recognition is needed.* I could never be so selfless.

I leapt from the escalator just before it swallowed my feet, and taking my lead from the other commuters, I fed Susan's Metro card into a mechanized turnstile. A smaller escalator brought me to the island of the platform, deep trenches on either side. I paced the middle of the platform, wringing my hands, trying to ignore the sight of the third rail. There was a troubling existentiality to the 70s-style hanger, the gray, corrugated, seemingly acoustically-modeled canals, the brown obelisks that served as station markers, and the blinking, circular, yellow lights that preceded the strang and thrum of an approaching train. I never imagined such violence.

The other commuters made a show of reading newspapers and books, but when they looked up over their raised collars, I knew they were watching—yes, all of them—the ones in headphones receiving secret instructions. I knew how things worked—I was always sure to tear up and flush any correspondence bearing my Social Security Number—so when the train thundered to a stop and its doors gasped open, I stood still.

People pushed their way each way through the doors, but I hesitated. Each car only held 5,250 cubic feet of air, which, divided by fifty-three passengers, meant less than twenty-seven moles of oxygen per person. For the second time today, I struggled through visualization exercises, trying to summon that mountain lake. *Go, go, go!* shouted a woman behind me, knocking me forward. I held my breath as the doors closed. With no empty seats, I stood in the aisle and clutched a metal pole with both hands.

Perfect Practice Makes Perfect

My treatise had determined that a player's speed around the base path was overvalued, but standing on the train, surfing the bends of its track, I had to admit some comfort in velocity. An MTA train could reach fifty-nine miles-per-hour, and I willed the train to move even faster, not minding the bump and buckle of fellow passengers who were dancing the exact same steps as me. I imagined the treatise in my hands. I imagined Susan, her strong arms around me as the two of us bundled up in bed and blocked out winter's woolen days. At the next stop, I stared at the Metro map and settled on players who represented each of the five lines: Cal Ripken Jr. the affluent Maryland suburban red, Boog Powell the volatile green of south-east D.C., Brooks Robinson the bland but dependable yellow line towing the center of the city, Eddie Murray the orange's workman-like northern Virginia corridor, and Jim Palmer the blue's upscale extension through Crystal City. I diagramed it all out on the receipt for the champagne.

At Ballston, a woman in uniform boarded and moved to stand next to me. She wore a blue-on-blue military uniform, bars on her shoulders, and close-cropped brown hair. I remembered the army captain who'd approached me in Ann Arbor at the close of my PhD. *You're special*, the captain had told me. *We value special people like you.* He wanted me to model the effectiveness of government weaponry even though I'd been researching the extinction rates of Chilean sea bass. I turned down the money. I had other visions. Susan never forgave me for this.

The military woman looked a bit like Susan, especially from the neck down, but something about the woman's head—a scalloped set of ears bookending a flat, expressionless face—made her look more butch. Could physical characteristics serve as determinants for sexual orientation? With no room left on the champagne receipt, I made notes on the back of Susan's Metro card. The military woman—whose nameplate read "Kowalski"—eyed my writing.

"Are you Polish?" I asked.

The woman responded with a curt nod.

"My wife's from Krakow. Her grandparents, I mean."

The woman nodded again and then turned to the train's dark window.

"You're a dyke, right?"

"Excuse me?"

"You can tell me. I'm a scientist."

Silence.

"Look. There's nothing wrong with woman-woman love, or man-man love for that matter. What is cunnilingus and fellatio and penetration but attention? Love is attention. The end of attention is the end of life."

"What are you saying?"

"It doesn't matter what I'm saying. Life cannot be broken into words. We need to *embarrass* words, embarrass them into confessing their pigments until the colors run from our hands." I shimmied and swayed with the train, releasing the handrail and raising my arms. Words clung to me like a burning robe. I gave over to their momentum. "Do you know how much I've seen? How many innings, hours, outs? I've recorded them, been good to them, treated them like I want to and deserve to be treated. You see, Adam didn't doom us by eating the apple. Abraham did it by refusing to slaughter his son. He disobeyed God. And God is not pi. He's not irrational, an infinity of digits. He's rational, as rational as 1-2-3, a concrete, undecimaled force.

"Look, you can't back away from this. When you bend the world with your eyes, you see the curve of the world, and that's where God lives. He's lives here—in every car of every train, all 662, in each one of these 86 stations, in every inch of 106 miles of electrified rail. You see, it's a fluid system. Every piece of flesh and metal is accounted for. I know. I've done the math."

"You need help," Kowalski said. She made fists with her hands.

"No." I took a deep breath and placed my hands over her breasts. "I need love and love is all we need."

The chorus of the train lulled any sense of danger, so when the punch came, it caught me full on the side of the head, the force of the blow dropping me to my knees. The pain was tremendous but I kept talking, even as people jumped from their seats to hold me down. "I'm going to Fairfax," I said. "I've been fair, and the numbers have been fair, so please be fair to me."

Thirty minutes later I was handcuffed to a chair in the fifty-by-fifty foot security room of the Falls Church Metro station. Sitting across from me was a uniformed officer sorting through a pile of papers. The officer was heavy-set and black with glasses and a fine, light-gray beard. On the other side of his desk, a 12-inch TV broadcast the Orioles game.

"What's the score?" I asked, tasting blood in my mouth.

The officer shook his head. "Boy, you are a piece of work."

My jaw hurt and I remembered the time during my limited, real-life baseball playing days when I took a grounder to the face, my two front teeth busted out. My father had coached all my teams, starting me at second base regardless of my average or on-base percentage. He yelled at me for poor hitting, for not sacrificing my body to the ball, and since I couldn't hit a curveball, I never made it past Little League.

"Just tell me who's up. I can't see from here."

The officer shook his head but this time he smiled. I tried to lean toward the TV but the cuffs cut into my wrists. They were attached in front of me to one arm of the chair.

"Look," I said, "at least give me some ice?"

The officer sighed. He opened the cooler under his desk and tossed an icepack into my lap. Despite the handcuffs, I managed to hold the icepack to the side of my head. The walls began closing in.

"You know," I said. "I built this place. There's one every three stations on the Orange Line."

"Anyone could know that."

"I guess." I would have gone on and reeled off everything else I knew—the date the room was constructed and the hours of the officer's shift—but I was tired and my head felt like an echo chamber.

"I need to get to Fairfax," I said. "I need to make a call."

The officer chuckled. "You need to get hold of your business. I haven't seen a brawl like that since '98, when Armando drilled Martinez."

"May 19th. A Tuesday. I was there."

"Yeah?" The officer's eyes lit up. "Remember Lloyd running in from the bullpen to get in some licks? And Strawberry's sucker-punch? Jesus, he fell right into the dugout."

"Munoz replaced Benitez. Gave up a two-run homer."

"But that fight! Who was it who slugged Strawberry?"

I switched the icepack between hands. "I don't know. I missed that."

"How does anyone miss that?"

"I was keeping score."

"Keeping score? People still do that?"

"I do."

The officer looked me over. Then he turned back to the game, shaking his head at the TV.

Listening to the announcers, I tried to picture the game, but all I saw were peanut shells and pencil shavings. When I made a move to wring my hands, the cuffs held me back.

"How's Cabrera?" I asked.

"His heater's going. But Thomas is coming up."

"Can I watch?"

"Yeah. All right." The officer sat up and turned the TV so I could see the mountain of a man tower over the plate. Frank Thomas was the only player in major league history to have seven consecutive seasons of a .300 average and at least 100 walks, 100 runs, 100 runs-batted-in, and 20 home runs. But that was in the nineties. This season, his on-base percentage had dropped from the 400s to the low 300s, and his walks had dropped from the 130s to the 80s. His waist had swelled and though his arms were still Hulk-like, his legs looked less like cudgels than fatty shanks of meat. Thomas knocked his bat against his cleats and then home base, bringing forth a cloud of dirt. For the first pitch, he didn't even lift his bat up off his shoulder.

"Don't worry about Thomas," I said. "His strikeout-to-walk ratio is the highest in the league."

"I don't know," the officer said. "He's still the Big Hurt."

"Wanna bet?"

"Bet what?"

"If Thomas strikes out, you let me go."

The officer ran his pen over his paperwork. Then he took off his glasses and rubbed his eyes. "I'll think about it."

Thomas called time. He stepped out of the box and adjusted the plastic armor covering his left arm. He tapped his helmet over the massive dome of his head and then took a wide stance. His eyes narrowed and his nostrils flared, and when the next pitch came, Thomas' body unwound, the colossus of arms and legs and hips let loose like a coiled spring. I held my breath until the ball disappeared over the deepest part of the field.

"Wait." I strained against the handcuffs and tried to stand. "That's not supposed to happen."

"I told you so," the officer said. "He's still a tough out."

A tough out? I shifted in my chair and the icepack fell to the floor. We were all tough outs—I was an out and Susan was an out, just as Stephanie and Horvitz were outs, and on and on and on. Thomas dropped his bat and rounded the bases with a slow, measured gait, and I saw the hint of a smile crack through his stony face. Susan had smiled like that the first night in our house. With everything still in boxes, we sat on a bed sheet and watched the game on her tiny black-and-white, the one with bunny-ears and tracking problems. We sat Indian-style on the floor and ate fried chicken with our hands, my fingers too greasy to keep score, our mouths too full to talk. It was just Susan and me, the treatise still unborn, our degrees newly minted, the only light in the room the gleam of the TV, the game a mere reflection in my wife's wine-dark eyes.

"The Big Hurt," said the officer, tugging at his beard. "Wow, the Hurt."

"Yeah," I nodded, sinking back in the chair. "He's still got it. It's still there."

The Neighbors
Frank Tavares

Newt Snyder took his time aiming. He was in his driveway leaning against the side rail of his Ford pickup. The streetlamp had been out for weeks. He was in the shadows, just like they'd trained him for Iraq. He took a low breath, let it half out, and squeezed the trigger. There was hardly a sound. The drone of his neighbor's air pump covered the pop of the silencer. Right between the eyes. The head snapped, then wobbled. A second shot and it started to deflate. In less than a minute, the whole thing would be over.

Newt lowered the rifle and retreated into his house. It was a small place, cheaply built in the early fifties—a cottage with city water and sewer, gas, two bedrooms, a leaky roof, and a car port: like all the others on the block. He tossed his coat on the couch and watched from behind the curtains as the inflatable Santa-on-a-motorcycle pancaked onto the snow. Three other airless Christmas figures lay in puddles of light around it, each aglow from a bulb under the plastic. One had been a snowman, another a tree. The largest had been a four foot snow globe with a carousel inside—three little unicorns carrying an elf, an Elmo, and some other critter Newt didn't recognize. They had revolved inside the transparent shell while Christmas music played from a speaker sitting on the side step of a big, red Peterbilt cab backed into the driveway. His neighbor's front door burst open.

"Aw, shit!" the man yelled and spiked a beer can into the snow.

"Goddamn fuckin' kids."

Newt's neighbor Frank Brevic wasn't a tall man, but he was built like a bear—barrel chest, short legs, big arms. He walked like a bear, too. Except for the mullet, if you covered him with fur, he'd fool a naturalist. The man seldom wore a coat. He favored vests that showed the tattoos on his biceps and forearms. If the temp dipped close to freezing, he'd wear a sweatshirt underneath, but that was it.

"It's all in the head," he'd once said to Newt. "You just concentrate on not shivering. That's where you lose your body heat." Brevic had been army. Two rotations in Iraq just like Newt. No shivering there.

Newt opened his door and yelled across the yard. "Hey, Brevic. What's the problem?"

"Fuckin' bastards." He stood in the snow, hands clenched in fists. "No fuckin' spirit of fuckin' Christmas."

Newt put his coat back on and went outside. Brevic was examining the Santa head. "Look at this," he said, sticking his finger into the hole between Santa's eyes. "Fuckin' head shot."

"Clean."

"You got a gun, Newt?"

"Yeah. Why?"

"Cause if you see the bastards before I do, I want you to shoot their fuckin' balls off." He threw the plastic to the ground then yanked the power cord off his porch. The music stopped and the pools of light disappeared, but the front of Brevic's house was still illuminated with rows of white bulbs that traced its outline. They were strung along the soffits and around the frames of the windows. The chimney was highlighted with a Santa display, the old fashioned kind, a rigid plastic 3-D figure lit from the inside and fastened to the brick with a clothesline.

Brevic kicked the snow. Newt noticed he was barefoot.

"Feet cold?" Newt asked.

Brevic looked down at his toes in the snow. "Can't tell anymore," he said. "Since Iraq, I don't have any feeling in 'em."

Newt grimaced. "Want a beer?"

Brevic shrugged but followed Newt into the house leaving wet footprints all the way into the kitchen. Newt took two bottles out of the refrigerator. They twisted off the caps and clinked the necks.

"Merry Christmas," Newt said.

"Yeah, what's left of it."

They each took a healthy swallow.

"Shame about your yard display," said Newt. "You gonna replace them?"

Brevic shook his head. "I've patched them twice already. That's enough. Maybe I'll just get more lights for the house."

Newt nodded.

"So how come no feeling in the feet?" Newt asked.

Brevic shrugged again. "Nerve damage. Last tour. Shrapnel in my back. Pretty numb from the knees down."

"I'm surprised you can walk," said Newt.

Brevic smiled. "So are the sons-a-bitch docs." He took a sip. "I'm not supposed to be barefoot. Too easy to hurt 'em without realizing it."

Brevic looked out the window. "Hey, you can see right into my kitchen," he said. "That could be embarrassing."

Newt looked away. "Don't worry. I got better things to do."

Brevic looked around the room. "Opposite layout to mine."

"I think they just had one basic floor plan and flipped every other house," said Newt.

"Same gas stove." They sat at the table. "Yours work?"

Newt nodded.

"Mine's got a leak," said Brevic. "Landlady's too cheap to replace it, so I just shut off the damn valve. Been using propane and an army camp stove."

"Better than MREs," said Newt.

"Sometimes," Brevic said and looked down the hall. "Two bedroom, right?"

"And one tiny bath."

"Ever think about getting outta this fuckin' neighborhood?" Brevic asked.

"All the time," said Newt.

Brevic leaned forward, elbows on knees. "Me too. All the fuckin' time. I think that's why I stay on the road so much. Fantasize sometime about just going AWOL and not coming back."

Frank Brevic was an independent. He owned his own rig but contracted with the majors, spending three weeks a month hauling auctioned cars all over the map.

"Ever have one fall off the back?" Newt asked him once.

"No, but I seen it happen," Brevic had said then laughed as he told about some twenty-year-old forgetting to chain a high end SUV. "First bump out of the yard and that fucker slid right off. Slow motion like. Last I heard, the kid drives fruit and shit."

"Brevic, you in here?" a woman's voice yelled from the front door.

"Yeah?"

"You driving me to work or what?"

Brevic grimaced and looked at Newt. "Yeah, I'm driving you." He downed the rest of the bottle and got up. "Wife's car is in the shop. Gotta go do my husbandly duty. Thanks for the beer."

"No problem," said Newt as Brevic barefooted it back into the snow.

A minute later, the Peterbilt fired up, and Frank Brevic pulled out of his driveway with his wife Chelsea in the passenger seat. Newt watched from his front door.

Chelsea Brevic was a looker. Taller than Brevic and ten years younger. She bleached her hair and favored bright lipstick that left pink rings on the filters of her cigarettes. She wasn't overweight, but had a fullness to her that stretched her clothes. Especially the tops. Chelsea was a waitress at a truck stop just off the interstate. It was a super stop, everything from Chelsea's restaurant to showers to truck detailing. Even mini-rooms where drivers could catch a couple of hours sleep or cheat some time with a working girl. Lots of traffic. An oasis in the desert of boredom for those riding the big rigs. It's where Frank Brevic met

Chelsea Khalil almost six months earlier. And where Newt Snyder had met her a month before that, her first night on the job. Newt had taken a fancy to her. She reminded him of a woman he had flirted with during his tour in the Green Zone.

"Chelsea's not my real name," she had confessed to him the first time they had sex. She had a Middle Eastern accent that bordered on the exotic. "My real name is Iraq."

"That's your first name?"

"My father was a proud son of Iraq," she said as way of explanation. "He honored his homeland and cursed me with a stupid name. So I changed it when I came to the United States. I like how it sounded so American. Not like refugee."

Newt was an overnight mechanic at the truck stop. It was a trade he had adopted in high school and which had served him well after the army pulled him off patrols. He became a diesel specialist, something that translated into job security when he came back to life as a civilian. A couple of times a week, he'd take a 3:00 a.m. lunch at the restaurant. The night he met Chelsea, he was the only one at her counter. She made a point of leaning over so he could see down her blouse. It was an obvious move, but Newt liked the obvious. She told him she was going on break and invited him outside for a cigarette. They ended up in the sleeper of a five year old Kenworth that Newt had been servicing.

"Do you know why I decided to fuck you?" Chelsea asked after their frenzied first coupling.

"Why?" he said and stubbed out his cigarette in an ashtray on the floor.

"Your hands." She laced her fingers through his. "Your strong hands."

"You like my hands?"

"Hands of a man. Someone who could take care of a woman. I wanted to know what they would feel like on my body."

"They feel okay?"

She answered by kissing him and pushing him back onto

the mattress.

"We need to get out of here," he said in response and sat up to pull on his jeans. "I told Bill I'd have this piece of shit out of here by now. He'd burn my ass if he found us ballin' in a customer's truck."

She had Newt on his back three nights in a row before she asked him for money.

"A hundred dollars," she said. "Just for tonight. The first two nights I fuck you for love." "You crazy?" he asked. "I'm not giving you any fuckin' hundred dollars." He was surprised that she looked hurt.

"Do you love me?" she asked.

"No, I don't love you," he said.

"Do you want to be my boyfriend? Take care of me?"

"Hell no."

"Then you should pay me. That's how things work. I give you sex, you pay me."

"Jeez," he said and looked out of the window. Bill was at the end of the bay hunting for something on the bench.

"Look, Chelsea," Newt said. "We had a good time. I didn't know you were on the clock. I'm sorry for any misunderstanding but I ain't fuckin' paying you."

"Seventy-five," she said. "Or I'm telling Bill."

"No."

"Bill!" she yelled.

"Wait," Newt said and clamped his hand over her mouth. He looked out the window. Bill had turned toward the truck. Chelsea started to say something beneath Newt's hand. He shook her. "Quiet!" he rasped.

Bill turned back to the bench, picked a wrench, then left.

Newt took his hand away.

"I think you should pay me the seventy-five dollars now," Chelsea said as she buttoned her blouse.

Newt stared at her. He took out his wallet and rifled through the bills. "I got thirty-six," he said and threw two tens, three fives and a single on the mattress. She took the money, stuffed it in her cleavage, then climbed out of the cab without another word.

"Fuckin' bitch," he said.

Newt stayed away from the restaurant for a good week until one slow night when Bill dragged him across the lot for breakfast. Newt steered them to a booth away from Chelsea's counter. After they ate, Bill gave him the rest of the night off and headed back to the garage. Newt stayed, drank coffee, and watched Chelsea flirt with a driver at the counter. He saw her leave with him and return alone twenty minutes later. An hour after that, she left with another. When she returned the second time, she made eye contact with Newt just long enough to mouth a curse and give him the finger. That was almost seven months ago. Just before Frank Brevic took her bait.

Brevic had rented the house next door about the time Newt Snyder had been hustled by Iraq Chelsea Khalil. Newt admired Brevic's Peterbilt. The man had customized it nicely and kept it clean. Lots of drivers didn't keep their rigs clean. Brevic was not too long back in the states. Kept to himself. It was two weeks before he mumbled a hello when Newt waved one morning coming home from work.

Newt was in the restaurant the night Brevic met Chelsea. He watched Brevic pay his counter bill and duck out the side door with her. But this time, she didn't come back. Newt stopped in an hour later to fill his thermos. Still no sign of her. "It was slow," said the other waitress. "She left early."

Later that morning after Newt was home, he caught a glimpse of Chelsea in Brevic's kitchen. She was laughing. A week after that, Chelsea Khalil had moved in. She and Brevic were married before the end of the month.

Now half a year later, Newt never caught anyone laughing in the Brevic household. Brevic was sullen and Newt knew that Chelsea still moonlighted amongst the rigs outside the restaurant.

"You're a sorry bastard," Newt said as he watched Brevic's taillights disappear down the block.

Newt pulled on a black sweatshirt and went outside. He

stood for a moment in the shadows by his truck. With the dead streetlight, it was pretty dark, even with the holiday bulbs that hung from Brevic's house. Newt went to the end of his driveway, then followed the sidewalk onto Brevic's porch. The door was locked, but the cheap hardware was easy to defeat with a putty knife that Newt slid into the crack between the door and frame. The door opened and Newt slipped inside.

It wasn't the first time Newt had reconned Brevic's house. He'd slipped in once before when Brevic was on the road and Chelsea was working the restaurant. That time, she almost caught him when she came home with one of her customers. He barely made it out the back window. He had rewarded himself by hanging in the yard and watching through the gauze of Brevic's bedroom curtain as Chelsea earned her money. Afterwards, he felt exhilarated. "Like being shot at," he wrote in his journal.

Newt headed for the bedroom. It was a mess: unmade bed and dirty clothes on the floor. He looked in a nightstand drawer. Same pills he'd found before. Two bottles with antidepressants, an expired antibiotic, and a wheel of birth control. She was almost out. The prescriptions were written for "Iraq." He hadn't noticed that before. He reached further into the drawer and found a vibrator. "This is new," he said and turned it on. The batteries were low. "Well, Brevic, looks like you ain't getting the job done." He shut it off and tossed it back. In the other nightstand, he found a pack of condoms and a pack of cigarettes.

Newt checked the bathroom. The sink was small like his. Two worn toothbrushes were on the rim fighting for space with a deformed tube of toothpaste. In the cabinet above, two sets of shaving supplies, an open package of tampons, and half a dozen bottles of pills— two for Brevic, the rest for Iraq: pain killers and other medications he didn't recognize. A hair dryer was on the back of the toilet along with a bottle of contact lens cleaner and a box of tissues. In the linen closet, Newt found Brevic's gun in a stack of towels. It was loaded. Newt checked the safety and shoved it back into the terrycloth.

He returned to the bedroom and went through the dresser drawers where he had been interrupted the last time. Hers were on the bottom, sexy lingerie and skimpy panties. He held up one pair, a leopard print with a thong back. He pocketed them and felt through the rest, finding another vibrator nestled among the underwear. In the next drawer, he found two envelopes. One was stuffed with cash. He counted it out—over eight thousand dollars in mixed bills. He wondered if his thirty-six were among them.

The other envelope was a collection of Polaroids. They featured a naked Chelsea in a number of poses with and without anonymous partners. Newt sat on the edge of the bed and thumbed through them. The photos were crude and amateur, but their effect was electric, and Newt enjoyed feeling their energy. Until he got to one surprising shot of Chelsea playing alone on a couch. It was the couch in his living room.

Newt jumped when he heard the rumble of Brevic's truck pulling into the driveway. He stuffed everything back into their envelopes and shoved them into the drawer. He unlocked the window, but it wouldn't open. It was stuck, frozen by the ice that coated the outside sill. He heard the truck rev, then go silent. Newt tried to loosen the window by pounding the frame with the heel of his hand, but it only cracked the pane. He heard Brevic unlocking the door. Newt turned his face away from the window and elbowed the glass. It shattered.

"What the fuck?" Brevic said from the kitchen. Newt heard him coming down the hall and slammed the bedroom door. He jammed a chair under the knob and dove out the window.

"Shit!" he said as he hit the ground harder than expected. He got up and staggered across the snow in the direction opposite his house. He made it across three backyards before he realized he was limping. He turned into the street. No sign of Brevic. Newt kept to the shadows and circled the block, approaching his house from the side away from the neighbor's. He let himself into the back and stood in his kitchen, hands on knees, catching his breath. "Shit!" he repeated between gasps. "Too close."

The overhead light flickered on. "Closer than you fuckin' think," Brevic said behind him. Newt felt the pressure of a gun on the side of his neck. "Move slowly," Brevic said. "While you're down there, take off your boots."

As Newt untied his boots, he saw blood. One of his pant legs was slit. He had cut himself jumping out the window. The adrenaline had dampened the pain during his flight, but now in his kitchen, he felt it starting to burn.

"Turn 'em upside down," said Brevic. "Let's see the pattern on them soles."

Newt did as he was told.

"You fuckin' asshole," Brevic said as he kicked Newt to the floor.

"Jeez, man!" Newt yelled as he tried to shield himself.

"What the fuck you doing in my house?" Brevic was barefoot, but let go another kick that connected with Newt's injured leg. Newt rolled in pain. Brevic kicked at him again. "Fuckin' going through my drawers!"

"What the fuck you talking about?" Newt said, trying to protect his bloody leg.

"What the fuck I'm talking about?" asked Brevic. "What the fuck I'm talking about?" He reached down and yanked Chelsea's panties out of Newt's pocket. "Fuckin' pervert." He got ready for another kick.

"Don't!" yelled Newt curling up to protect himself. "Stop!"

Brevic hesitated. "Aw, fuck," he said. "I broke my fuckin' toe again." He sat on the floor with a thud. Newt looked over. Brevic's big toe was bent sideways. "Shit."

Newt sat up against the refrigerator. His leg was throbbing. His hands were bloody. He could see the gash in his leg. It was big enough for stitches. He grabbed a dishtowel hanging from a drawer and pressed it over the wound.

"Doc's going to fuckin' kill me," said Brevic. "She told me not to go barefoot." He lay his gun on the floor and reached for his toe. He jerked it back into place with a snap. Newt grimaced. Brevic picked up his gun. "I should just fuckin' kill you and be done with it."

"Don't," Newt said, raising a palm toward his neighbor. "Please." Brevic held the pistol at arm's length aiming right between Newt's eyes.

"A nice, clean head shot," said Brevic.

Newt raised both hands in surrender. "Look, man," he said. "I'm sorry. It was a dumbass thing to do."

Brevic held the gun steady for a few long seconds, then bent his elbow, and fired into the ceiling. Newt flinched. Plaster snowed over them and a chunk the size of a dinner plate fell onto the floor at Brevic's feet. He kicked at it with his heel. "Fuck."

Newt reached back to his leg. The bleeding had stopped. The two men sat there for a moment. Brevic smiled.

"What was you planning on doing with them panties? Wear 'em?"

"I don't know," said Newt. "I wasn't really thinking."

"She told me about it, you know."

"What."

"How you fuckin' stiffed her."

"I didn't stiff her. We just had a little misunderstanding."

"Yeah," said Brevic. "Thirty-six dollars." He reached toward Newt's leg and lifted the towel. "Shit, man. You need to clean that thing and get it sewed up. You got some isopropyl?"

"In the bathroom."

Brevic got up. He came back with the bottle and a roll of gauze. He grabbed a knife off the counter and knelt down. He slit the rest of Newt's pant leg and exposed the wound.

"This might hurt a bit," Brevic said as he unscrewed the bottle top.

Newt gasped as Brevic poured the alcohol over the gash.

He balled his fists and concentrated on staying conscious as the pain seared up his leg and into his gut. He was sweating. Brevic wrapped the bandage around the wound and tied it off. "That'll hold you till we get there."

"Get where?" asked Newt, his hands shaking.

"The fuckin' VA, man."

"I don't need the VA."

"Suit yourself," said Brevic. "I'll sew it up here for you."

Newt looked at him.

"I can, you know. One of the many survival skills I brought back with me."

Newt shook his head.

"Then get your boots on."

Newt struggled and Brevic helped him tying the laces.

"Come on," Brevic said pulling him to his feet.

Newt's leg was on fire but he made it to Brevic's driveway and into the Peterbilt. Brevic fished a pair of socks and boots from behind the driver's seat and put them on. "If I walk in there barefoot, they won't let me out," he said.

Brevic started the engine. They rolled onto the street. Neither said a word for a block and a half.

"I ain't much good below the waist," said Brevic. "Fuckin' shrapnel numbed everything."

Newt sank into his seat.

"Chelsea's been real good about it. She don't really expect anything from me in that department." Brevic maneuvered the Peterbilt onto the boulevard that led downtown. "We play around with her toys and shit, but when it comes down to the nitty gritty, she just needs a little outside entertainment. Letting her keep working, well, seems the least I can do. Fact she gets paid for it's a fuckin' bonus."

Newt lowered the window to let the cold air dry the sweat on his face. "Why you telling me this shit?"

"To let you know that I know," said Brevic. "Let you know she ain't doin' stuff behind my fuckin' back."

Brevic stopped for a light. They sat in silence until it changed. "It don't bother you?" asked Newt.

"Fuck, man. I didn't say that." Brevic started through the intersection.

"I saw the pictures," said Newt.

Brevic shrugged

"You take 'em?"

"She likes to pose. Keeps hoping to get one in Hustler. You know, 'photo by husband.'"

"You took one on my couch."

Brevic laughed. "That's the one she wanted to send in."

They parked in a lot across from the ER. Newt's leg was aflame. He could barely put pressure on it. Brevic helped him down from the cab. Newt leaned on Brevic more than he wanted. By the time they got inside, Newt was dripping in sweat. A nurse got him a wheel chair. Brevic got him some water.

The ER was crowded. Damaged vets in all states of disrepair. It took close to two hours before someone looked at him. The pain had settled into a steady throb, nothing he couldn't handle with concentration. He'd been hurt worse than this. The bleeding had stopped but the wound was deeper than he thought. When the doc started examining it, the fire returned. Newt gripped the sides of the table and lay back on his elbows gritting his teeth. The doc emptied a syringe with multiple stabs around the gash until the fire went out. There was embedded glass the doc had to remove and then a dozen stitches. By the time they were finished, Newt's leg was wrapped tightly, an ace bandage holding it all together.

"Try to stay off it for a couple of days," the doc said.

Brevic wheeled Newt back to the truck and helped him into the cab.

"Thanks," Newt mumbled after they'd settle into the seats.

"No problem," Brevic grunted and started the engine.

They got back to the boulevard before Brevic said, "But you could do me a favor."

Newt shrugged.

"Help me kill her."

* * * * *

It had snowed again. A good six inches. It had been four days since Brevic had asked Newt to help him frag his wife. Newt was pretty much back on his feet but avoided going outside for fear of running into his neighbor, even after the guy cleared both their sidewalks and driveways with his snow blower, finishing off the front steps by hand.

It was six p.m. Newt had to go to work. Bill had threatened to can him if he took any more time off, leg or no leg. Newt eased on his boots. He looked out the window to check Brevic's driveway. The Peterbilt had been gone all day. Chelsea's car was back from the shop: a ten year old beater with a driver's door that didn't match. As long as she parked in the driveway, Newt knew Brevic was on the road. Newt was about to open the door when he saw Chelsea heading toward her car. He'd wait until she left.

She slid behind the wheel. The motor barely turned over. It groaned a couple of times then stopped altogether. She got out and slammed the door. He was surprised when he saw her cross the driveway toward his porch. She rang the bell.

He stood still, hoping she'd give up quickly. But she knew he was home because his truck was outside. She rang again then knocked. He took a breath and opened it.

"You going to work?" she asked.

He nodded.

"I need a ride."

She didn't say anything for half the trip. She sat next to him, seatbelt tight, arms crossed. At a stoplight he caught her looking at him. She smiled.

"I still like your hands," she said.

It was warm in the truck. Chelsea unzipped her coat. Beneath the winter padding, she showed cleavage.

"Don't you get cold?" Newt asked.

"I keep a sweater at work," she said. "Besides, being in and out of the kitchen keeps me hot."

He shrugged.

"How is your leg?" she asked. "He told me you hurt it."

"Leg's fine," he said.

"He told me you hurt it in our house."

"It's fine," he repeated.

"I am embarrassed," she said. "He told me you saw the pictures."

Newt looked at her. She looked away.

"He makes me take the pictures," she said. "It's not my idea." She looked at him again, no trace of a smile.

Newt stopped for a light. "Didn't look like you were objecting too much," he said.

"He beat me if I don't pose for him. Pictures don't show that." She crossed her arms again.

Newt pulled onto the highway. "So the hustling part's okay," he said. "Just not the pictures."

"I marry him," she said. "I thought I have someone to take care of me. Someone who understood. But he chooses men for me to bring home. Makes me do things."

"Like play on my couch?"

She looked out the side window. "I told him you and I were lovers once. So he broke into your house and had me sit there. He was going to give you the picture to show you're no longer the big man."

Newt shook his head. "Chelsea," he said. "You're so full of shit I'm surprised you don't choke." Before he could say anything else, she punched him in the face.

"Jesus!" he yelled as he swerved onto the shoulder and back. "Fuck, woman! You trying to kill us?" He touched his jaw where she connected. "Fuck." He raised his arm when he saw her move again, but nothing happened. He looked over. She was crying, sobbing into her hands. "Oh, Jeez," he said. "I'm the one should be crying."

"You don't understand either," she said between sobs. "You just think I'm a whore."

"Well ain't you?" He thought she was going to hit him again, but she took a tissue from her pocket instead and blew her nose.

"You don't know how hard it has been," she said. "I come here alone. No family. No friend. No dollars. I do what I need to stay alive. I look for someone to take care of me so I can be normal. But I made a bad choice." She blew her nose again.

Newt looked at her. She pulled another tissue from her pocket and dabbed at her eyes.

"Nicely done," he said. "You almost convinced me."

"You are a bastard," she said and started to cry again.

He slowed for the exit. By the time they reached the truck plaza, she was quiet, facing her window. He parked near the garage and shut off the engine. She didn't move.

"We're here," he said. She turned to him.

"I am sorry for what you think of me," she said.

"Well," Newt nodded. "Maybe you can't help it. I'm sorry for making you cry."

He opened his door but she reached over and put her hand on his leg. "Wait." Newt held the handle. "I have to tell you something," she said.

He closed the door. "What?"

"He is only half a man. From the war. He can't be a true husband."

"Chelsea, that ain't none of my business." She moved her hand up his leg. He grabbed her wrist. "Look," he said. "I know what you're trying to sell here, but I'm not buying."

She smiled at him. "Did you like when we were lovers?"

"We were never lovers," Newt said and put her hand on the seat.

She moved her hand back to his leg. "Sex, then. When we had sex. Did you like our sex?"

Newt looked at her. The smile had faded. It was a real question. "Yeah," he said. "It was good."

"Thank you," she said and pulled her hand away.

"You're welcome." He started to open the door again.

"Wait," she said.

"What?"

She rested her finger tips on his thigh. "May I give you a kiss to thank you?"

Newt chuckled. "You gonna charge me for it?"

She leaned over and kissed him. It was a gentle brush at first. But she slid across the seat and kissed him again.

"Shit," Newt said. She kissed him a third time. He felt himself warming to her touch. He reached up and put his hand against her cheek. She sighed. He moved his hand to her breast. She whimpered then took his hand in hers.

"This is not a good place," she said.

"You want me to see if we got a sleeper in the garage?" he asked.

"No," she said. "I don't want to do that."

"What then?"

"Maybe you give me a ride home after my shift?"

It was a slow night. For all his harping, Bill had little for Newt to do. By midnight, Bill told him he could leave. Newt's leg was throbbing but he walked over to the diner. He sat at Chelsea's counter. She leaned on her elbows in front of him. It was hard not to look at her breasts.

"I can get off early," she said. "Have something to eat then I'll meet you at your truck"

He ordered one of their specials. When he finished, he paid the bill and waited in his truck. He was listening to an '80s station when she opened the passenger door and climbed inside. Without a word, she pushed herself against him and kissed him, pulling his hand against her. "Take me home," she said.

They rode again in silence. This time she was close to him, nuzzling his neck, her hand inside his thigh. When he pulled into his driveway, she led him into his house. "Did you like my pictures?" she asked as they balled on his couch. They did it again in his bed. Afterward, they shared a cigarette.

"Thank you," she said.

"For what?" he asked.

"For making love to me."

He didn't argue about her choice of words. She took a long drag and blew smoke over his chest.

"Can I ask you something?" she said handing him the

cigarette.

He flicked the ash into a bedside ashtray. "Sure."

"A favor," she said as she nestled her body against his.

"You can ask," he said as he handed her back the cigarette.

She took another drag. As she exhaled against his ear, she whispered, "Will you help me kill him."

* * * * *

Brevic was back. His truck was in the driveway and Chelsea's car was parked at the curb. Newt felt a prisoner in his own house. At work the night before, Chelsea had stopped by the garage twice looking for him. Both times, he saw her coming and hid behind a rig.

"You got something going on with that bimbo from the diner?" Bill asked after her second visit.

"We're neighbors," Newt told him. "Probably looking for a ride home."

"I'm not so sure," said Bill.

That morning when he drove home, Newt parked down the block from his house and snuck in the back door. The Peterbilt was in Brevic's driveway. Newt kept his lights off and watched the street from behind his curtains. Chelsea came home just before dawn. Newt moved to the kitchen. He watched from the shadows as she rinsed a coffee cup in the sink. As she turned off the tap, he saw Brevic slip behind her. He put his arms around her and kissed her neck. She turned and embraced him. She left the cup on the counter as Brevic led her out of the room.

Newt managed to avoid them for another day. But returning from a beer run, he saw Brevic's Peterbilt in his mirror. His neighbor followed him all the way home and pulled into the driveway as Newt was climbing out of his truck.

"Hey, Newt," Brevic waved from his yard. "Haven't seen you for a while. Come on over. I owe you a beer."

"Can't right now," Newt said. "Maybe a little later."

Brevic came across the drive. He glanced over his shoulder. "I got it figured out." But before he could explain, his wife pulled up in front of the house. "Shit."

Chelsea took a grocery bag off the passenger seat and started up the driveway. When she saw Newt, she went back to the car and got something from the dash. Newt shifted his six pack from one hand to the other.

"We have some of your mail by mistake," she said. "I was going to stick it in your slot, but since you're here." She handed it to him.

"Thanks," Newt said.

"Well, good to see you," said Brevic. "If I don't catch you later, thanks again for the beer." He turned and headed toward his house. Chelsea started to follow but hesitated.

"I have something to tell you," she said then looked over her shoulder after Brevic. "He beat me again last night. I am afraid."

"Chelsea?" Brevic yelled from the porch. "You gonna fix dinner?"

"Yes," she called back. "I'm coming." When she turned back to Newt, he thought she was going to cry. "I know what I need to do," she said, then ran across the driveway and into her house.

Inside his kitchen, Newt took a beer from the six pack and twisted it open. He took a long drink and sat at the table. He looked at the mail Chelsea had handed him. One envelope was without a stamp. He opened it. It was the photo of her naked on his couch.

"Shit." Newt stuffed the picture back into the envelope and took another drink.

He had the night off but shortly after dark, he moved his truck down the block and snuck back into the house. He didn't want Brevic banging on the door after Chelsea left for work.

Chelsea did leave but was back a couple of hours later. She parked behind Brevic's truck. She wasn't alone. Someone slid out behind her and arm-in-arm, they went inside. Newt checked the view from his kitchen, but the lights were out.

He finished another beer and crawled into bed. He could

still smell Chelsea on his sheets. It stoked his curiosity about what was happening a few dozen yards away. But he was tired, and before his fantasies could play out, he was asleep.

The explosion threw him across the room. He was under attack. He found himself pinned to the floor. Alarms whooped as he struggled to free himself. His bed was on top of him. He managed to push aside the mattress and box spring and elbowed himself across the floor as a second explosion blasted outside the perimeter. He covered the back of his head as debris rained over him, then he rolled to safety in the hall. His heart was pounding. It took a moment to get his bearings. There was glass on the floor. He looked through his bedroom door. The window had blown in, bringing part of the frame with it. But instead of the cold of winter, there was heat, intense and searing. Brevic's house was on fire. Flames shot twenty feet in the air. Newt grabbed for his jeans and boots.

He made it onto the street, then stood and watched as Brevic's house deconstructed. By the time a fire crew arrived, the dwelling was a flaming skeleton. The crew kept the blaze from spreading to Newt's house, but it was clear that the water damage to his place would leave it uninhabitable. After the fire was out, the crew chief let him throw some things in a suitcase then surrounded the site with yellow tape.

"What caused it?" Newt asked.

"Too early to tell for sure. Started in the kitchen. Gas leak, maybe."

"My neighbors," he said, not sure how to finish the sentence.

The chief pointed across the driveway. Two men were carrying a covered body on a stretcher. A second stretcher followed.

Newt felt his legs weaken. He sat on the curb.

"You okay?" asked the chief.

"Yeah," said Newt. "Yeah, I'm fine."

"It never gets easy," said the chief.

"You need someone to identify them?" asked Newt.

The chief shook his head. "Not enough left."

The tears that came surprised Newt. They burned his eyes as he squeezed them away. He got to his feet and walked down the block. He threw his bag into his truck and headed to the garage. He'd stay there for a night or two until he figured out what had to be done.

* * * * *

Three months had passed. Newt had repaired his house and replaced his damaged furniture. When the last piece was delivered, he tacked Chelsea's picture above the dresser.

Brevic's landlord had the remains of the house bulldozed. She sold the lot to a local developer who had already started construction on a small cottage. Between the insurance and the sale, Newt figured the old lady wasn't too sad about the fire.

At the end of each day when the construction crew left, Newt walked the shell and fantasized about moving up. Maybe it wasn't so bad here. He liked the neighborhood. It was quiet and easy to get to work. Maybe it wasn't that crazy an idea.

The day he made an offer on the house, he received a plain, hand lettered envelope in the mail. There was a Mexican postmark but no return address. He sat in his kitchen and opened it. Inside, folded in a sheet of plain paper, he found two ten dollar bills, three fives and a single.

He spread the bills evenly in front of him then got a beer. He raised the bottle in a silent salute and took a long drink.

The Walrus and the Tub
Kendra Langford Shaw

The only bathtub on the island belonged to the high school, and no one—not even the old natives—knew exactly where it came from. It wasn't easy to get a head of fresh lettuce that far into the Alaskan passages, let alone an antique French tub. A few suspected the Russian mafia had smuggled it over during the turn of the century, when they'd built a fur empire in the southeast. Others thought it had simply washed ashore one day, the rusty remains of a luxury cruiser sunken in the Aleutians.

In the past, the tub had belonged to Principal Amelia Baranoff, the last of the great Alaska Baranoffs. She was an eccentric woman who ate clams three meals a day and died from an allergic reaction to the shellfish (or so they'd always assumed) which had turned her skin a puffy pink. At the time of her death, she bequeathed her estate to her pilot son, who disappeared in the bush some years later, leaving the bathtub—as a tribute to his mother's memory—to the entire high school staff. There'd originally been talk of bronzing it, setting it up as a statue near Swan Lake, but the practical need for warmth settled in their winter bones, and they reconsidered. The high school administrators worked out a yearly schedule, and the tub had been home to nearly every oily bottom in town over the years. Aside from one incident with Andy the crabber, they had been peacefully rotating the tub for thirty-four years the winter Principal Love stole it.

The theft, surprisingly simple to accomplish, happened one Tuesday in December. Principal Love was supposed to return the bathtub on Christmas Eve, but that morning when he saw it steaming happily in the corner, he couldn"t imagine ripping out the plumbing just to hand it over to the Johnsons, a young couple who probably didn"t even get cold. At their weekly staff meeting, he announced he needed the tub a little longer, for an experiment. (Marty the science teacher mocked him, putting "experiment" in air quotes. But the joke was really on Marty, who"d lost fingers to frostbite—or a shark?—and looked like he was trying to pinch Principal Love.) They gave him until New Years, citing his old, rheumatic bones. That evening, as he happily toweled off his red body, he noticed that his skin felt thicker than usual, and his throbbing pulse took longer to quiet.

During the Christmas vacation, he bloated and stewed and pruned. He spent long afternoons—then whole *days*—in the bathtub, until his skin creased like good linen. He began to develop—*symptoms*. New teeth pushing through his meaty gums. A carnivorous inclination. He'd munch through fifty pounds of salmon in a sitting, a sore jaw the only thing stopping him from eating more.

At the first staff meeting of the year, the teachers seemed anxious, like nervous creditors who knew they'd being hustled. Still, he asked again—begged, really—for more time. By then, he could swim just a *touch* faster than the average 63-year-old. He'd been the high school dive instructor before his principal days, but the water had never slid off him with such ease. Now, when he dove in the bay in search of abalone, he was furtive, lithe, his 300 pounds menacing. No longer did he awkwardly propel himself forward with plastic flippers. With his own secret stopwatch, he timed himself able to out-swim the state champion.

One night in early February, soaking in water so hot it made his blood pump—and maybe boiled him, just a little— he thought to himself (as they all had in the throes of winter) *Well, what if I just didn't give it up at all?* And that's how the whole slimy mess started.

"I'm not giving it up at all," Principal Love said at the February staff meeting. In the back corner, the secretary loudly—angrily—stapled the fish plant's brochures. "I'm an old man," Principal Love said, "and I've had my moment of clarity. All I want is some peace and hot water at the end of the day."

It had taken Principal Love 14 years to get the bathtub in the first place, and if it took him another 14, he'd be in his seventies, too old to install the tub himself. If one of the young guys tired to snake it out from under him, what could he do but hobble after him, throwing his cane like a shooting star? There was really no other way about it. It was winter and this was Alaska and any moment one of his loose joints could slide out of place.

Cecilia, the traveling music teacher, said, "What do you think happens to the rest of us when we get old?"

"Wouldn't it just be easier for everyone to buy their own bathtubs?" Principal Love asked.

"A new bathtub. Special ferry fees. Plumbers," Cecilia said, ticking these off on her thin fingers. "Are you going to pay for each of us?"

"It's time to be adults. All this swapping has gone on long enough," Principal Love said. "You can come to my house and bathe there if you must. Can't you learn to live like this?"

He was the Principal—weren't his decisions supposed to carry heft? If your king told you he was taking a few peasants off your land, did you whine and grovel like these poor teachers? The secretary walked around the room, passing out the fish plant brochures. Principal Love rubbed his hand over the smooth picture on the front of Marty the science teacher in a wet suit holding a purple octopus in front of him like a trophy.

Lately, soaking in his tub after a long day, Principal Love had begun to picture himself as a sea creature—his figure, already broad, stretched to accommodate the hulking muscles required to maneuver flippers, his face covered in a thick brown hide. He"d be able to out-swim a leopard seal, go diving after salmon for his fellow teachers, like a team player. He could open tuna cans with his tusks! His whiskers, little more than a runaway handlebar mustache, would make him more distinguished.

"You've taken away our hope, our light in the long winter," Marty said. "Where will I wash my clams?"

"Gross," Cecilia said. "*That's* what you've been doing with the tub?"

"A citizen may do as he pleases in the privacy of his home."

"I think we should vote Marty out of the schedule," Cecilia said, raising her hand. "Who else uses the tub to wash clams? What other nasty things do you people do in there?"

"Well it won't matter now," Principal Love said, "since I'm keeping it."

"And what disgusting practices do you have?" Cecilia asked. "Please tell us you have an exotic illness, so we can feel sorry for you. And not like to we want you to freeze to death."

Principal Love paused, unsure whether to continue. "I might be turning into a walrus."

Cecilia sniffed. "That'd better not leave a stain."

An old native could get away with talk like that—already had: the tales of the blueberry rain, the 106-year-old who turned into a polar bear. When he looked back on his life, it seemed inevitable, the result of saltwater swims, island living, oyster parties; he was surprisingly unsurprised by the whole ordeal. As though he'd known all along people who go against the group turn into monsters.

Saturday, Principal Love drove out to see Charlie the vet, who doubled as the island's only registered nurse. The vet had pigment issues so his hair and eyelashes were bright white, ghost-like, as though somehow he'd convinced God to give him a jellyfish wig. Charlie's office was a slope-roofed attachment to the ferry terminal and smelled of cat urine and something faintly dizzying, like a sugar buzz. While Charlie calmed down the owner of a missing black lab (who later hobbled into town on a broken hind leg),

Principal Love waited next to a woman stroking a bright orange tomcat. Out the window, he watched the ferry crew lower a new skiff into the water.

Charlie came out of the back room with a syringe. "Did you hear the story about the bear?" He squeezed the syringe and a trickle of liquid dribbled down the side. "This bear, stalked into town and ate poor Miss Carrie's dog right off its chain. He snapped the head right off. Something was wrong with that animal."

Charlie lunged forward and plunged the syringe into the rump of the orange cat. The cat's green eyes bulged round like marbles, then settled back into their sockets. "It's dead," Charlie said, and the woman began to cry. "Get that thing buried quick, Mrs. Williams," he said. Mrs. Williams furiously smoothed the cat"s ears, something it would never had allowed while alive. She took a small canvas bag from beside her chair, delicately lifted the cat, and placed it in the bottom of the bag. The orange tail stuck out the top like a feather.

"We're friends, Charlie, aren't we?" Principal Love asked. A long time ago, when Principal Love had just moved to the island, he and Charlie had run a charter fishing business. They were a frightening pair, the Principal big as a walrus, and Charlie pale as cancer. It hadn't gone well. Tourists left them *get well* notes attached to bottles of brown hair dye and yoga instructional videos.

"Cecilia told me about the meeting," Charlie said. He put his hand under Mrs. William's elbow and helped her to her feet. More pushing than guiding, he led her out of the vet office. Principal Love stared at Mrs. William's back. She wore a lumpy brown jacket that bunched around her shoulders like plumage.

"Can I give you some advice?" Charlie poked the tip of the syringe along his thigh absentmindedly. Then he waved it under Principal Love's nose. "This isn't like being a policeman or a leprechaun. Do you realize what you're asking of us?"

Principal Love shrugged. He cuffed his right sleeve to expose his forearm, then took a pencil out of his back pocket and rubbed the tip against the thick hairs on his arm. It came away sharp as a sewing needle. He held the tip up for Charlie to examine.

Charlie leaned in and whispered, "Do you think you might be losing your mind?"

Principal Love cocked his head to the side, and the extra skin on his neck bunched like leather. "I think you should check me out."

"I could cover my couch with all this skin around your neck," Charlie said.

In the back room, Principal Love sat on the black examining table. Charlie took a stethoscope from a shelf that also held dog muzzles and an empty aquarium. He huffed on it twice and then slid it between the buttons on Principal Love's shirt.

"Symptoms, symptoms," Charlie muttered, his eyes closed. His hair, as though alive in and of itself, waved like seaweed. Principal Love had a nearly overwhelming urge to run his hand through it. Charlie tapped at his lips with a long wooden stick. "Open up."

The vet shone a flashlight into the deep recess of his mouth. "Smells like fish in here," he said.

"Increased appetite."

"Is that a bone?" Charlie whispered. Using the wooden stick to push Principal Love's upper lip against his nose, Charlie rubbed his own thumbs along the Principal's gum line. He pulled back suddenly, a sliver of blood on his finger pads.

Principal Love rubbed his sweaty palms against his thighs. "Did my tusks cut you?"

"How did this start? Did you get bit? Did you—" he gulped, unsettled, "*eat* walrus recently?"

"I've been taking a bath every day. I started diving again—I've become very fast."

"Based on my knowledge of the *animal*, I'd say you have

about a month," Charlie said.

"What's my diagnosis?"

"Let's just say you should get your affairs in order," Charlie said.

As Principal Love struggled back into his coat, Charlie looked furtively out his window, drew the shade, and, red-faced, mumbled, "Say, while you still have the tub, can I come over tonight for a bath?" He laughed. "We old guys have to stick together."

When Principal Love got home, he found Cecilia and Marty on his front steps, Cecilia gripping a red bucket with crab legs sticking out the top, Marty dressed in a full wetsuit. As he unlocked his door, Principal Love motioned for them to follow him inside. The house was a shoddy attachment to the boy's dorm, and the walls had a layer of newspaper paper machéd across them as insulation. When you leaned up against a doorjamb, the faded black ink rubbed off onto your clothes like wet paint. In the kitchen, a meat-stained roll of butcher's paper for wrapping fish leaned against an industrial-sized stainless steel freezer. Above it hung a rack of knives that ranged in size from a steak knife to a harpoon.

Marty hopped up onto the freezer and his black wetsuit squeaked across the top. "Larry, don"t you think you're being the least bit selfish?" Marty asked

"Look," Cecilia said, peering into the bathroom, "just turn off the water, and I'll unhook the tub and take it to my place. We can put this all behind us."

Principal Love shook his head. He stared at Marty's nose, big and bulbous as an oxygen mask. "Marty," he said, "when you turn into an octopus you'll understand. You'll want to be surrounded by your natural habitat."

"I'm turning into a water flute," Cecilia said. She pulled a crab leg out of the bucket and used it to point accusingly at Principal Love. "It's *true.*"

"It's a gradual process," Principal Love said.

Cecilia tapped the crag leg against her open palm. "Walruses live in *cold* water, Larry," she said. "We all know this is just a ruse. An elaborate, *mean* ruse."

"Enough," Principal Love said. "I'm still the principal." He reached out and snatched the crab leg from her hands. He snapped the spiny bicep against his knee and used his thumbs to yank out the sinewy white meat in one long strip. The empty shell clattered on the floor like cheap plastic. Tipping his head back so his jaw opened wide enough to expose his burgeoning tusks, he slid the meat down his throat without chewing. That was a new development, not needing to chew. Cecilia froze for a moment—perhaps imitating a water flute?—and then crossed her long arms.

"I'm not unhooking the pipes," Principal Love said. He stepped on the discarded crab shell, and it broke into pieces. "And if you rip it out, you'll flood the school."

"We'll call the water company ourselves," Marty said. "'Cut to the source.'" He leapt off the freezer and shuffled in his flippers across the room. After a few minutes on the phone, he covered the mouthpiece. "They can only take orders from the person whose name is on the invoice."

Cecilia walked over. "Yes," she said into the receiver, "this is Principal Love's wife." Then after a pause, "Oh, damn you, Dale, I hope you know this means Kenneth's getting a D in music." She hung up.

They looked at Principal Love with fishhooks in their eyes. He spread his hands—flippers, he supposed—and shrugged. "This is not an elaborate prank," he said.

"No one's going to believe you're a walrus until you surrender that tub," Cecilia said.

Marty took the remaining crab legs out of the bucket and tossed them across the room as you would toss a stick to divert a dog. Principal Love's eyes tracked the legs.

"I hope you know this means the fish plant is off limits," Marty said.

It's important to know the story of how Andy the crabber made off with the bathtub. Andy had lived in a dog musher's shack out near the ferry port and the barbeque hole. At the end of his turn with the tub, he asked for an extension. Carl and Vesta, the Tlingit couple next on the list, quietly asked Principal Love to "involve himself,"" to recoup the bathtub for the sake of the whole staff. Andy, feeling betrayed, cold, and alone, slid the tub out onto the harbor ice like a giant skate and slept out there with wolf pelts packed around his torso. When Carl and Vesta went to the lake's shore the next morning to lure the crabber away with hot crab bisque, they found a smooth hole where the bathtub had been, the black winter water taut as a bed sheet under the ice.

No one could prove—or rule out—sabotage. The ice around the hole hadn't cracked, as it would if a whale or wayward seal had thwaped the surface. Instead, the hole was clean, smooth as icing, with no sign of Andy or his furs. Naturally, they suspected each other. The staff nosily invited themselves to each other's houses, looking for proof someone had monkied with the hot water lines or left a sloppy wet trail up from the basement. The cold made them grumpy, and they slammed their doors on each other. Everyone assumed the tub was gone, sunken with the lead-bottomed icebreakers, oil-soaked birds, and faultily-wired salmon skiffs. They would have been upset with Andy, and probably stolen fish off his line at night, except that they presumed he was dead. Nobody could survive in a winter ocean.

Then that summer when Marty was out looking for an octopus for the second grade class pet, he found the tub not twenty feet offshore, green as a sunken ship, barnacles covering it like warts, hot pink sea anemones waving like mermaid hair. Andy the crabber"s body was welded to the porcelain frame, his skin hard and red as an exoskeleton, his hands curled in on themselves like claws. After seeing his frozen body, it took many of the villagers weeks to get up the courage to boil crabs for dinner.

Even after they thawed out Andy, his shell was still stained red like a nasty sunburn. *Or a crab*, the high school students whispered to each other. Of course, everyone

The Walrus and the Tub

knew that was hyperbole and folklore. Only the very old people still swore that it had once rained blueberries when they were children. The fruit splashed and broke on their faces like raindrops. One old woman had an Africa-shaped blue stain on her right thigh. Of course, any Alaskan would argue it was probably just frostbite.

It took five scuba divers to retrieve the tub. The staff found a huge winch and the divers tied a noose under the bathtub's collar. Everyone waded into the waves in their black rain boots, grasped the line, and heaved. The island's reporter took a photo for the front page. The bathtub surfaced with a family of orange sea slugs in its belly, and the children grabbed for them, waving them like trophies. Principal Love had been in the after-care group, and as the women moved in with steak knives to pry off the barnacles, he took Andy's frozen body and propped him up by the bonfire. Throughout the night, he stuck toothpicks into Andy's fingers, testing to see if he was done.

Monday, Principal Love drove over to the fish plant to check out the high school interns. They sent a dozen students every semester, and it was his job, his *responsibility* to monitor their progress. Principal Love sampled as he walked through the gutting stations, asking for a taste of fresh meat at every station. He watched students slice salmon thin as paper, and then they held the pieces up to the light, checking their translucency. Out of the corner of his eye, Principal Love spotted the smooth glint of a fish skin, and he whirled around. In a corner, a freshman with stringy blonde hair pried open clams with a letter opener and pulled out their meaty tongues. Behind him, two boys stuffed sardines into pickling jars, and it took a moment for him to control his wild eyes; they wanted to follow the fish from bucket to jar, bucket to jar, bucket to jar.

A senior carrying a tray rippling with fish eggs walked past, and Principal Love got distracted by the jiggling mass. Then a fish hit him in the back of the head. Before it could drop to the ground, Principal Love twisted his arm behind his back and caught it in his massive paw.

"Cool," the senior said.

Principal Love bared his teeth. The tusks pushed painfully against his lips, and freeing them felt like uncurling your legs after a long car ride. Deep inside himself—in his heart, his liver, his enlarged stomach—he felt a deep pull to stick the fish into his mouth. In the hot water of the bath, his blood boiled and popped, and he felt the same heat rush now, his face red and murderous.

With two hands, he heaved the fish onto the tray of eggs and dodged into the smoke hut. A charcoal fire sizzled, casting a faint orange light into the room. Principal Love could just make out the shadows of two boys wallpapering the room with halibut the size of second graders. When their backs were turned, Principal Love pulled a juicy halibut off its grappling hook, and then devoured it. When he finished, he wiped his greasy palms on his suit pants, smearing the evidence. The fish left his mouth feeling abused, distended, and he sent his tongue to dislodge a finger-length bone lodged in the muscle of his cheek.

The fish plant was no place for a Principal who had to hide out in the smoke hut, feeling his skin dry and crisp like bacon. As he headed toward the back door and the safety of the salty air of the bay, he spotted a young native boy feeding hunks of multi-colored meat into a metal shoot. When it came out the other side, a girl caught the ground meat in a large plastic sack. They both had chunks of pink meat stuck to their lips and eyebrows, like the flakes of white fish in Principal Love's stubble. The girl caught Principal Love looking at her and smiled. "Dog food," she shouted over the whir of the machine, and the boy laughed.

"I'm Principal Love," said Principal Love. "Checking progress. That's all."

The native boy, his hands waxy with fish bits, dropped the lump of pink flesh he was holding and walked over to Principal Love. He reached up and put his hands on either side of the Principal's face.

"Has your blubber started coming in yet?" the boy asked.
Principal Love drew a deep breath. "Has anyone ever
gotten *hurt*? While this happened?"

The boy shrugged. "You'll get used to it."

When he got home that afternoon, Principal Love found
his bathtub full of starfish. A note taped to his mirror read:
Need a hand moving the tub? Underneath, a small P.S. in block
print: BRING THE TUB TO THE MEETING OR ELSE
scrawled in soft pencil.

Principal Love stuck a finger into the tub and put it
to his lips. Someone had gone to the trouble of hauling in
saltwater; someone who didn't want to kill forty starfish.
Marty. As a child, Principal Love had found starfish
frightening, like an organ suddenly exposed to the light.
Their ability to re-grow themselves kept him up at night.
What if they found ways to replace their arms with claws?
Or shark teeth? They were the color of fruit—bright
purple and orange—except unnatural, chaotic, a strange
cross-breed between a tongue and a gourd.

Principal Love plunged his hand into the water, locked
his fingers in the creases between a starfish's legs, and pulled
the creature to the surface. In the air, its skin felt warty,
diseased, and Principal Love almost let it go. Gripping the
starfish's body, he tugged at the thin skin between its legs.
Before he knew what he was doing, he pulled a little harder,
heard a satisfying rip, and dug his fingers into the tendons,
prying them apart. A leg came loose in his hand, and he
set it next to the faucet. Then he gently lowered the body
back into the water, on top of the pile, where it stood out—
partly from its red color and partly because it had been
mutilated, changed, made into something the other starfish
didn"t recognize.

He removed the rest of starfish gingerly, as one might
handle a closet full of musty hats. As he dropped them into
the buckets and slung the load over his arm, he thought
about simply taking them out to the sea. He could slip into
the water for a *second*, nose around for some oysters. But

then the clock in the kitchen chimed, and he realized he was late for a staff meeting.

"We are sobered by the knowledge that you are handling the situation with less *panache* than one would expect from a man of your—*ahem*—maturity," Brenda the secretary said at the meeting as a way of introduction.

Principal Love took one of the sloshing blue buckets and heaved it on the table. A boisterous yellow starfish curled a hand over the bucket's lip. "There's five sides to every argument," he said.

"You have a rare gift of candor," Marty said.

Cecilia fingered the leather of her trumpet case. "What did Charlie have to say?"

With his thumbs Principal Love nudged his upper lip into the cleft made between his gum line and his nose. Two gleaming, thick tusks exposed themselves.

"Good god, the apocalypse is upon us," Brenda said.

"Please give Principal Love a hand," Cecilia said. "Best Halloween costume I've seen yet." She gave a few half-hearted claps to the quiet room.

Lately, everything had begun to sound muffled, as though Principal Love had two seashells pressed to his ears. His world had begun to sound like the ocean. "It's not a costume," he said.

Marty flipped through a planner. "It's also March."

Cecilia rubbed her temples. "I *know*," she said. "For heaven's sake, we all *know* it"s *March*."

"Are we finished here?" Marty asked. "I have a cold shower waiting for me."

Principal love reached into the water and grabbed the starfish missing its leg. He tossed it between his hands for a minute, flicking water angrily on those sitting near him. Then he rolled his shoulders back and hurled the star over everyone's heads. It hit the ceiling with the wet smack of a kiss and suctioned itself up there next to the ceiling fan.

No one could find the janitor that evening to unlock the ladder closet, and when they all finally left, one of its legs had peeled off and hung limp, in danger of being chopped to bits by the fan's blades. The next week, when Principal Love was long gone, it turned the sickly green of a bruise and fell onto the table, startling the teacher's sipping their morning coffee. For years after that, they could see the faint outline of the four-legged starfish on the ceiling. Cecilia was once heard to tell a new math teacher, "I *know* it doesn't look like a starfish, but it was. *Something* bad happened to it. We didn't want to watch it die, so Marty flung it back into the ocean. And we all feel very sad about that."

Principal Love began to see walruses everywhere— in the clouds, on signs around the ferry terminal, in his dreams. He had a vivid dream of stepping into a lumpy brown walrus hide, putting on a furry head and wandering onto the basketball court during a game, the school''s mascot. In another dream, he wore the same costume to a staff meeting. They gave him rolls of uncooked spaghetti to shove up his nostrils like tusks. They applauded when he smacked his flippers together. He was a spectacle. A *star*.

It wasn't long before he could no longer squeeze into his suits. Then he stopped going to the school altogether. Like a teething child, he stuffed ice cubes under his upper lip, trying to soothe the itchy red welts the tusks had made when they carelessly pushed his gums aside. One day in desperation, he went to the dentist.

The dentist ran a one-room business out of the back of the Russian Orthodox Church. You could have a crown replaced and attend mass all in one morning. He was a short, stout man with khaki colored-hair and chocolate wool suits. When the dentist had him in the chair, he jerked on the right tusk, and Principal Love roared in pain. It surprised both men, who looked warily at each other. The receptionist peeked nervously around the corner, but when she saw Principal Love's huge pelvis tipped up at that unnatural angle, his neck fat spilling off the sides, she put her hand over her eyes and backed out of the room.

The dentist snapped a few X-Rays, and together the men

stared at the films, which were propped up on a small white box that looked like a little girl's makeup mirror. They had to whack it periodically to keep the light from flickering.

"You have tuscular teeth growing," the dentist said, pointing at the dental records.

Principal Love ran his tongue over the tusks. The skin bulging around them itched like a bad scar. "You've seen this before?"

"And other odd things. You wouldn't believe the things people put in their mouths."

"Is it supposed to hurt like this?"

The dentist peeled off his gloves and tossed them into a bucket at his feet. "You're getting old."

"I'm sixty-three," Principal Love said. "That's not old anymore."

"It's not *just* that," the dentist said. "Your body's going through its final growth spurt. Belated growth. It must know you're going to die soon."

"Charlie never said anything about *dying*."

"Well," he sighed, "Charlie's carrying around a horse gauge needle full of tranquilizer. He's preparing for *something*."

By the time Principal Love left the office, it had turned dark. He drove home by way of the harbor, and as he swung his car along the shore, his beams raked the bay and lit up dozens of ice skaters. In the glare coming off the ice, the students looked ethereal, misty, their edges melting into the silver edges of frost, their earthy moose wool sweaters and red snow pants the only tangible things about them. He turned off his head lights and rolled into a gravel parking lot.

Looking down, he could see the whole town gathered as spectators at the party to which he had not been invited. It was almost April, but still cold. The harbor had frozen over half a dozen times that winter, and the town hadn"t been able to put in the skiffs they used to take the summer tourists fishing. The trees were leafless, and snow still covered the

Totem Poles built on the hill as sentinels. Frozen ice floes jutted up where the harbor met the shore, and the students skated between them as though on an obstacle course.

On the pebbly beach, his staff stood around a fire. A few people took sips from bottles covered in brown paper sacks. The old natives sat bunched far away from the ice, their backs propped against the base of the hill on which Principal Love stood. A few of them had dogs on leashes, and they threw frozen starfish just out of the range so the animals jerked at the end of their ropes, whining, learning they couldn't have everything they wanted.

A few pilots had brought a case of creamed corn from Anchorage by mistake, and periodically the staff took a can, shook it, and sprayed it into the air like fireworks. Charlie the vet carried around an octopus suctioned to the black rubber glove on his right arm. With his keen eyes, Principal Love could see the bulge the tranquilizer needle made in his front pocket. While Principal Love tried to decide what to do, the dentist pulled in, and nodding at the principal, walked past, picking his way down the hill.

Principal Love got out of the car and stood at the top of the hill long enough that his whiskers frosted over and when he breathed, his nose hairs crinkled. The native boy from the fish plant looked up and waved, then put his hands in his pockets and nonchalantly skated away, his red scarf flapping behind him like a flag. Principal Love watched as the boy, out near an outcropping of slate-gray ice, peeked over his shoulder, then brought his right skate to its toe. He pivoted in a circle, twisting faster and faster as he picked up speed. Soon he was just a blur of colors, his long ponytail wrapping around his body like a second skin. When the boy stopped, he stepped off the circle he'd etched in the ice, lifting his skates delicately, as one would treat a set of expensive knives. Then he reached down, pried up the edges of the circle, and lifted the whole hunk of ice right out of the ground. He looked around for a minute—warily—and then dove into the hole.

For a moment, all Principal Love could think about was the hole in the ice after Andy the crab—wait, *crabber*—had sunk with the tub. Then he was running down the hill, the loose skin around his ankles and wrists flapping in the breeze, his frozen lungs pumping. Principal Love pointed, and like a school of fish, the crowd whipped their heads toward the harbor. There were no words for the hole in the ice, just the feeling that someone had dropped a trap door, leaving them dangling in mid-air.

As the crowd rushed to the hole, they let out quick steamy breaths, fogging the ice. They toed up to the edge, and the icy blue water peered back at them like an angry pupil. There was no trace of the native boy, no symbolic, floating skate, no fingers frozen to the lip, trying to hoist the rest of him out of the water.

Principal Love saw the boy's hair fanning out like a cape, enveloping him. The shift of his facial features as his nose and jaw puffed out, his skin mottling itself gray in the water. His skin would thicken instantaneously against the cold as he shot out after a school of sardines. For don't we all wish that the people we've lost have simply found a better life, that the drowning victim became the dolphin that guides the shipwrecked crew to shore? Instead of wasting away old and pruned in nursing home beds, old people could simply drop out of airplanes, and instead of face-planting on cow paddies, necks broken, they'd never come down, but instead migrate north the next summer as Canadian geese. Simple, happy, capable of doing something they could never before have imagined.

"Walrus man will save him!" Cecilia called, igniting the crowd.

Marty the science guy poked him in the back, his finger rumpling Principal Love's skin like a pile of leather. "Was stealing the tub really worth all this?" he asked.

It seemed no one had asked Principal Love such a complicated question. "This is the proof you need?" he asked.

"Huzzah!" shouted the teachers.

It was another couple of days before Cecilia and Marty could get in to reclaim the tub. They brought a chainsaw, a tool belt from the shop teacher, and Cecilia's brain, which remembered not only the snub from the water company, but Kenneth's abysmal year-end grades. They found the tub right where Principal Love had left it—scummy from the starfish, but otherwise intact. Hot water lines connected. A ring of dried salt crusted around the drain.

Before he dove under the ice, Principal Love tried to reason with them. They could have the bathtub back in the summer. They could make a big 4th of July spectacle. He'd pay for the parade! Surely, as winter melted away, his whisker line would recede, his tusks would burrow back into his gums, his flabby, sea-thick skin would tighten and grow taut like any normal human's. Charlie the vet said he had *every hope* for a normal recovery.

"Do you recant?" Cecilia asked. "Tell us everything is normal and we'll let you go."

"You still have time," Marty said.

Principal Love looked into the hole. His eyes, never before able to distinguish the silver scales of a fish from the deep navy knit of the water, caught a glimpse of a furry flipper. This time, the color nearly blinded him, shining in his eyes like a quarter left in the sun. The ice began to crack under his enormous sumo-walrus weight. Then there was a great shift, a jostle that dropped the crowd a few feet. The gasps caught in their throats, and suddenly, water from the open hole spilled over and ran toward their shoes, wicking up their pant legs. A few people froze in place and had to abandon their expensive boots. All ran back for the shore. The hole started to gurgle like an unplugged drain, and Principal Love could feel the tide pull at his own flippers. Suddenly his sweater seemed too heavy, itching against his skin. He pulled it over his head and tossed it behind him on the ice. As he dipped a naked toe in the water, he was surprised to find it warm, the lip of the hole curving smooth as ceramic as it melted into the hot water. He held up one arm in a wave and then gracefully, as though he'd been practicing his whole life, dove into the hole with the ease of a walrus going after food.

Genetic Drift
David Naimon

For the first two years in our new house, I was unable to successfully grow a tomato. It prompted me to listen to the gardening show, despite the host's ludicrous name. On Herb Potter's advice, I took a handful of soil in my hand and squeezed it, watched how it clumped and how it broke apart. I smelled it to see if it had a "fresh earthy aroma." I moved the tomatoes to more or less sun, tried them from seeds and from starts, added additional compost made from mushrooms and bat poop, sprayed the soil with emulsified fish oil, and brought home a bag of organic llama feces from the farmer's market and turned it into the soil at the base of my robust but fruitless plants. I set slug traps of cheap beer, light, amber, and dark, and then, in desperation, a series of gourmet ones, brews by Belgian monks and local beers made exclusively by solar power. I even kept my cat, Henry, inside for a whole summer in the hopes that come fall I would be buried in tomatoes, spending my free moments cooking them down in to sauce, making caprese salads, chutneys, gazpacho, and bloody marys. Even the soil sample I sent to the laboratory showed a good pH and a soil free of significant levels of lead. And the plants looked great for all the effort. They were huge and sprawling and seemed to ache in our shared desire for fruits. Who knew that those scrawny little sad excuses, those ugly wrinkled yellow tomato flowers that I picked off with relish *became* the tomatoes? I certainly didn't. My now ex-wife, while she had little interest in gardening, put two and two together, when in a gesture of reconciliation after a rather hellacious fight, I floated a handful of tomato flowers atop a cup of water on the toilet tank in our bedroom bathroom.

So, yes I was green but I didn't have a green thumb, that is for sure. I was immature and unripe like my perpetually frustrated tomato plant. And perhaps that is why my wife and daughter now live next door.

It seemed the most reasonable of solutions at the time. When she declared, *this just isn't working for me anymore*, there was no anger, no lack of tenderness, just a sense of exhausted resignation. When the house next door went up for sale, we both thought we could co-parent Delia best as neighbors. Essentially, we had been amiable roommates for years now. Shuttling our daughter back and forth across town based on some arbitrary custody agreement seemed pointless. Instead, she would see us both every day, and Delia could stay at either of our places as she saw fit. And it worked well, just as we imagined it. Until Leonid that is.

I haven't dated since our divorce. My libido has never been the same since an unfortunate episode of testicular torsion several winters ago. I'm not entirely clear on the details to this day. If I had to paraphrase my poor understanding of Dr. Mikelson's explanation, things can twist and contract due to cold weather, particularly in men who have "bell clapper deformity," which apparently has something to do with how and where all my parts attach inside my scrotum. That there were more than two parts in there was news to me. And because I waited a day to go to the doctor my testicle had died. I didn't know they could do that. I still have one, a living one. But it doesn't seem too interested in anything.

My now ex-wife started dating Leonid soon after she moved. He owned a gas station and had reprimanded one of his employees for giving my ex-wife a hard time when she forgot which side her gas tank was on. Leo refused her money and washed her windshield with royal aplomb. His bulging, veiny Ukrainian bicep had a tattoo of King Kong holding his dainty human woman aloft in his large and primitive fist. This had aroused some long buried part of my now ex-wife, like a dormant seed waking up and germinating after a forest fire. Before I knew it, Leo had become part of our family, Delia would come home from school and complain to me about how stinky he was, his sweaty feet that smelled like milk that had gone off in the back of the fridge, the fermented oregano-esque smell of his armpits, and his exclamatory farts reminiscent of smoked jerky.

"I'm afraid to ask how in the world you know his feet and armpits smell at all …"

"Dad!" she defended herself, "he's always shlumping around with no shirt or shoes."

"I've seen, believe me. A hairy fellow that Leo."

"*All* over his back."

"Like a monkey."

"Like an ogre."

These were good times for me and Delia. We bonded over our discomfort as Leo, without either of our consents, inserted himself into our lives. It seemed that no matter where I was on my property, Leo was assaulting one of my senses. If I wasn't watching the back of his bald head and the tufts of curly hair stuck to his sweaty back as he cleaned my ex-wife's car or checked her tire pressure, if I wasn't subjected to the Ukrainian ogre's King Kong tattoo as it hung across the shoulders of my ex-wife on her porch, his thick short fingers fisting a can of beer after a day's work making something, anything, better at her house, if I was inside my own house minding my own business, sleeping, watching Herb Potter on public television, listening to Beethoven's late string quartets, Leo found a way to declare himself present. Chopping wood early on a weekend morning, running an outboard motor in a tub of water in the driveway, listening to a Russian death metal band called Azazelo while he stripped the paint off her garage with the assistance of an open flame blowtorch, Leo was in my face and affronting all its orifices.

But life is never simple. It would have been simpler if Leonid could have been summed up by this wellspring of irritating activities that he took to like an ant to a picnic, but the problem was he was a good-hearted soul. We'd often greet each other across the fence. At first it would be his disembodied voice,"That's what that I sniff?" when I was picking basil for my pasta, "Working hard like soldier, no?" when I mowed the lawn, or oddly "You, Olympic!" when he saw me high on a ladder harvesting figs. And if I came out bleary-eyed at dawn on a Sunday morning with a poorly hidden tone of exasperation in my voice, asking him to wait a couple hours to break twigs and branches into smaller and smaller bits and pieces of twigs and branches, I was immediately disarmed by his effusive agreement, "Must that be pushing you crazy! So stupid of Leonid Dmitri Kosvloshenko to not think before you. My mother would have ..." Okay, okay, I'd think to myself, I get it, but he would hold me captive on the porch in my pajamas far after he had made his point.

Leo drove me crazy but drove my daughter into my arms. Delia was in that awkward post-puberty phase where parents were poison, and all the camaraderie she had had with my ex-wife as a young girl had evaporated, seemingly overnight, replaced by a stiff and chilly tension between her young adult self and her now too motherly mother. Leo's clumsy attempts to be fatherly had unexpectedly turned me from my daughter's father into her friend. When Leo took her aside to talk about the feathered birds and the bumbly bees, I did not rise up in anger at being usurped, because I cherished her outrage, tears, and laughter that she sought me out to share.

One finds that things, good things and bad things, tend to happen in threes. It took me three years to grow a tomato, three months to conceive Delia, three consecutive wonderful weeks of my daughter staying at my house every night before what seemed too good to be true became so. On the twenty-first day, we learned that Leonid was moving in with my now ex-wife.

"And with Lukas," my daughter spluttered through her tears. "His son. I don't want a brother, a stinky, gas-pumping brother."

"A hairy, stinky, gas-pumping brother," I added, succeeding to resuscitate that nearly snuffed out sparkle in her eyes. The phone rang before she could answer. Expecting my ex-wife, I picked it up, "Silverstein Home of Neglected Daughters, how may I help you?"

"Dad!" Delia lunged for the phone, mortified.

Oh, uh I'm sorry. I think I, uh, I think I must have the wrong number … click.

"Who was it?" she asked.

The phone rang again in my hand. The same thin, warbly adolescent voice on the other end. *Is a Mister, a Mister Silversteen at home?*

"Stein. Like a beer stein. Silver beer stein, without the beer. Yes, this is he." I spoke this more to my daughter, performing an old ritual for her pleasure—correcting a caller for the umpteenth time on our family name—her tears now dry, her brow scrunched and quizzical.

I know, sir, I know this is a, a weird question to ask. And I apologize for interrupting you at your home.

"Just spit it out now, son."

I'm sorry Mister Silverstein. Excuse me but did, did you donate, did you donate sperm, your sperm, in 1988? Or '87?

"What the …" I muffled the phone against my chest. I could feel my heart ka-clunking against the receiver. "Go to your room, Delia. Dad needs to take this call."

That marked the end of my three week honeymoon with my daughter.

Fifty bucks went a long way in the 80s. My work ethic twenty years ago was wanting, to put it kindly. I dabbled as a product-tester for home abdominal toning devices, a guinea pig for medical students learning to draw blood, listen for bowel sounds or insert a catheter, and a participant in studies testing yet-to-be-approved pharmaceutical medications. It was there that Piper, a volunteer lucky enough to get the placebo in a study where an unlucky 14%, myself included, developed "anal leakage," boasted of how much money she made harvesting her eggs for infertile couples, scoffing at those naïve souls who relied on the measly return from donating blood or selling used books. "You could drip me dry of every drop, and still I wouldn't have as much as from one of my precious little eggies. I'd be vacationing bloodless in New Jersey rather than short an egg on the shores of Jamaica." This inspired my brief foray into self-selling. But as I found with my other ventures into easy money, it all either came at too much a cost or too little a benefit. Methodically, I worked my way from the top down. First, I grew my hair, twice, to sell it to Schleimel's, a factory specializing in wigs for Orthodox Jewish women. But one can only produce so much hair on a yearly basis. It wasn't until I reached my loins that I thought I had stumbled across a true income generator. In contrast to my grades, my scores here were high. They evaluated my celery sauce every which way, starting macro—volume, color, consistency—then micro, orchestrating a census of my groin—how many tadpoles were there, were they shapely (one round head, one svelte tail), did they swim, how well? And without even trying, the answers were stellar: a lot, white, creamy, millions!, 90%, indeed, very well, thank you.

My dabble in loinal donation was short-lived, however, despite my pride at effortless excellence. The discomfort of being offered porn with my collection cup by my nurse who expected me to masturbate and then, upon return of my "sample," look her in the eyes as if nothing had happened, despite her knowing that everything had, was just too much. My female friends unanimously scoffed at my awkwardness. Now you know what it is like for us every time we have to put our feet in stirrups for our female exam, they would say. No, I'd answer, it would only be equivalent if you had to masturbate to orgasm before the exam, the doctor knowing exactly why your cheeks were so flushed as he snapped on his rubber gloves.

I zipped up my career in easy money and closed up shop, took my fifty bucks and bought a Zippo lighter, a vintage one with a sexy woman on it, leaning forward on her high heels into the wind, lighting a cigarette. Over the years I learned how to light it in countless cool ways, snapping my fingers against the flint wheel, rolling it down my thigh, flicking open the lid and flipping the wheel in one well-practiced fluid motion. When I first met my non-smoking ex-wife she was initially amused by these moves weaved into our courtship, but it was quickly clear that my smoking days were numbered. My Zippo's spark no longer necessary, it became a mere mantelpiece knickknack.

I learned a lot about Josh in our increasingly frequent phone conversations. His mother had just passed away from breast cancer. He had been estranged from her and his father, an "amoral corporate whore" who worked in agribusiness. Josh was taking a long break from school, where he dabbled in environmental studies, not because of his mother's death—he was already taking a break when she died—but because he needed to figure out who he was. He blamed his parents for his diabetes, for not breastfeeding him, for introducing cow's milk as a substitute. An ardent vegan for two years, he not only now avoided meat, fish, eggs, and milk but also honey and surprisingly many wines and beers. Gelatin from sturgeon bladders, from cow and pig hooves and connective tissue, he explained with an air of outrage and disgust reminiscent of my own early twenties passionate obsessiveness, were used to remove impurities in the alcohol before being filtered out themselves. Could some miasm of my own youthful kookiness have been passed down to him when I ejaculated into that cup during a time in my life when I too was lost and desperately seeking to avoid the responsibilities of adulthood? I balked at trying to answer that question, still unable to truly believe this was a lost son of mine.

How many more sons were blowing in the wind? I had no time to wonder, not with Leo's sudden shift since moving in with my wife. Still friendly and loud he now displayed an unneighborly territorialness. The first time we met at the fence line after the Ukrainian invasion, he broached the subject of my dwarf magnolia hedge. "Don't get the idea wrong. We neighbors now. I cause no harm my son Lukas cutting branches or leafs that cross or touch our side across property. I cut straight up, just keeps simple for you." Leo said this so matter-of-factly, without aggression, without any trace of evidence that these confrontations pained him, or were even confrontations at all. I wanted to educate him about the city code, that he must respect the health of the tree even when pruning it on his side, but it was easier to grumble to Delia about these conflicts or inconveniences. Whatever these encounters were, they were multiplying, they were more than the sum of their parts. A Leo and a Lukas didn't make for double the pain but instead brought it more alive, with an added quality as if hearing the same song but in stereo for the first time.

"Delia, when you bring in the salad greens and carrots, make sure you wash them extra well. Lukas is up on Mom's roof tearing shit down around the chimney and throwing it over the edge into the back of their pick-up."

Delia, just weeks ago, would have said something snide about Leo's pick-up truck, with the American flag flapping from the antenna, the *Love it or Leave it* bumper sticker and the Playboy bunny mud flaps. But all she pushed out was a perfunctory "so?" as she grabbed the garden scissors. Was it Leo moving in with Mom? Was it Leo moving in with his son in tow? Or was it Josh? Or perhaps it was just too much to get a stepbrother and a half brother the same week, the same day. Perhaps she didn't know why herself, but if she did, she wasn't saying.

"Soak the greens in vinegar water, rinse 'em well, twice, and make sure to peel the carrots and potatoes. Construction dust is wafting over our garden beds as we speak, every time Lukas drops another load from the roof. Dust of who knows what: lead paint, asbestos, napalm, plutonium."

Delia didn't even crack a smile. She hadn't cracked one since the day we learned Josh was coming to meet us, traveling by Greyhound bus as we spoke. I busied myself in anticipation of his arrival. My ex-wife's sewing room was adjacent to Delia's bedroom. Now absent a sewing machine and loom, the room was unused, unfurnished, and useless, a vestige of my married life, an evolutionary dead-end like a tailbone. But I now had the excuse and motivation to revive it from its ghostliness. I went futon shopping, bought assorted furniture at IKEA, scattered various magazines I thought Josh might enjoy around the room, and stocked the refrigerator with soy cheese, rice milk, soy-rizo sausage, non-dairy ice cream, and a tofurky.

When he showed up with two suitcases worth of clothes, I fretted over Josh's expectations, of how long he expected to stay, a topic that was never broached on the phone. But we quickly established a rapport, and frankly, the timing couldn't have been better. My ex-wife asked me, understandably, to take care of their house and yard while her and Leo and Lukas went on a week-long camping trip. Of course I was thrilled at the prospect of a serene, lawnmowerless, outboardmotorless, toxic dustless, Leo-at-the-fenceless week. But my ex-wife mentioned that Delia had asked if she could come along. I could feel Delia slipping away from me but could not imagine her freely electing to be trapped in the backwoods with the Cossack King Kong and his spawn.

Fortunately, my life wasn't merely withering away like a wrinkled, ant-eaten fig, or a testicle twisting itself dead from its own source of blood. New life and opportunity was also sprouting up around me, was sitting across from me at my patio table, the sired son I never raised.

"I was in their backyard watering their tomato plants. By the way, their tomatoes are huge. Unnaturally so. Attack of the Killer Tomatoes so. Colossal, Dad." An awkwardness fell down upon us like pigeon shit. *Dad.* We both knew he had said it. And I wish I could have shoved it back in his head. But Josh paused and cocked his head sideways, like an abandoned puppy at the pound. He looked so pathetic I expected him to perk up his ears, let his tongue droop out of his mouth, and wag his behind. "Can I, can I call you Dad, Dad? Howie? Do you mind, sir?" I smiled and nodded my assent, genuinely, my resistance melting away. He continued, perking up. "I was suspicious of those tomatoes, Howie, Dad. So I rooted around in their garage and found all sorts of horrible things. They have a toxic poison for almost every living creature."

"Ex-husbands?"

Josh smiled. "I didn't see that, but bugs, slugs, and rats, for sure. And dandelions. You should keep Henry from going over there. Pets that roll around in that shit get lymphomas."

Finally, a boy to my heart. He got it. He got that there was a hypocrisy in Leo's wanting to be literal and inflexible about the property line while letting all the intangibles— his noise, his dust, his chemicals—float over into my life. I brought Josh inside and took the Zippo from the mantel. "This, son, is the Windproof Beauty." I spun it around between my fingers making sure he saw it from all sides, and the engraving in all its wind-blown sexy splendor. "Stand back, amigo." I palmed the lighter upside-down, hinge side toward me. And pointed two fingers of the same hand at Josh as if I was pointing a gun. "I've got you now, you big Ukrainian slug!" I swept my free hand toward me as if cocking the gun, knocking the lighter open and lighting it at the same time. The flame leapt upward as if coming from my hand. Josh looked mesmerized. "That is 'The Gun,' and this," I slapped the lighter into his palm and pressed it there, "is for you."

Josh began practicing "The Gun" move immediately, aiming at Leo's pickup truck or at the corn stalks in my ex-wife's garden that looked awfully tall this year. I even caught him aiming at his own reflection in the mirror in the bathroom, his legs stanced ready for a shoot out at the O.K. Corral. That was my boy. Heading over to bring in my wife's mail, I imagined Josh courting a girl someday with my Zippo of old.

As the week neared its end, I had trouble enjoying its final peaceful moments, much like a beautiful fall day that hints at the winter to come. I mistook a rumbling engine for Leo's RV ready to hover over our backyard once again, but it was the UPS truck. I accepted a large cardboard box, three feet by four, for Josh with no return address. Had he mailed this to himself before he left to come here? The door to his room was ajar. I watched him sitting on the edge of the bed, rolling his pant leg up mid-thigh, and pinching the muscle in his hand. He held the needle up with his free hand and uncapped it with his mouth. Casually, without hesitation, the needle disappeared into the flesh of his leg and he emptied the plunger while staring at a National Geographic splayed open on the bed beside him.

His head tilted as he recognized he was being watched.

"How often do you have to do that?" I pushed the door open.

"Just once a day for this. The long-acting stuff." He cocked his head to see what was behind me in the hall. "Hey, my first package arrived"

"What'd you get?"

"Stuff," he dragged the box into the room, now suddenly full of silence. An awkward unspoken cue for me, the Dad, to leave.

It wasn't Leo or Lukas or even Luther, the German Shepherd puppy they came home with, that brought our week to a close. Oddly it was happiness, Delia's, whistling from the kitchen. "Oh, Dad, it was the best. I saw an otter and an eagle We ate a deer and it was so good. And Lukas knows how to move quietly in the woods. You just have to see it."

I wasn't sure how to respond, so I helped her put sliced

ham, cottage cheese, and eggs into her backpack. "What are we doing exactly?" I asked squatting beside her in front of the open refrigerator.

Delia looked at me with pity in her eyes. "Oh Dad, you look so kerfuffled. It was fun, that's all."

I looked down at the now half-full backpack and back up at my daughter's face.

"I'm moving some of my food over to Mom's. Not all of it. See, I'm leaving the grapes, and the peanut butter."

"What do you mean, *your* food?"

"Dad, you know exactly what I mean. You pushed all my stuff into the back corner of the fridge last week."

"I pushed our stuff. He's a vegan. I didn't want to offend him."

"You just don't get it, Dad."

"I don't get why you went on vacation with them."

"God! Get a clue!"

Grow up were the last words I heard as Delia stormed out of the house.

A wicker basket left on the countertop spilled over with vegetables. The tomatoes, a blemish-free, uncanny red, ready to burst forth in fertile glory, surrounded a watermelon-sized zucchini and two exemplary ears of corn, each kernel as plump and yellow as the next. A card written in my ex-wife's girlish hand, the dots over the "i"s and "j"s hollow like little bubbles, thanked me. *Howard, thank you for watching the house while we were camping. Enjoy our bounty!*

Henry brushed against my leg, meowing an "I know just how you feel" meow. We went out into the backyard to inspect our garden. Leo's RV now casting a shadow over my south facing raised bed for several hours each day, I had an abundance of perpetually green tomatoes, several small squash persevering, if not growing, despite the leaves succumbing to powdery mildew and the squash flowers serving as a boarding house for itinerant slugs. I plucked two ripe tomatoes and collected salad greens and parsley. Meanwhile, Henry grumpily wedged himself between the side of the house and a blueberry bush to fertilize the soil, flustered and off-put by Luther's yapping from the other side of the fence. "There is only so much we can do, furry man," I lamented to my feline compatriot.

Inside, I threw two ears of my wife's corn in boiling water, cooked up some chili with texturized soy protein, and took out the tub of non-dairy margarine in anticipation of Josh returning for dinner. He said he was looking for a job.

"I'm famished. I looked into some canvassing jobs with Greenpeace and PETA, but they require *a lot* of work for very little pay. I think I'm gonna step back and consider my options before looking again. It's exhausting."

I plopped down a steaming ear of corn on his plate. He chomped at it with verve and industry. I sat down and spread the margarine across my kernels. Josh looked up while I did this, smiling from behind his cob, but then his eyes looked past me. Perplexed, they squinted, then went flat and unfocused as he processed something in his head. All at once they snapped awake, growing large and alarmed. His nostrils flared and a weird gurgle came from his throat as his shoulders curled forward. A stampede of half-chewed corn kernels fought to be the first to exit his mouth. Some froze mid-air, momentarily suspended by strings of saliva, others tumbled, en masse, onto the plate, like a flow of undercooked chowder. Josh pushed back from the table and stood up, wiping his face with his forearm. His outstretched arm pointed and shook. Henry hurtled through the pet door.

I looked behind me expecting to see something to warrant this disgusting display, but nothing was there.

"Is, is that, is that corn Leo's?" Josh said, but pointing at the remaining zucchini and tomatoes in the basket behind me.

"Jesus, man. Get a grip. We got the food as a gift. I washed it. It isn't possible to be pure, Josh, to avoid all exposure to pesticides all the time."

"You don't und—"

"You don't need to act like an animal. It's a gift."

"Fuck you, Howard!" he said storming to his room.

I could hear him talking to himself, pulling open and slamming drawers closed, stomping back and forth in his room, while I sponged down the table. *Howard.* That stung.

I heaved the basket of remaining vegetables on to my shoulder and walked them out to the compost pile in the far corner of the yard. I rolled the giant zucchini and fire engine red tomatoes, one after the other into the rotting mass of leaves, grass, and food waste. This super race of vegetables, for all their symmetry and perfection, would soon be like any other, food for the bugs and worms. A perfect waste of perfectly good food.

I sat down on the bench beneath the cedars at the back of the yard and lit up a cigarette. Spider web silk glittered in the early evening sun. A meaty brown spider did maintenance on her web as it swayed, suspended between the fig and vine maple. Another sat at the center of her elaborate mesh, motionless, waiting for her food to be delivered. I remembered when we first moved into this house, before these trees were even planted. I was convinced someone was stealing our lilies, surreptitiously surveying our home and cutting them when we weren't around. A blush of shame colors my face even today when I remember the makeshift sign I hung on the lilies still blooming, devised from a note card and twine: *I know what you are doing. And I will catch you!* I could never live this down with my wife. She would bring it up—this and the tomatoes—whenever we fought. "You are the most unseemly combination of paranoia and incompetence!" she would say at her most exasperated moments.

But the lessons most deeply learned are those from the most painful mistakes. I would never forget—never ever— that the tomato flower became the tomato fruit or that the stems of our lilies, once the blooms had fallen, looked as if they had been cut, but truly had not been. Josh must be caught in the grips of a similar delusion. What else could explain his corncob conniption? I hoped for him that he would learn as enduring a lesson from it as I had from mine. I watched a cloud of cigarette smoke drift toward the house and wondered what exactly that lesson would be.

"You don't get it," Josh said upon my return inside, waving a National Geographic in front of him. "I'll bet my left nut those are genetically modified vegetables. My dad, he brought home ones just like it from his freak experiments at TerraViva Technologies."

"Cool your jets, cowboy. I composted them."

He beelined to the compost pile. I followed, catching the screen door before it slammed in my face, incredulous that he didn't believe me. But instead, oddly, he pulled out the zucchini and tossed it in the trash can, and then gingerly extracted tomato after tomato as if they were delicate porcelain and splattered them unceremoniously atop the zucchini.

"Smoke?" I showed him the pack of organic, additive-free cigarettes, and he joined me on the bench.

Josh unfurled the National Geographic as if to read to me but mostly shook it or waved it in front of him as he spoke. The article, Seeds of Deception, was about the creation of the terminator seed, a seed that only bore sterile fruit, created to prevent farmers from saving seed for next year's crop. Each year, the farmers would have to buy the seed anew from some greedy corporate behemoth like Josh's father's, seeds that not only were reproductively impaired but genetically modified and patented.

"Even if you are growing totally organically," Josh said, his eyes wide and ablaze, "100% responsibly, minding your own business, if pollen blew from a field of Frankenfood on to yours, your plants would be owned by TerraViva Technologies, and they could sue you." His voice rose in a swell.

"I get what your saying, son. It sounds horrible, it does. But realistically, nobody is going to sue me or some other backyard gardener if Leo's pollen drifts over here," I protested. "It's not a reason to spit your food all over the place Josh. C'mon now."

Josh's face flushed. He pointed at Leo's corn peeking over our fence. "Pigs eating GMO corn have trouble getting pregnant. Farmers say some of theirs are giving birth to sacs of water. And, and farmers in the Phillippines, I think, got sick from breathing corn pollen, and, and," he furiously flipped through the magazine, "here it is, '*And the modified genes, altered for antibiotic resistance, have been found in the DNA of human intestinal bacteria. The implications of this are yet unclear.*' Do you want me to go on?"

I admit, I was impressed, proud of my son's smarts and on the verge of being downright scared, that is, until his impassioned plea devolved into science fiction, about as believable as a lily bandit stalking someone's house day after day. I shifted uncomfortably as Josh described a food supply so divorced from nature that we now put honeybees and salmon in trucks, that we drove them around like harried soccer moms, shuttling insects from farm to farm to pollinate our crops, careening down the interstate with carpooling fish to bypass the dams responsible for their dwindling numbers.

I rested my chin in my hand, arranging my fingers across my mouth, in the hopes of hiding my disbelief at his description of overworked honeybees revolting, going on strike, leaving their hives in increasing numbers, their populations plummeting across the country, our food supply teetering on the edge of collapse because of it.

"And, and amazingly, only a few people are standing up to this at all," Josh said. "In Europe, they've lit GMO fields on fire and driven bulldozers into McDonalds."

I must have smiled at this point, a wrong sort of smile, I suppose, because Josh looked me square in the eye and said in a tight and reedy voice, "I swear, Dad, I'm gonna prove it to you." He flung his arms into the air and broke one of the spider web's silken anchors, causing it to flap lazily like a flag in the wind.

"Maybe we could erect some sort of mesh to keep the pollen from coming into our yard?" I offered half-heartedly, thinking of the spiders but realizing how stupid it sounded even before it left my lips. But Josh was already gone, having stormed back into the house. I took a deep drag on my cigarette and blew the smoke after him. The spider hung tight to its partially unmoored home. Leo's corn stalks swayed uneasily in the wind across the property line.

Upon returning to the house, I discovered the Zippo lighter back on the mantel, as if it had been tossed there without a thought, lying askew against a photo of 6-year old Delia in her theatrical debut as a munchkin in an elementary school play. Yet I knew it had been returned there with painful purpose and in anger. Josh had held tight to his new talisman from the moment I had slapped it in his palm. And yet here it was, a mere mantelpiece knickknack once again.

It was just Henry and me now. Over the weeks, Josh became a skulker, a shadow who hugged the walls, who sulked in corners, or played angry songs in his room on the guitar that had arrived in the mail shortly after our argument. Delia, annoyingly happy, flitted in and out of the house like a hummingbird, a fleeting glimpse of her here and there. She gathered her cheer mostly elsewhere. Henry and I, two aging bachelors, devolved on the couch, watching reruns of Herb Potter, napping, eating pizza. I peeled off the cheese for Henry, but now and again, I'd eat some, or even order half the pizza with sausage and think "Take that, Josh!" each time I plucked a piece of meat from the gooey surface, plopping it into my mouth instead of Henry's.

During the day, we dove into gardening to implement Herb's advice from the night before. Henry chased moths and bees while I pruned, he munched on weeds or turned the soil while I added coffee grounds around the rose bushes. Leo and Lukas, waterproofing the front porch of my ex-wife's house, stirred buckets of stinky sealants and waxes in the driveway abutting my property. But I was at peace with it because I knew it could be worse. At night, I had nightmares of Delia atop my wife's house, throwing chunks of asbestos over the edge, wiping beer foam off her upper lip and belching. Or I'd discover her checking the tire pressure of Leo's pick-up truck, her butt crack leering over the top of her pants as she polished his hubcaps, prompting me to lurch upright in my bed in terror, the image of King Kong on my daughter's burgeoning bicep tattooed indelibly on my brain. I was grateful each day for the status quo, what little remained of it and its diminishing returns.

One day, Leo was waiting for me by the dwarf magnolias. I knew something was up before I approached. He stood stiffly, as if fighting himself still, his arms akimbo, his jaw set, his face drawn.

"Neighbor!" he waved me down. Lukas, squatting by a bucket, stopped stirring the goo inside it as I approached them. "She said it's greater if she talked to you. That I don't control well. But, it's greater still man facing man."

"I'm not following ..."

He scooped up his puppy Luther and wedged him in the nook of his elbow. "Someone's been inside the house." I watched his stubby fingers pull at the loose skin behind Luther's ears, kneading it. "Someone moves things. Someone opens things. Someone spilled seeds in our rooms."

"Seeds? Leo, I don't follow."

"Neighbor. I believe fair and square. Your side, my side. You come my side, it's square no longer. You mess my side, we have big, big problem." His eyes ceased to blink. His bicep flexed. A big tortured vein popped up in exclamation above Luther's ears.

"I don't know what you are talking ..."

Leo's fingers unconsciously clamped down on Luther's head as I spoke. The puppy let out an anguished yelp.

"You understand me?" Leo said to me. The dog squirmed out of his grasp, tumbling to the ground.

I nodded.

I was still nodding, stunned, as I burst into Josh's room. He had been napping, loosely clasping the guitar across his chest. He yelped as the door banged open, instinctively grabbing the guitar neck as if ready to wield it as a weapon. He loosened his grip and sat up when he saw who it was and cradled the instrument against him like a breastfeeding mother.

"Were you in their house?" I yelled, lifting a stack of his folded shirts to see if there was anything hidden beneath. "Were you?" I pushed over a chair and walked into his closet. I rifled through a stack of papers, peered inside his shoes, looked behind a tin of cat treats. I didn't know what I was looking for. I figured I'd know it when I saw it.

"It's over here. It's by my CD play …"

"Have you been feeding Henry?" I came out of the closet with the tin of chicken livers. "I swear I don't know what the hell you are doing in here half the time. He has started begging between meals."

Josh stood and lifted up a big bag of seed from beside his stereo. "This is why I was over there. To prove it to you. That it is all Frankenfood terminator shit. Just like I thought."

He pressed the bag into my hands. I didn't look from his face.

"Aren't you going to say you are sorry?" Josh asked.

"Me?" I guffawed. "Me say I'm sorry? *You* broke into their house, not me. And I'm supposed to apologize? You are going to march over there right now, young man, and admit what you did, and then you are grounded. For two weeks." I grabbed his guitar from the bed and held it behind me.

"Give me back my guitar." He stepped toward me.

I shook my head and widened my stance. "Give me back the key to their house and go apologize."

"Fuck you. You were the one who didn't believe me. You should be grounding Delia not me after what I caught her doing with Lukas over there." I slapped Josh hard across the face. He staggered backwards and I slammed the door shut.

"And she wasn't sucking on a lollipop, Howard," Josh yelled from the other side of the door.

"I want you out of my house by morning," I yelled back, though immediately I wondered if I was going too far.

That night, Herb Potter's words ran through my brain with a new meaning, a soundtrack to the unceasing images of Leo's son defiling my daughter in every way imaginable. *When saving seeds, pick the healthiest, most robust specimens. Do not save seeds from spindly, poor performing plants. They will pass on their unwanted characteristics to next year's crop.* Loud, boorish Neanderthal genes—genes damaged from years of pumping gas, spraying pesticides, eating genetically modified food, thinking stupid thoughts, and inhaling fumes from endless inane projects—mixing irrevocably with mine, strands of our DNA intertwining in one long embrace for generations to come. Anger buzzed through me like a swarm of fed-up bees. Henry jerked and shook next to me, deep in a dream, chased or being chased, while I ruminated, burping up, again and again, the coupling of Lukas and Delia, of Kosvloshenko and Silverstein, like a cinematic Kama Sutra from hell.

Henry usually awoke with the birds. Just before the dawn, they would sing and he would meow for breakfast. I would typically stumble downstairs and feed him and roll back into bed for an hour or more of early morning sleep. But on this sleepless night, I was up and around, unusually active before the dawn, before the birds, before the fire engine that illuminated the still dormant neighborhood with its swirling beacon of light. I walked out onto the front porch. Many neighbors also on their porches or peering through parted curtains watched one of the firemen speak to someone at the front door of my wife's house. Josh shook my shoulder from behind in a panic. He pulled me back into the living room with him.

"I didn't do it. I swear. I, I swear Howard, Dad. I didn't do it." He glanced repeatedly at the mantel. "I swear, I didn't take the Zip …"

I turned his face back toward me and held it between my hands, his cheeks still plump with baby fat. "Josh, I believe you. I know you didn't. I've been thinking, what sort of father would I be if I didn't trust my son." I could see his packed suitcases just inside his open bedroom door. "Hurry along now and go unpack your things." I pinched his cheeks and let them go. "We'll sort things out over breakfast."

My ex-wife, huddled within a baby-blue terry cloth bathrobe, nodded to the fireman's questions, a police officer filling out a form behind him. It wasn't long before she noticed me watching her. The fluffy ears of her rabbit slippers, the ones I had bought for her during her depression after Delia's birth, flopped up and down, as she traipsed to the near end of her porch, until I could see the whites of their plastic eyes, their pupils swirling in opposite orbits with her gait.

"I told the police about your son."

Her stern face, girded against her susceptibility toward feeling guilty about disappointing me, the same face she assumed when she needed to muster a determined resolve, the you-are-driving-me-crazy-but-I-feel-bad-having-to-tell-you face, the this-isn't-working-anymore face, a face that had hardened into a permanent mask since she had left.

"*My* son?" I said, supremely irritated. "Why Josh?"

"Don't play dumb, Howard. This has all happened since he arrived. Someone could have died."

"And you call me paranoid! Why not Leo's son? This has all happened since he arrived, too. C'mon now, Carol, you have always scolded me to not jump to conclusions. I'll vouch for him."

…pizdu……fucking zalupa!…….bzdenok

We could hear Leo's curses from the backyard, going off like fireworks amidst the early morning birdsong.

A smile flitted across Carol's face and vanished. "You

should be glad he doesn't know you are here, Howard. This is as bad as I've seen him."

"Is that a threat? Am I supposed to be scared?" The idea of Lukas atop my daughter, inside my Delia, inoculated me from fear.

"No …"

"Then, why exactly were you smiling, huh? Because your boyfriend could beat me up if he wanted to? Is that it?"

"Howard! Get a hold of yourself." She pulled the bathrobe tighter around her. "I smiled because he basically called you something in Russian that translates as 'little old man who farts frequently.'" She wanted me to laugh. She smiled again, meekly, testing me to see if we could find common ground. But I wasn't amused.

I caught a glimpse of Henry walking towards our backyards, atop the fence between our houses. I leaned forward and looked down the side of the house. The back of Leo's bald head glowed a purplish red from the first rays of daylight, that fleshy Ukrainian orb hovering over the fence where the corn stood just hours ago. The fence, now blackened in places on my side—my cat walking nobly atop its uncharred top edges—was much worse from where Leo stood. One solitary black stalk of corn wobbled feebly in the wind.

I spoke without looking at her, watching daylight capture the orange in Henry's fur. "Your boyfriend's seed has been blowing all over my yard. I'm going to have to dig up everything and start over."

"Howard, what in God's name are you talking about?"

I turned back to look at my ex-wife but could not see her face. The sun blinded my eyes. I stared into it instead, the first fiery red edges of a new day, and did not answer.

"You are so fucking impossible!" she growled.

I shielded my eyes and watched her walk away from me on the porch in a huff, the two bunny tails, the same ones our baby girl once called *boonies*, bobbing a furry farewell.

"Hey, Carol!" I yelled, as she reached the screen door. She

Genetic Drift

paused in the doorway. "Do you remember this? From our first date?"

I fondled the still warm Windproof Beauty in my right pocket, nestled next to my still living testicle. I flipped open the lid, for the second time that day, and let the flint wheel graze my thigh as I brought the lighter into view. I leaned into the breeze, the spark, the flame, the day glowing anew.

The Intelligentcia
Bill Lawrence

I guess you could say the Thirty Minutes to Save the World Scenario came into play today.

What a mess.

We ended up having to torture a guy.

We didn't want to. We're basically a good and decent people, and we don't ever want to have to be seen as torturers. But this was a thirty minute deal and—whatever. People's lives were hanging in the balance.

So we tortured this guy who I'll call Abdul, but which is not really his name. Unless I'm wrong and that just happens to be what his name really is. What I'm saying is that I'm not really sure *what* his name is, but it's probably not Abdul.

But it might be.

Doused him. Had to.

One of those situations where there's nothing else *to* do. Thirty minutes till a bunch of people are going to be blown up and you pretty much know this guy might very well have some info that could possibly end up saving a bunch of lives. What are *you* gonna do?

Not waterboard him?

Some people say it's torture and some say it isn't really. I don't know. I don't make those kind of judgments. I do know that it's not a lot of fun. For the guy that's getting doused anyway. And it usually ends up getting them to at least say something. So when it's all over, even if the people you were trying to save get all blown up and shit anyway, you can at least say you gave it a shot and you didn't just stand around with your thumb up your ass.

How it all started out is—last week, as soon as we found out there might be a plot to blow up this coffee house in

Hamburg, which is a city in Europe, well—we took Abdul down to interrogation, which is this little sealed off room at the end of the cell block with no windows and bare walls and chairs and a table and a sink. Then we started asking him if he knew anything about the Hamburg coffee shop thing. We asked him if he'd like to be a sport and help us out a little bit on this one. You know—treating him like a fellow human being and all except that he was tied up and had a hood over his head. We told him we might be able to help him out when he finally goes to trial. He didn't seem any more interested in making a deal than he has been about anything else over the last couple of years, so we decided to put his skinny little ass back in his cell and let it slide until we heard something more.

Well, we didn't hear anything more till about forty minutes before the stupid bombing was supposed to take place. All of a sudden, we get this call, and it's like, "CIA really thinks that Abdul knows more than he's telling."

And Captain Deaver, our Company Commander, calls a couple of us in his office and he's all like, "Fellas, we gotta get that intel from Abdul pronto, or there's gonna be some serious Hamburger blood on our hands." Yes, he actually said that. "Hamburger blood."

Corporal Lynch and I are all, "Well, gosh Captain Deaver, what do we do?"

Deaver goes, "Shit, I don't know. It's all supposed to come down in like, about thirty-five minutes! Get Abdul into the interrogation room!"

So Lynch and I roust Abdul out of his rack and shuffle his ass down the hall, and Deaver's just going ballistic.

"I want you guys to help the CIA guy to get the location of that coffee shop by *whatever means necessary,*" trying to sound all Malcolm X-ish and all. Deaver's half black and he really likes to highlight his black side.

This CIA guy, who's about twenty-three years old but looks like he's fifteen, meets us in the interrogation room.

We've seen him around but he only talks to officers. He's wearing these Italian suit pants and a white tee shirt and trying to act all above the fray and all. Adjusting his glasses and sighing like he's really put out to have to deal with this petty shit, you know? Smoking a cigarette and it looks like he just learned how to smoke last week. Guy's like one year out of college, and he's walking around like he's auditioning for a role in "24," or something. I'd tell you his name, but we're not supposed to do that, and I don't want to get put on some list. Suffice it to say that this guy's about as bogus as they get.

So right off, it's not going well. Abdul's going all limp and everything like he always does and acting like he can't wake up. On top of that, somebody forgot to bring in the plastic wrap to seal off his nose for waterboarding purposes. So anyway, we're all, "Abdul, you'd best tell us everything you know about whatever the fuck is going to happen in that coffee shop in Hamburg. If you don't, we're going to bring your daughter in and shoot her right in front of your eyes!"

Then I realize we still got a hood on him and I'm all, "Oh, yeah—and we're gonna take your hood off before we do that." And Corporal Lynch is all, "Yeah! So you'll be seeing all that bad stuff we were just talking about!"

Dumb. I don't think you should ever talk about what they're *going* to see until you take the hood off, but that's just me.

Whatever.

Abdul usually keeps his eyes closed most of the time anyway.

Thirty minutes. Abdul's all mumbly and like, "I don't have daughter."

And CIA frat boy is trying to act all stoic. Filing his fingernails and sighing really loudly.

He goes, "Hhhheeeeehhh. Daughter. Son. Wife. It really doesn't matter much to us, Detainee. We *will* bring a family member in, and we *will* shoot them in front of your very eyes if you do not cooperate."

Detainee?

Shit. What a wad. Great time to get all formal and all.

"Umm, Jack Bauer called, Sir. I think he wants to do lunch. That is, when you get done with the *Detainee.*"

Bogus asshole.

Deaver sticks his head in the door. Motions me over. Whispers.

"Is it working?"

"Is what working?"

"The threatening and all."

"No."

"Did you do the thing where you say a big black guy is going to come in and rape him?"

"Sir, they say that only works if you've actually *got* a big black guy."

Deaver's all, "In case you haven't noticed, Lance Corporal—I happen to *be* black!"

Captain Deaver gets highly pissed when people don't take note of his blackness.

"What? You mean we're supposed to threaten him with *you*, Sir?"

I'm sorry, but Captain Deaver weighs about a buck ten, and he is one of the most non-threatening looking people I've ever met.

"Fuck's wrong with that?"

"With all due respect, Sir ..."

"What?"

CIA comes over and whispers to Deaver. "Mark, you're only half black and you are *well* under six feet tall. You hardly qualify as a big black guy."

"Oh, so I'm incapable of being threatening? Is that what you're saying?"

Captain Deaver's all offended and everything now. He's not really even supposed to be in here, but you can tell he *so* wants to be part of the thing.

"Abdul," he yells in this really deep voice, "I am a large black man, and I'm gonna come over there and give you a good ass rapin' if you do not tell us whay dat coffee shop is."

He sounds a little like Gary Coleman when he used to scrunch up his face and say, "Whatchoo talkin' bout, Willis?" I can see Lynch smiling a little, and you can tell he's trying to keep from laughing.

CIA guy is all, "Mark, there's no time for ass raping right now. The best thing you could do in this situation is run down to the mess hall and see if you can find us some plastic wrap!"

"Let's let the Captain run with the ass raping threat and see where it gets us, why don't we?" says Corporal Lynch.

I forgot to mention Lynch is a big time ass kisser.

"Shut the fuck up, Lynch!" says CIA guy.

"What? I'm not allowed to say anything?" says Lynch.

"No! You're not!"

"Oh, of course not," says Deaver. "When it's something *I* want to try, nobody's allowed to be supportive, are they?"

"It's not that, Mark," says CIA guy. "It's just that Lynch used the words, "ass raping *threat*." So now the Detainee knows that you wouldn't really ass rape him."

"The hell I wouldn't!"

"Let it go, Mark."

"All right, but let me just add one thing ..."

Deaver gets really dramatic and gets all up in Abdul's face.

"I am going down to the mess hall, Abdul. And there, I'm gonna get us some plastic wrap so we can waterboard the shit out of you. And you know what? I just might ass rape you *while* we're waterboarding you!"

Abdul's moving his head around like he can't tell where the voice is coming from.

Then Lynch goes, "Actually, Sir—that probably wouldn't be possible because he'll be on his back and ..."

"Spare me the logistics, Lynch!" Deaver screams. "I think I know a little bit more about ass rape than you do!"

"But, Sir ..."

"Lynch! Shut the fuck up," says the CIA guy. "Mark! Just

go and get us the plastic wrap!"

"Okay," Deaver says, backing away and jabbing his finger at Abdul and trying to look all threatening, which is pretty stupid considering Abdul still has the hood on.

CIA guy goes, "And hurry, man! Time is of the essence!"

"Time is of the essence." Spare me.

Captain Deaver slams the door shut, and all of a sudden it's quiet as can be.

"Lay him down and place his feet slightly higher than his head," says CIA guy.

"Lay him down on what?"

"The table."

"Oh."

Deaver sticks his head in the door.

"Hey, if they don't have plastic wrap, should I just get some baggies, or what?"

CIA guys all huffy and shit and like, "Right, Mark. Like a mess hall isn't going to have any plastic wrap."

Then Deaver really gets pissed and he's like, "You know what? Why don't we put a lid on the condescending tone! I'm in the military and you're not! I think I might know a little bit more about what a mess hall might and might not have than you do!"

"Secure it, Mark. I don't want to argue."

"Well then—why don't you just stop scoffing at my suggestions? I'm just trying to help."

CIA guy sighs again. Lowers his head like he's trying to be patient.

"I know that. I apologize. Yes, just bring baggies if they're out of plastic wrap."

"Okay."

Captain Deaver leaves.

"And bring some bottled water!" CIA guy yells.

"Oh my gosh, *bottled* water?" says Lynch.

"Fuck yes, bottled water. What's wrong with that?"

"That shit costs a dollar per!"

"Not the Poland Springs."

"Yes, it does. Disbursing told me that a case of Poland Springs is twenty-three bucks! That's almost a dollar per!"

"Yes—it is," says CIA guy. "For *you*. If *you* want to buy some for *yourself*. To *drink*. For interrogation purposes, we charge it to Uncle Sam and get it for about twenty-three cents per."

"Okay, now you're fucking with me."

"I'm serious as a heart attack."

"That's a good price."

"I know."

"Especially for Poland Springs."

"You know what's funny? It all tastes exactly the same to me."

I finally pipe up.

"Hey guys, we only got like twelve minutes left."

Then Lynch turns on me because he's all buddy-buddy with CIA guy all of a sudden.

"Lance Coporal Brewster, will you kindly do us a big favor and shut the fuck up? We can't do a damn thing until Captain Deaver comes back with the plastic wrap and the bottled water! We might as well shoot the shit until he gets here."

"Maybe we could soften him up?"

They just both start laughing at me.

CIA guys takes his glasses off, and he's like wiping tears from his eyes.

"Brewster—we don't 'soften up.' Because softening up would imply torture, and we don't torture people."

"Well, we do torture them in cases like this," says Lynch.

"Oh yeah! Absolutely! When you're in like a thirty-minute scenario," says CIA guy.

"So—let's soften him up," I say.

"Well, okay—I guess we could do a little of that," says CIA guy. "This isn't exactly fate of the world hanging in the balance stuff, but I guess it kind of qualifies. What should we do?"

"I've only softened up using waterboarding," says Lynch.

"Oh! I know!" says CIA guy. "We could do this one thing

we used to do during rush week for Alpha Kappa, where you make the guy carry an ice cube between his butt cheeks, and if he drops it, you spank the shit out of him with this big effin' paddle!"

I say, "I don't know if we'd have time for that."

CIA guy's not even listening.

"This fucking paddle's got *holes* bored through it so it cuts down on wind resistance and it's like—whooooosh, thwack! Stings like a motherfucker! I know. I went through the initiation. It's like, on the first night they get you together in this room all buck naked and shit…"

I say, "We've only got, like—what? Ten minutes left?"

CIA guy's like, "Yeah, I guess you're right. Still. If we had some ice cubes here right now, I'd do it in a heartbeat."

Lynch goes, "I could run after Captain Deaver and tell him to bring some."

"No. It's no good without the paddle anyway. Let's get the Detainee into pre-operations position."

Pre-operations position?

Spare the living fuck out of me! He probably calls it "Pre-op-po," when he's telling his girlfriend about it.

Pathetic, really.

So we get Abdul all positioned, which is a bitch because he doesn't feel like getting waterboarded today, and Deaver finally shows up with three bottles of water and a roll of Reynolds Wrap.

CIA guy's just about fed up.

"Reynolds Wrap?"

"Secure the fucking attitude, please! They didn't have any plastic wrap, as you so adamantly insisted they would, Mr. Knows Everything."

"Okay," says CIA guy, "but it's your ass if any water seeps up into his nose."

"That's a risk I'm willing to take at this point."

"I don't think the citizens of Hamburg will begrudge us a little water up the nose," says Lynch, chuckling.

"Lynch, shut the fuck up and hold his legs still," says

Captain Deaver.

"Detainee? At which coffee house in Hamburg is the bomb set to explode?" asks CIA guy.

No response.

"Hand me that Poland Springs bottle," says CIA guy.

"They didn't have any Poland Springs, so I swung by the Officers Quarters and ripped off some Aqua Fina," says Deaver.

"That Aqua Fina's some good shit," says Lynch. Lynch sees himself as kind of a bottled water expert.

"I swear to God, except for the labels, I can't tell the difference," says CIA guy. "Hand me one."

"Aye aye, sir. Just let me get the lid off here," says Deaver.

"I know what you mean," says Lynch. "Those plastic caps are a bitch."

"They are!" says CIA guy. "And, you know, what are they trying to protect us from? Deadly Mountain Spring Water?"

We all laugh but it's a nervous sort of laugh.

"Detainee, we are about to douse you. If you feel like telling us what you know about Hamburg we *will* stop dousing. Do you understand?"

Abdul starts shaking his head.

"No."

"Spare us the bogus comments, Abdul!" screams Deaver. "I'm getting ready to unzip my trousers for some ass rape!"

"No, Mark," says CIA guy. "One technique at a time."

Deaver slides up to the CIA guy and whispers,

"Sorry. I just thought that if he heard the sound of my zipper being undone, he'd crack."

"He's not going to all of a sudden hear your zipper and start giving us locations, Mark."

Deaver sighs loudly and zips up his trousers.

"Well that might be true and it might not be true, but we'll never know now will we? Because as I was just now unzipping, you covered up the zipper sound by shutting me down with your, 'one technique at a time,' comment."

CIA guy looks at the ground and pauses for a sec.

"Mark, we're getting down to business here. Now, if you want to hang, fine. But I'll need you to simply hold off on the interjection of comments and let me be in charge during the interrogation."

"Okay, smart guy. Knock yourself out."

Captain Deaver is playing along but you can tell he's pissed. He stares straight ahead.

"Douse him," says the CIA guy, which is kind of funny, because he then proceeds to douse Abdul himself. He pours the water into the washcloth and squeezes the foil around the base of Abdul's nose to create a kind of seal. Abdul kicks like a motherfucker and tries to shake his head, but we hold him tight.

No response.

"Ooops," says Lynch. "Looks like some water got in his nose."

"Tough shit," says CIA guy. "I'll say I'm sorry later."

"I'll say I'm sorry too," says Deaver, *"While I'm ass raping him at the gates of hell!"*

We all look up at Captain Deaver.

Long pause.

"Douse him again," says the CIA guy.

After about the fifth dousing, Abdul heaves like his heart is coming out of his chest, and you can tell he's screaming underneath the washcloth. His back arches like he's a wrestler trying to keep from getting pinned by his opponent, and then he makes these really guttural whimpering sounds. Then, finally, he says he'll talk. So we remove the foil from around his face, and he says that the bomb isn't set to go off at a coffee shop in Hamburg, but at the McDonalds, next to the coffee shop in Hamburg.

"Douse him again," screams Deaver. "There's no friggin' McDonalds in Hamburg!"

"The hell there isn't!" says Lynch. "They got those things everywhere!"

"You're right, Lynch! They went international in the early seventies!" yells the CIA guy.

"And think about it," says Lynch, "Hamburg—hamburg-er."

"That's just the kind of logic that would appeal to these animals," says CIA guy. "Douse him again!"

"Why?" I ask. "We've got the location!"

"Oh, right," says CIA guy. "I see your point."

"Right next to the *Hamburger* place in *Hamburg*," says Lynch.

"That's viable intel! Good work, Lynch!"

Deaver raises his hand.

"And also, what about this? Ham—burg—*ler*,"

We pause and look at him.

"Mark, you said you'd secure it."

"I said I'd secure it *during* the interrogation."

CIA guy is shouting orders to everyone now. Go phone this in. Check this out with Langley and shit. He doesn't even wait for them to say, Aye aye, Sir. And by the way, what's with the Italian pants and tee shirt look? Is this some new thing?

Bogus.

Deaver's all, "It's only going to take us about *seven minutes* to check your story out, Abdul. And you'd best not be lying, or in the name of Allah, I will march every single one of your family members into this room and oh my goodness, the Poland Springs shall flow like the Nile and the ass rapings will be plentiful."

And Lynch goes, "Aqua Fina, Sir."

"What?"

"We, umm, used the Aqua Fina instead. Remember?

Deaver looks at the floor and shakes his head.

"Lynch, could you *just for once* let me say something without having to top it off with some bogus comment that makes what I just said seem less threatening? Is that even a *remote* possibility?"

"Sorry, Captain."

"Fuck you are! You do it intentionally!"

"I'll secure it."

"Do so. Immediately."

The Der Raskeller Coffee Haus in Hamburg did not

explode six minutes later. Fourteen innocent Germans had some coffee and then went home. Turns out there wasn't a McDonalds within two miles. Also, once we got a reliable interpreter, we found out Abdul said the same thing about McDonalds on another occasion and it turned out that he had been trying to say that he'd give us some intel if he could have a cheeseburger. So while we did get some answers out of Abdul, they were sort of tainted with a wrongness that just couldn't be verified in five minutes. And since the US is now saying it doesn't torture for punishment, Captain Deaver couldn't really follow through on his rape threats, and Abdul just got to go back to his cell.

Still, the *detainee* ate no cheeseburgers on that day.
Detainee.
Spare me.

The Bleach Keeper
Jane Hoppen

Before dusk that first night, Sergeant Diana Hunt was unable to fulfill one of her primary duties, she stood outside of the tent she was in charge of, stared. The sand land was table flat, caked, and cracked, and it moved on into forever, pushed past the bland horizon, hung and hovered just as time did, going nowhere. Sergeant Hunt had begun to feel like a sand mite, grit settling in her mouth, her saliva so thick she couldn't spit it out. Heat scratched her skin. There, everything, everyone crouched low to the ground as if Earth was somehow safe. The jigsaw puzzles there were made of body parts. Some nights, she could hear the soldiers calling through thin air from the roadside past the camp after a bombing. Or two or three. Open the door and throw out an IED—made up shit-bomb carving through the bodies.

Diana was a Signal Systems Analyst and a shooter for special missions stationed at Camp Anaconda in Balad, their own Hell Away from Home. The base décor consisted of bunkers and sandbags flanking each tent and facility. Every day, soldiers accessorized with a weapon and ammunition and despite the desert inferno, the ground a furnace beneath their feet, they wore flak vests and helmets, donned gas masks during code reds. Sweat evaporated even before it was mist on skin.

Diana had found an even more important mission within Operation Iraqi Freedom, though: filling buckets with bleach each night, the buckets carefully placed in the tent of the female soldiers under her command. She took that duty seriously. Each woman, like her, had left some kind of life behind. Private Penny Baker, a cocky nineteen-year-old from Chicago's south side, would stretch out on her cot and describe in intimate detail the makings of a deep-dish pizza with the works, every woman present salivating with hungry discontent. Corporal Paula Lawson kept a bent and misshapen Gumby doll that belonged to her five-year-old son Bennett beneath her pillow. Sergeant Honey Kay Welk had a personal supply of canned Kim chi, claiming to have fallen disastrously in love with the volatile concoction after doing a tour in Korea. Every woman had a story.

> Two old ladies lying in bed
> One rolled over to the other and said
> I want to be an airborne ranger
> Living a life of war and danger
> I want to go to old Baghdad
> I want to kill a towel-head

Whenever Diana stretched out on her cot, that cadence call from basic training preyed on her mind—play, rewind, play—and she kept thinking: *I don't want a war. I'm in the wrong place. I've made a mistake. I'm not an old lady and I'm not lying in bed. I don't want to be a ranger of danger. Do I look like a ranger of danger?*

She didn't. Diana was thirty-seven, soft, with a Betty Crocker style. Her weak coffee brown hair fell even with her chin, an erratic mix of curls and frizz. Her eyes were the same color as her hair. She was medium in size, five feet five inches, with only a slight ripple of muscle veining along her arms and legs. She in no way resembled a ranger of danger. She was a single mother of two, Ariana, nine, and Tara, six.

Diana had joined the National Guard in 1999 after she and her husband divorced and he spent a year not spending money on child support. Diana felt she had no choice. Her six-to-two job as line chef at the Pancake Palace in Minnehaha, Wisconsin, didn't provide enough for the survival of three. She thought the decision was a safe one. The National Guard stayed stateside, on call for riots, domestic security, natural disasters. She served only one weekend a month, went away for training two weeks each summer. That was what she wanted to be, needed to be—a weekend warrior, nothing more. She never thought she would go to war. But she did. And every day, every night her gut was a snake den of knots. And that song—every time her head hit the cot: *Two old ladies lying in bed.*

*

Balad was under mortar attack each day. Mortars were the daily forecast, the explosions rattling through the base, rumbling Earth. Soldiers covered their ears, braced for the impact. They joked about it, sang the Burt Bacharach melody: Mortars keep falling on my head …

*

The brainwashing at basic training was evident from the beginning, that ride in the cattle car from the airport in St. Louis to the reception station on Fort Leonard Wood, an immediate erosion of ego, and within days, each day became a string of rote behavior—one, two, three, four: eat, pee, sit, shit, stand, march, run, shoot, shit. *Should I sit or should I shit?* Never think. Thought was the forbidden fruit, the enemy, to be broken down into shredded threads.

*

Sergeant Hunt went to sick call one morning for medication for a migraine, and beside her sat a woman no older than eighteen, tired and distressed, her eyes gone dead. Diana wanted to console her, the misery molded on the woman's face, but she couldn't speak, the pounding in her head erasing all words. She said nothing. The woman stood and walked out into the scorching slant of sun. Diana learned later that day the woman had left sick call, returned to her tent, burned her bible, put a bullet in her head. Diana never knew her name. Two days, later she couldn't recall the face.

*

Diana had eleven women to protect, including herself, and the first woman to go down was Private First Class Lucy Price. The second was Private Penny Baker. The attacks were well executed, coincided with the outgoing mortars, when no screams could be heard. Private Baker was raped as she exited the port-a-pit. The soldier had grabbed her from behind, dragged her down, torn at her clothes with scaly hands, the weight of him pushing into her until her mouth opened, a silent cavern, the red of her blood soaking into the brittle brown dirt. Sergeant Hunt wasn't going to let a third fall. She thought of her own girls back home. *No way, Jose; not on my shift.*

The female soldiers reported the rapes. They were sent to the Army hospital in Baghdad where rape kits were available. The rapists reverted back to pure soldiers and returned to work, weapons in hand: War is war. After the rape of Penny Baker, the tent went quiet, each women recollecting the ingredients of those deep-dish pizzas. *Did she say roasted peppers, or was that zucchini?* Diana went to the chain-of-command. She had faith. She had been told it was a chain of leaders.

She went to the sergeant and he sent her to the captain. She went to the captain and he sent her to the colonel. She went North, East, South, and West. She did her best. She reached out to a world no longer there, to a world only a presence in a newspaper, an image on a screen, a place on a separate plane. She walked another Earth.

Enter the colonel's office.

Attention.

Body straight and tall, hips level, stomach tucked in, chest lifted and arched with shoulders squared. Touch heels of boots together, feet at a 45-degree angle, body weight resting equally on heels and balls of feet, legs together and straight.

Salute.

Place arms straight at your sides along the seams of your pants, keeping thumbs pointing downward along the seam, curling the fingers loosely toward the palm. Look straight ahead with head up, focusing eyes directly in front, keeping face straight and relaxed. No smiling allowed.

Raise the right hand smartly until the tip of the forefinger touches the lower part of the headdress or forehead above and slightly to the right of the right eye. Extend and join thumb and fingers, palm to the left, upper arm horizontal, forearm at a 45-degree angle, hand and wrist straight. Turn head toward the colonel. Complete the salute by dropping the arm to its normal position by the side in one motion, turning head and eyes front.

"Sergeant Hunt reporting, Colonel."

"At ease, Sergeant."

Clasp hands behind back, relax upper body, shoulders slack.

"You have a problem you want to discuss?"

"Yes, sir. My women are getting raped when they go to the bathroom at night."

"I understand your concern, Sergeant. The matter has been brought to my attention. But it's not yet been proven. Until then, my hands are tied."

"There are allegations, sir."

"It's a matter for JAG."

"And until then, Colonel?"

"Until then?"

"What will my women do, sir? How will I protect them?"

"Protect them from what?"

"My women are being raped, sir."

"Those charges haven't been proven, Sergeant. There is nothing I can do."

"But it is the truth, sir. They won't drink water anymore. Last week, four went on sick call for dehydration. They're in the desert and they're not drinking water. The port-a-pit is a pit of hell."

"Well, you can't lead horses to water. Can you, Sergeant? The issue will be dealt with. It's a matter for JAG, Sergeant. Is there anything else?"

"No, sir; but ..."

"Dismissed."

Salute. About face. Exit.

Diana stopped behind the mess hall after she left the colonel and scavenged two large white plastic condiment buckets, and then she stopped by Supply and hustled two bottles of bleach from the Staff Sergeant on duty.

"What do you need it for?"

"My soldiers need to wash their undergarments. There are hygiene problems."

"Like what?"

"Take a guess, Sergeant. You can't even get us an adequate amount of menstrual supplies. We have to write letters home, ask people back home to send us tampons and pads."

"Guess that's why women shouldn't go to war."

"The bleach?"

He slammed two bottles down on the counter.

"Don't come back."

She signed for the bleach and grabbed the bottles.

"I'll be back."

That's when bleach became the essence of all existence. The white curved bottle with the blue label—Clorox. She was Diana Hunt's goddess—Goddess of Staunch Acid. Take a whiff of acrid sweetness. That was their salvation—a bucket of bleach. And Diana was the gatherer, the keeper. She needed two buckets of bleach, two buckets of bleach each night, to keep her sister soldiers safe. Two buckets of bleach for serenity.

A convoy was hit with an IED one night on a road about fifteen kilometers away, and soldiers from Camp Anaconda were sent to clean up the mess. They were rushed to the site, ordered to scour the area, searching for body pieces of disintegrated soldiers. Hey, Sarge; I got someone's hand. Can anyone tell me whose hand this is? It's got a ring. Someone's torso is over here. Each part found its way into a black bag—a mismatched menagerie.

Diana was able to hoard enough bleach initially for the first three months as the justice cogs of JAG barely budged. She had worked out a deal with the Supply Sergeant—a bartering of goods her soldiers received from home for precious bottles of bleach. One week, the trade would consist of packages of beef jerky from Sergeant Woods' folks in Michigan and bags of red, white, and blue M&Ms from Specialist Carter's grandmother in San Francisco. Another week, it was orange marmalade from Private Martinez's aunt in Miami and canned bread from Private Wilson's mother in Vermont. Even Sergeant Welk donated much-coveted cans of Kim chi.

In that matter, the buckets of bleach remained full. The women relieved themselves in the tent from dusk to daylight, the buckets resting behind a dusty-gray olive-drab blanket. A growing ripple of unrest traveled through the camp, gathered, and spread like the silt of sand. Word of the slipping camp morale was a topic in formation.

Sergeant Hunt sensed the uneasiness and that morning after three months of peace at the port-a-pit, she went to supply, her rucksack packed with home goods, and her request was denied. The Supply Sergeant told her they had begun to question his requisitions. She returned to the tent empty-handed—no bottles of bleach to fill the buckets. The few women in the tent when she returned said nothing, and for a long, wordless time, they avoided one another's eyes.

Diana looked at her watch. Night had evolved into blackboard darkness: 20:00 hours. At home, it was 4:00 in the morning, and Ariana and Tara would be sleeping snugly, the night light glowing in the bathroom, their grandmother in her bedroom down the hall. Diana went back into the tent, knowing it would be a long night. She sat on the edge of her cot, tired but refusing sleep, not wanting to hear the song in her head: *Two old ladies* ... She never could stop thinking.

At 23:00 hours, Sergeant Hunt heard rustling in a corner of the tent and turned toward the sound—Private Martinez pulling on her boots. Diana watched as the private readied herself and headed to the tent entrance, hesitating, feet not progressing forward. Sergeant Hunt sat up on her cot, whispered loudly, "Wait." She had stretched out with her boots on, dangling over the edge of the cot: She was ready to roll. She joined Private Martinez, rested a hand on her shoulder.

"We'll go together."

"I drank too much water," Private Martinez said apologetically. "It was so hot. I was arched. But I should've known … I forgot."

"We'll go together," Sergeant Hunt said again, pulling back the tent flap.

They heard muffled sounds then and both women turned around, the other soldiers in the tent shoving feet into boots. Not one woman muttered; no sighs escaped. They all realized they now had a new duty.

"If you go," Sergeant Welk said as she approached Sergeant Hunt and Private Martinez, the other soldiers falling in around her, "we all go."

The soldiers filed out of the tent—one, two, three, four—and they marched, formation proud, to the port-a-pit: *How did we end up in this war within a war?* Diana glanced at her watch. At home, it was 7:00 in the morning. The girls would be getting ready for school. Ariana would be donning a meticulously matched outfit that she had spent time preparing the night before even though she would be destined to tweak the outfit by morning time. Tara, on the other hand, preferred a disarray of rainbow colors that she both assembled and crawled into in seven minutes flat. Their grandmother would be making them breakfast—Ariana insisting on eggs over easy and toast, Tara calling out for Lucky Charms. Diana could see their faces clearly—Ariana's oval green eyes and tightly pursed lips, Tara's deep-set dimples. Diana gritted her teeth to hold back tears. At home, her girls were safe.

What Really Happened to PFC Quinos
Vic Sizemore

The truth has to be told, so I'm finally going to tell it.
It was 24 FEB 91. The USS Tarawa was off the coast
of Kuwait. At 0430, Gunny Reed shouted, "Drop your cocks
and grab your socks." The berthing area lights blasted on
and every Marine jumped. Nylon and canvass hissed, gear
popped, ALICE packs thumped on the deck. Murmured talk
and laughter rose, undulating. An excited buzz was in the
air, like a locker room before a big game. They were going
in-country, going to get combat action ribbons. Corporal
Kline was packed. He lay in his rack and recorded everything
in the journal he kept in his cargo pocket.

At 0440, they ran through the ship's passageways and
chugged up stairwells—gear swishing and thumping, rifle
butts banging against steel bulkheads—and ran into the dim
hangar bay and curled around the heavy bulkhead and up the
ramp to the flight deck and across the tarmac and onto the
46's; the helicopters lifted and swung out over the Persian
Gulf. Out the back of the 46's, the Tarawa's two and a half
acre flight deck shrunk to the size of a breath mint. The
ship disappeared as the helicopters swung toward the sandy
theater of war.

Corporal Kline had found *Red Badge of Courage* in
the ship's library: Glory was a whore. Every one of the
reservists wanted a piece of that whore, especially since the
air war had softened Saddam's troops and the ground war
was going well and the risk was light. It meant breathing
real air and seeing the sky as well as getting a combat action
ribbon.

The helicopters jerked and lumbered. Their ass-ends
bounced like being dragged—as if they might fall out of

the sky any minute. Sometimes, they did: the Tarawa's search and rescue helicopter had crashed during training op's, killing all four men on board.

They flew in under the brown-black smoke of burning oil wells. The wells were glowing dots on the horizon with smoke widening upward like still photos of tornadoes. The smoke drifted and spread low and wet as they flew farther in—it was like they were under water looking up at a heavy oil slick; through the oil, the sun was reduced to a pale dish.

They ran off the 46's and stumbled under their gear in swirling sand. They fanned out and set up a perimeter. Nuclear winter it was being called back in the States; it looked like a movie-set surface of some bleak alien planet.

Combat engineers, they were reservists from Cross Lanes, West Virginia—college kids and working guys. Gunny Reed was the sheriff of Wayne County. The platoon was to be pulled apart and attached by squad to Golf Company platoons. With real ammo this time. Not only did they have permission to kill—to actually take human life—it was a stated part of the mission.

Corporal Kline dropped to his knees in the sand and fell forward, aiming his rifle out to the barren sand. His 60-gunner Ski dropped to his right, followed by the rest of his squad, dropping as well rehearsed as a chorus line to the prone position and aiming outward, fanning into a circle to spot threats coming from any direction, though there was nothing but dunes and wadis for miles.

Gunny Reed shouted, "Squad leaders, count your Marines."

Kline's squad was accounted for, curved at his right in the same order they stand in morning formation.

Then PFC Quinos—Kline had forgotten about Quinos—dropped heavily at his left. The helicopters lifted and withdrew toward the Gulf, their engines' hum chopped by rotors; from a distance, it sounded like boys hollering through window fans.

Kline pulled his olive drab bandana over his face and straightened his tinted goggles. Quinos lay beside him like a sea lion; he looked down at the sand and wheezed through his bandana.

Kline felt his cargo pocket for his journal. He planned to write a history of Desert Storm, an insider's perspective. He was studying history at WVU; he was going to teach high school and coach, just like his dad, except his dad coached wrestling, and his sport was soccer. His dad had edited history texts; he was going to provide the actual account. He was carefully studying everything to be accurate with the facts.

"Here we are," he said to Ski on his other side, "watching history happen right in front of us—and we're part of it."

"Damn straight, we are," Ski said. He set his M-60 machine gun on its tripod, and swiveled it around to scan the empty desert.

"Dude, I ain't supposed to be here," Quinos said. "I'm a truck driver." His goggles cut into his face. He coughed. The ejection port on his M-16 was open.

"If you don't want to fucking die, you'll take better care of your rifle," Gunny Reed said as he strode behind them.

Quinos flipped the ejection port cover closed. It made a gritty scrape.

This was it. They were in-country and when the Hummers got there, they would be heading into real combat. The categorical moral imperative had been suspended: their rifles were loaded for men.

It was 15 NOV 90 when the platoon Gunny Reed had cobbled together from the Cross Lanes unit of the 4th Engineers flew out of Charleston. They arrived at Camp Pendleton, California one driver short of a full platoon, so an active duty platoon sent them Quinos. He was a driver; he was as wide as a hospital door, fat and unsat'. As he stowed his gear in the squad bay, Gunny Reed said to his squad leaders, "In the old Corps, we didn't mind the big boys.

Those big fuckers can hump the heavy loads."

On 1 DEC 90, the platoon loaded onto the Tarawa and sailed for Hawaii to load an air wing. Christmas was spent in the field at Green Beach, Subic Bay, Philippines. New Years Eve, they partied with the bar girls in Olongapo City.

The morning after, the platoon was in formation on the dock in front of the Tarawa, still drunk and reeking of booze, but clean-shaven and in uniform. Gunny was going over general information: third squad was on head duty, the chow hall needed two PFC's for scullery duty.

"Kline?" Gunny said.

"Yes, Gunny."

"Send two of your Marines down to the chow hall this morning."

"Yes, Gunny."

Then Gunny's eyes rose and looked out over the platoon, his creased face distorting into astonished disbelief. Kline leaned out and looked down the row of Marines. Quinos, wearing shorts, a stretched white t-shirt and tennis shoes with no socks, had just stumbled in from liberty and fallen in at the end of his squad. He had an embarrassed grin on his puffy pie face.

Gunny Reed marched over to Quinos, grabbed a fist full of his shirt and bitch slapped him. Hard. The crack of it echoed back from the iron hull of the Tarawa. He shouted, "Where the fuck do you think you are?"

"Sorry, Gunny, I—"

Gunny slapped him again, harder, and shouted, "Shut your cock sucker." He let go of Quinos' shirt and slapped him on the other side of the face, making him take a step back. "If you're ever late for formation again, I swear I'll fuck you up."

Gunny took two steps back, looked down at the deck, and then said in a quiet, almost conversational voice: "What do you think we're going over there to do, Quinos?"

Again Quinos began, "Sorry, Gunny—" but shut up when

Gunny stepped toward him cocking a fist behind his hip.

"Some raghead is going to put a bullet right in your fucking skull, and it's not going to change your brain waves." Gunny put his finger in Quinos' face. "I'm not going to let you get one of *my* Marines killed." He returned to his place in front of the platoon, letting his shoulder slump. "Go square yourself away," he said in a calm and weary voice.

"Yes, Gunny." Quinos ran for the Tarawa's loading ramp, loose civilian clothes and fat swinging on his frame.

Ski stood beside Kline shaking his head. "Jesus, Joseph, and Mary," he said. "How'd that sack of shit even get through boot camp?"

Ski was what Gunny Reed called a hard–dick Marine. His grandfather had been in WWII and his father in Vietnam. He was tall and lanky, all points and angles, as if he'd been drawn with a ruler. He kept his hair cut in a high and tight, a sharp horseshoe on top of his head, the stubble above his ears only slightly heavier than that on his jaw in the evenings.

This was his war, as he'd said, just the way things were supposed to be, each generation getting their shot at glory. He was in ROTC at Bowling Green and was planning on going to OCS. He studied his Green Monster; he worked out with Kline in the ship's gym. He was collecting memorabilia: a desert camo New Testament, letters addressed to any serviceman coming from the patriotic frenzy back home, any extra gear he could pick up.

Gunny Reed turned his back to the platoon; he seemed to be addressing the gray side of the ship, "In 'Nam, we fragged unsat' motherfuckers like that."

Ski nodded his enthusiastic agreement.

After formation, as the other squad leaders walked up the loading ramp, Gunny Reed stood almost touching noses with Kline, breathing his boozy breath into Kline's nostrils; snuff spittle flecked Kline's lips as Gunny carefully annunciated: "Corporal, don't you fucking ever make me square away one of your goddamn Marines again."

The next two months were spent in periods of classroom instruction: minefield breaching Vietnam style with the obsolete mine detectors they still humped; first aid topics, such as how to use an ID card to treat a sucking chest wound and how to use a gauze bandage to put internal organs back into someone without getting sand in the body cavity; desert survival classes, like how to make a solar still to purify urine for drinking.

In his free time, Kline tried to read through what classics he could find in the ship's library. He wanted to be ahead of the game when he got back to school. He worked out every morning with Ski, trying to stay in shape for soccer. He kept notes in his journal for his history of Desert Storm. It was a Moleskine and fit in his cargo pocket.

Tetris on the new Gameboy was the rage in the berthing area. Marines were obsessed with the hand held video game. When scullery duty came back around to Kline's squad, he assigned Quinos. Quinos didn't show, and instead of letting Gunny Reed find out about it, Kline went down and washed pots for twelve hours himself. When he came back up to the berthing area, Quinos was in his rack playing his Gameboy.

The berthing area reeked of body odor. As Kline sidled into the berthing compartment, Quinos lifted his leg and farted. His berth was the bottom of four, flush on the deck.

Kline bent over, grabbed him with both hands and dragged him out. "I just pulled your scullery duty, Quinos."

Quinos's rolled onto a knee, then slowly stood and mumbled something in Spanish. He was suppressing a grin and his breath was hot and moist and smelled of beef jerky.

Kline hit him with an uppercut into his solar plexus, which doubled him over, then hit him again, square on the left eye socket. As he swung he said, "I am not your fucking baby sitter, Quinos." He made contact with Quinos's gut on the *not* and with his eye on the *fucking*.

Quinos fell back against the bulkhead, ripping one of the girly pictures that were taped up. His Gameboy hit the deck with a sharp crack. He slid down, pulling the photo with him, and sat on his ass, his hairy knees out like frog legs. He put both hands over his face.

Kline's squad had all taken off their earphones and stopped playing Tetris to stare out of their berths. Ski nodded with a satisfied smile.

"You cannot do this to me," Quinos said into his hands. "I got rights, Corporal Kline. You know. I got rights. You and Gunny. You got no right—"

"You ain't got no rights, *Queeno*," one of Kline's squad members shouted.

Quinos was silent.

Ski's grin stretched tight and toothy across his skull. "You fell, PFC," he said. "I saw it. Corporal Kline wasn't even here—were you Corporal?" He gave Kline a nod of hollow-eyed innocence.

"Yeah," another squad member said. "Nobody hit you."

"You fell, Quinos."

"Tough shit, Quinos."

"Lose some weight and maybe you wouldn't fall down, dude."

Kline silently unlaced his boots, pulled them off, threw his shower shoes onto the deck, stepped into them, grabbed his toiletry bag and towel, and stalked to the head. His shower shoes slapped at his heels.

On 24 FEB 91, after the helicopters were gone, Gunny shouted, "Form it up," and they fell into platoon formation and humped across the desert hour after hour, following the boots in front of them, heels chewed down from snappy marching on Paris Island parade decks. "Keep it moving," Gunny Reed shouted. "You'll pass out before you'll die." He made long strides; everybody made long strides; the war was going well and they didn't want to miss it.

Seven endless hours of humping through soft sand, then the platoon crested a wadi, and the staging area appeared out of the blank desert, from behind a dune. Hummers and six-bys and heavy equipment all surrounded by concertina wire and 50-cal gun emplacements built of fresh blond timber. The platoon hummers were waiting there, gassed and staged, ready to roll. They staged their gear and slept in and around the trucks and set out at 0430 the next day.

Kline sat in back with his squad on wooden benches. Quinos drove. They fell into line with the other two Hummers and the platoon from Cross Lanes, West Virginia, joined the race to the front. It had already become a running shooting gallery as Saddam's troops collapsed and waved white flags and abandoned their tanks to flee.

The minefield had been breached as wide as a four-lane highway, and they cruised through at 60mph. The terrain was hard and uneven so that Quinos kept hitting spine-jarring potholes. Marines listened to their Walkmans and played Tetris. On either side of the breach, three-pronged anti-personnel mines perforated the stretching desert. Six-bys coming the other way were loaded so full of surrendered Iraqis that in the dark of the oil smoke, their heads looked like piles of black melons stuffed into the backs of the trucks.

An endless line of trucks. Scuttlebutt was that Sadam's tank army was crumbling, his elite Republican Guard imploding. "Combat action today," Ski leaned over and said to Kline.

Quinos hit a bone-jolting hole.

"God damn you, Quinos," a Marine shouted.

Ski pulled his headphones down around his neck. "I'm going to frag your ass, Quinos." He pulled his headphones back on and looked back down at his Gameboy. He said, "Shit, I wish we'd get there."

"The war's gonna be over," another Marine said.

Kline rifled around in his asspack and pulled out *For Whom The Bell Tolls*. He hooked his flashlight in the chin strap of his Kevlar helmet and began reading. They pulled through a fueling station and everyone got out and pissed and grabbed bottled water from a pallet beside the tanker as the Hummers refueled.

The day was not getting too much brighter with sunrise because of the oil smoke; the dark was shifting from black to brown-black. They pulled back into the line of trucks racing toward the war. It was as busy as an interstate highway, headlights one direction, blurred red taillights the other.

At 1200, for reasons known only to Gunny Reed, their three Hummers veered out of the line of trucks and drove across the dunes for a while and stopped. "Form it up right here," Gunny shouted, and the Marines clambered out of the Hummers and fell into formation. Quinos unfolded himself from the front and rubbed his back and his eyes and fell in at the end of Kline's squad; he let out a wide yowling yawn and stretched his arms into the air. Ski slung a bandoleer of M-60 rounds over his shoulder and stood tall.

"Shut your pie-holes and listen up," Gunny shouted. He had his 9mm out; he waved it towards the dark shapes behind him, twisting on his toes like a ballerina, and said, "Behold what's left of the fifth largest tank army in the world."

Iraqi tanks, Soviet model T-62, sat abandoned all around in the midst of small square structures with their gun barrels pointing off in every direction; some were intact, some had huge charred holes bored into their centers. Some were ripped in half, the turrets popped off like bottle caps.

"Fuck with the bull," Gunny said with satisfaction, "you get the horns."

He turned to the platoon. "Our job is to clear these bunkers. There isn't likely to be anyone left alive, but don't let your guard down. Booby traps are always a possibility, so if you don't want to leave a leg here, watch yourself. And I said there probably aren't any ragheads left alive. We don't know that for sure—that's why we're here. Ackmed might be hiding down there waiting to Jihad your ass." Gunny paced, stopped, and waved over the area again. "Spread out and clear these fuckers."

The bunkers were dark squares against the rolling dunes; whether the wind had uncovered them or there was rock under the sand here, they were half exposed. Shelter from sandstorms maybe, but certainly not aerial bombardment.

Ski adjusted his goggles and said through his brown bandana, "We have arrived."

"The supply bunker is mine," Gunny shouted. He pulled his empty pack out of the front of the first Hummer and strode toward what appeared to be the center structure; it looked like eight or nine of the small bunkers pressed together, the roofs not quite matching up, like shantytown row houses.

Marines rushed to empty their packs into the backs of the Hummers making room for war booty. Then the only movement was the members of Kline's platoon, spreading from the parked Hummers, half-running, stumbling over sand, toward the abandoned fortifications to gather or kill any hangers-on and to collect souvenirs. As they moved away, they lost detail under the oil smoke, becoming shadowy, ghouls in the dark, out rummaging for loot.

Quinos settled against his Hummer's back tire and started eating something—beef jerky—yanking at it with his teeth; he twisted a bottle of the Saudi Alwadi health water into the sand beside him until it stood on its own.

Kline yelled, "You coming, Quinos?"

"I been driving since zero four thirty," he said. "I'm tired."

Kline pulled out his light and trudged to the nearest tank. It had been blown in two: the turret was upside down beside the tracks, a burnt and hollow shell. The tank itself was peeled open, wires and metal melted together, a light coat of sand blown over it.

Beside one of the tracks were several metal ammo boxes a little bigger than car batteries. One of them was open with a white plastic grocery bag in it, full of dirty potatoes and one tomato gone soft and black on the side and ready to explode. Other ammo boxes actually had ammo, what looked like 20mm rounds, big as a man's middle finger. Strands of rounds were strewn all over; old pineapple shaped fragmentation grenades lay apparently where they'd been dropped.

Ski jogged up and stood beside him. "Corporal Kline, if we find any ragheads alive, let me kill them." He held his M-60 at his hip.

Kline pulled his goggles up onto his Kevlar helmet and readjusted the Velcro on his Kevlar flak jacket. "Do you have your G-2?"

"My what?"

"Your Interrogator-Translator card. From 1st Marines."

"I'll let Christine here translate for me." Ski patted his 60. "She knows the international language."

Kline shook his head and stepped over the scattered ammo and walked toward the bunkers to the right of the supply bunker; they dotted the sand unevenly about every two-hundred yards, running out into the dark desert. Jets roared overhead above the oil smoke.

Ski skipped up beside him. "Tell me she doesn't, motherfucker." He squatted and hefted the machine gun onto his skinny leg as if ready to let the rounds fly.

They approached two dark humps on the sand, piles of rags or something. Ski pulled his goggles up and his bandana down and squinted. Kline trained his light at them.

"Mary, mother of God," Ski said. "Kline, you see that?"

The two walked up to the first humped mass and stared down.

"Ackmed don't look too good," Ski said.

The Iraqi soldier lay on his back with his hands at his waist as if hiking up his pants. His face was black and crusted like the charred skin of a roasted pig. His open mouth was full of sand. At first it looked like his head was half buried inside a little hole, but it wasn't. His head lay flat—shrapnel had clipped off a clean chunk right behind his ears. Other than that, he was pretty much intact.

Kline stared at the dead man, running his light slowly over the figure.

"Shit, Kline, come look at Hagi." Ski had moved on to the

second clump.

Kline stared at the spot on the sand lit by his flashlight as he walked the small distance until the other Iraqi slid into the beam. The dead face bore a maniac grin, all top teeth and gums. The bottom teeth, lips, and chin were gone. One leg was gone altogether. An arm lay about thirty feet away, with ragged clothing and meat hanging off one end of it; at the other end, the hand was curled into a gentle fist with index finger out, like a sleeping baby's; there was a thin white stream of sand along the crease of the palm.

Ski turned toward the other figures moving behind them among the bunkers and tanks. He shouted and waved his arms until the figures began to turn and move in their direction.

Kline's squad arrived first.

"Holy shit."

Ski said, "This is Hagi." He pushed the carcass over with his boot heel. The torso was ripped open, and as it stiffly turned, a twisted bundle of intestines and organs blobbed out, picking up a coat of sand like fish rolled in corn meal.

The Marines fell into a party of hoots and cheers. A Marine squatted and dug in Ackmed's pockets. "Hell yeah," he said when he found Iraqi coins and dog tags. He stood and shoved them into his own pocket. Another Marine nearly had to take the laces out of Ackmed's boots to get them off his hard feet. He shoved them into his pack. Two other Marines took Ackmed by his arms and shoulders and lifted him like a piece of lumber. They both dug in their ass-packs for cameras.

Gunny walked up and stood at the edge of the revelry, setting down his pack, now stuffed full, and crossing his arms. He blew a burst of air out of his nose, which appeared to momentarily throw his head back; then he stood and watched with an expression of bored indulgence.

Upon seeing Gunny Reed, Kline counted his Marines; his squad was all there, except for Quinos, whom he'd left sitting on the ground beside the Hummer.

One of the Marines with Ackmed accidentally pulled out his Gameboy. He laughed and said, "Wrong thing," shoved it back in, and found his camera.

Kline's platoon took turns standing with their arm around Ackmed's shoulder like he was an old school chum, his dead eyes squeezed shut in his cooked face, his sand-filled mouth open.

A Marine pulled the boot off of Hagi's one leg and set out looking around. "If anybody find's Hagi's other leg, I call the boot," he shouted.

"Kline, here." Ski was holding out his camera. In his other hand was the severed arm. He stepped back and posed with it as if he and the arm were shaking hands; he had a wide toothy smile on his sharp face.

"Okay," Gunny Reed yelled. "Fun's over." He stepped in between the two Iraqi's. Ackmed was again on his back. A Marine unzipped the pants and tugged them off Ackmed's hips, then alternated legs, jerking the pants off.

Gunny stepped to Hagi. With the heel of his boot he rolled the teeth-grinning carcass over and stood with his hands on his hips looking at it.

Ski said, "My dad said that in 'Nam they'd cut off ears and dry them and wear them around their necks as trophies. You ever do that Gunny?"

A Marine unsheathed his K-bar. "I'm gonna get me an ear," he said.

"I want one," another Marine said, also unsheathing his K-bar.

Gunny said, "I told you the fun was over. Get back to the mission."

"Gunny," another Marine said. "Let me get a shot of you and Ackmed together."

Two Marines again stood the cadaver up, now naked from the waist down. The penis skin had shrunk up tight, and the thing looked like a hard little mushroom cap under a mat of black pubic hair.

Kline turned and looked out at the desert; the bunkers

stretched on. The platoon dispersed back toward the shattered tanks and the supply bunker, laughing and chatting.

Gunny put his arm around Ackmed's shoulder and said, "Fucking cheese."

Two hundred yards and more between them—Kline walked past two bunkers, then three. Then four. He walked into the dark desert. He came to the last bunker in the chain; there was nothing visible beyond it but white dunes and wadis under a brown sky. Jets flew above the smoke. Kline stood till the last of their sound had been swallowed by the gusting wind.

The last bunker was like the others: square, cinderblock with a corrugated tin roof held down with more cinderblocks thrown across the top. Above the entrance, the tin roof was ripped; it banged against itself every now and then when the wind picked up. Two more pineapple shaped grenades lay on top of the bunker roof, and a bent piece of pipe with a bicycle handlebar grip pushed onto one end.

Down four cinderblock steps was the entrance. At the opening, a plywood floor was visible with a threadbare rug on it. The rug had an orange and yellow pattern of lined up diamonds with four smaller diamonds inside each one.

Kline stepped silently down to the entrance. He shined his light in, backed away and waited.

Nothing.

He shined his light in and turkey-peeked.

Two cots. Shadows.

Again he leaned back and waited.

After a couple of minutes he shined his light in and looked around: cots, rug, a blanket folded on one cot, a small box under the same cot. Nothing else.

Kline stepped inside. The air was heavy with the smell of human sweat; the animal gone from the lair, but its smell still strong, the living dangerous animal—sweat: not the smell of dead men, but men very much alive.

He sat on the cot and let his eyes adjust. From inside, the weak, smoke-filtered sunlight appeared as a pale rectangle at the door, brown sky on the upper half, cinderblock steps on the lower. What Kline thought was a folded blanket turned out to be a wool sweater; it had the imprint of a head on it. The sweaty smell rose from it. Kline shoved it into his pack.

He pulled the box from under the cot. There was a coffee mug behind it. It was white and said *Ovaltine* on one side. The other side said presumably the same thing in Arabic. The name *Benny* was scratched with an ink pen on the bottom in English. He shoved that into his pack too.

The box was a green cardboard box, six inches square, bulged out on the sides from having something stacked on top of it. Kline stuffed the flashlight into his armpit and gently shook the top off, the bottom dropped onto his lap.

It was just full of toiletries. A tube of toothpaste, the old kind in the aluminum tube that holds its shape when its rolled up. The brand name *Amber* was also printed in both Arabic and English, made by the Iraq State Enterprise for Vegetable Oils. Smelled like mint: smelled like toothpaste. There wasn't any toothbrush.

Two old razors both with faded and cracked plastic handles, one red, one green —the kind with a two-piece metal top that screwed apart and off the handle for changing blades. The blades were the old flat kind people in movies used to slit their own wrists. They were rusted in spots and there were no replacements.

With the razors was a lather brush with a broken wooden handle, blue paint crackling and breaking off in tiny chips. Papers with Arabic writing. A small leather bound book in Arabic, the title on the back, the back of the book being the front, the language so indecipherable that Kline couldn't begin to guess what it was, as he could have with German or French or Spanish.

Kline undid the Velcro of his flack jacket and pulled his Alwadi water from his pack.

Inside the book, possibly being used as book marks, there

was a 25 Dinar bill, crisp and unfolded, and a flyer that had been dropped by aircraft. The 25 Dinar was turquoise and had a picture of a young Saddam Hussein looking out over a mass of Arab warriors on horseback riding hell-bent into battle.

On one side of the flyer had two cartoon pictures: in one picture, an Iraqi soldier is surrendering and presenting that very flyer to an Arab-looking Coalition soldier; in the second picture, the surrendered Iraqi soldier is with other Iraqis, wearing now instead of helmets, turbans, boots off, sitting around a huge tray of fruit, drinking tea. The Arabic Coalition soldier stands with his arm out, apparently having just finished a joke, as they all seem to be laughing.

The other side of the flyer was covered with writing over a watermark of the Joint Forces symbol: the earth under small swords and cradled by what looked like fern fronds—olive branches. Kline took out his journal and slid the papers in.

The only other thing in the box was a small photo of a soldier. There was some kind of rank insignia on the collar of his white shirt. He had a thick mustache like Saddam Hussein. He was attractive, had chiseled jaws, a cleft chin, and serious, deep eyes. Impossible to know if he was Hagi, but he wasn't Ackmed. His jawbones were too thick and strong.

Someone approached above, heavy boots and rattling gear. Kline flipped off his light, buttoned his journal back into his pocket and sat in silence. The boots pounded, a purposeful stride.

Kline laid his journal on the cot and pulled his M-16 around and sent the bolt home, chambering a round. The ejection port cover flipped open on his thumb, the crack of the bolt rang in his ears. He set it on three round burst.

The boots stopped.

Kline slowly raised his rifle and aimed at the rectangle of brown light. His rifle smelled of CLP cleaning oil. He twisted to better face the door. His heart pounded in his ears.

The boots took a few more scuffling steps and were above the entry.

Kline sat in silence. Breathing. Slowly breathing.

The person above shuffled with gear, un-slung a jangling weapon; it sounded as if he were sitting down, settling in. It could be an Iraqi coming back from the desert, unaware that his comrades have died or surrendered, the man who made the sweat smell that seeped now out of Kline's pack, the owner of the toiletries spread beside Kline on the cot, the owner of the cot. The strong-jawed Iraqi in the photograph.

Kline's back began to ache. He stood slowly, slowly as to be silent. But the plywood warped up and banged the cot pole. There was sudden boot-scuffling movement above. He was trapped. One of those grenades chucked down is all it would take—Kline would be done for, his carcass ripped open and his guts spilled out like Hagi's.

There were more interminable minutes of silence.

By the time the wide, backlit form came huffing down the cinderblock steps, Kline was in a state of sheer, unthinking panic. He pulled the trigger four times.

Quinos's Kevlar flack jacket was hanging open, but at such close range it wouldn't have stopped the rounds. All twelve cracks hit his chest. The dull light seemed to wrap around Quinos as he fell, his head canting back. He landed on his knees so hard his jowls jerked and shook back into place. A slimy wad of chewed gorilla bar was lodged between his teeth. Carbon hung heavy in the bunker like fireworks residue. Kline climbed over the body and ran out across the dark desert screaming over and over again, "Shots fired, man down," as if he were in a television cop show.

Operation Desert Storm ended on 28 FEB 91. The platoon of reservists from Cross Lanes, West Virginia, went back to the staging area and set up their hooches in tank traps. They celebrated with Tetris tournaments and football. They sat around drinking the bottled water from Saudi Arabia, *Alwadi Wadi Fatima Water Makkah*, as if it were cold beer.

Kline sat on his Kevlar helmet and watched his platoon playing ball against a Golf Company platoon. The other guys were skins; their upper torsos were sweaty and covered in sand. The field was marked off by tent poles with olive drab skivvies shirts flapping on top.

Gunny Reed strode up from behind him and squatted, balancing elbow on knee. He had traded his Kevlar helmet for his soft cover, and his desert camouflage uniform was clean and pressed. He brushed sand off his shined boots, took out a can of Copenhagen, dipped out three fingers full of snuff, and pressed it between his bottom gum and lip.

Through snuff-tightened lips, he said, "Kline?"

"Yes, Gunny?" Kline stared at the football game. Gunny held the open can of snuff in front of him, and he said no thank you without looking away from the game.

"Here's how it happened," Gunny said. "Quinos was ordered to stay back at his Hummer. He didn't. Those two ragheads shot him, and we blew the hell out of them." Gunny chuckled and said, "You should see what a SMAW can do to a body at thirty yards." He flicked snuff off his fingers and almost lost his balance. "The report's been filed. It's already in the books," he said, "Understand?"

"Gunny—"

"Goddamn it, Corporal, get your shit together and listen to me: This was war and these things happen." He dropped his snuff into the breast pocket of his camouflaged blouse and shifted his weight to the other knee. "Nobody has to go down over this. It's over and we're out of this God-forsaken desert. You hear me? We're headed home." He spit and it rolled to a sandy pebble in front of Kline. He said, "Lance Corporal Kawalski has already testified."

"Ski?"

"You change your story, and he goes down. I've written the report. You're going to sign it. Understand, Marine?"

"Yes, Gunny."

Gunny said, "Where's that little damn book you write

in?"

"Left it."

"In the raghead's bunker?"

Kline nodded.

Gunny Reed nodded. He watched the ballgame. A short PFC from Golf Company made an end-run and streaked down the sideline and scored. Gunny laughed and said, "You see that motherfucker run?" He stood up and adjusted his cover. He said, "Good God, he's a fast little fucker."

The teams separated to their respective ends of the field and lined up between the green skivvies flapping on the poles. A Marine kicked the ball and it wobbled high over Kline's platoon. A PFC scurried back and snatched it up, and the others formed a wall for him, and he curved in and ran behind them. Gunny Reed laughed and shook his head and slapped Kline hard on the shoulder. The two sides came together, grunting and slinging one another down in the sand.

My name is Robert Kline. My life since has been a good one. Two marriages, three fantastic children, two of them up at WVU, and one at Poca Middle School.

I don't believe in heaven or hell. Quinos—I never knew his first name—has been dead for eighteen years. I shot and killed him.

Cambodia, 1981
Staci Stokes Morgan

In the winter of 1981, my daughter's mother was born. Her mother had crossed the border between Cambodia and Thailand and finally collapsed there in the no-man's land of tent villages and shanties. She was shaking from pain and weak with malaria and starvation. The father of my daughter's mother, an American serviceman from Detroit called Tex, neither knew nor would he have cared about the birth. By the time she delivered their baby, he didn't remember the woman, and he had never known her name. My daughter has her grandfather's wide, broad nose.

My daughter's mother was nursed by another woman after her mother died. The delivery was difficult; the baby was too big for her small, angular body. She died the day after my daughter's mother was born. The woman who nursed her raised her as her own daughter in Shinoukville, where they returned when the Khmer Rouge had been driven out of Cambodia and into hiding in the jungles of Thailand.

When my daughter's mother became pregnant at fifteen, her foster mother forced her out of the home she'd grown up in. My daughter's mother promised that she would give the baby up, but her foster mother suggested it would be better to drown the baby in the Mekong river. My daughter's mother thought about this a long time, but she finally left home to deliver her baby away from the temptation of the river. She had nowhere to go—no family other than this— and she delivered my daughter in the back room of the bar where she got a job selling drinks or, maybe, herself. I have a picture of her holding my daughter, her nails and lips a rich, ripe red.

* * * * *

In the fall of 1981, my daughter's mother was born. By this time, the Khmer Rouge had been chased out of Cambodia, though some of them had remained behind immune from prosecution because of the fear they had so thoroughly instilled in their countrymen. My daughter's grandmother was married to the son of a former Khmer Rouge, and they lived in luxury compared to other Cambodians. They often had clean water to drink and a toilet they flushed with a bucket. They had a television, run by car battery. Their house, on stilts, was protected from the seasonal flooding in Shinoukville, and they received yearly tributes of money the villagers paid to the family out of fear or loyalty, or habit.

My daughter's mother was delivered into the hands of a midwife, even though most Cambodians with medical knowledge had been killed starting in 1975, hacked to death with hoes after digging their own graves because bullets were too expensive. Midwives were an exception, though, as long as they didn't have glasses or speak English. Women kept having babies, Communist or not, and someone needed to catch them and clean up the messes the women made.

The midwife wrapped my daughter's mother in soft cloth and put her on her mother's chest where she began to suckle. Mother and daughter gazed into each other's eyes as the midwife cleaned. When my daughter's grandmother died, she did it silently in a gush of blood, the baby slipping from her arms. My daughter's mother wasn't hurt, though, because the mattress was thin and resting on the floor, but her mother was dead, and someone had to take care of her. Poor motherless girl. Is this why, sixteen years later, she carried her own baby to the gates of an orphanage and left her there?

* * * * *

My daughter's mother was born in a hospital in Thailand

in 1981. Her parents had crossed the border from Cambodia in 1977 at the height of the destruction and genocide. My daughter's grandmother was a surgeon, educated in France and fluent in four languages. Her husband, another surgeon, was half French, tall with dark hair and glasses. He could pass for a foreigner and could have left the country safely without his wife and children. After being forced from Phnom Penh and onto a collective farm, he knew they must leave or they would be killed. A slip of the tongue, a phrase in French or English, the eye glasses he couldn't force himself to destroy, all death. They pretended to be peasants. The children, a son and a daughter, had been taken from them and sent to a reeducation camp.

My daughter's grandfather spent fourteen months trying to farm without his glasses, hacking accidentally at edible plants and unable to see the weeds clearly before he and his wife left the country. They were afraid to take their children—afraid the children would denounce them to the party after their reeducation—so they left them behind. After walking for days without food, his wife's eyes leaking tears for their abandoned children, they crossed the mountains into Thailand.

At first, my daughter's grandmother refused to have more children. She busied herself treating the refugees from Cambodia and dreaming of her lost boy and girl. When she fell pregnant she was terrified of losing another child.

My daughter's mother was just fine, hearty and robust as an infant, rebellious and athletic as a teenager. When she became pregnant at fifteen, she tried to hide her growing belly from her parents, and they pretended not to see it. She paid a Khmer taxi driver forty dollars to take the baby and leave her at the gates of an orphanage in Shinoukville. My daughter was abandoned, like her aunt and uncle before her, as if abandonment were contagious, her birthright. My daughter's mother kept whatever she had called my daughter to herself, and so the taxi driver named her. The name, Branett, means wealth in Khmer, and we didn't keep it, not even as a middle name.

* * * * *

My daughter's mother delivered my daughter in the night in the shanty she shared with her parents, her grandparents, and her brothers and sisters. Her grandmother caught the baby, and her mother, white-lipped and angry, never said a word or tried to comfort my daughter's mother. Her parents had been angry about her pregnancy because they intended for her to marry someone else. They forbade her from seeing the father of her child and insisted she give the baby away. She was not driven from her village in shame. She was not damaged goods. She was not able to keep the baby, but she was allowed to marry the boy of her parent's choosing. No one mentioned my daughter.

* * * * *

My daughter's mother was sent from her village to Shinoukville when she was twelve years old. She was a virgin and worth plenty to the woman who had paid her parents two hundred dollars for her. They hoped she was being sold as a servant, but they had seven other children to care for and didn't ask many questions. She was sold by the hour to tourists, some American, some Thai, some Chinese. Because she was so small, she bled a lot, and not just the first time. The woman who owned her was able to sell her virginity several times over before my daughter's mother stopped bleeding and screaming and the men no longer believed in her innocence.

My daughter's mother didn't know the father of her child, but it could have been anyone.

* * * * *

My daughter's mother had four other children and was

Cambodia, 1981

pregnant with my daughter when her husband was killed, beaten to death with a hoe after an argument. She and the children already worked every day, she sewing and the children selling candy on the busy streets of Phnom Penh. She didn't know how she would continue to feed herself and the children without her husband's income. She wanted an abortion, but she couldn't afford it. Her brother, a taxi driver, offered to take the new baby and find her a good home. My daughter's mother considered drowning my daughter in the Mekong river, but instead, she gave the child to her brother. He took the baby to an American run orphanage in Shinoukville, where he was paid a one hundred dollar finder's fee. He gave the baby the name Branett, wealth in Khmer, as a joke. He didn't share the money with his sister.

* * * * *

My daughter's mother was a whore.
My daughter's mother was a child.
My daughter's mother is alive, or maybe she's dead.
My daughter's mother was motherless, or overprotected, or she was neglected, or she was pampered.
My daughter's mother never thinks of the baby she gave away.
My daughter's mother thinks of the baby she gave away every day.

Do Over
Moira Crone

Lila McHenry might listen to the Mayor of New Orleans, but she refused to obey him.

"Folks may feel re-traumatized. Signs of trouble include inability to finish tasks, make simple decisions. Offer to help. Make a plan. And leave early." On TV, he was pleading with people in advance of Hurricane Gustav. It was August, 2008.

The screen's scene switched: the indigent, the old, the sick were getting plastic name bracelets at the train station, soon to be hauled away by Amtrak. The governor called the exodus, *"Well under control."* None of 2005's mistakes. Lila was happy to see it, though she had made her decision. This was hype.

For Katrina, it was different: she'd experienced true dread. William, her ex-husband, refused to hear her until the very last minute. And then, he hardly packed, insisted their part of town didn't flood, they'd be back in days. The trip was awful: clogged highways, filthy rest stops. They slept in twenty two different places over a fifty day exile— never again.

Even worse: the desolate evening they drove in past National Guard tanks to see their ruined, water-logged house. They slept in one of the drier upstairs rooms, but at daybreak, Lila woke unable to breathe. It was another hell, trying to find a doctor. The mold brought her childhood asthma back. She had to flee.

Once she arrived at her brother's in Massachusetts, her wheezing cleared. After months on the road, she slept for a week. When she finally got out of bed, she discovered the charm of being alone. Her brother, a pilot, was never around.

She liked not having anybody telling her what to do, her

husband's specialty. She liked not having a job, rethinking all that. She liked not fighting, for they fought constantly on the road. Katrina scrambled her life, left things exposed.

"Give me a break, going Garbo on me, honey?" William said when she suggested they separate. "Katrina divorces are such a cliché. It's not that bad here. You don't *really* want to be alone."

"You don't know what I want," she said. "I know you better than you know yourself."

In the end, her brother's lawyer wrote the letter.

Her mother died after a long illness when Lila was a teenager; her father drank himself into a black hole after. She left for college in New Orleans—as far away from Boston as she could get. William was her drawing teacher when she was nineteen. She'd had a crush. He seemed exciting. Three years later, he came up to her at a gallery. "Excuse me, beautiful? Weren't you in my class when you were even littler? That *Lila?*" People usually called her "petite," "piquant," sometimes "scrawny," rarely "beautiful." In no time, she was in his loft— lured to the nest of a bowerbird—his sculptures, his big, semi-amazing messes, his towers of shiny objects. Three days later, he said, "We go perfect." She was incredibly flattered.

Her girlfriend said, "Mr. Bickham? The artist? You'll be his wife? How cool is that?"

And it was in a way. She walked right into his bohemian existence—and sort of disappeared she felt now.

The divorce went through the second spring after the hurricane. She didn't think she'd return to New Orleans, but then she got a job online with a new charter school in the city. When she ran into him downtown, William said he would have done anything to keep her. He had once been handsome for a big man, and very proud. That night, though, he seemed exhausted, needy, wrecked.

"It's not me you need," she stood up for herself. "It's me-in-your-life." But she felt selfish, guilty, a little cruel. "What is the difference?"

For a moment, she wasn't sure. He still had that effect on her.

"Some shrink in Boston told you to leave me, right?"

How did he know? The therapist had said, "We have to sort out the current crisis from the old losses it stirred up. Your feelings now are like an echo, copies of an original." And slowly, carefully, they started the process—going back, peeling away layers. Before she left Massachusetts, she made one decision: To live that limbo where you test yourself, find out what scares you. She'd skipped it when she was younger, rushed into William's arms.

*

Around three, Lila went out on her porch. The city was too quiet. She hadn't expected so many empty driveways, so many houses boarded up.

To Lila's relief, Alice from across the street appeared in Capri pants, holding a beer: "I saw the Weather Insider website. We're cool. The rest on this block are scaredy cats."

Alice's son Julian wandered in barefoot. On his laptop he pulled up "the cone of uncertainty," the long funnel that indicated possible storm paths. Alice said, "Wasn't it closer to us before honey?"

"No, momma," he said. "This morning, it was farther away."

"I'm still not going through all that. For what?" Alice said. "You staying too, right Lila?"

Lila confirmed. Upon leaving an hour later, Alice added without any nod to her contradiction, "If things get bad, come to Memphis with us."

Something inside Lila's chest did a small, discreet flip, and then flipped back.

At five, Alice called again: "The cone has us, babes. Memphis, I'm afraid. Come." "It's still just a category two, right?" Lila said. She wasn't changing her mind. She wasn't.

"For now," Alice said. "I mean it. Come with us. Follow in your car. You don't want to be on the road alone, later, nowhere to go."

Alice was headed to her mother's cramped house, which she'd described in great and awful detail in the past. Lila would be on a couch in the TV room full of ashtrays, the only guest not part of the extended family. She'd been a refugee before. She told Alice, "I'll be fine here. Really, I will." But when she watched her favorite neighbor pull out two hours later, she had more than a few doubts.

She went out for a walk about nine to see if anybody was around. After many empty blocks, she came upon a lone green station wagon. Tarps on the roof covered coolers. Three children snuggled in the backseat, already sleeping. Extra gas cans, ruby red and glowing in the night, were tied on the back bumper. The father came out, said, "Goodbye," to Lila, and suddenly as he pulled away, she was ambushed by fear. It was as if she were suddenly the last woman in New Orleans.

What happened next seemed uncanny: an old red truck turned off St. Charles Avenue and drove right to her, stopped. The driver rolled down his window. "You staying for the storm?"

"How are you here?" Lila said to William, her ex, whose house was miles away in the Bywater.

"Dropping off my keys at Luke's. You know Luke Ward on Constantinople? The cop? He has to stay."

"So you are leaving?" she asked.

"Have you looked at the cone?"

"I saw," she said.

"I mean in the last half hour?"

"I was walking." She wondered if he could see the look on her face. She hoped it was too dark.

"Well, it's coming. It could overtop the Mississippi levee. Get us good. Mayor's been saying it's the 'Mother of all Storms.'"

"You believe him?" her voice was faint.

"Me in my attic: can't get the picture out of my mind. Early morning—won't be so crowded. The traffic is awful now. I got to clean up my fridge, clear the yard."

"Where are you going?"

"Friend of mine rented a three-bedroom in Pensacola for the weekend with friends, but he left for family in Arkansas. Gay couple there. I don't know 'em. Two bedrooms vacant."

"Two?" she said.

He stared at her. She could tell he wasn't going to ask. She would have to. So she did.

He paused, looked over to the side, and down, gave himself a moment, then said, "Sure. Like, why not? The couple are friends of Jerry Jewel. Remember Jerry? I'll tell 'em."

"Thanks," she said with great and unexpected relief. "I have my own car."

"Well, yeah." he nodded.

"Thanks, I appreciate—"

"Look, it's okay. It's fine. It's a free room. It's not like I don't know you. Pulling out at four. I mean, we caravan?"

"Yeah," she said, thinking how odd that seeing William could be lucky. "Till then. You know my house?"

He said he did.

So she had to go home to prepare her place for the worst—take things off the porch and the patio, empty her refrigerator, select pictures and favorite clothes for plastic tubs that floated. Her possessions were pared down after a hurricane, a flood, two moves, a divorce—but that made it harder, not easier. She hated not having any idea where she would be in three days, not knowing if this were the first act in a comedy or a tragedy.

Three-fifty in the morning, William stood on her porch in a rain slicker and cowboy boots clutching a road atlas and evacuation routes. He looked haggard, tense. She wondered what she was in for.

She said, "I thought you would have your girlfriend." The second to last time she'd seen William, he'd been with a gap-toothed woman in a full skirt and braids.

"Amelie?" he said. "What was I going to do at Burning Man? I'm nearly fifty, remember?" he smiled. Lila knew right then he wasn't going to give her a hard time. He'd try to be decent on this trip. He seemed humbler. She wondered if he'd gotten used to being left. There had been two others before Amelie she knew of. Maybe someone with a bit more backbone who could stand up to him. He seemed lonely. "Sides, I would have missed hurricane season and evacuating with you," he snorted.

What did he mean? "Look," she said.

"That was a joke," he snorted again. "Really."

She always thought his snorting was cocky before. Now it seemed lame.

He changed the subject, a good idea. "You watch on TV how they are doing everything right this time? Republicans talking about how much they care? Every homeless guy hauled off to bum fuck? They think it's like a do-over?"

"I had to turn it off," she said. They were still on the porch. She made no move.

"Well?" he finally asked.

A big step, letting him inside. He'd never been in her new place. He didn't sit. "On the way over, I started to think—the traffic for one thing. And Pensacola's in some trouble."

"But didn't you spend all night packing?" She was eager for resolve.

He looked around at her plastic tubs, seemed impressed. "So did you. But we are so late, like last time," he said.

"This isn't last time," she said. But she was thinking it was a little. She was accustomed to his scent, his size, how he talked, how he moved his big hands. She had the feeling of being surrounded. Also of being safe.

"I know. Believe me," he said.

She found that comment hard to read.

"What will you do if it's longer?" she asked, recalling how opposite they were in a crisis—she was shy, tentative, frozen, indecisive. He was adamant, ferocious. He had gained thirty pounds. She'd lost ten.

He shrugged, "Vermont?"

Lila didn't like the reference. In 2005, her cousin had

offered them a ski house for as long as they wanted. William said he couldn't be "taking vacations." He was more loyal to his roof, his sculpture studio, than his wife she felt.

"Look, Look, I'm just—I'm thankful. I am. But, like, I'm not up for—going back over—"

"Joke." He raised his two hands, "I know, I know. I'll shut up. A room in a condo in Pensacola. That was the whole offer. You want it? No historical references, how about that?" His mustache sank a bit into his bottom lip—he did that when he was really sorry. "Got essential papers? Insurance policies? Passport? Divorce certificate?" he asked.

She was glad he mentioned that last item.

He took a deep breath. "Inhaler?"

"I don't think I'll need it," she said. She didn't say her asthma had disappeared after she left him. "But I'll take it."

Outside, Lila was surprised by what he was hauling. The truck was loaded down with power tools, torches, scrap metal, three duffel bags. For Katrina, he took a knapsack. He gave her the address in Pensacola. She put her single, carefully packed suitcase in her Toyota and got in. They'd keep in touch by cell, meet at the condo if they were separated.

This was it.

Lila got queasy when she pulled out into the empty streets. Other than William's truck, there was nothing moving. On the highway, he called. The radio announced the interstate into Mississippi was closed to evacuees. Everybody had to drive north. He knew another way.

First exit, he went south to the old coast road. Lila followed. The traffic was light at first, but around the entrance to a state park, they came to a dead stop. Cars ahead as far as they could see. People got out, walked their dogs, waited. Were they being turned away? Someone said there was a one-lane drawbridge. The coast guard had ordered craft to inland harbors. It would be a while. Now and then, they climbed back in and crept along past fishing camps with twisted roofs from three years ago, a half-recovered neighborhood called Venetian Isles, beige stucco houses on stilts. The pink tinge in the sky slowly became a full blown August day. They went over a few bridges that crossed narrower channels and finally approached the Rigolets Pass Bridge, over the waterway that led from the Gulf of Mexico to Lake Pontchartrain. Another stop. Lila got out this time and went to William's truck, said she was taking a little walk.

"Go for it," he said.

"You seem different," he said, when she came back. "Calmer."

"We weren't comparing," she said, but she was not as bothered as before.

"Innocent observation. And you never used to wear skirts."

"I knew not to wear pants when you might have to squat to." She grinned.

"I guess we learn," he said.

Around eleven-thirty, they made it into Mississippi. The first service station over the state line was swarming; queues wound out the doors— the old, the young, babes in arms, people in wheelchairs. A woman in white pants started screaming at Lila about the gas pump not taking her credit card, then left to complain to the cashier.

White pants returned, demanding Lila's pump, threatening her. Just as William got close to intervene, Lila stretched her own nozzle over to the woman's Honda, gave her ten gallons. The guy in line behind applauded.

When the woman was gone, William said, "That could have been ugly. You did good."

Lila said, "You seem surprised," though she was glad he'd seen her handle it. He always said she couldn't deal with things, she needed to be protected. In the next moment, however, she thought she should have gone with Alice. Anything with William was going to stir up everything else with William. She didn't want it.

On the Mississippi coast, the huge, rebuilt casinos dominated; they had the beach to themselves now—the cottages were still missing. One p.m. in Alabama, another full stop. They worked out a new route, but in the rolling hills above Mobile among horse farms and subdivisions, they got completely lost. Lila called to tell him they should ask for directions, dreading his response, for he used to hate to do that. But he pulled over immediately into the empty lot of a church. A red-haired Baptist minister walked up between her Corolla and William's truck. "You all from New Orleans? Went to seminary there. Loved it. So sorry about what you been through."

They chatted, answered questions. How was the city?

"We are stronger," William said. "It was good for us."

"Your wife believe that?" he nodded over to Lila.

"Not married," William said before Lila could. "Old friends."

"Well good. Couples always fight on road trips."

"Don't I know it," William said.

Lila shook her head, laughed. Strange how this trip was easy, she had to admit.

The preacher gave them directions. Lila wrote everything down, thanked him, pulled into the lead. Forty minutes later at the Florida line, a mechanical voice broke in on the FM station: "*Attention Gustav evacuees. Do not stop. Tropical Storm conditions in the Pensacola area. Repeat, Hurricane Gustav threatens the Florida Panhandle. Keep driving.*" On the phone, they agreed to take back roads to avoid the state police, meet up at the condo.

Exhausted, Lila pulled up at the rental around six.

A three hour trip had taken fourteen. The place was concrete, raised up off the ground, a pink rock with windows. The other occupants, Richard and Neil, two lawyers in their forties, met her at the door in Hawaiian shirts.

"William Bickham get here? Big truck?" Lila had lost him hours back.

"Jewel's friend?" Neil, the shorter one, asked.

"I'm William's, who is Jewel's," she said. All this was familiar—depending on offers hosts might regret later, housekeeping with strangers. "He tell you I was coming?"

"We thought you decided against it. Some weather here,

you see. God, how many hours were you on the road?" He said Gustav was churning up the whole Gulf.

She told her story, leaving out that William was her ex. She liked them, they liked her. When Neil showed her the rooms, she picked the one with bunk beds and a sea view. They offered her a Bloody Mary—they were pretending this was an ordinary Labor Day weekend vacation. Later, they asked her come along to a Chinese restaurant—she said she would wait for her "friend."

When they left, she went out on the balcony, took a deep breath, and called William's cell—no answer.

If people had told her thirty six hours before that she would be on Pensacola Beach waiting for Hurricane Gustav and her ex-husband, she would have said they were crazy. But she had to allow that if you looked at the whole process step by step, it all made sense—except the part about how she felt.

Around eight, his truck.

"What happened?" she didn't conceal her concern.

"I stopped for one beer," he said. He looked sheepish, confused.

There had not been a single night in her married life when he'd chafed under her interrogation like a teenage boy. She didn't have the authority then. It was funny. "And?"

He paused and she saw his old charm. "I fell asleep in the car. Conked."

"Lord," she laughed.

"Can't do all nighters now," he shrugged.

She broiled the steaks from his cooler. He made a salad. They'd always cooked together well.

Dessert was a joint on the balcony. After several tokes and a long, long silence, he said, "You were right to leave me. I was an asshole. I know it now." He nodded his big head to emphasize.

It was all she had been thinking about, but she protested, "I believed we weren't going to go over—"

"Break the rule," he said.

"Okay. You didn't get me, no, you didn't. But I'm over it. Don't berate yourself."

He insisted on explaining. He had felt he was in a war after Katrina. Something kicked in. He thought he'd give way, everything would.

"We did," Lila said. "We gave way." She felt like she might cry.

"But why did we?" he asked.

"You know," she said.

"Yes, but is that an absolute reason or a relative reason? I mean—"

"Absolute," she said, but she turned away. She knew he could read her face. She pointed out how the Gulf was liquid pearl after the sun went down. And did he notice how fast the clouds were moving across the sky in the winds? He said yes, the scene was incredibly beautiful, and then he kissed her. As kisses go, it was sweet and not very demanding—not very William.

The strangest part: she reached up and held on, kissed him back hard.

"What was that?" he said, pulling away. "Lila?"

She only shrugged. She really didn't know.

"Lila?" Disbelief.

She said truthfully, "I'm not sure. Sorry." Something came over her, something in her wanted to hold him.

"Don't have to be—"

"I think I am," she said, and not long after, she found her room, closed the door, climbed in the bunk. Through her window's thick glass, she watched the surf threaten to come over the road. She felt she was in a cocoon, a womb. Her mother used to tell her that when she was just born, she could have hidden Lila in a teacup.

Monday morning, she woke to cheering in the living room. Landfall was west of the city. New Orleans unscathed. So this was a comedy. Lila decided she should have trusted her first instinct, never left. But she had such a hard time trusting, being sure.

To avoid William's glances, she stared at CNN-Republicans in Minnesota at their convention, concerned about poor New Orleans. Richard said, "Tiny Tim Town. God Bless us everyone!" then threw his flip flops at the screen. Geraldo Rivera traipsed across the Ninth Ward holding a pinwheel, apparently praying the levees would break. Local news said the city had a schedule for allowing people back in. It would be a while before they could leave.

William was silent; so was Lila.

She looked outside. In daylight, it was easier to see where they were—the last building on a narrow strip between sea and sound. Across the way, the ocean sloshed under the houses. When it cleared for an hour, she went by herself to the little pool on the opposite side of the complex right at the edge of the bay— no beach on that side at all. A woman resident came out to walk her poodle. They chatted. She told Lila she got the condo in her divorce. "The road there," she went on. "See? It's closed. It used to lead to an old fort. But you can't drive there anymore. Hurricane Ivan split the island. All the buildings past here fell into the Gulf. This is the last one standing."

"Did you break up after Ivan?" Lila asked.

"What honey?"

"I mean, with your husband?"

"No." She shook her head. "It didn't have anything to do with the hurricane."

"Aren't you frightened to be living here?" Lila asked. "It's like you are out in the ocean."

The woman said, "Been through it all, I figure. So I know what I can take." She paused. "You said you live in New Orleans?"

The rain started up again but Lila couldn't go inside. She had to know what she'd say before she talked to William. She went past the state bathhouse and found the "CLOSED TO ALL TRAFFIC" sign.

The sun faded and parts of the huge sky melted into a single purple pool. The wind was so strong the rain drops flattened like snowflakes. Rough, thick rollers from the Gulf and smaller, milder ones from the bay came together in a moving V that merged at the horizon. Ahead, a few figures marched on the submerged road, silhouettes in the swirling blue. At a place like this, Land's End on Cape Cod, Lila walked with her mother for hours at low tide once. When she was four, Lila knew exactly whom she loved.

Above her head, the sky kept changing, changing—huge gray fists opening to reveal bands of gold, clear patches. Lila climbed over the barricade, stepped on the sunken asphalt. She still couldn't decide what to say to William.

She was standing there, water swirling around her ankles, angry with herself. What did she really want? She thought she had figured a few things out in three years. But in truth, she wasn't certain of anything—not until William came upon her from behind, touched her, said, "You going to walk into the Gulf of Mexico, Lila? The Gulf of fucking Mexico? Or you coming back inside with me?"

Wishing Well
Kirk Nesset

A girl threw a penny in a wishing well, then sat by the
well on a bench and dozed in the sun and awoke to find
a basket of pennies beside her. Later she dropped in a dollar
and waited while clouds floated over, and though no basket
appeared, they were soon swimming in money, the girl and
her mother, richer than butter, thanks to luck (a dead hit in
the lottery). So they sold all they had and caught a plane,
chastened somewhat, determined to cultivate good, commit
humanitarian acts everywhere possible, and did in Zimbabwe,
Burundi, New Guinea, Peru, and apparently drowned in the
Philippines in an overfull ferry on Easter with eight or nine
hundred people whose bones have yet to be raised.

Others telling this tend to differ dramatically. The girl
threw bill after bill in the well, they will say, and the well kept
coughing up cash, which the mother buried; later, the bags
were dug up by dogs, bags containing not just money but
guns, poison reptiles, and drugs. An eyelash fell in the well
with a bill, some insist, and the girl awoke to find herself
pregnant—nay, partly swollen with child—which isn't right,
since the girl at the time was barely ten.

Some say she pilfered and stole, the well itself having no
bearing. She worked with a child hoodlum called Fruitrag
or Fruitrock, charging staggering fees in neighboring fields
for a "living miracle show" involving latex garments and
finishing nails and a stuffed poodle. Others claim she and the
boy hitched to the city to lurk in parks and waylay passersby
with knives, a drama they staged in which the girl served
as bait. Still others who tell this, determined to see only the
world's ugliest side, claim she visited neither park nor field
nor well but was herself that dark place, spurred on by her

whore-mistress mother. Well-wishers called at the cottage in short. The girl was clearly a year or two older; the basket in fact was a pot.

More versions keep trickling in. The girl guided by the voice of Jane Seymour, the short-lived British queen (she ate only quail, apparently, during her pregnancy): the girl not a daughter but a fraud, an itinerant midget: the girl not a girl at all, but a ghost, even while living, a kind of angel in sojourn. Our banks, pubs, and pool halls are brimming with people eager to argue these stories. Controversy is good for the town. Our inns and cafes are full to bursting. We're doing almost appallingly well, selling gas, selling food, selling the little wooden well-replicas, key chains, figurines, maps, lockets, bracelets, amulets, talismans, baskets of candy money. So many wayfaring souls, dropping in offerings, standing in lines stretching the whole way down the hill. So many tokens enter the well, hour by hour—coins, bills, keys, toenails, bits of hair, panties—we have to suck the thing out with an industrial vacuum. Now and again, people wish in less than dignified ways (multiple tosses, monopolizing the well-mouth, and so on) and quickly lose loved ones and gain in heartbreaking ways. Be careful what you wish for, we say. An elderly Kentucky man lately asking for freedom from pain and peace with himself was within the hour struck and killed by a bus. A woman threw in a bundle last April, intimate feminine items we dare not describe, and found herself pregnant with triplets: not one infant survived.

Where do we stand? We stand by the facts (girl throws money in well, mother wins lottery, both disappear in the Philippines) and leave it at that. We don't enter the fray and haven't. And would refrain from doing so now if nonsense weren't aimed at the town.

We flatly deny any and all wrongdoing, any intent to commit unseemly acts. If the girl and mother indeed didn't drown and are back, we haven't seen them. Why would we hide them? To let rumor build, as the tabloids will have it, and to time the release of the pair to advantage? Do we want more people here, really? Night and day, people pour into town. Many have nowhere to stay; they sleep in their cars or in buses or vans; they raise tents in the park and churchyard or on lawns by the library. We're up to our gills now in traffic and feces and garbage. So preposterous some of this is, it doesn't merit response. But answer we will. Why would we kill them? (Assuming what's dead is alive or was again, temporarily.) To keep the world from hearing the well's just a well and a penny a penny, to drown them again, silence them utterly?

The truth is they've always been here. They're in the air, in leaves and sunlight and stone, in the dust floating over. But the intensity's grown. Prayer feels like white heat, like fever, like burning. Corn ripens too quickly. Deer and raccoon stand around dazed. The ground is unsteady, righteous with nettles and ooze. The stories are running things now. This is not something we chose.

Inch up the path to the well and you'll know. Inch up at dawn, eyes cast on the dirt or on the next pilgrim's sandals. Wear the schoolgirl attire if you wish (plaid skirt, saddle shoes, pennies jingling on belt) or scrape on knees the whole way, wearing custom-fit kneepads; come clad as young Fruitrock, polyvinyl ensemble, sans poodle, blurring versions of versions of tales. Pause where each and all pause, taste the air there, gaze out over town—church steeples, rows of roofs, the heads of magnolias and elms.

The girl and mother are here and not here. If you look with your guts, you will see them, the basket they began with now overwhelmingly full. They linger in glimpses, in echoes of phrases and words, in folds and heel-ends of tales that can't and won't end, that will not conform or confirm.

A Wooden Nickel Life
Marc Watkins

It's tomorrow and I'm still here. Though I have a hard time accepting I'm alive in the present, my wife does not. She's profoundly religious. Chides me for my lack of faith. Puts all of hers into Jesus and the gospels. But not once has she ever questioned her own life. I've never accepted mine. The way I see things, trusting that you're alive is a bigger leap of faith than believing in the resurrection.

She drops me at the doctor on her way to her weekly meeting of The Daughters of the Gloriously Departed—the support group for women claiming to be descendants of Confederate veterans. I tell her I'm due for a checkup, that I worry about a decline in my virility. This is a lie. I lie often.

Truthfully, I can't stand her war meetings. No one knows what they do to me. Her especially. I feel alive in the past—more than a century ago—riding atop a horse with Quantrill during the struggle and charging in and breaking the Federals' line than I do in this world of digital gossip.

Her girlfriends speak of epic battles.

I participated in none, only in raids.

Of the few men I killed outright in combat, all were shot in the back after we set them to flight. And while she and the other hens serve tea and share sexual fantasies about what it must've been like to own slaves, I remember firing a barn with the family still trapped inside. The taste of ash is still fresh on my tongue.

The doctor is an old fishing buddy of mine. Right off, he asks my quality of life.

So I tell him, "I'm in a middling sort of way, I guess."

He smokes in his office, two packs a day of unfiltered

tobacco. "What ails you?"

I have three children, a son, a daughter, and a third child I will not acknowledge in public save to say he bears my last name.

"I'm nostalgic. I can't stand the past anymore."

"Simple case of melancholy," he says. "No more beer, then. Drink only bourbon." And he writes me a script for two bottles a day. Then the doctor confesses my chances of making a full recovery are in doubt

The last time I drank so much was with Bill Anderson after the raid on Lawrence, Kansas. A hundred of us rode into the town after a dozen of our wives died in a Yankee internment camp. They burned to death, tragically. We expected to meet a full Union garrison to revenge our dead womenfolk, not a town full of old men and young boys. Still, we spared none, not even the livestock. Once the men were dead we turned our lusts to the women. I wound up taking a bony middle-aged gal. She was Mormon, confident in being saved. I think I may have crushed her youngest son's skull when I smashed him over the head with my revolver. I don't recall apologizing. She was a quiet sort. There was only a limp struggle.

Bill and I drank the liquor we stole on the ride back across the border into Missouri. It helped take the heat away from what we did. We drank till we fell off our horses, laughing.

But that was then and I find it too much to bear now. There's too much joy in it.

The funny talking lady behind the pharmacy counter refuses my prescription on grounds of moral turpitude. The lady, a morbidly active sort who corrects her speech like a grammar school teacher, calls me a fool. A drain upon society.

I've worn many names, most of them aliases to mask the truth. Fool was never one of them, though it seems fitting. The slew of names I carried around in my pocket with me when I was a Bushwhacker were mostly Indian, heathen sounding names. The only one I kept and use today is what my family calls me, the most terrifying alias of them all: Father.

It's a brisk walk to the liquor store up the street where I'm sure no one will decline my medicine. People don't walk around town anymore. They sit in traffic and glare at you from their cars. A few sips of bourbon later and I don't mind being stared at. I'm just so damned afraid of making a spectacle of myself.

This fear comes from my first wife, a lazy feminist who concerned herself more with being socially graceful than properly taking birth control. In this day and age, men are supposed to accept equal responsibility when it comes to conception, but I'll never forgive her. She put me through too many false pregnancies, always drinking at lavish social gatherings till she passed out and forgot to take the pill the next day. Or she waited until she was out of them for a week before she ordered a refill. Frightened the hell out of me. I even made her douche with a bottle of vodka once after we had sex.

But old wives' tales don't work. And after our first child was born, there was no stopping her. We had the next two in quick succession. She never asked me if I wanted children. I believe she knew the answer.

When she was carrying our third child I refused to have sex with her. She accused me of discriminating against pregnant women. Then vainly inquired if I thought the pregnancy ruined her look.

"Don't I turn you on no more?" she asked me during the seventh month, belly swole up like it held a coiled eel.

"I've got gas, that's all."

"Are you pooping good?"

"Now just what does the movement of my bowels have to do with it?"

She flipped open Cosmopolitan magazine and expertly narrated an article on how irregularity can affect a man's sex drive. Ever careful and always thoughtful in her ways, even as she gave a very measured description about what she thought was destroying our marriage.

But she never once fought with me, not even in private. Said it would be rude. I didn't earn so much as a click of her tongue.

Then the baby came. It was our last and I was determined never to have relations with her again.

She tried for twenty years, but I stood firm in my zeal.

My wife's name was Carmine. I abandoned her publicly at one of those socialite functions she so fabulously attended. Suppose it was the bastard in me who knew if I did it there, she'd not make a scene. The only reaction I noted in her was embarrassment, a slight reddening of the cheeks, like they had been freshly slapped. It's hell being right.

I finish the first bottle of bourbon and move to a bench in front of the doctor's office. Soon, the only people on in the street will be those from my distant past.

There were other wives a century ago, though Carmine was my first divorce. I can still recall the years directly following the war and the passion I shared with my homestead wife. Even though I've forgotten her name, I cannot forget the pain of losing our child to scarlet fever, the disease brought on by chronic malnutrition. She passed of sorrow shortly thereafter. I was only able to survive because I had lived through the same illness after our sides' dreadful defeat outside of Springfield.

The focus of my life used to be as keen as a knife. Now it takes everything to not let the past smoother me. Oh, God. This liquor isn't enough to keep it from screaming out of mind and coloring everything.

Some men hold their present depends entirely upon their past. This makes me feel good to think about, but it's only true if a man can measure the balance of his life against his legacy. And I know all those memories about the war don't make sense. It's not my job to make sense out of them. Go on and judge me and my questionable past. I've no future.

Three children are my legacy.

My oldest is a graduate of Washington University. His

education was paid for by me, exclusively. Recompense was doled out when he stuck a metal rod through his nose during his first semester, then announced to the family at Thanksgiving his sexual partners run from male to female given his mood. Carmine wouldn't let me stop payment on his tuition. She argued upon his behalf eloquently. When he chose to make money on the side as a male escort, Carmine told me it was our parental duty to support him. The last I heard, he's living in a motel in East St. Louis, servicing the occasional truck driver during the day so he can afford his habit of gorging in the particular affections of large Negro women come evening.

The middle child is my daughter. She will not go to college. Gifted only in having a bleak and charmless personality blacker than a starless night sky. Only carnal pleasure with men, any men, can fill such a void. How many she's been with must range into the hundreds.

One evening I returned with Carmine from an engagement with her high society friends to find our daughter unconscious on our front lawn. She was fifteen, surrounded by the varsity football team, the JV squad, and the marching band from a neighboring school who'd just been trounced by our boys. The band belted out an awkward version of Wagner's "Flight of the Valkyries."

It was an inspired score.

They were all nude and ran as soon as I pulled my car in the drive. Carmine and I walked through the piles of discarded jerseys and balled up jock straps until we came upon our naked daughter lying atop an altar of shoulder pads, spread eagle.

Upon closer inspection I found evidence of a lightning bolt shaved into her private hair.

Her lusts cannot be satisfied.

What's more, a gynecologist found she cannot bear children. I only tell you this so you sympathize with her. It's important you do because I no longer can.

I won't say I haven't considered renting a young bull

from a neighboring farm and tying her beneath it so she can get it out of her system, but I'm afraid she'd drain all the worldly essence from the animal before it could calm her heated desire. And it would be a social faux pas for Carmine to find her only daughter crushed mid-coitus beneath an exhausted bull.

I refuse to have any children with my new wife.

She arrives directly from her DGD meeting, face fully flustered when she finds her husband intoxicated on the street. Unlike Carmine, this wife and I fight daily. It's a beautiful feeling. I no more set foot in the car, and we're at each other's throats. And she may be high on the religion, but there's nothing socially graceful in the words she uses on me.

"What a shiftless, indigent old man I've married."

I love her more than anything for saying things like this to me. "But, honey," says I, raising the bottle so the light passes through it. "The doctor told me its medicine. Even wrote me a note to prove it."

"I never," she says, putting the car into drive and starting home. "Well, I just never."

Her name is Mary. When we arrive home she leaves all talk of religion at the door. We find ourselves making up often. She gives me free reign in the bedroom. As she undresses, I admire her body still tight with youth, reminding me Mary isn't much older than my children.

She sits me on the bed, then calls me daddy and tells me she's going to fuck me. I have no say in the matter. She retires to the bathroom to prepare her body.

My third child is the youngest and my greatest disappointment. He is the only one I have disowned. His profession utterly disgusts me. He is a priest. We speak but once a year on my birthday. Our conversation was brief this year, as it is always. It began when he asked my health. I'm sure he wants me to die, so I humored him and said the end was in sight. Then I asked him if he had anyone in his life.

"Only God," was his answer.

"Really? Nothing on the side?"

"No, pop," he says. "I've kept my vow in Christ."

"Not even one of them little boys?"

The trouble began when he asked for my confession. He wanted to save my soul, to salvage our relationship, but I refused to ask absolution from a twenty-something virgin.

I hate him the most of all my children because he will never have any of his own now that he's taken to the priesthood. This makes him the smartest of the bunch. Brilliant compared to me.

Mary returns from the bathroom, perfumed and trimmed around her pelvis. She lies on the bed and waits for me to perform my husbandly duties.

Now I know she wants a baby with me. But I tell this woman that won't do, yet she refuses birth control, calling it profane. Yet she knows I can't refuse her body. She doesn't understand the pain children can cause. How could she?

I manage to finish first. I always do. And she lets loose a series of mournful sighs, wanting a release of her own. So I move between her legs—as I do every night at the end of our marital encounters—my tongue lashing the insides of her thighs with the promise of fulfilling her need.

Kinky is what she calls this. But a kink is something found in a hose. What I'm about to commit is an act of social responsibility.

I put my lips over her labia and suck out the wad I just shot in.

Children are the future and I want no part in this inevitable moral calamity other than what I'm already guilty of with my three offspring.

And you, you voyeurs want me to tell you what it tastes like. Well I won't do it. I still have some measure of decency.

Go out and eat your own salvation.

Year of the Demon Tree
Jesse Waters

January. Divorce. I transplanted the apple tree to my new solo place. The limb by limb bulk of her spread out across my yard and eventually up as it took to soil and made it its own. Each leaf would rattle in the wind, and at night in my cold, solo sheets, I would listen to that whispering and make out words. My old Labrador, Diggy, would whine as the last winter winds blew them loose and rushed them against the doors and windows of the house.

I'd found Diggy howling at my back door one night. I was crippled inside and unable to love, but in the end. I took us both in. Eventually, he did the same and we'd come to an understanding more than simply mutuality, food for love—I admit it, we shared a bed. But when the twitching of his dreaming would wake me, I'd rouse myself for just a few seconds, and rather than soothe him, I'd walk to the window and watch the growing arms of my apple tree waving in the darkness.

That February, I traveled to Europe to find the history of my family. No one in America knew much, and I wanted to be the first to know. We're Jews. Lynn, my ex, loved to see me in a yarmulke. "Your head finally looks perfectly round."

Nine hours in the air and forty-five minutes by bus and I'm in Dachau, where a host family, The Werkliens, has offered to house me. When I walk in, they're making apfelkuchen with bits of bacon, salt to match the sugar. Three daughters, Teilna, Sara, and Greti. Their mother Elka claps her hands and says, "All jewelry off—get your hands underneath the dough and make it paper thin—no tears!" Right then, I imagine my mother making gefilte fish at my house. I dare you to find one bone. Passover. Pass over. It's an odd word for a holiday.

I stay three days and find no information about my family. I go to the camps—who couldn't? I visit a small out-building, waist-high full of glasses, the kind you wear on your face, but waist-high, eye glasses up to my stomach. There's another thigh-high full of hair. I'm frustrated. I buy an apple in Dachau from a woman selling them out of a cart on a cobblestone back street. No one in my America knows much about my family, and I want to be the first to know *real* things, importance. But there's one family story everyone in my America knows:

My stupid Great Uncle Jolek didn't die in the Nazi death camps. Jolek, who was young, and stupid, did *not* die in the Nazi death camps. Instead, he cut off his own left hand around January 1940, at Birkenau, or Sosnowiec. Three feet from an infirmary, or a cafeteria, with a hatchet, across an Oak tree stump or a make-shift plyboard bench like an overgrown root, Jolek cut off his own left hand. He was still right-handed – with that good right hand he banged through the clinic (mess hall) doors, "My hand, my hand!" he cried, and they starched the wound closed, but no one would touch Jolek's lost hand back out in the cold. It lay there shivering. The Polish kapo who'd seen the whole thing had forbidden anyone to go near it, the story goes, and told his sergeant (after losing in cards the night before), who told his captain, who thought the story unusual, a Jew cutting off his own hand. This captain went first to Jolek in the infirmary and asked, "Why? Why would you cut off your own hand?" but Jolek had no answer, would not tell why, and the captain was so taken by the (lack of) story that once Jolek's arm had "healed," he gave Jolek the kapo position over ninety-five older prisoners, and Jolek beat them with his good right hand, beat them clutching his stump to his chest and made them jump and dance till they passed out sometimes, my Great Uncle Jolek did. But before all that, as that captain left the infirmary, he stopped to stoop at the

still-weeping, still-shivering left hand, "Look," he gestured
to the sergeant—actually a friend from Dachau, or Wiesloch,
from before the war—there in the web of Jolek's left thumb
and forefinger, in prison ink blue, was a dime-sized tattoo
of the Star of David, lots of Jews had them—in different
body places—and as Jolek's hand turned blue and the tattoo
disappeared, they watched.

I imagine it was an amazing thing. That captain and the
sergeant talked about it over the years and stayed friends
and thought a lot about being called upon to do something
bad—called upon by your country to do something bad,
because they were not animals or demons, but workaday
men and not sure about that even, I found out: I met them
both by coincidence, absolute luck, at a tram stop near the
Munich airport (moving through after a funeral for the one's
brother, or wife), and we just struck up a chat, in English,
and talked about the war because I asked. Compelled, I think,
by Jolek's hand, by memory, like breaking open, they cut each
other off telling me how this Jew named Jolek sliced off his
own hand with a hatchet, Jolek who wouldn't take the hand
back, Jolek with his left arm clutched to his chest the rest
of the year—how they'd watched the Jew in Jolek literally
fade from his body—Jolek, Jolek, Jolek, until I just had to
tell them—had to tell them about my Great Uncle Jolek,
young and mean and stupid, who did not die in the Nazi
death camps but rather cut off his own left hand, and that
no one in our family ever knew why, and it's true, it's true
I said, I wouldn't lie to you, and we sat quiet for a moment.
We embraced then. I hugged them each hard like I would
my father, and they hugged back hard. The one promised
to send me a photograph of my Great Uncle's hand. I kept
that one Dachau apple in my pocket all through the plane
ride home. I put it in my freezer when I get back to North
Carolina, and later on, it'll end up in my mouth. I won't ever
see that photograph. I won't ever really be convinced that
my trip to Europe taught me much about my family.

In March I waited for something and walked through the wet, changing streets, hoping for spring.

April came and I visited my father in Chicago. It was not named the windy city because of weather. I didn't know this until the pilot explained its political significance as we banked left behind the airport. The townhouse my father now lived in was half-full. He looked half-full himself. He'd transplanted a lemon tree into the puny backyard. A lemon tree in Chicago. It never really lived. One day as he overwatered it, I told him finally about Lynn. For the whole month I stayed, I watched him lug pail after daily pail down the Brownstone steps to the tiny backyard. He's not a dumb guy, my dad, "You know you're killing it" I said.
"I'm loving it the best way I know how."
"Then you don't know anything about love." We've known each other my whole life.
"You don't know anything about love."

All throughout the month of May, I dated a woman named Trina. But I was fickle as hell and didn't give anything. She took all she could of it and left me for another man, a mortician. "It's a gamble, that's for sure" she frowned, "but you're a sure thing."

In June, I flew to Las Vegas for two days and made a charcoal rub of the headstone at my Great Uncle Jolek's grave. He was born in 1911, in Sosnowiec, and died two years ago in Las Vegas. I couldn't make the actual funeral because the advertising office where I do freelance work on a regular enough basis was having a party for the retiring president, and I didn't feel, at that time, like my Great Uncle was a person I needed to know about. So I skipped it. My mother ended up filling me in on the details over the phone one Sunday during a long, slow North Carolina rain. Later, I did make the time for her funeral. Flying out of the Vegas airport, I thought about making that rub that night before.

Year of the Demon Tree

It'd been dark out but not night. I could make out the city's skyline about five miles south. The air was warm. The stone was cool and smooth as flour.

During that plane ride back, I thought about how important it would be for me to start truly remembering events in my life, not just things from the trip overseas, or to my Dad's, or anything in Las Vegas, but everything I did, or was. It struck me as important because of one story my family told about me getting bitten by the dog of a friend of my mother.

All the people in my family have a version, even people who weren't there. They all say I was poking at the dog—a small, tough Spitz named Tony—in his "spot," a stretch of rug under a pew in the friend's foyer. It was deep summer. After teasing him too much, they all say, Tony snapped at me and bit me on the cheek.

But none of them were actually there, I know because I was the only one there, and this is what really happened. I was sitting with Tony in the middle of the friend's living room *next* to the foyer where Tony's "spot" was, putting Lincoln Logs together, when the friend's son Michael jumped out from the dining room and scared the crap out of both me and Tony, and Tony jumped up and bit me on the cheek. Michael and I are friends. It's a funny thing between us now, even though he swears to this day he was nowhere near the event. Lynn and I wanted a dog but never settled on a breed. "You pick the kind of dog that would bolt in a second," she'd say, or "That one'll kill anything small." In a dry, wonderful way, it tears at me that I remember all this so vividly and terribly and so differently each time, so I want to make sure I get everything else right from now on. I buy a journal and vow to keep it with me. I write down the call number of the jet we're flying on back to Raleigh. I write down the names of the stewards and stewardesses on board and the kind of meal we have—little long strips of orange roughy and some pasty potatoes. As we eat, the guy sitting next to me pulls off his wedding band and slips it into one of the folds of his wallet.

When I land back home in North Carolina, in Wilmington, and pick up Diggy from Lynn's house, she warns me: "He's turned sort of ill." When people in North Carolina say ill, they mean mean, not sick. Lynn and I now each have dogs and trust one another to keep each other's pets when the other has to leave town. It's a grudging sort of situation, but it's enough. And too much and not enough. I get Diggy into the back seat of the car, and as I slide in on the driver's side, he leans over the ridge of the front seat and nips me on the ear. It doesn't draw blood, but it hurts. A dark red mark and a little purple bruise pop up by the time we get home, and the message light on my machine is flashing. It's from Lucio Floyd, one of my Dad's friends—he's had a heart attack.

I fly back to Chicago the next day. I don't even unpack my Vegas suitcase. In the hospital room where they have him hooked up to tubes and machines still, he squints up at me and sees my ear. "What happened to you?"

"Diggy bit me." He smiles and starts to laugh but catches himself and takes a deep, long breath that's not a sigh. There's a glass of water with a flexi-straw in it on the little drawer/table next to his bed, and I point at it, but he shakes his head. "How'd it happen?"

"I put him in the back of the car, and when I got in the front, he nipped me. I don't know. I picked him up at Lynn's after the airport, and she told me he'd been acting weird, but I didn't really think anything of it."

"Like I said—you don't know anything about love." One of his machines beeped and an IV filled with a lemony-looking liquid attached to his left arm began to drip. He closed his eyes. I wondered if someone could fall asleep so quickly, and it occurred to me that a person shouldn't really be friends with a parent. It's just too much, they know you exactly. And when they die, it's a double crush. But it wasn't my father's time, that time. Three days later I rolled him to my rental car in his hospital wheelchair and then home.

I stay July and August. I keep the yard clean, water the

plants, all that stuff—but not the lemon tree. As a result, it gets stronger. The roots dry out a bit, and some of the soil loses the moss and mold running through it, and so does the bark at the base of the tree. I call Lynn one afternoon—she tells me Diggy has bitten her, won't eat, and that I'd better fly back. I pack my things and do a little shopping for my father. Before I drive to the airport, I catch Lucio lugging a few pails of water down the steep back steps. I refused him. "Look," I said, "it's actually living, leave it alone."

"It's for your father," he insisted.

In September, the apple from Dachau was still in my freezer. That sentence popped into my head as I was reviewing some of my memory notes from these few trips, making sure what was in my head matched with the info I'd written down. The sun was going down and my father would be dead in thirty-seven days. I imagine a new couple that buys his house will ignore the lemon tree and it will flourish so passionately that when they have two boys who grind the pulp of those lemons into sweet juice for all the kids in the neighborhood, it'll make them popular and happy and total.

Keeping fruit in the freezer will not keep it. When I split open the apple from Dachau, after close to a half-year in deep cold, I see the black seeds inside have grown a tumor of ice in a ball around them and that their little huskshells have split. Through the haze of frost, I can make out the split strips bent back. It's fascinating and for the next few days, I try to translate its look into my journal. It's hard to live even one half-year of a long life. When I do taste the apple, there's absolutely nothing but texture, the one weather of the freezer has killed its flavor.

Please do not ask me about October.

On the first of November, my vet came out through a sleeting rain to the house to check on Diggy and happened to see my own apple tree. "It's got buds," he laughed. "You've got a demon tree."

"Demon tree?"

"My grandfather from Boone used to say that when a plant or tree bloomed out of season, it'd gotten the devil in it. He said his father used to call them demon trees. Apple trees are supposed to harvest in the fall, not bloom." He reached up a hand to touch a branch, and I pulled a longer branch down to my face. Sure enough, under the drizzle of that cold sleet, all along the wood were fat blossoms starting to show.

North Carolina winters here on the coast, low to the ground, are not severe, and the blossoms on the demon tree thrived through even December and January and February of the following year. But with no bees around to pollinate them, they simply swelled with tree-lust. Walking to the mail box, I swore I could smell apple. It made sense to me—fed on hunger and watered with thirst, it made sense that a demon tree should thrive like that. I thought of my father's lemon tree in Chicago, the block kids there now drinking their fill. Spring came. While mowing the lawn one warmer evening as the sun dropped down and let in just a bit of breeze, I cut into a long apple root close to the house. It bled a kind of clear blood. That night, I dream the soil transparent, that I am watching the first root of that blood take hold, deep down during the one transplant. In the dream, I squat down to get a close look. My mouth says, "I should have let love die before the harvest." The root answers in a female voice: "My center will be made from luck and lust," and I wake shaky in these cold, solo sheets—Diggy cocks his head at me in the way lovers and dogs will in half sleep when you wake them—those demon leaves whisper at me, "Bad Jew," or "You Knew," or "Tattoo," and I feel for the first time the earth's terrible rotation.

Year of the Demon Tree

The Devil's Circle
Bonnie Nadzam

The truest of all men was The Man of Sorrows, and the truest of all books is Solomon's, and Ecclesiastes is the fine hammered steel of woe. In it you will be reminded that during a wise man's lifetime of seeking, he will find one upright man among a thousand, but not one woman. More bitter than death is woman. She is a scavenger of beauty. She stands in the light of others that she may herself appear civilized and wise. She is a misfit, a rover, a split wreck. What after all is woman but a fleshed out rib wrenched from some other vessel? What but a soft and pretty container to be filled with the bodies and toils and fruits of men? How then is it possible that a woman be pure? Her heart is a snare. Only the man who pleases God will escape her.

When I met Ben Gordon, it was like being pulled from a tangle of barbed wire and washed in milk. Like being raised from death to life. It's an old song, really, a familiar story: dark of night, storm winds spiriting a ship away, huge wind howling forth. Great wheels of water churning and foaming, spinning the craft like a toy boat, bowsprit to the east, then north the long way around. Men flung overboard, their necks snapped in the wind. Despair, lament, gnashing of teeth. A broken mast, a ship driven fast upon the rocks. Then suddenly water smooth as oil. The muted cry of a single gull. Another. White skeins lifting in the clear light of day. And there—washed up on the sand, torn clothing dried in the sun and flapping in the breeze like clean feathers—lies our hero. A woman.

It was like that. On fumes of gas, I'd rolled down out of

the high cracked mountains, out of screaming white snow, and onto the even, verdant plains of eastern Colorado. I slept on the shoulder of a county road, my head in a bony pile of arms on the steering wheel. Wind drove the shadows of clouds over the fields like dark fish swimming beneath the blue grama. Violent green ribbons of prairie sandreed combed themselves through the short, yellow wool of the last year's grass.

I will not tell the story, here, of where I spent the night— or the week or the year—before I ran out of gasoline in front of his parents' house, set like a clean white island on a vast swath of green running silk. But I did tell Ben.

Your hair is like a flock of goats, he told me, listening as I explained how it'd been. What I had done. He traced my jawbone with his finger. Your teeth are like perfect rows of sheep newly shorn.

I told him everything. I'd been sealed up in my secret lives, kept in caves, and in the life with Ben, there would be no secrets.

It was he who'd found me in his parents' shed, looking for fuel to get myself back out on the road. He stood in the doorway watching me shake the gas can, watching me gauge it. Flycatchers and swallows darted like silver hooks in the early gray light behind him. He stepped inside, lifted my chin, and gazed upon my face. You need a warm meal, he said. He checked his watch. He took me by the elbow. I'll show you the shower and the guestroom. Inside, his mother brought me lavender-scented water in a beautiful handmade ewer and poured it out into a clean, white ceramic basin. Outside the bedroom door was soft country music: Kisses Sweeter than Wine, The Hurtin's All Over.

Be wise now, I told myself when I came down the stairs in his mother's loose cotton dress and an old pair of Ben's slippers. I was clean and my head was anointed with oil. Ben and his father stood up on the far side of the supper table when I entered the dining room. They had matching eyes of cornflower blue. A tall glass of yellow buttermilk beading with moisture sat before each dish. A bowl of spring green peas. A pile of golden chicken. A soft white heap of whipped potatoes. An iced chocolate cake.

Give her some more chicken on that plate, Ben's father said. She's skin and bones. Here. Two scoops of that. One more. They'd all waited for me, their faces calm and happy. Ben's cheeks a little pink. I couldn't look his father in the eye.

Stay still, I told myself. Ben pulled out a chair. Don't move from his side. Careful about the moon. Careful about the riptides of spring weather, of warm wet nights. But it was beyond me. What is crooked cannot be straightened. Round and round the wind goes. Night after night, the sun hurries back to where it rises, and the earth spins so fast beneath me it is like racing water, no steady place to plant my feet.

For a time, the stars seemed to cease turning up there. For a time, it seemed I'd landed someplace, was home somewhere, could learn to make latticed pies, cheeses of raw milk, mixed garlic and kelp for the free-range hogs. I could be the woman who made whole meals from scant goods: skillet bread and boiled dandelion greens, cornmeal cobbler with prunes. The woman who put every spoon in its slot and who hung her husband's shirts neatly in place and no mismatched socks and no spiders in the closet and pickled greens and honey-sweetened jams lined up in pristine cabinets and clean combs on the bureau and fresh sheets on the bed. I could be the woman who never lost her keys. Never tore at her nails. Never slept in the backseat of her car. Never met anybody at a truck stop. Never wrote a bad check for an alcoholic beverage, never stole her lunch from a gas station.

Ben and I spent the summer like children on his parents' farm. We walked the acres of green oats as they slowly rose and overtook the distant tree line. We tucked ourselves beneath the willow outside his bedroom window and followed the harriers and meadowlarks with binoculars and copied their whistles. At twilight, the red and swift foxes darted through curtains of grass carrying field mice, beetles, rabbits, and voles. We wrapped onion sandwiches in wax paper and brought them to the fresh stream behind the older barn and ate slowly and deliberately and folded the paper into little boats that we dressed in beeplants and pearly everlasting. We milked the grass-fed cows. We gathered hens' eggs, blew out their insides and painted the hollow shells with watercolors. We made a layered lemon cake when Mr. Gordon's mother visited from Las Animas. We sifted the flour. We leveled our measurements with the back of a butter knife. My gaunt face rounded. My elbows and shoulders softened. My lungs were scrubbed out with cool wind. I flossed my teeth and trimmed my nails. I bought plastic packages of clean cotton underwear from the dimestore, wore Mrs. Gordon's old flannel shirts and hand-knit cardigans, a pair of blue jeans that were Ben's when he was a boy. All the clothes smelled vaguely dusty: clothes for a ghost, clothes for someone who might disappear at any moment, whereupon they would be refolded and stored away for some other wandering wretch.

We married in October. Roasted a lamb and a hog and half the town came to the neatly clipped green square of buffalo grass behind the house. There was hot apple cider and champagne, silver platters of ripe figs and raw nuts. We moved into the tiny blue and white bungalow where Mrs. Gordon had lived as a girl. The beams of the house were cedars; the rafters were firs. It was newly painted and three blocks from the high school where Ben taught English. All the young women saw me and called me blessed. At daybreak, the vast flat world to the east opened before us like the smooth and easy page of a prayer book. Behind us, the Rockies were invisible in the distance, though still there, I knew. Still dark and still rising. Geologically complex. Crystalline cores guarded by uplifted walls of sedimentary rock slowly wearing themselves out.

Every Saturday afternoon, Ben's folks brought us a

whole roasted chicken and potato rolls and custard pie. We had a schedule, the four of us, a neat little routine: by the time his parents left their house, making the half mile walk or driving if there was snow or wind, we had lain together in our clean and narrow bed. Ben would lift me up, take me to our little white bathroom where he'd bathe me, comb my hair like a doll's. By the time his parents crossed the lawn of St. Augustine's Catholic Church, he was pulling on my socks, and we presented them with fresh smiling faces, love newly made all about us. I believed that in two years, there'd be children. I believed the moon would be fat and silver and still, the wind still. Mornings, Ben brought me glasses of apple juice and vitamins. I learned to braid bread for him and studded it with yellow raisins and smooth green pumpkin seeds. We woke at dawn. We ate all our meals at a little table of clean, blonde wood. I went down to the school during the week, and we'd picnic in the courtyard or on the smooth black lab tables in his classroom if there was weather. His students called me Mrs. Gordon.

But alas, I am a warning piece again to all those rash and ignorant. A woman such as myself recognizes a man like Jack Ryder. Pay attention to what I am about to tell you. This is the oldest part of this old song. And a woman such as myself ought to have recognized it, though a woman such as myself never does. It was the way he threw his head back, his shoulders back; it was the cocked smile, it was the hair that shot off his head like daylight. And a man like Jack Ryder would recognize a woman like me, however many salutary disguises of health and wholeness I might layer one upon the other. I even told Ben: Please keep me clear of that man. He's worse than the Nebraska one.
Worse than Nebraska?
Worse than Nebraska and New Mexico combined. Worse than Idaho.
How can you tell?
I can tell just how he would move.

How he would move?

Keep me away from him.

Sometimes on a Saturday evening, we'd walk to the Plains Bar and each have a glass of cold beer. Jack was often there. Shirtsleeves rolled up. His cheekbones and jaw planed and angular. His head thrown back. His arms thrown back behind his thrown back head. Legs crossed. Wherever he was from, I thought, it wasn't here. The men and women circled around him. Adored him. Made him welcome wheresoever he chose to sit or to stand. He almost always came into the bar with a woman—one of these sunny types who has loved with her body and with pleasure and is pleased with herself but who has never loved with misery. There's no misery in her body. None. She moves light as fine rain from one side of the bar to the other, making funny faces, smiling wide. She wears a ball cap. But it's not his, that I can tell. And I never saw them touch each other. Never even bump elbows. They weren't in love, I thought. They couldn't be. That's not what he was doing with her. He was doing something else.

But I was left to speculate about Jack Ryder's life, his plans, his girl. Left to keep lookout when I was about town, left to live on the heat of passing glances. When one evening Ben noticed me watching Jack walk from the bar to the rear door—a tall passage of lit blue pulsing in the dark back room, he stood up.

Let's go my little goose, he said. And leaned over the table and kissed my forehead.

Home?

Home.

I gathered my purse and ran my fingers through my hair and stood up. Ben took my hand and walked me out. The plan was he would buy a six-pack from the store on the way back. We could drink it slowly over the next couple Saturday nights. But when he came out of the corner store, he had a box of root beer. A carton of ice cream he would cut into small vanilla bricks.

A better deal, he said and winked at me.

You love me, don't you?

A hundred tons. And he moved in to kiss me, and I turned and gave him my cheek.

So it was that we spent our Saturdays that late winter and early spring. At home we sat on the porch as the sun melted behind the old granary, and in the distance, the grass was coming up like pale green water, white vapor rising from the center pivots beyond. Ben tucked me into an afghan on the porch swing, and we sipped our cold root beer in the chilly wind as he read me stories of heroes. Character-building books. Thousands of pages of men pursued by shadows. Of men fleeing devils. Of men converting savages on strange and distant shores. Of men who won the battle once and for all, claiming their own souls and settling down with girls bright and bendy as young olive trees, empty as big-eyed birds. Of a young man who lived years alone on a distant island with no company but his own God and who slowly built a little empire among its palms, upon its sand. Of a man who finally returned home after ten or twenty or thirty years away, his wife and his cattle and all his flocks and his fruit trees and his concubines restored to him. Of a man who at the end of the tale floats calmly away from the shipwreck, everyone else eaten by the sea, his sleeping face pressed up against a splintered coffin, sun warming the back of his golden head like recognition of the only creature on the planet worth sparing.

By the first night in May, the branches of the wild plum tree beside the porch were cobwebbed with white blossoms. Music sifted through the newborn leaves, some band of high school kids playing on Main Street. Or maybe it was live music at the Plains Bar. Maybe in the center square. Jack would be there, dancing with his girl. He'd put one hand on the small of her back. Drive the other one up into her hair from behind. He'd wheel her into the shadows beneath the starlight, reach into the waistband of her jeans, open her mouth with his own. I pulled Mrs. Gordon's shawl tighter around me and listened to my darling read: all the days I should now live would be as good as the days that Lazarus lived after his resurrection: a supplementary clean gain of so many months or weeks as the case might be. I survived myself; my death and burial were locked up in my chest. I looked round me tranquilly and contentedly, like a quiet ghost with a clean conscience sitting inside the bars of a snug family vault. Now then, thought I, unconsciously rolling up the sleeves of my frock, here goes a cool, collected dive at death and destruction, and the devil fetch the hindmost.

Sometimes after Ben stopped going with me to the Plains Bar and while he was at school, I'd go alone. In the daytime. Jack Ryder was, I supposed, a man of some profundities. The kind of fellow who might come in for a cold beer in the early afternoon. He worked at the small shop doing metal work and car and tractor repair. There were probably days without any work at all. Jack was the kind of guy who'd put in four or five good hours and wash his face and find himself thirsty. I knew it. It was a matter of time and chance. So on these days when I ventured out alone, I'd have a small chaste beer and a grilled cheese and eat very slowly. Maybe once a week. Maybe Mondays, sometimes Wednesdays, occasionally a Friday because a Friday afternoon would be a likely time to leave work for a beer. I'd sit at a table facing halfway toward the windows, my heart in a fat, warm knot, watching. Eating slowly, my head and chest and hands emptied out by the time I'd filled my belly. I couldn't possibly eat any slower. I'd be home to greet Ben at the door. We'd fix a small glass dish with white rectangles of farmer's cheese and yellow tomatoes sliced into circles, and he'd grade any papers he might have to grade, and I'd do something—laundry or reading or rolling socks—and then I'd fix dinner. One of his mother's recipes for meatloaf or city chicken or potato dumplings sliced and fried with turnip greens in bacon grease. And we'd drink our buttermilk and sit on the porch, and he'd read to me from his books.

When I finally did see Jack in the Plains Bar, it was almost June. And a Friday. Summertime rising in my blood. Weedy yellow prairie rockets and pointed red sky rockets rising and heating and pricking my blood like an unstoppable and fragrant and perilous tide. He stepped out of the day and into the cool dark and sat down, leaned way back in his chair, legs splayed, boots filthy. Without a moment's hesitation, I ordered him a beer from my table. My pulse quickened, my face flushed with fever. It was not the sort of thing Ben Gordon's wife did. But it was the sort of thing I'd always done. It was what the woman with no face always did. I straightened my posture, and when the glass was set down before Jack beside the one he'd already ordered, he stood up with them both, cool as morning, and brought them over to me and sat down. I extended my hand like a man would. Of course it was too early for a beer, he said and grinned and ordered me a second.

You live beside the granary, he said, yes?

I told him we did.

Have you been up in there, yet?

I told him no. Maybe I asked him to show me. Maybe I led him there myself.

There are missing stairs, he said. Watch out.

I took his hand. He paused, then continued up.

I've been watching you, I said.

I think I know that.

Here, I said. Stand here. Like that.

We adjusted our feet.

At first slowly, by degrees—and then suddenly and stealing my breath—he took over.

In a rectangle of spring light on our clean white bed that morning, Ben Gordon had called me his Rose of Sharon. Kissed my forehead. Kissed my chin. In the shadows in the empty grain elevator beside the derelict tracks, loose teeth of sheet metal swinging in the wind, Jack Ryder's fingers dripped with myrrh. Your name, I whispered, Christ. Your name is like perfume poured out upon me. He drove the heel of his hand into my mouth. Outside, thunderheads were roiling up to the west. I ran my fingers along his teeth. He swung his head in the dark like a horse. He bit my neck. He pressed his grin against my mouth and reached into Mrs. Gordon's shirt and pinched me twice so hard my breasts would bloom into green and purple hyacinth blossoms. I cried out. These were the marks by which my beloved would discover me. Outside, the leaves and shrubs were neon green against a racing black sky. Heaven and Jove and all the other gods would punish me.

This can't be happening, I said.

But it is, he said, and he smiled in the dark.

I made it back to the house I shared with Ben in time to greet him at the door, take his satchel. The shoulders of his jacket were wet with rain. He followed me into our kitchen. He refreshed me with apples. Outside the window behind his head, the trees blew sideways in dusty green light. Jack put his hands in his pockets and disappeared down the narrow cracking sidewalk. The hail came. We huddled in the center hallway, our heads in our arms. I trembled and sobbed and Ben stroked my hair. It's only rain, baby, he said. It's only thunder and wind. In running itself out of town, the storm stripped all the new life from the trees.

All night long from my bed, I looked for him, out the window for him. I told myself I would get up and go about the town. Through its streets and squares. So in my heart, I went out into the last cool film of rain. In my heart, I circled the town till morning. In my heart, I walked as far out as the Grain & Feed and repeated the same circumference over and over and over again, searching. The night was transparent and black. Across Gessing's fallow field, a spotted horse was tearing across the dark. Overhead, the stars burned and spun. Nightcrawlers all about my bare feet as though the earth itself had turned inside out. The universe repeated back to itself in puddles, lining the center of Main Street like a

strung out necklace. I am dark, I told the night, but I am
lovely. Tell him, tell him. I looked for him beneath the lamp
posts. In the doorways. Expected him on upon the back of
that magnificent and terrifying horse flashing past. But the
streets were empty. The fields were empty. The trees shook
aromatic rain from their boughs. Show me your voice, I
breathed, let me hear your voice. But I couldn't find him. Tell
him, I whispered into the wind through the open bedroom
window, my throat bare to the watery night, tell him I am
faint.

It was two days following when next I saw him in front
of the post office between the Stage Stop Motel and the
Depot Museum. A boy screeched past on the sidewalk on his
rusty tricycle over a glittering green spill of broken glass.
The wind blew my hair across my face.
I won't be seeing you again, he said.
Okay.
You can have the Plains Bar.
I don't want the Plains Bar.
I won't be there.
Okay.
Don't look for me.
Okay.
We probably shouldn't be in the same places.
I understand.
Don't speak to me.
Okay.
Don't look at me as if you know me. And don't call.
He had already turned his back and walked ten feet away
when I heard him say: Good to see you. A pleasantry I will
never again hear without flinching.

Such bottomless, appalling beauty in these men—dressed
in the flesh of Gessing's shining, shadow black cattle, rich
with dark blood and marbled with fat. Dressed in alfalfa, in
clover, in triticale, oat grass, and forbs. In the water shot

in circles from the great center pivots to the north. Each toils and eats in the daylight. Each has in his way found favor in the eyes of the Lord. But this woman—God will put me back out to sea. Send me over the rim of false indigo, rising like a blue shadow out of the ditch water. Send me back to the broken hems of the Front Range. A very great work it is, going over hills and mountains in an endless track where the rocks are impassable and the precipices such as no enemy could possibly enter or indeed climb up, or where if they did, no wall could hinder them. Trouble will find me in Denver. Trouble will find me in Salt Lake. Trouble will find me Phoenix. It always does. It gathers about my heart in a quick rush like the soft pleats of a dark skirt lifted up over my ribbing.

I've been driven out of town before. Not by men on horseback, not at gunpoint. But by women who pull their shades down when I come up the walk. By the fathers of young men who cross their arms, shut their doors. I set my bedroll in the dust behind the grain elevator, the clean line of center pivots spraying a fine white mist over the green surf. Ben wasn't two hundred yards away, inside what used to be our house, in some inner room. His parents were in there keeping the doors locked against me. Answering the telephone. He don't want to hear your voice, his mother said. You just go back to where you came from.

But there's no single place. I leaned against the rusted metal of the empty elevator. My mouth was bitter. The center pivots always wheel back around to where they started—slowly and over the course of several weeks, as if steered remotely by some unseen hand. Or say, rather, it is a beginningless spin, an inescapable watery ring, the perverted and unnatural condition upon which life out here paradoxically depends.

An hour passed. Two hours. Ben finally opened the window of what had been our little white bathroom and looked out at me huddled against the grain elevator. The sun was going down.

You can come back in, he said. His voice cracked. If you come back and promise you'll never—go out again.

I looked up at him. I said nothing. The wind moved through my hair, cold fingers across my throat. He closed the window.

It was dark enough by the time I walked into town that the windows of the Prairie Street Cafe hung like perfect, pale golden rectangles across the street. And there he was. Not waiting for me in the shadow, not beckoning from a distant estuary of earth and sky, but sitting in a red vinyl booth right in front, clear as if he were standing before me. He was sharing the booth with a woman, but it wasn't his girl. It could only have been his mother. She was leaning forward, hands folded before her. Two ceramic brown mugs between them. She was small and lovely. Her hair soft and thin and lightly gray. Jack Ryder had perhaps lived here all his life. This was his hometown. These were his people. I was an alien and a stranger among them.

She spoke slowly, looking at her son directly. He was holding his head in his hands, shaking his head in his hands. I knew the story he was telling. He would not lift his head. I could guess what he'd lost. Just look up once, I thought, imagining I could will him to do it. Just look up once. Look at me. I'll take you with me. I stood there on the sidewalk across the street in the shadows waiting until I got it. Until I saw the curve of the back of his neck, felt what the weight of his head must have been.

So continues my disordered flight, the devil in his long strides racing alongside. I fly like the wind over the land in my old and glittering Chevrolet. The sky reflected somehow in waving blue asphalt before me, as if I were upon some haunted freshet coursing west. I passed the broken spine of a long connected line of center pivots twisted and flattened by the storm. A three or four hundred thousand dollar loss, a wreck of metal strewn across the rye, and I felt a sickening echo in the center of my chest, an empty hollow five thousand fathoms deep. A familiar need to outrun my own body, to rush continually across the moving plains, which permit no record. I was seized by pale fear. My heart was as if it were dead within me. But this feeling goes away, I told myself. It goes away, it goes away, it goes away. The life comes back to it. I have been here before. I have told myself these same words before.

False Gods
Kelly Cherry

It had been a mistake, she realized—of course she realized this: did you think she was a fool?—to lend him money. It was not that he wanted more, however, but rather that he now seemed to think he owned her.

As if, lending him money, she had given him herself.

Henrietta was sixty-six; she had retired last year, a single woman in Richmond, Virginia, once the capital of the Confederacy, staid and conservative, belated in so many ways, now a place where you could actually buy a drink. Or go to dinner with a black man.

He had been so sweet in the beginning. He wasn't *un*-sweet now; he was just clinging and pressuring and wanting to get too close too fast. She had met him in the park near the Mosque. She had been eating a chocolate bar and had forgotten that she was still holding it, watching all the young people strolling or hastening by, young people with lives of adventure and passion. She had thought she would have adventures, too, and passion—how could there not be passion? Everyone's life had passion. Everyone's but hers, as it turned out. Going to work in the bank each morning, returning home to *La Petite Maman*, who needed dinner, some conversation, and later on, to be moved from chair to sofa to bed, and later on than that, to be turned in the bed, massaged, medicated, to have her thin white hair combed, her face washed and teeth brushed, to be changed, to be sponge-bathed, to be this, this, this, and this until the *this*es ran together into one long hiss like the sound of air escaping from a tire, life going flat.

Henrietta, lying on the hallway floor just inside her front door, was getting a stitch in her right side and rolled to the other side. Now she was facing into the living room. She had lived in this living room for over forty years, first as a trainee fresh from Mary Baldwin, her diploma framed and hanging on the wall alongside the class photograph taken on graduation day all of the girls in cap and gown and the snapshot of the synchronized swim team she had been on every year of her college career, and then as she made her way up through the bank's ranks, as a single woman looking after her mother. Her girlfriends used to tell her she needed to look after herself, but someone had to look after her mother, and it clearly was not going to be Bob or Clinton, both of whom had been in favor of putting their mother in a rest home as soon as the home would take her. *La Petite Maman*, as Henrietta, following family tradition, had come to call her—because she wasn't quite five feet tall and had the dainty, painted porcelain features of a doll—needed company and attention and, finally, care. Henrietta couldn't bear the thought of her sitting unspoken to all day long or plopped down at a cardtable to fill out a bridge set. Children owe their parents. Think of all those years of instructing, protecting, entertaining, think of all the Christmas presents and Easter baskets, the pets who had to be fed and walked and came to a bad end anyway (run over, stolen, lost), the report cards that had to be signed, the lunches that had to be packed, the clothes that had to be washed, the advice, the tears, the hopes. Children owe so much. Children pay so much.

Girl children, anyway. Bob and Clinton had got off almost scot-free. Henrietta pressed a palm hard against the floor.

La Petite Maman would never have thought of it like that, but she had expectations, that was for sure. She expected certain things of Henrietta. Things she didn't look to her sons for, such as attention or companionship or, finally, care. Or the time of day! Bob and Clinton sent their mother money, and later they began to send it to Henrietta, counting on her to use it wisely. They knew her as a fiscally responsible sister. She had welcomed each niece and nephew into the world with a General Electric stock certificate. She had never played bridge for real money. She paid her credit card balance promptly upon receipt of the bill. Could there be a more fiscally responsible person in the whole trickle-down goddamn world?

The chocolate bar had melted in the hot sun, and she had said, "Oh!" when she discovered that her fingers were covered with chocolate. He had been walking past just then, and he took in her predicament and offered her a tissue. "Thank you," she said. In spite of herself, she hesitated before taking the tissue, but she really had no choice unless she wanted chocolate all over her skirt.

"You're welcome," he said.

"You are not from around here," she observed.

"I've come down from Providence," he said.

At first she thought he was some kind of crazy preacher.

"In Rhode Island," he added.

"I know where Providence is."

She was trying to decide how old he was, but he could be fifty or seventy-five. His hair was gray.

"Ah, yes. I should know by now never to underestimate a Southern woman."

It had been a while since anyone had made much of her Southern womanhood. Being Southern was practically the same as being an anachronism these days. Not even Southerners were very Southern anymore. Even Henrietta had changed.

At one time Henrietta had been a believer in states' rights. She *had* thought restaurant owners should serve blacks, but because blacks were human beings and it was the morally right thing to do, not because someone in power said they had to serve them. After all, it was the restaurant owner who owned the restaurant, not the federal government.

She would not admit to anyone now that she had thought that. Now she was ashamed of her ignorance, ashamed that she had been prejudiced and didn't even know it. She hid it the same way she hid the information that she was a descendant of slave owners. There had been plantations, ladies in hoop skirts, dreamy gentlemen who could recite Latin poetry and oversee the tobacco harvest, and Henrietta had never doubted *La Petite Maman* when she told her that *her* mother, Ma'am, had said the slaves were so well treated that after the war they didn't want to leave *Grandmère*. (Her friend Betsy said that all formerly proud Southern families consoled themselves with this myth.)

"We've had to learn to make our way in the world," Henrietta said.

"It must not have been easy but I can tell from your red hair that you have a lot of spunk."

Henrietta stiffened. She thought he must be making fun of her.

"You have beautiful hair," he said.

"I want you to tell me," Henrietta had instructed her hairdresser repeatedly, "when it is time for me to stop dyeing my hair red. I don't want to become one of those little old redheaded ladies!"

Her hairdresser, an overworked survivor of two marriages with three children, two of whom were in college and the third of whom, six years old and not yet in school because his birthday fell in April, she brought to work with her, would not tell Henrietta that she already had become one of those little old redheaded ladies.

"Hon," Henrietta had said to the six-year-old, "I don't think you should play with the scissors."

The hairdresser had snatched the scissors from little Leon's curious hands and replaced them with a toy video game.

Henrietta did not understand video games, toy or otherwise, and she did not know how to talk with a child, although she was vaguely acquainted with several. Among her friends were whole families, and there was nothing provincial about them. One family was Cambodian; another had come from Saudi Arabia. But their children waited in the background, seen, not heard.

If she thought about it, she had to admit that she couldn't stand that kid, the hairdresser's kid, Leon. She had once heard him ask his mother why she was fixing the hair of "that old lady." "She'd look better with a bald head," he had said, laughing at either his wit or the image—who could tell with children. Boys were brutes. His mother had smacked him on the top of his head, but he just stuck out his tongue at his mother when she turned her back on him. Henrietta had seen it, the disgusting, bumpy pink tongue. "You look like a frog," she had said to him when his mother went to mix the color, "a stupid frog with a stupid long tongue. If you don't watch out, you'll catch a fly."

Leon had started crying loudly. The hairdresser rushed over. "What happened?" she asked Henrietta.

"Nothing," Henrietta said.

"She called me a frog," Leon said.

"A frog?" The hairdresser raised her eyebrows at Henrietta in query.

"Children," Henrietta said. "They have such wild imaginations."

Leon wouldn't speak to her after that. He didn't even look at her again until his mother had rotated Henrietta in the styling chair in front of the big mirror, holding a hand mirror up in back, waiting for Henrietta's approval. "A good job," Henrietta pronounced. The hairdresser sighed a sigh of relief. She went to the cashier to give her the total while Henrietta gathered her purse and glasses and magazine. Before she followed her to the counter, Henrietta stuck out her tongue at Leon.

Thank god she had never had kids. Girls were no better than boys, just different. The girls were liars. How could she not know this, having been one herself? To fool people, to hurt people, to make people feel *good*—girls told lies because that was the only kind of power permitted to them, the power to alter the world of appearances.

Jesus, did her hairdresser really think Henrietta should still be dyeing her hair red? Did she really think Henrietta did not know she was a pathetic, skinny-ass spinster who should have quit wearing high heels a century ago? Did she really not know that her son was a six-year-old creep with a scissor fetish who in all likelihood tortured small animals for amusement?

The black man sat down beside her, which was somewhat forward of him. Though it was, after all, a public bench. "Let's be realistic: time gets to us all but I can tell that you were a beautiful woman. Still are, if you ask me."

She took off her glasses so he could see her eyes. She rubbed the top of her nose where the glasses pinched so he wouldn't think she had taken them off just so he could see her eyes. She placed the glasses back on her nose. She had recently been toying with the idea of having Lasik surgery.

He leaned farther back into the bench, stretching his legs out. She could smell the sweat on his skin, see the muscles moving in his neck. But he was not a teenager, not one of those young men who travel in packs for the express purpose of frightening women, but a middle-aged, well-spoken African American (such a mouthful to have to remember!) gentleman. He took the used tissue from her and wadded it up and set it down on his side of the bench.

"Thank you for assisting a lady in distress," she said, drawling only a little more than normally and cocking her head to the side and smiling slightly to let him know that she was being ironic.

Wait! Wait, now! Henrietta was *not* a fool: She thought women should get equal pay for equal work. She thought there was nothing a man could do that a woman couldn't do, and if she found modern technology perplexing and untrustworthy, she had friends her age and older who could email their grandchildren, take digital pictures of their trips to Europe or the Orient, trade stocks online. But a man was not a piece of technology, and neither was she. She was a graduate of St. Catherine's and Mary Baldwin. She had made her debut in 1953 in a strapless white tulle with black velvet sash, and she hadn't needed glasses yet, and although her father had not been able to attend, it was because he was in Washington on important business at the State Department, and her brothers had been there to act as escorts. That had been a night—the air scented with lilac, all the debutantes in white or pastel, their skirts swishing over the dance floor, rose petals floating like dream boats in crystal bowls on white linen tablecloths. Henrietta's red hair, natural then, made her shine as bright as a candle as she danced, as if she were a moving flame. She had felt dangerous and even powerful in a way she had never heard anybody talk about.

Things had been lost that could never be recovered: private nightclubs where you could wear a cocktail dress and smoke with a cigarette holder; a respectful, exciting flirtatiousness; the reciprocal promises of submission and protection. How Henrietta longed to be have someone at her side, a defender, a companion. She had been on her own all her life, not counting *La Petite Maman*; but how she longed for company, a partner, as one might long for a cup of cocoa on a cold day or money in the bank.

"I've had my eye on you," he said. "I've seen you around, walking into that bank you like to go to."

And right then a warning bell had gone off in her head. How could it not?

But he said, "I just couldn't take my eyes off you."

"Do you really expect me to believe that?" she asked.

"Believe it or not, it's true," he said.

She knew it was not true but nothing about flirting had ever been true, had it? The whole point of it was that it was a game. And how could she argue with him? If she did, she would appear needy and desperate, hungry for compliments. Which maybe she was, but she would not allow herself to appear that way.

He offered to walk her home. At first she demurred, unsure whether she should let him know where she lived, but then she remembered the speaker system, her friends in the building, his thoughtful tissue, and allowed him to accompany her. She was as liberated as the next woman.

When he held out his hand to say good-bye, she looked first at her own, turned it over as if inspecting it for chocolate stains, laughed lightly, and then shook his hand, thanking him sincerely.

Then, before he turned away, he asked her out for a drink. "I do love a cocktail," she murmured, remembering that in the old days it had not been possible to go out for a drink in this city, but now it was, now there were singles bars and theater lofts and jazz clubs and karaoke. Now there were poetry slams and cineplexes where the soundtrack from another movie was always leaking in from the theater next to the one you were in. In the movie you were watching, a man and a woman would be speaking quietly, urgently, their monstrously long legs and arms entwined with one another and the bed covers, and next door you heard gunshots, heroes and villains slugging it out on a cliff or suspension bridge, a car chase. Now the once-glorious azaleas in the median strip on Monument Boulevard were pinched and scrawny (they were aging, she thought, like herself).

She remembered having read at Mary Baldwin a description by Henry James of her city's "historic poverty" and her professor's explaining that James had meant that Richmond's history had been one of worshiping idols. *False gods.* She remembered that phrase. Now that she was old enough to have a history of her own, she could see that it was just like James had said Richmond's was. She had always valued the wrong thing, and by the time she realized it, it was always too late to redeem herself.

So of course—of course!—she said yes.

A shooting pain in her left hip woke Henrietta around three in the morning. She woke up breathing wood. She listened carefully for any noises from the outside hallway. There were none so she stood up, wincing as she let her weight settle on both legs evenly and compressing her lips to keep from groaning. There were rails in her panty hose. She crept to the door, put an ear to the crack. Still nothing. She looked out the peephole. The hallway bent and curved as if she were viewing it through a fishbowl, but Bill was gone. All the same, she did not want to risk turning on the light—he might return—and felt her way to her bedroom in the dark. She got into bed still in her clothes and pulled the top sheet up to her chin, clutching it with both hands. The window's drawn shade had begun to define its oblong shape, the sky beyond it lightening, before she fell asleep again.

The first time Bill picked her up at her apartment, he was wearing brown trousers, a blue shirt with a tie looped around the open neck, loafers, and a brown leather jacket. "You look nice," he said to her.

They went to a restaurant in a mall, a place more comfortable, more for older people than the restaurants in her neighborhood, which were always crowded with students shouting over the earsplitting music. They chatted over drinks and then he urged her to stay for dinner. He told her about growing up in Providence, about his physician father and seamstress mother. He had been an only child.

His attractive appearance, the drink, the baked swordfish, the murmurings at adjacent tables, the reduced lighting, his soothing voice, good manners, soft laugh—all these worked in her a mood of relaxation. She let her hands linger on the tablecloth and he reached over and clasped both of them in one of his. She had a B&B. He paid the check.

She didn't invite him into her apartment, and he seemed to respect her for it, but she was in turmoil. She had gone to her gynecologist for her annual checkup. Her gynecologist had talked to her about vaginal atrophy and had given her a prescription for a medicinal cream that was to help her with that—because when she asked Henrietta if she'd like something for that, Henrietta had said yes, because you never knew—and Henrietta had gotten the prescription filled but she'd never opened the box. She dug the box out of a bathroom cabinet and read the instructions. The box warned her against using the cream for very long. Death was a possible side-effect. She put the box back in the cabinet. She would wait to see how things developed.

She went out with him several times—to the park, to the museum, to a movie—and then he began to turn up unannounced. At first she liked this, liked that he felt close enough not to stand on ceremony, liked that he liked to be with her. She thought he might be falling in love with her. He might even want to marry her.

At this late date! But Henrietta thought, Well, it's my turn; it's my turn to have some happiness. She thought about Bill all the time. She thought how she'd show people, getting married at last. She thought about his good manners, his take-charge profile, his large, capable hands. She began to forget that he was black, or, no, she began to think that if she were married to him, she would never again have to wonder if she was a racist. She began to appreciate the distinguished sound of "African American." She might be falling in love with him.

But then he told her he needed money to pay off debts, to clear his name—Bill Crowe was his name—so he could find a job. If his name were cleared, he said, he could find a job as a night watchman, a campus security guard, a crossing guard—things he had done before. (He was good at protecting.) "What have you been using to pay for our dates?" she asked him bluntly, modernly. "I saved some cash before coming south," he said. By then she was ready to believe anything he said. It never occurred to her that he might have conned it out of another woman.

At first, it felt like she was paying him back what he'd spent on her, and that was all right; she didn't mind going Dutch. And at first, she had given small amounts to him over deli or sushi or miso in her apartment or at a neighborhood restaurant, but he began showing up at all hours, leaning on the buzzer and banging on the outside door until she had no choice but to let him in, and frequently he was high. That was where her money was going, of course, crack or pot or pills or something she didn't even know the name of. She no longer let him into the apartment. She suggested he might get help. She threatened to call the police. Her neighbors complained to her and told her that if she didn't get rid of him, they might have to take the problem to committee. But she had been in this apartment forever! Henrietta would wait until the banging and shouting stopped. When it was clear it was not going to resume, she would get up from the floor and go into the living room. If she were the type she supposed others thought of her as, she would pour herself a drink, and it would be on top of others, but she was not the drinking type. You couldn't be the drinking type and still lay out your clothes for the next day. She had *absolutely no vices*, she thought, seeing the words like the lead in an ad. *La Petite Maman* would have told her that it was high time she got some.

He wasn't always high. Sometimes he was as courteous as he had been that day in the park. When he was, it made her heart ache, an actual pain, as if someone had hurled a baseball smack into her chest. A pain that tore at her all the more because of the hopes she had had. But sometimes at night, he would wait until someone was entering the building, and he'd come in with them, and then he'd talk to her through the door about how much he wanted to make love to her, and she would curl up on the floor inside where she could listen and not have to do anything.

Perhaps, she thought, her apartment was a bit fussy, cluttered with the memorabilia of a lifetime, perhaps a stale odor had settled into the corners of the kitchen, and perhaps the picture frames had dulled, the hall floor sagged. It was hard to see these things when you lived with them, but she saw them from the perspective of her position on the floor behind the closed front door.

She didn't call the police. She couldn't stand the thought of the humiliation that would cause her, plus she didn't want to get Bill into more trouble than he was already in. Maybe, she thought, he had planned something like this from the beginning, picking her out as an easy mark, but she remembered the things they had shared, the meals they had eaten, and she worked hard not to believe this of him. At the same time, she could not bear the thought of moving out of her apartment building, so she continued to give him money just to make him quiet down. She would slide an envelope with cash under the door to her apartment, and he would seize it as soon as the tip of the envelope appeared on the other side. Then he would crouch down and talk to her some more through the crack under the door. "Henrietta," he would say softly, "sweet Henrietta, don't you miss seeing me? I miss you. I miss you so much."

In the beginning, he used to joke about how they could hold up the bank where she had worked. "I'll drive the getaway car," he said, "and you'll come out with the money and we'll drive away to California." Was he joking or was he serious?

What she needed was a man—not money, not cocoa. Feminism was good but the only thing that protected you from a man was another man.

Or a woman so old that no man wanted to have to deal with her. If *La Petite Maman* were alive, Henrietta would not have to lie on the floor like this, rigid and breathless, until he got tired of trying to entice her to open the door and left.

La Petite Maman had known how to handle men. She had known how to keep men at bay. And even when she didn't— even after her mind had failed and she had forgotten who her daughter was—Henrietta had known how to use her to keep men at bay.

La Petite Maman had made decisions, acted, started things and put a stop to them. *La Petite Maman* was never at a loss, and she had made sure Henrietta wasn't either. If *La Petite Maman* were still alive, Henrietta would not be in this predicament, this absurd predicament. If only *La Petite Maman* would come back to this world right now, scold Henrietta and say, "Go wash your face, dear, and comb your hair nicely; I need you to accompany me to Mrs. Lipschitz's house. She's not doing well and we must cheer her up." If only *La Petite Maman* would say, "Henrietta, stop this this minute. Get up off that floor and call the police or a friend. Get hold of yourself." She would say, "What do you think you're doing, crawling down the hallway as if you were a soldier in enemy territory. You live here!" And so on. "Don't you dare walk down the hall to the liquor closet, don't you dare open that bottle, don't you dare pour yourself a drink, don't you dare, don't you dare."

But it served *La Petite Maman* right if Henrietta crawled on her stomach. *La Petite Maman* was not around to tell her to stop being afraid.

La Petite Maman was not around to stop her from giving money to Bill Crowe.

La Petite Maman was not around to tell Henrietta that if she was smart enough to become a bank manager, she was smart enough to make some new friends and forget Bill Crowe. (Until she retired, there had been co-workers.)

La Petite Maman was not around to buy her a Valentine's Day card. One that said something like, "To my beautiful daughter."

In the morning Henrietta dressed in the outfit she had set out the evening before: a pale yellow wool suit with brass buttons on the jacket and gold braid edging the slanted pockets; a crisp white cotton shirt; bone-colored heels and matching stockings. February in Richmond was chilly and often rainy, and sometimes there were sudden deep snowstorms, but today the sky was bright blue, and there would be neither snow nor rain. Crocuses were pushing their way up through the small patches of lawn in front of renovated townhouses in the Fan district, and cherry trees and dogwood were poised for spring, bark of bare limbs glistening, buds swelling. A few porch lights left on all night, by design or because someone had forgotten to turn them off, flicked off now. Cars seemed to awaken with a slight shudder, a soft moan, as if the night's dreams had been indulgent and persistent, hanging on a moment longer.

Not long ago, Henrietta would have walked from her

apartment building to the bank where she worked, stowed her purse in the bottom righthand drawer of her desk, and reviewed her file of current work while drinking the cup of coffee she allowed her assistant, Owen, to bring her. Owen was now Ralston 's assistant. He greeted her warmly as she walked through the doors and across the lobby to his desk. "Henrietta! What brings you here? Shouldn't you be on a cruise, or at least sleeping in?" She had started as a teller and worked her way up to manager of her branch.

Owen was twenty years younger than Henrietta. When he first came to work at the bank, she used to hope he'd ask her out, but there was not only the age difference, there was the fact that she was his boss. She thought he might be homosexual, but then again, maybe he was just a bit effeminate. Many men were, just as many women were masculine, and it didn't necessarily mean anything.

"I need to make a withdrawal," she said.

"Didn't you make one last week?"

She did not answer him. It was not his place to note how frequently she did or did not make withdrawals from her account. She adjusted her glasses and gazed at him expressionlessly, something she had learned to do when she was just starting out and had to find a way to handle the men who were her superiors and wanted to sleep with her and the ones who were her inferiors but would soon climb past her up the ladder to success. Early on, she had decided she was not going to be used, but she also wasn't going to make enemies of people who would be in a position to help or hurt her career. And then later, she had *La Petite Maman* to look after, and she felt it was important to focus on her career since a man wasn't likely to propose if it meant having to support them both. Betsy had questioned her strategy. "Do you seriously think being an independent professional woman is a way to attract a man?" she'd asked Henrietta. "You don't think that when a man is attracted to an independent professional woman, it's in spite of her being independent and professional?" But what was a girl to do? When her father died, *La Petite Maman* discovered that his money had vanished (like the old Richmond, it had been lost and was unrecoverable); what remained after a series of bad investments had trickled-down straight into the hands of probate lawyers and real-estate agents. Vassar had gone out the window and she'd enrolled at Mary Baldwin instead.

Owen, who surely knew before he asked about the withdrawal that he should not have asked but honored friendship above business had run after Ralston, who came out to say hello to Henrietta and invite her into his office for a cup of coffee. The sun was shining straight through the bank windows onto Ralston's face, and she could see all the pores in his nose as if someone were holding a magnifying glass up to his face. His cheeks were crisscrossed with thin threads of broken capillaries. She followed him into his office. "Henrietta," he said, softly, "how are you?"

"Why, Rals, I'm having the time of my life," she said. "I spend my days doing only what I feel like doing. Retirement is great! You should try it sometime."

"When you have a family—" he said.

"Oh, I know, we can't always retire as early as we'd like. I had *La Petite Maman*—"

"Henrietta?"

"If I hadn't had *La Petite Maman*, I swear I would have taken down my shingle long ago!"

"Henrietta, I certainly wouldn't ask you this if you were just a customer, but we've known each other for a long time, and I can't help worrying about you. Nor can Owen. You're family to us. We've noticed that you've been making frequent withdrawals. Forgive me but you're not in any kind of trouble, are you, Henrietta?"

"Now see here, Ralston Quivey. I appreciate your concern and all, but what business is it of yours when and how much of my own money I withdraw?"

"It's none of my business, I admit. I just don't want you to have to be a bag lady, Henrietta." He smiled to suggest he was exaggerating. "I certainly hope you are going to live another forty years—"

"Time enough to wander in the wilderness!" she cried, suddenly wondering if the yellow suit with its brass buttons and gold braid was too brazen with her red hair. Why did she say that, she wondered. Didn't she sound hysterical? Didn't she know that a professional woman must never appear hysterical?

Ralston leaned back in his managerial chair, looking at her managerially. "I guess so," he said.

"Richmond was such a proper place forty years ago," Henrietta said. "Prim and proper. Even after the marches and riots started elsewhere, you couldn't get anything going in Richmond. Nothing organized, anyway. People didn't want to muss their clothes is all I can figure."

"That was a long time ago."

She was observing that Ralston was in a pinstripe suit, the tie red with dark blue diagonal stripes. "I knew a girl from a very wealthy family who never wore new clothes in public. She would wear her new clothes indoors for a week, until they had gotten rumpled and the shine was gone so when she went out in them she would not look as though she were showing off. This was because it was bad form to display your money. You could have more money than your neighbors, but you weren't supposed to act like it."

"I'm just trying to look out for your best interests, Henrietta. It's what you once said you wanted me to do."

"Oh, it is, it is. I just—it's just—things come up, you know?" She spread her hands in a gesture of helplessness, a gesture she had made so often in her life that it now occurred to her that she was acting a role, something staged and set and not particularly meaningful anymore.

"Well, you were a manager before I was, Henrietta. I imagine you know what you're doing."

"I imagine I do," she said, as sweetly and dangerously as Scarlett O'Hara might have said it, but on the way out, she saw herself reflected in the polished elevator doors and thought, Scarlett O'Hara! Baby Jane in *Whatever Happened to Baby Jane?* is more like it! And the thought made her so sad that instead of going to the park where she still liked to sit watching the students and noticing all the latest fashions and ornaments—even with shaven heads or green hair, they looked so beautiful, full of life—instead of going to the park, she went back home, where she took the money from her purse and slipped it into a plain white envelope.

But after her neighbors threatened to call the cops themselves if she didn't put an end to Bill Crowe's loud intrusions, and she stopped giving him money, Bill stopped calling. A year later, her heart lurched like a sailor on shore leave when she spotted the card under her door. She opened it with shaking hands.

It was a valentine.

A week late, but a valentine.

Sweet Henrietta, he had written. And he signed it *Love, Your Bill.*

She showed the valentine to Betsy at lunch.

Betsy ran her fingertips over the paper lace edging.

"He signed it 'love,'" Henrietta said.

Betsy handed the card back to her. "Henny," Betsy said, "sweetie, you know that doesn't necessarily mean anything."

Henrietta's face felt as fragile as fine stemware; it felt as though any expression she might make would shatter it to shards, and she tried to show nothing. "I guess not," she said. They had both ordered chicken croquettes and the house salad with ice water to drink. She had never told Betsy about the sums she had lent—given—Bill.

"It could, though," Betsy said. For thirty years, Betsy had been the secretary for Epiphany Episcopal, and Henrietta had often thought that her voice had acquired a sort of carpeted sound, a hint of the vestry, something efficiently organized and quietly liturgical. "I had an aunt who fell in love and got married at eighty-eight."

Every time Henrietta left or returned to her apartment,

she thought that this time Bill might be waiting for her. She kept an eye out for him when she went to the bank. With the valentine in her purse, she had been relieved and rejuvenated to think that he had not been after her only for her money but had indeed been smitten by her, had maybe even been in love with her. As time passed, she began to hope—how could she ever explain this to anyone—that what he had wanted *was*, after all, the money, because she still had money in the bank, but every day she lost a little more of her looks. If he waited too long, he would run in the opposite direction when he saw her. If he waited too long, she would be eighty-eight.

Sometimes Henrietta bought herself a chocolate bar and ate it while she sat on the bench. She couldn't always finish it and pitched the uneaten part into the trash bin. Brand-new spring leaves put in an appearance and deepened into dark green as summer came and went. The grass became brown. Fallen leaves were raked. Corn husks and snaggle-toothed pumpkins turned up on front stoops. It turned cold. Now there was an electric candle in every window, and through some of the windows you could see Christmas trees or a menorah on a mantel. Henrietta understood that Bill Crowe was never coming back.

"I should have trusted his feeling for me," she said to Betsy over the phone.

Betsy didn't say anything.

"I should have married him," Henrietta said.

"Sweetie," Betsy said, "he didn't ask you. You have to tell yourself the truth about this, Henny."

"He might have. You don't know for sure that he wouldn't. I should have slept with him."

"You didn't?"

Now Henrietta was silent.

"You really didn't?" Then Betsy laughed. "Now that was probably a mistake."

Henrietta told her hairdresser about Bill and they talked

about the vagaries of men, how even the best of them needed a woman to provide them with a sense of direction. "A moral compass," Henrietta said, remembering that her father had thought that weasel McCarthy was right about the Communists. He had also thought J. Robert Oppenheimer was a security risk. He had been a warrior for The Cold War. But who was she to be angry with him for his bad judgment? Her father's daughter had always been a step behind the march of time, too. Freedom riders had been shot while she was *dancing*. There had been rioting in the streets while she was taking a seminar in *mutual funds*. And you couldn't blame it on merely being a little slow to catch up; she was not a good person. She knew it by the way she kept tripping over her own emotional circuitry, setting off alarms and starting small fires that she had to rush to put out. She knew it and knew it was something she had to hide from others.

With a well-tailored suit. Classic gold jewelry, including an expensive but unostentatious watch. Good shoes. Good manners.

Yes, she had tried to look after *La Petite Maman* better than her father or brothers had, but only because society said it was the daughter's responsibility to look after the mother.

She had tried to hide that, as well—hide the resentment she felt—but *La Petite Maman* had known, she was sure of it. Had known and had found every possible way to flay her daughter because of it. *Bring me an iced tea. Wash this blanket. Come here. Do that. Don't do that. Do this. Bring me an iced tea. What a pity you never married, then it wouldn't be just the two of us. Come here. Bring me an iced tea.*

The hairdresser spun her in the chair. "How is Leon doing?" Henrietta asked, thinking how much more pleasant her salon appointments were now that he was in school.

"Oh, he's reading like a house afire."

"No more video games?"

"Well," she said. "I don't think I'd bet on that." She blasted Henrietta with the hair spray. "You think he'll be back? Mr. Crowe?"

"What do you think?" Henrietta asked, knowing the answer would be a lie but wanting to hear it and take heart from it anyway.

"I think that if he could see you now—"

She wandered down to the bank for a visit. Were they weary of her, she wondered, but she had nothing else to do. She was reassured when at the bank, Ralston said to her, "You always brighten our day."

Owen came into Ralston's office and handed her a cup of coffee. In a real china cup, not Styrofoam. Not a mug. He stood by her elbow while she stirred. The spoon clinked against the saucer. "How are you, Owen?" she asked.

"It's not the same place without you," he said. "It never will be."

She peered at him through her new glasses. She had splurged on the frames, gold wire in the small, rectangular shape that had become fashionable. She took a good look at him, trying to decide if he was a homosexual.

It was no use. She just couldn't tell.

"You're looking well," Owen said—ungrammatically, in Henrietta's opinion, but she didn't say anything because she knew the modern world didn't care that *well* was an adverb.

There was a time when she would have said, "I should hope so, Owen! These glasses cost me a fortune!"

"Your hair is lovely," he said.

Rals Quivey tapped his pen against the edge of his desk. Maybe, Henrietta thought, he believed his assistant was being too forward with her.

She put her cup and saucer on his desk and stood up. "It's always nice to see you both," she said.

"You too, Henrietta," Ralston said, also rising.

"Owen," she asked, turning to face him, "won't you see me out?" She slipped into her red coat, which she'd never really taken off but had kept draped around her shoulders.

"Of course, Henrietta!" Owen held out an arm for her. Maybe she was an old fool, looking for love in all the wrong places, but she had once been a show-stopper in a one-piece swimsuit, and weren't those suits, not the tank suits that squashed you up top and sagged in the seat but the ones the Mary Baldwin team wore for their end-of-year performance, with structured cups, and crotches tucked away beneath the latex sheath, weren't they more tantalizing than a Brazilian thong? She had once been a redheaded show-stopper, a dancing debutante, a graduate of the class of 1957, and a sleek and lively teller tackling a man's world of privilege and perks, and there was at least as much hope for her as there had been for Betsy's aunt. She took his arm but in the lobby Owen reclaimed it, said "Don't be a stranger," and turned back toward the elevator. She was on her own.

She experienced again that sensation of performing a role for the umpteenth time, of pretending to be herself. That old worn costume, her body, weighed on her, dragged her down. Would she be able to make her arms and legs go, could she ever say anything she had not already said? She felt trembly and faint, or maybe just faintish..Cold and sweating, she put out a hand and touched the outside wall of the bank to steady herself and then made the mistake of looking at her hand. The skin was thin, the blue veins raised like elevated trains. Her knuckles had thickened with arthritis. She was old. Too old to begin again. What was she to do? How would she traverse the long, lonely, empty years ahead? She took one step, then another. Ahead of her, a young mother pushed a pram. A cat slept on the sidewalk in the shade of a parked truck. She stopped where she stood, watching the carriage recede, the cat uncurl and stretch. Oh, she felt lightheaded and dizzy, and for one wild moment, as she looked around, she did not know where she was.

Louring Age
Laura L. Sullivan

*It is folly alone that stays the fugue of Youth and beats
off louring Old Age.
Erasmus – In Praise of Folly*

You would think our lives expand as we age, but no. Mine began with the world and contracted to a hypodermic prick in my vein.

In 1918, not that I knew anything then, being an infant, I sailed to India with my diplomat father. In 1919 it was China, in 1922 when I was just beginning to awake to the world, it was …

Nasty little thing, look at him, with his pug. What kind of dog is that for a healthy young man? Hate dogs altogether, but anything I could kill with my heel is the limit.

"Hello, Henry!" I called merrily. "How are June and the Giblet?" One of the many blessings of advanced age lies in being able to say unpleasant things with a smile and get away with it. Their offspring looked like a fat slimy red piece of turkey viscera, and so that's what I called it. Fool took it for a pet name and beamed at me.

"Oh, swell, swell," he replied, too loudly. I'm not deaf, you cat's turd. I narrowed my eyes menacingly at him but realized he would only think me nearsighted and gave up.

"I'm going to India tomorrow," I lied, tired of being predictable.

"Oh, swell, swell," was all he said.

Then Russia until I was ten.

"Oh, I'm sorry, did I tread on dear Pug's foot. My, what a voice he has!" Wretched brute. I know he digs up my daylilies.

What a treat Russia was for a young thing, all troikas

and skating and notes passed in fur muffs. Is there still a Russia? Even then we had just started calling it the USSR, and of course Daddy had to call it that in public, but he was a Romantic, and at home it was Russia til the day he died.

What came next … Poland? No, that was later, just before the war. Oh, of course, Italy. Then we all skittered to London, Daddy and his old maid daughter. What was that about leading apes in hell? Old maids, or virgins, or were they once presumed to be one and the same? Then the bombings and I went to America, the homeland for which I had no proper accent. To this day, no one can quite tell where I come from, aside from the nebulous *somewhere else.*

Certainly not here.

There's that odd little teenaged creation, sitting on her rock. I wonder if she'll acknowledge me? You never can tell. Most of the time, she's in her own private sulk, but occasionally, she sounds a proper little lady. Probably when she's high. Someone should tell her you should never smoke pot before dark.

"Hello, Mrs. Millais." High.

"Hullo, dear, how goes the egoistic self expression?"

She looked at me blankly. Today it was pitchy hair with an underpaint of violet, and if I'm not mistaken, a new piercing. Not to my taste but then I am from a different era. In my late teens, I took up with a clan of artistic naturists who with deliberate, elaborate nonchalance, would strip for *un petit dejeuner sur l'herbe.* A daubed memoir of my rebellion is still on display in the National Gallery.

She looked at me with exquisitely rehearsed pathos and said, head cocked a-side, "I think old people are so brave." I do believe she sighed.

I almost looked about for an old person, then realized. Ye gods and little fishes. Is that what they think of me? Brave old Millie hobbling along on her walker to buy gin?

"Fuck you," I mumbled, but at ninety-three such a thing was so improbable I think she willed herself to not understand.

"You're welcome," she replied and started to paint her toenails.

She probably thinks I should be in a home. Look at me in this tiny little life, almost poor, almost dead. Brave? If I was brave I'd pack up my kit bag, cash in my IRA and go to Tibet or Cuba or Iran or wherever you can't go today. Brave? I once rode across the Sahara, some of it anyway, on camelback, now I live in fear that one wrong step will break my hip. Sometimes I forget what I am and start to cut a caper, then almost have apoplexy when I think what could have happened.

If I was brave I'd chuck it all. But it's so much easier to be comfortable, safe.

Brave? Leave me alone, you horrid young thing.

How on earth did I fall into all of this? This sameness, this smallness.

And here's the zoo of nincompoops and ninnies, of those unfortunates who, unlike me, have lost their brains to age. Or maybe they never had any to begin with, and they too use age as an excuse.

Those with more stake in the future fought against its construction, the way one might object to an insane asylum or a crematorium in one's backyard. They didn't want to be constantly depressed by the sight of their own futures, an institution of senile Cassandras harping on their fates.

The Restful Glen Home for the Aged. Unspoken is added the Decrepit, the Enfeebled, the Fossilized, the Geriatric Dregs. Every person in there—if indeed they still count as people—has the scourge Alzheimer's.

What a traitor the mind is. Worse than the body, for even in youth, an ankle will twist or a tooth ache, reminding us of our mortality. The mind should be the divine essence, incorruptible. But no, even gods die or prove greedy or gluttonous or just plain stupid. The Greeks knew that, and the Norse. Why are we still learning?

Poor wandering souls. I walk my two miles, my two hours, every day, but they just mill without even a bottle of gin at the end. The grounds are lovely for the sake of visiting relatives, but do the inmates even see it? Or, oh joy, do they see it afresh each moment, reawakened? Suddenly I'm drawn to them, as if they are some odd biological specimens, great apes, like and not like.

They are confined by a simple gate, low wrought iron with a u-shaped latch. I lift it and enter, feeling like the interloper I am. Some officious nurse will shoo me away soon, like an ogling old man at the playground. But no one notices me.

Of course. They do not know that I am really a gamboling girl of sixteen at a ball in Vienna. They only see the ancient hag with a walker. I am one of them. I am accepted.

I feel ill.

No, no, I am in disguise. This is an adventure. At once I see the possibilities. In the kingdom of the blind …

I spot a woman at a table alone with a deck of cards. She is laying them out in a haphazard way that smacks vaguely and inaccurately of solitaire. I sit down with a flash of good intention, but soon my devil takes over. I make up a game, I explain the rules. She smiles, nods, seems to understand. I let her win. I ask if she has any money. Two twenties, folded impossibly small in a change purse. I win them. I ask if she has any more money. She smiles, beatific, blissful, fumbles in her change purse, a gift from some grandchild, and says, "I thought I had some in here." She frowns. Am I discovered? No. "It must be in my room." She wanders off and does not return. No matter. I have found a lovely addle-pated old man at the shuffleboard court. He only has twelve dollars but soon it is mine.

My heart quivers like an incipient infarction. This is wrong I suppose but so was smoking opium in China. So was seeing a pony show in the Philippines, cheering the poor whore on to greater exertions. So was stealing Vera's husband then dropping them both in boredom. This is a victimless crime. I am alive, thrilling. I am young.

Moving among them, like one of those wooly dogs

raised with their flock of sheep, I fleece those fogies the world would call my peers. But see! I am not like them! I have sharp teeth!

I've reaped more than two hundred dollars by the time I feel the insistent whimper of cocktail hour calling me home. I will do this again. Not too soon. Whenever I feel low. Whenever some chit tells me old people are so brave. I roll across the sward on my walker, feeling lissome as a schoolgirl.

"Where are we going now, Margaret?" a saccharine voice cooed, and firm hands spun me effortlessly on a new trajectory. A colored woman—I can't break the habit of calling them that, though I marched in Mississippi—wearing scrubs with some grinning yellow cartoon character on them, shoved me gently toward the main building.

"I'm not Margaret," I told her crossly, refraining by superhuman effort from calling her a great sow.

"Who is it today, dearie? Agatha? That's your sister you know. Or the queen? Come along now. Suppertime."

I stared at her for all I was worth and said, "My name is Anne Millais. Take your hands off me."

But she didn't look at me, wouldn't look at me. Couldn't look at me. I was just an Old Person.

She got on a little radio clipped to her hip. "Could you send some help? Margaret's getting ornery again." She looked, not at me, but at my ankle. "Where's your bracelet, Margaret?" She sighed. "They get them off all the time, then the admin blames us if they escape." I was they to her, a lump of congealed years.

She tried to pull me again but I batted her hands away and began to curse with the ease of a diplomat's daughter in six languages. "I'm not Margaret, you ignorant negress," I said at last. Even this didn't touch her. She locked on to me and waited for her backup. I gave her the old Pug treatment and stepped on her toes. She squealed and let go and I, struggling for freedom, found myself falling in that terrible slow motion of inevitability. I knew how it would be before

I hit the grass. Bone popped and cracked, and there was a grinding more than a pain as my hip broke.

"Now you've gone and done it," the nurse said. I forgot I was a lady and spit at her.

They carried me, screaming and cursing, inside, calling me Margaret all the while and when I slapped another nurse they strapped me down and jabbed that serpent's tooth of Versed into my vein, and everything was gone.

Over the next week they kept me well-drugged. I suppose there was a hospital but other than a sense of whiteness and a bleach and urine smell, I don't recall it.

Here I am, in Margaret's bed at Restful Glen. Where are you, lucky Margaret? Did you slip your ankle bracelet and get past the alarm, the electric dog fence? I like to think of her at a casino, winning piles of nickels and seducing some fat young Indian, but she's probably in a retention pond being eaten by alligators. No, she's alive. She is me. If I'm alive.

I tried to tell one nurse—they're all large, solid, colored, indistinguishable—about Kafka, but she smiled and nodded and didn't look at me as she made the bed with me in it.

Unlike me, Margaret has a family, but they haven't found time to visit. They sent flowers, which went to the lobby, and candy, which was taken away. Apparently I'm diabetic.

Here's one in her cartoon scrubs. Spongebob she says his name is. She rolls me and sops me and changes my diaper. I wept the first time. Now I accept that I'm just a meat vegetable that for reasons beyond me must be kept alive. Shut up, I'm not feeling sorry for myself. This is temporary. Wait til I can walk.

I tried all forms of reason. After the curses that is. I told them where I live, less than a mile away. They were gentle and calm, and sedated me again. Margaret is known for the elaborate precision of her delusions. I have no family who could vouch for me, but I gave them Henry and June and the Giblet's names. Henry came by one day, looked at me sadly, and said no, that can't be Mrs. Millais. She's in India. I'm taking in her papers for her.

I vaguely remembered the lie. The one time someone listens to a fogey. It figures.

I cursed him and his pug and his ugly wife and his grotesque visceral infant, and was sedated again.

Now I'm crafty, a prisoner of war. I mend. I wait. I palm my pills. Two months, then I am able to get out of bed.

I walked three steps and had to sit. I could see my legs, mottled sticks, but for all practical purposes, they were gone. It was another month before I could stagger on my walker, my dancing partner, out to the garden.

They're all around me, prison bulls. One catches my darting alert eye and I deaden it, make it vague, and smile absently as if in the throes of some memory. Their alarm subsides, for they know I'm only another dodderer.

I walk to the gate when no one's looking, but this fool body of mine starts to shake. I have been coddled so long. Can I make it home? I'm disoriented. Where is home, anyway? Damn those drugs, fuzzing my brain. Give me a good sharp quick cocaine high any day, like we had in Paris, but saints preserve me from those deadening drugs. Tomorrow I'll be ready.

Tonight I fumble with my ankle bracelet, but my hands have turned to knotty unbendable wood and I tear off a nail. In the morning, I wrestle a blade from a safety razor. These nurses aren't as smart as prison guards after all. I saw through all the way to my skin and beyond, but the razor is still sharp and though there is a lovely scarlet rivulet it doesn't hurt.

I have a word with a jolly, clueless inmate. I tell her there's a birthday cake for her just outside the back gate. When the staff converges on the escaped criminal, I slip out the front gate. My entire back tingles with the prey's fear, and I know, I know, that teeth will sink into me. They won't let me escape. A gentle hand will ask Margaret where's she's going, not listen for an answer, and lead her back. And I will go, damn me.

There is a wail, heartbreaking despair. Emily may not have her cake. She sees it plain as day in the field across the street, white with roses just like I told her, and her name on it in pink icing. She weeps. So close, but not for her. I turn the corner and I am free.

The mile home is the Spice Road for me now, long and arduous, beautiful, so profitable if traversed, so brutal if I fail. It is nighttime when I get to a house overgrown with morning-glory vines, their closed buds awaiting the day. The hibiscus are leggy and the pansies have withered in the heat, but someone, probably Henry, has been mowing the lawn.

Almost safe, but even now they could snatch me up. I don't dare admit who I am by looking over my shoulder, but once I'm inside, I run to the window and pull the curtain aside to thumb my nose at them. Then, having taunted the gods, I tremble again. I'm safe for now, but what about tomorrow? If I walk to the store for my gin (how I miss gin!) they'll see me and recapture me. If I so much as check my mail, they might be waiting.

It's like the Blitz. I don't think I slept for months then, until finally I went to America. Even on the still nights, you were always listening for the steady drone of a German plane, the up and down wail of the air-raid siren. Then, if by some miracle you slept through the warning, the all-clear would wake you up for sure.

They didn't come for me that night, but certainly, they would come in the morning. I hadn't thought ahead to my escape, back then. Would they remember my ravings and check the address I'd insisted repeatedly was mine? The cottage cheese was blue and the bread green. I broke my fast on a can of stewed tomatoes.

At ten, there was a knock at the door. I'm sure it was a Mormon but I couldn't help it—I crouched down behind my bed for half an hour, and when I tried to rise, I couldn't feel my legs.

I shut the curtains. I shut the windows. My home became a musty sarcophagus, I the living dead. Mold covered all the food and I hardly had the strength to turn the can opener. What had happened to me in those three months? Already it was almost a blur, though a peaceful blur. The drugs again. At least I had my three squares there. I opened a can of salmon halfway and drank down the juices, a lamprey, then used a fork to drag shreds and crumbles of flesh through the crack.

A day of darkness. I dare not even turn the television on. My own neighbor did not know me, the man I had been insulting for ten years. I might as well be Margaret. At least she saw the sun every day.

The food is gone now, unless I can make myself believe the moldy bread is penicillin, and life-giving.

I can never go out again, can I? Or they'll catch me.

I know what I should do, what I should have done long ago to make this tiny life of mine explode like the expanding universe. I'll do it: I'll call a taxi, pack light, and drive to the bank. I'll get all my money and go to the airport. Where next? Who knows. The world is large. I'll flip a coin, ask what's leaving soonest, follow a handsome pilot or attach myself to some émigré family returning to their natal soil. I'll be free, expansive, living every one of my years. What's ninety-three? The beginning. Me and Daddy, roaming the world again.

But what if there aren't ramps in Afghanistan? Or support bars in the bathrooms? What if I break my hip again in a third world country? Who will change my diaper? Who will fan away the flies? What if I end up an oddity, a white crippled beggar in the Orient?

Stupid woman! Where is your pluck?

My hip aches. I'm hungry. I'm frightened.

I've seen the world. Do you think it's any better now than it was then?

Buck up and live the way you want to, old woman.

I pushed my walker over the threshold—they'd given me eviscerated tennis-balls for my walker feet, and it made the going easier—into the glaring sunlight. Just one mile, and I know the route well. Suddenly there's nothing fuzzy about my mind. I'm almost swift and I make it there in three quarters of an hour.

I'd forgotten how green the world is, with fritillaries among the greenery, laying their eggs on passion vines. Summer is falling off and it's almost pleasant to be outside as the first faint breath of autumn tickles me behind the ear, coy and lover-like. This old body isn't up for nude lunches alfresco anymore, but it will be nice to sit sur l'herbe again.

"Margaret!" a voice shrills nearby. "Judith, call the police and tell them to cancel the bolo. Margaret's back! Where you been, sweetie? You ok?"

All solicitous kindness, she lets me lean on her arm and escorts me to an Adirondack chair near a lavender garden abuzz with bees. There was one just like it in Hampshire, where Daddy taught me croquet and Lord Litchcombe's son taught me to smoke.

"I'd like some tea, please," I say, and the colored nurse runs to fetch me some.

For a while I just bask in the sun, in the ease. Then I look around. There's a whiskered man next to me, oddly familiar. I close my eyes and from somewhere a mockingbird sings a soothing chorus of the same three notes, over and over again.

"Oh daddy, you take me to the nicest places," I say. I know he isn't daddy. I'm not that senile yet. But he obviously can't be handsome young Roddy Litchcombe, and it is soothing to pretend.

The old man plays along or believes it, I don't know which. He pats my hand as the nurse brings out biscuits and a light wrap against the breeze. "Thank you, darling girl," Daddy says. "So nice to be appreciated."

It won't last. Margaret will turn up, or bits of her will. Or her family will be shamed into a visit and know me for a fraud. Or will they? If a stranger was in my grandmother's bed, a wolf in a bonnet, I'd probably pretend nothing was amiss. One old lady's as good as another.

It won't last forever. Neither will I.
"Some lemon?" I ask, or order the nurse.
I could be anywhere, but I happen to be here.

The Little Things
Kyle Lang

When David calls early in the week to see if I can come to poker on Saturday, I ask my wife. Elle gets frustrated when I ask her for things like that, as if I need permission and she's my mother. But it's a simple courtesy. Better to err on the side of caution, I say. She drifts into the kitchen, answering that it's a good night, and I relay the message to David.

The Saturday morning of the game, I find Miriam and Elle in the dining room coloring at the table. Elle's coffee is colored with a touch of Bailey's—a habit she's taken to since Miriam was born, a nip of the good stuff on Saturdays and Sundays. I try not to preach about drinking before noon.

I watch Miriam color a horse leaping over a garden gate and kiss her on top of her head. She mumbles something I don't quite catch.

"Good morning," I say, and Elle shrugs.

"There's coffee," Elle says and takes a sip. She looks drowsy.

"Thanks." I pull a clean coffee mug from the dishwasher and pour myself a cup. Elle's gaze shifts between me and the dishwasher. I open it again and put away the clean dishes.

"Are we going to Nona's house today?" Miriam asks. It's a loosely held tradition that we visit Elle's parents one day on the weekend, and Miriam looks forward to her grandmother's doting and chasing their old beagle, Baxter, around the lawn.

"Not today, honey," Elle says, reaching out and smoothing Miriam's hair.

I finish with the cups and move on to the bottom rack

where I see the knife—an old, wood-handled one that has been passed down to Elle by her folks. Half of the handle is missing. It lies on the bottom of the dishwasher. I freeze. I reach down to touch it, confirm it. The blade is cool against my fingers.

I pull the knife from the dishwasher and fish around in the bottom for the rest of the handle. I turn my back and try and piece it together, but water has worked into the wood and split it clean. It's like joining oil and water.

"What are you doing?" Elle asks. She is up from the table. I turn to her with my palms open, offering up the remnants of the knife. I'm trying my best to wear my own disappointment on my face, but she doesn't give me a second glance. "Oh," she says, "what happened?"

"It went through the dishwasher," I say, shrug my shoulders and set the remains on the countertop.

"What did I tell you?" she asks.

"No knives, no wooden utensils," I say. "I don't know what happened. I don't remember putting it in there."

She takes the pieces in her own hands, fumbling with them, trying to realign them. "It's ruined."

I back away, lean against the counter. I cross my ankles and wink at Miriam to show her nothing's wrong, but she's heard her mother's tone. She turns back to her coloring and I face up to Elle.

"This was my mother's knife."

"I know," I say, "but it's just a knife, right?"

Elle's face screws tight, her eyes and lips drawing into thin slices. I wait, arms behind me, hands holding onto the counter, but I know I must wait this out, wait for the bright slash of her anger before she'll settle into herself again.

"It was my mother's," she says again, working it out in her head. She's still playing with the pieces of the handle.

"I'm sorry," I say. I pick up my coffee mug, see Miriam knock a crayon to the ground with her elbow and bend to pick it up. I sit next to Miriam, opposite Elle, and watch her color. She smiles and moves her elbow so I can admire her progress. It's a cheap out, using Miriam like this, and I can tell Elle's fuming, but I don't want to get into it. I take a drink of coffee and fix my eyes on Miriam. I hear Elle sigh and the trash can open. She takes a long string of paper towels and rolls it around the knife blade before she nests it in the trash as if she's burying a pet. The lid closes with a click.

Elle walks out of the kitchen and down the hall in the direction of our bedroom, and I know the day is tainted by disappointment. Elle's moods, once set in motion, are hard to derail. I think about going after her, decide against it, and grab one of the coloring books on the table. I glance over my shoulder occasionally, looking for Elle, but it is the furnace ticking on or a bird in the eaves above the front door that I hear, and the hall remains a darkened aperture that I'm reluctant to enter.

Miriam finishes her horse picture, a frog prince, and is working on a mermaid when I refill my coffee. Elle hasn't reappeared. I know I'll find her lying on the bed, flipping through the channels, watching nothing in particular. I give up and go down the hall to talk to her.

"You okay?" I ask, sitting on the edge of the bed. Her back is to me. I place my hand on the blanket above the rise of her hip.

"Hnn," she says, "Fine."

"You're upset." I run my hand down her thigh and back. There's a static energy to the blanket that is either dry air or Elle's mood.

"It's fine," she says again.

"Sure it is. Why don't you tell me and we can talk about it?" I'm goading her. I want this over. Like a band-aid. Do it quick.

I sit there a moment before she says, "I can't have anything nice."

"Of course you can," I say, "just not until Miriam grows up and moves out." Elle doesn't smile and I rub her thigh again.

"Everything I like gets ruined and you couldn't give two shits."

"That's not fair," I say. "I like nice things."

"No you don't. Something gets ruined you just buy a new one. You don't take care of anything."

"I take care of stuff."

"Oh, really," she says, rolling over in bed and leaning against the headboard. She looks at me like she looks at our accountant. "The pair of wine glasses I got you for your birthday?"

I knew it. I knew it was going to be those wine glasses. I want to tell her, number one, that I don't think people should spend $30 a stem for wine glasses and, two, she was the one who got me drunk that night, filling my glass before it ever emptied and smiling across the table at me like she had plans.

"It was an accident, Elle."

"You didn't have them a day and you broke them."

"What do you want me to say? I've apologized for the wine glasses."

"It just shows what I'm talking about."

"Fine," I say, adopting her own mantra. "What if we go buy you a new one? A really nice knife. We could splurge. It'll be fun. We'll all go to the mall and get you a new knife."

"That's not the point," she says, "What happens when that one gets ruined? It's a waste. I just won't have anything nice anymore." She crosses her arms and turns back to the television.

"Well, I can't fix it, so, it's either a new one or nothing at all."

"Forget it," she says, setting her jaw.

"Fine, no knife." I get up off the bed, shaking my head.

"What?" she says, her voice growing louder.

"Nothing," I say and leave the room.

We stay home all day. Elle moves about the house, saying little. She brightens for Miriam's sake, coos over her pictures, reads a story at naptime, and watches from the patio as Miriam and I ride bikes in front of the house. When it creeps toward six and I've exhausted all the yard work I can think to do, I come back into the house and tell Elle I better get ready.

Miriam is playing on a blanket in front of the television. It's tuned to a nature program that Elle pretends to watch, and she shrugs her shoulders. I wrestle with the idea of asking if it's okay or just leaving.

"Are you sure it's okay that I go?" I ask.

"I said it was fine, didn't I?"

"I'm making sure. What are you going to do?"

"We're just going to hang," she says. "Go. Have fun." She doesn't look away from the television.

When I get to David's house, the driveway is full of pickups I know at a glance. I walk in the front door, knocking as I enter, and hear Addison holler for me to come on in.

"The boys are downstairs waiting for you," she says. She's wearing a tight, black cocktail dress and her hair curls around her face, showing the high line of her blushing cheek.

"You look nice," I say. "You get dressed up for us?"

"No, I'm going out with some girlfriends. You boys will be entirely un-chaperoned this evening." She tucks her hair behind her ear. "I expect the house to be standing when I get back." She laughs, a cascade of high notes that twitters on the edge of nerves and then, as an afterthought, adds, "Keep an eye on David, will you?"

I don't know what to make of the comment, so I nod and leave her standing in the kitchen. The stairs open up into the basement, and I peek around at the stacks of laundry by the washing machine, bags of toys ready for the Goodwill, and in the corner, what looks to be a stack of boxes, one of which is marked "Girls' Room."

"Wait, wait, wait," I hear Bernie say, "How much did you buy in?" I can imagine him reaching across the table for someone's stack of chips to verify the count. It's an informal game, but Bernie scolds us that it is a gentleman's game. The rest of us are just looking for an excuse to get out of the house.

"God forbid we come up a quarter short," I say, stepping into the tiny cinderblock room that serves as our poker den.

"It's about time," Bernie says without looking over his shoulder and sure enough, he's bent over the table, reaching for Ezra's stack of chips. Ezra leans back in his chair, lifts his ball cap, and runs a hand through his hair. Bernie draws the chips across the table and counts them out into even stacks. Ezra's buy-in is square and Bernie pushes the chips back toward the center of the table.

"Satisfied?" Ezra asks, drawing his chips back to his side of the table and aligning them by color.

"There's a chair over here," David says and then adds, "What time are *you* going out?" I hadn't noticed Addison coming down behind me, and it takes me a moment before I realize he's talking to her. I can't help but notice how the *you* rises out of the question and becomes an accusation.

"Eight. Why? Are you trying to get rid of me?" She crosses to his chair and puts her hand on it. She makes a face at the back of his head, arching her eyebrows and sticking her tongue out at him. She flicks him on his ear, eyeing the rest of us.

"Now why would I want to do that?" He tips his head back and seeing her all done up, twists around in his seat, eyeing her up and down. He shakes his head and turns back to the table. Addison looks over at me and shrugs.

"You let your wife go out looking like that? I have two words of advice for you, David," Ezra says, leaning forward, "Muu muu." David shoos Addison from the room and she feigns insult and saunters out.

"I have to say, David, you got balls," Ezra says. Ezra grabs a deck of cards from the center of the table and starts shuffling. Bernie's rapt attention is on the carrying case of chips, and David sits back in his chair, lacing his hands behind his head like he's the king of poker-dom. His only response is a juicy belch. I seat myself between Bernie and David, drop a twenty dollar bill on the green felt and wait for Bernie to count out my chips.

The night runs standard. I start off slow, folding two low hands that could have taken the pot before I realize that these guys are full of shit and rarely have anything to back their bets. It's a bluffing game with these guys, and we play dealer's choice for most of the night.

Eventually, I get lucky and score the pot from a five dollar all-in tournament and the chips stack high next to me. I'm doing good, up a little on the night but not drawing too much attention to my chips.

"Read'em and weep, fellas," Bernie says laying out a full house—queens over eights.

"Son of a bitch," David says throwing his cards into the middle of the table, "Jacks over fives." He's down to his last two dollars in chips and he pulls his wallet from his back pocket, searching for more cash.

"What can I say, boys, I got the touch tonight," Bernie says. We eye his pile of chips, plotting against him. So far, it's a losing battle. David slouches against the table, his hand against his forehead.

"Fuck you, Bernie."

"Time to break into the college funds, boys." Bernie stacks his chips with a smile that grates on us all. He's the only one without a wife and kids, and he clicks each chip down on top of towering stacks with a righteousness employed only by the single or the evangelical.

"You're such a prick," David says reaching for a fresh beer.

"Ah, don't be a sore loser, David," Bernie says. It's Bernie's deal and the rest of us are stuck waiting for him to arrange his chips. David watches Bernie with a look beyond envy.

"Like you need the money," David says. He sits back in his chair, glowering now and a little of the smugness drips off Bernie's smile.

"Just a friendly game, David," he says, but he pulls the pile of chips toward him, leaving the rest of the stacking for later and takes up the cards, shuffling quickly and dealing them around the table. The room has gotten quiet except for the radio playing "Sister Christian."

"Texas Hold'em," Bernie says, bringing the second round of cards around the table. Everyone picks up their cards and holds them tight to their faces. I can see Jesse's eyes, blank with beer, passing over Bernie to David and back again. He looks confused and I'm wishing him silent with a single thought, *don't*. It's like he hears me because he turns his eyes back to his cards and waits for the betting to begin.

"I fold," David says, pushing back from the table and leaving the room. We watch him go, not a word passing between us.

We hear him mount the stairs and when he is out of ear shot Bernie says, "What was that?" We stare at our cards. Adam avoids the question by betting fifty cents, Jesse sees him, Ezra splashes the pot with his bet, and I tuck my cards, face down, into the pot. I push myself up, feeling the tightness in my knees from sitting too long, and go after David saying, "I'll be right back, deal me out on the next round." I hear a door close somewhere upstairs.

I can't find David in any of the open spaces upstairs, and the next place I check is the bathroom. The door is open and no one is inside. Moving through the kitchen, I peek into the backyard and see David sitting in the girls' swing set. He holds his head in his hands and leans forward as though he's inspecting the grass.

Outside, the night has grown colder, and the air hangs thick with impending rain; clouds creep across the sky. There isn't a star to be seen, and the only light comes from the streetlights behind the neighbor's house. In the dim glow, David is an outline against the pruned row of arborvitaes. He rocks himself in the swing but his feet remained planted.

"You all right?" I say, stepping toward the swing set and leaning against one of the uprights.

He tells me he's fine, but the word stumbles over a thickness in his throat. I watch the dark clouds slip across the sky, moving east toward the mountains, and I ask, "You sure?"

"I hate that guy," he says.

"No you don't," I say, "It's Bernie. He's a lousy winner."

"I could give a shit if he wins a couple of bucks off of me. It's his attitude. He's a smug little bastard."

I shrug. "You're preaching to the choir," I say. "I wouldn't trade places with him." I stop myself and wonder if it's true. If I could erase the last few years with Elle, with Miriam, and be Bernie, would I do it?

"It doesn't mean anything if it's easy," David says. He lifts his head, squinting at me, and the shine of his eyes make him look empty. "Addison's leaving," he says. I turn my gaze back to the sky and settle against the upright, bracing myself against the news. "She's moving back in with her folks, taking the girls. She's already packing," he says.

"What the fuck," I say. "What's going on?"

"She's out right now with her girlfriends," he says, "probably trying to find some sap to take my place." He laces his fingers together between his knees and stops rocking in the swing, steadies himself, head bowed, praying against the darkness.

"What happened?" I ask.

"I don't know. She says it's been coming for a while. It's the little things. Lots of little things, she says." He studies his hands as if the answer is written in the creases of his balled fists.

I find myself wondering what Elle's doing, if she's sitting in bed, reading, watching her cell phone to see if I'll call sloppy drunk, wanting a ride, the evening having gotten away from me.

The tendons in David's neck rise against his skin, and he squeezes his hands together until the color bleeds out of them. I reach out and put a hand on his shoulder, and I hope he'll relax.

"Look at this place," he says. "What a pain in my ass. Do you know how much time I spend out here? Planting bulbs, weeding, spraying? I spend more time in this yard than I do with my own daughters. Isn't that ridiculous? She's always telling me that I don't spend enough time with them. But when I get home, what does she do? She puts me to work out here. Tells me it's got to be done. Got to, get it? Mandatory, no argument, no debate." David swings his arm over the beds. "Do you see all these ferns? Addison had me dig them up and transplant them here from Mount. Hood. Couldn't buy a fern, had to dig the fuckers up. It's how *she* wanted it. And what do I get for it? Nothing. Now she's taking the girls." He stands up, and I straighten, but he only looks out over his perfectly groomed yard. How ridiculous that I envy it so much. I'm constantly fighting moss and dandelions, but his yard is a smooth plain of green that ends in abrupt edges. The smell of mulch rises up into the night. The beds are clean of weeds and I can make out the red of the bark he's laid. The rhododendrons are trimmed and fresh with the first blooms of spring.

His eyes are shaded but I can see his forehead wrinkle with a frown and he steps up to a rhododendron, reaches out his hand as if to pluck one of the blooms, but he wraps his hand around it. "And this little bastard, trimming and mulching, trimming and mulching. Got to trim these bad boys right after they bloom, you know? Typical. Wait until their all used up, and then it's snip, snip, snip." His hand closes over the flower, the petals pressing out between his fingers. He pulls at it, plucking it free. He reaches for the branches, his hands sliding over them. He reaches again, grabbing deeper into the bush, snaps off a branch and throws it onto the mowed grass. Again and then again he reaches for the bush.

When I realize what he's doing I decide against interfering. When he has ripped one side of it apart, he settles to his hands and knees and starts in on the daffodils, sinking his hands down past the bark and into the dirt, digging up the bulbs, tearing new growth out of the ground.

He talks in a low voice but it grows louder with each new handful. "I didn't want this," he says. I watch his neighbors' darkened windows, waiting for lights to switch on or for faces to appear floating behind glass.

"I didn't want this," he repeats, but this time it is as if something has torn loose inside of him. His voice raises an octave and then he's swearing at the plants, throwing handfuls of bark and dirt. Digging up plants whole, he's up to his forearms in dirt. He reaches for one of the ferns, pulls the fronds loose, digs at the dense center with his fingernails. The fern holds. He pulls and grapples with it, but its heart is solid and firm.

When he finally gives up—winded, sweating, bits of dirt in his hair—he sits in the bed, leaning against the house. He rests his elbows on his knees, and his hands forage around in his thick hair, grasping at it as though to uproot it as well. His eyes glass. I stand in the center of the lawn, the carnage of his yard strewn around me and feel the first drop of rain.

"Better?" I ask.

David nods and looks at his hands. Another couple of rain drops fall, I can feel them on my scalp through my thinning hair. I look up at the sky, grown darker with the storm, and sit in the grass across from David, picking up a frond of the fern, and running my fingers over the underside, feel the spores. Goosebumps rise on my arms and I look at David. "That's it?"

"That's it," he says, and his eyes drift away from me toward the streetlight.

"So, what's next?"

"We don't exactly have a plan."

"Are there lawyers or just talk?"

"Just talk." David wipes under his eyes and leaves a smear of dirt across his cheekbone.

"That's good. Keep it simple."

David looks up at me and I can tell he's pissed. "What is that supposed to mean? My fucking wife is leaving."

"You're right," I say, "I'm a dick. I'm a great big ole dick."

David's mouth twitches but he doesn't look at me.

"I'm a great, big, hairy, low-hanging, wide-swinging dick.

You got me nailed."

We laugh but it falters quickly. "What would you do?" he asks.

"You mean, if it was Elle?"

"Yeah."

"I don't know. Sometimes I think I'm just buying time, running from one narrow escape to another. They get so mad over piddly-shit."

"It's the little things," David says and leans his head against the siding. The rain is coming a little faster now, but neither of us makes a move toward the house.

"I ruined a knife," I say.

"What?"

"I ruined a knife, old wood-handled thing. Put it in the dishwasher. Now we're fighting. She can't have anything nice, ya know?"

David laughs. I smile but I'm serious. It's the moods. One mood can last into weeks of facing Elle's sleeping back.

"Don't let it go too far," he says.

"Sometimes nothing helps."

"Hmm," David says. I lie back in the grass and watch the rain fall down on me; the drops appear out of the gray night just a few feet from my face like bubbles rising in water. We sit for a while like that. I can hear the guys in the basement arguing over a hand. Bernie is the loudest. He's trying to mediate the racket.

Bernie can cut and run, get while the getting's good, and I think David envies him that now. I'm not sure I don't.

The sky opens and a single sheet of rain that is everywhere at once drenches us. We stay where we are and David hoots out into the night. I answer with a short call of my own, and soon we're baying and howling up into the rain, calling it down on us. I wish for it to wash away the debris in the yard and repair the gouged earth, but I know it's a false hope.

If the guys come looking for us, they'll wonder what we're doing sitting in the rain, but I can bet they won't ask questions. I imagine them joining us, sitting in the rain like fools, grown men out of their minds, sopping wet, and all of us hooting into the night. But it's a moot point because no one comes for David, or for me, and the rain continues on until I can't see.

David quiets, holding his knees tight to his chest and looks at the scarred mess of his flowerbed. The wet soil blooms out of the red bark.

"I'm soaked," David says, and it sounds remarkably like a laugh.

"Yeah. Me too."

I smile at David, wipe a wet sleeve across my eyes.

There's talk when we go back downstairs about us standing in the rain, but David dismisses it. He doesn't mention the ferns. We play a couple more hands, but the evening is broken, and I'm too wet to pay attention to the cards flying around the table.

On the way home, I'm aware of each bump and turn in the road, no longer on autopilot, and I can feel David's house receding into the night. In the darkness of the four lane highway, not a street light for miles, I think about Elle and Miriam and how I would react if we were in David and Addison's shoes: split incomes, split houses, split child even—gearing up for even more complex negotiations than marriage provides.

There will be visitation schedules, planned payments, and holiday itineraries to navigate, and it seems like trading the beast you know for one you don't. Like I said, I'm not a gambler. I turn on the radio but in the late night hours, there is nothing much but ballads and hip-hop. I turn it off.

I know these roads. The abandoned marina, the woodworker's shop carved into a forested bank, and the river turning and falling away behind the run of hills. When I drive these roads, banking the car through turns before I realize what I've done, I get nostalgic for the things I know, which aren't many. I know that Adam will try and buy the pot time after time with a hand full of nothing, that David is the best player at the table when he has his head about him. I know that Ezra and Jesse are there for the beer, Bernie loves bragging rights, and that I wouldn't give a damn about poker if it wasn't these guys sitting at the table. I know that even knives are important.

I pull into the driveway of the house, careful to shut off the headlights so they don't shine into Miriam's window, and I kill the engine before I can even put it into park. The storm darkens everything and my house is a shapeless black form in the night. By memory, I make my way to the back gate and let myself into the backyard. I find the leather strapping threaded through the hole in the post, a thin thread that opens the first glimpse of my life, my property. The dandelion spotted lawn, the weed filled beds, and a failed patch of dirt that had begun as a garden. The rain gathered in the leaves of the dogwood double their efforts to wash me clean and what little dryness I've achieved in the drive home disappears. The patio light shines out over all of this. Elle has left the light on for me.

Inside the house, I strip down in the mudroom and throw my clothes into the hamper by the washing machine. Naked and shivering, my hair dripping down the nape of my neck, I make my way down the hall. I watch Miriam sleep from the doorway of her room. She sleeps open-mouthed and she smacks her lips, a habit left over from her thumb-sucking days.

I sneak into our bedroom and find Elle curled up, the covers pulled up to her eyes. The dim glow from the street presses through our blinds, and I can see a tousled crop of hair. I stand above her, shivering, listening. She fills the room with her breath. That's one thing I can add to the things I know, I know her breathing while she sleeps, the smooth slide of air. The shifting under the blankets that lets me know she somehow senses me here, standing above her. I'm tempted to rouse her, to tell her I love her, but I don't. I watch the soft rise and fall of her breath. I know I'll wake in the morning and find my family gathered here, but even the things we know, things we've known for years, the slight bends and turns like the rise of a hip under a blanket, these things can at any time appear uncertain, even perilous.

Swan Song
Frank Dineen

B abe says, "Ah, here we go," and starts reading from *To Hellas and Back*, her well-thumbed bible for this trip: *The Antikythera Young Man emerged off that Aegean island in 1901 and is one of the most accomplished classical bronze sculptures to grace the National Archeological Museum of Greece. His outstretched, open hand once held a spherical object, inclining scholars to identify him as perhaps Paris, awarding the Apple of Discord to Aphrodite, or…*

On she goes in her schoolmarm cadence. Sam, befitting this tipping-time in her twelve year-old life, muses that if she were male, and an old statue, she'd for sure want to be a bronze one, because *the things* of all the marble guys were snapped off. When her mother pauses, she jumps in.

"My feet hurt."

"Well, miss skimpy sandals twined up her calves." Babe directs this mostly to Rus, because he had let Sam buy them at some cluttered trap in the Plaka.

They permit photos here, just no flashes, so Babe goes to work on hunky Mr. Antikythera. One of them may end up in the travel section of their Philadelphia daily, where she'd done what she considered serious education reporting, before its drastic cutbacks. She tries to see journalism as her lark now, and Sam her vocation, but it's not always easy. She circles balletically, snapping away. Babe knows the cute verdigris phallus will never see print, but she likes capturing it anyhow.

"A couple of you two," she says, directing them to stand in front. Sam slips an arm around her father and nestles into his chest. They touch less and less. He wraps his arm around Sam and inhales her, flesh of his flesh. Babe says, "Good, hold that pose," but it doesn't feel like a pose to Rus.

***

Babe in the lead, they hop a trolley bus to the base of craggy Mt. Lykebettus. During the ride up in the funicular, Babe whips out the guidebook. The ascent is steep and dramatic. Rus can see that Sam is enjoying it. He blurts out, "Like an eagle riding an updraft!" which, it comes back to him now, Leda, his new-found fellow backpacker, had exclaimed, nearly 30 years ago. Leda had been a student like him. She was from Tarpon Springs, where her dad ran a fish restaurant and her grandfather told and retold grim tales of sponge divers succumbing to the bends off Kalymnos, an island near Turkey. She'd struck Rus as just what he was not—spontaneous, mysterious—and had taught him some Greek, among other things.

At the top, the hot wind nearly makes off with Sam's jaunty fisherman's cap, another Plaka buy, and would be whipping Babe's highlighted hair back and forth like the pages of the guidebook, if it weren't pulled back so tight. A white chapel to Saint George crowns the terrace. Below, the bleached city smothers the Attic plain like scattered teeth. Babe is gazing beyond it, westward.

"Way out there is the Acropolis of Corinth," she says. "Says here that on good days you can see it. What about it, Sam?"

"About what?"

"Corinth, Samantha. Can you spot it?"

"It's not a good day. This old town is polluted, mom."

Actually," says Babe, looking at her guide, "ancient Corinth was the place to go for real pollution. As in big wine and gambling parties. As in the one thousand priestesses of Aphrodite's temple there."

"That's a lot of priestesses," Rus says.

"A lot of *prostitutes*," Babe says, her eyes on Sam, as if to say: history, boring? "The money they raked in kept the temple looking spiffy."

"The Vegas of its day," Rus says.

"Not quite," Sam says. "What happened in Corinth ended up in your guidebook." Babe laughs. She likes to think of her daughter as precocious.

They flee the gusts and the screaming everywhere light for the tiny chapel. Inside, they don't move for a moment, waiting for their eyes to get the message. Gradually, the joined blur of votive candles recedes into discrete points of light. Wood pews appear in shadow, then the ecclesiastical gloss of silver, brass and bronze. As their gleam grows, Sam imagines invisible hands still buffing away, all to please them. Babe informs them it's customary for visitors to light a candle and to kiss, or at least glance at, the bold fresco of St. George slaying the dragon. Several visitors are queued up to do just that. "I'm not going first!" Sam hisses. Babe tells her don't be silly, nobody's going first. The Sproats are not a churchgoing family. Sam's not even baptized. Rus doesn't think about this much, but he does now. Since arriving in Greece, he's found himself ruminating more. It must be the distance from their everyday lives. He sees Sam just now beginning to assemble the person she'll live and die as. At her age, he was frightened of Hell. At night in bed, worried for saying fuck when he'd missed a jump shot or for trying to see up a girl's dress, he tried to make what they called a perfect Act of Contrition. *Oh my God, I am heartly sorry for having offended Thee, and I detest all my sins because I dread the loss of heaven and the pains of hell ...* He remembers striving for purest sincerity, chewing on each phrase until he tasted the fear and guilt in it, believing that the more regret he felt, the cleaner his soul became. *But most of all, because they offend Thee, my God, Who art all good and deserving of all my love ...* Babe, the product of a secular home, considers that the telltale residue of such superstitious ardor is a certain meekness in her man—the last trait she wants her daughter saddled with. Rus knows this and generally agrees. He sees the sense in letting Sam find her own spiritual path, if she ever bothers. Nevertheless, standing beneath this chapel ceiling plastered with biblical scenes, at this highest point of the city of Socrates, that open-eyed questioner, Rus wonders about Sam eventually stepping out into the world minus any sense of tribe, or tradition, or what it feels like to believe in mystery, or to hold something sacred and worthy of awe. Just this spring, she asked what she was—Christian, Jewish, what? Babe told her she could decide later, which had turned out to be sooner: within days, she'd proclaimed herself Jewish and asked her parents to stage a Bat Mitzvah for her, approaching in lavishness the bash she'd just attended for her schoolmate Miriam, the daughter of two radiologists. Not that the matter of Sam's identity is a real big deal to Rus, a monkey on his back or anything. He just doesn't like the thought of his daughter wondering where she fits in or whether she's part of anything. The world can be pretty chilly.

***

Sitting across from the Acropolis, Sam has finished jotting down notes of her daily impressions, a chore negotiated with Babe in exchange for a bit of slack about makeup and impulse buys. Sam is featuring Cleopatra-black eye liner, which she imagines fits with the distant, vaguely alluring sound of "Greece." Rus thinks she looks cute, in a raccoon way. Sam had asked that instead of handwriting notes, she take along her laptop and blog to her friends. Babe might have gone along, but Rus wouldn't hear of it. He didn't want her face buried in a screen during this trip. There had been no laptops in his day. He wanted her *present* with him and Babe and all that together they might imbibe from this consequential land.

Their order arrives: ouzo for Rus, retsina for Babe, Coke for Sam. Sam sniffs the licorice and pine of the drinks and wrinkles her nose. "You never drink that stuff back home," she says.

"When in Rome," Babe says.

Sam spreads her arms on the table and lays her head down. Rus cuts his ouzo with a splash of water. It clouds to mother of pearl. Babe sips her retsina, which tastes better to her in context like this. Around the Acropolis, flood lights come on, imbuing the Parthenon with theatrical magic. "Wow," Babe says. She and Rus smile and raise their glasses. They'd like to share this moment with their daughter, but she's asleep already. This impresses Rus, her dropping off so fast, and amid all this racket. Is there a noisier city than Athens? All around them, horns honk, jets scream, motor bikes rip, vendors squawk like kicked fowl. Everybody's talking as though they can't be heard, and when they run out of words, they snatch up a newspaper, chewing on the latest political scrap until it strikes a fresh nerve, then ejecting renewed indignation into the warm diesel Athenian air. They enjoy it all immensely, Rus can tell. Their endless fascination with the doings in this small plain of Attica, as though it were the whole world. He wonders whether democracy was born here as an excuse, rather than a sanction, to bicker. Babe opens the notebook and reads Sam's impressions of the Parthenon. She marvels that even this cultural icon is unable to evoke from her surely precocious daughter any bouquets less insipid than amazing, awesome and incredible. It doesn't occur to her that Sam's remarks have been crafted largely for parental consumption, and that in fact, the Parthenon has had a queer effect on her. She'd already had it processed as an image, and the real-life honey marble flesh of it had struck her as not quite right.

Babe closes the notebook. Rus moves Sam's untouched Coke out of spilling range, then drapes his jacket over her shoulders.

***

Sam's riding shotgun, absorbed in her indigo toenails; they're splayed on the dash, hot to her touch. Babe's at the wheel. Rus, in back, has been assigned guidebook duty but finds nothing of note about this endless drab sprawl of Athens. At last, they begin to climb and turn curves until the stony hills of Attica are all around them, starkly *present*, in the most oddly transparent atmosphere. Sam takes her feet down and looks out at the rocks and clinging shrubs and the

Popsicle!" she says. The Ghinekon has done her wonders.

"Tell mom what you called the kids."

"A school of fish."

"Ha!" Babe says.

***

At Olympia, Babe has informed them that during the ancient games, women were excluded from these sacred precincts under penalty of death, prompting her, in retroactive nose thumbing, to challenge Sam to a footrace in the excavated stadium. Since no one's there right then, Sam goes along. At the far end, Rus waits poised with camera. He calls out ready, set, go! and Babe blasts off, her elbows uppercutting like a boxer's. Sam, already a decent hockey player, lopes along with easy animal grace. Babe wins by a hair.

"Did I get it?" Babe asks. She leans forward, hands on thighs, sucking air.

"It was close," Rus says.

"Photo finish," Sam says, catching her father's eye. "But I think the gold is mom's." Rus winks.

"Yes!" Babe exclaims. She raises her arms and twirls in a little victory jig. Rus snaps this moment, too, and as he does, sees Sam, an old woman, showing it to somebody and saying, That was my mother. My father took it. We were in Greece. It was amazing, awesome, incredible. Doesn't she look happy?

***

They're on a car ferry, leaving the Peloponnesian peninsula behind, wending their way to Delphi. Rus the navigator, head back and mouth open, has slipped into a doze. Babe is inclined to let him catnap; his sleep in a series of strange beds has been sub prime. Babe has quietly passed their one cell phone to Sam, hand-signaling that she doesn't want Rus to find her with it. Babe wouldn't call Rus a Luddite; he just seems not to get that the clock time he and Sam abide by is misleading, that her world is not his, not its present, past, or future.

Sam is texting Miriam, whose first few days at camp have been a mixed bag. Stuck in Maryland's buggy woods with a bunch of lil kdz, she is bordsilE, but her Norwegian counselor, Nils, is gorgES, 2D4. W00t, Sam texts. She's a wee bit competitive with Miriam and tells her that Greece is amazn, orsum and NcreDbl and that she's been sipping retsina wine in tavernas. The placid ferry has floated Rus back to freshman high school math class. Math comes easy but bores him, just as his it's-a-living actuarial work does now. A buff young Jesuit named Father Rosato has unfurled a thorny quadratic equation across the blackboard and ordered Rus to step up and cut it down to size. Rus has not heard him; deploying both pen and pencil, he's whittling down his list of greatest rock groups and is part way through penciling in Fleetwood Mac when a flying stick of chalk explodes against the edge of his desk. Looming over him now, Father Rosato examines Rus's Final 15, nodding with terrible appreciation, then takes up Rus's dense school bag and shakes it out over his head. Rus, in his doze, feels it. *Caesar's Gallic Wars.* Ouch. *Elementary Biology.* Wham. *The History of Western Civilization:* Ka Boom!

He's snoring now. It irritates Babe. So does the clicking of the cell phone's keys. It sounds cryptic, out of reach, like a rodent in the walls, or the course Sam's life will take. She takes a couple of deep breaths. For this little family of hers, she would willingly submit to Sinis the Pine Bender, if she isn't already.

***

Babe says, "Rus, turn in here. Photo op, maybe."

It's a bumpy dirt path cutting through an olive grove. Sam has been spreading bottled water onto her neck and arms because her father resists the air conditioning because it shuts them off from the countryside because this ain't no TV travelogue. They stop and get out.

"Nana's hands," Sam says, running her own over a gnarled tree trunk.

Babe is crouched, snapping. "The silver leaves in the

light," she says.

Three wiry little men appear at a crest up the path and scurry down into the grove. They spread out to form a circle. They're shirtless. They're shouting back and forth. They have knives in their belts. Rus grabs Sam and runs for the car.

"Wait! It's okay!" Babe yells. She takes off toward the men.

"It's a rabbit!" Rus says.

The men are whooping it up. They close in, each in turn heading off the darting brown blur. One lunges and gets hold of a rear leg, which sets them laughing and yelling Opa! but when they see Babe coming, they go stony. She waves Rus and Sam over. One of the men stuns the rabbit with a short punch to the head.

"Yasou!" she says, pointing at their catch. This delights the young men. She requests photographs. The prospect of their prowess being immortalized delights them more. Rus and Sam watch as they take turns displaying the rabbit stretched out in front of them. In good English, the one with a still eye explains that they're farm hands, that over the crest are fruit trees and corn and tobacco, and would the Sproats honor them by sharing this savory gift, prepared by them on their very own spit. The rabbit, all ears, starts twitching strenuously. The Zhivago lookalike unsheathes his knife.

"No no!" Rus says, pointing at Sam. "Efkaristo, efkaristo, but we must go now. Kalimera sas!"

The young men understand. They smile, wave a special goodbye to Sam, and head back over the crest.

***

Rus is filling the tank, wincing as the euros pile up on the meter. Babe's visiting the station's unisex head and is unlikely to emerge in a lightened mood. Next to it is an automatic car wash, prompting him to tap the rear window and point it out to Sam. Back home, the two of them used to have a ball as his porous vintage Mustang inched through its bi-monthly bath. It was like a funhouse to her. The Hidden Serpents showering venom down upon them. "It's inside, Daddy, get it!" Sam cried, handing her father the bath towel they were obliged to take along to avoid a soaked dashboard. Then the churning attack of the Whiskered Meanies, Sam hiding her eyes as though at a scary movie, followed by the menacing hula tentacles of the Giant Octopus, sending her diving into the backseat, and the final ordeal of the People Sucker, glomming onto the windshield to inhale them, Mustang and all, into oblivion. The names, the whole fantasy, nearly all Sam's invention, and as they escaped out into the sunlight, a theatrical pressing of her cheek to his, exclaiming, "It's a miracle we survived!"

She was little then. Now, seeing her father pointing at the car wash, Sam shakes her head and mouths, "It's not that dirty."

***

In Levadia, Rus has split off while the girls shop. He and Leda had ended up here, very late one suffocating night in 1977. They'd detoured from their own pilgrimage to Delphi, to check out the fabled springs of Lethe and Mnemosyne, Oblivion and Remembrance, which Babe and Sam have just dipped their feet into. The town, aside from its feral cats, had been asleep that night. Following signs, they'd passed over a stream on a fairytale Turkish bridge, then gone part way up a dreary gorge to a little waterfall spilling over from a pond. This is it, Leda had said. It's older than ancient. Bubbles up from Hades, is the tradition—from Lethe, the river of Forgetfulness. We must go in!

She'd undressed then, and directed Rus to do the same. He hadn't seen her like that before. They'd agreed back in Athens that physical intimacy and companionable travel were oil and water. But something had come into her eyes now—a glaze, a pagan fleck. He'd gone ahead and stripped, trying to feel alone, to avoid seeming shy. When he straightened up, Leda had admired him boldly. He was twenty. He'd never felt like a man before. And her ripe perfection simply stupefied him. Leda took his hand and they waded in like God's first couple. The chilly water quickly rose to touch her breasts

and Rus thought, who could blame it? Leda dove beneath
for several seconds, and when she emerged, right in front of
him, her spiky hair gave her an even wilder look. She pulled
him to her and wrapped her legs around him. She felt like
a creature of the water, cold, instinctual, enormously vital,
compelling the animal in Rus to respond. Not a Herculean
task. For several minutes, the only sounds were the tame
waterfall, the slap of flesh on water, and a frog. Cheering
them on?

They'd spent that night farther up the gorge, in the
courtyard of a deserted Frankish castle. Rus looks up at it
now, then into Lethe's forgetful, memorable waters. This
spot's been gussied up for tourists. He doesn't remember the
restaurant over the water, and there are guided tours of the
castle these days. He'd woken there alone next morning and
looked for her around the town, but she was gone.

Where is Leda now? he asks. She's between my ears, he
answers.

He meets the girls on the Turkish bridge, festooned with
dense Flokati rugs. Sam's excited to show off her latest:
earrings of woven red bead, telling her father they're "after
the Minoan style." Babe's eager to show him a small painting
she fancies at one of the galleries. She's in a good mood. This
detour to Levadia's mythic springs was Rus's idea. She likes
him to initiate and wishes he'd do it more often.

***

Even from a distance, the first sight of Parnassus and
the mountains massed around it strike the Sproats as a realm
apart. All at once the imposing peaks are simply there.

"It looks fake," Sam says.

"It would through celluloid eyes," Rus says. He's hungry.

"I know what you mean Sam," Babe says defensively. She
takes up *To Hellas and Back: Receptive travelers may sense the
extraordinary atmosphere of grandeur and mystery which haunts
Delphi. At few other places will they feel so utterly apart from the
everyday world and transported to the very center of things that
matter—into the navel of the earth, as the ancients said.*

But Delphi doesn't work out so well. The road at the base of the sanctuary is clogged with tour buses, and the crowd of stout Germans at the Kastalian Spring is enough to put them off, weary as they are at this final stop. They poke about in the ruins, where Sam makes a mental note about the Lesbian Wall. She'll tell Miriam it has zip to do with you-know-what, and actually commemorates the freed slaves of Lesbos, which is a Greek island, which will be news for sure to brainy miss bat mitzvah. The Sproats are becoming quieter now. Their real lives are leaking back in. They have a plane to catch tomorrow. In the museum, Babe gamely feigns interest at the size of the fabled stone navel, a massive missile-head of a stone, and Sam has enough left to remark on the sharp sandals of Sisyphus, a general missing his head and arms. After a while, Rus trails off on his own.

Later, in their hotel room, Sam's in the shower, but Rus and Babe can't hear her singing. Sam always sings in the shower. The privacy and the siss and teem of hot, clean water flood her with a sense of animal well-being, and further down than she can tap, with an inexpressible joy at the sublime arrangement of her earthly home, its nourishing air and sky and light and living things. It's a mayfly blessing, worthy of awe.

Rus presses his ear against the bathroom door, and waves Babe over. They can just make out Sam's song.

December
Eliza Victoria

I *know a place*, Gabriel told him, and he came to him, the old man's trusty helper in that small store, as they always did, like children to the Pied Piper. Rats to the Pied Piper. Jeffrey, his name was, serving in that store too small to carry paints and brushes and heavy muslin. But the store carried the usual necessities—instant coffee, instant noodles, sugar, chips—and Gabriel found himself walking the two blocks to get to it, entering its door almost every day. The old man (Gabriel couldn't remember his name) had a different helper before, a young girl who looked like she didn't shower much. The girl didn't interest him, even as an experiment. Then the girl was replaced by Jeffrey. He could have easily lured Jeffrey out of that store if he wanted to, there was no need for the small talk and the eye contact and the small sighs and chuckles, but Jeffrey actually responded to the game. So Gabriel said *I know a place* that morning a storm was brewing in the atmosphere, that day the old man, frightened, ordered his helper to close up shop, saying, "Who would want to go out on a day like this?"

At the edge of town was an estate covered with trees, and on the spot where the trees met the road was a vast lake and a ramshackle house. Probably a guard's house years and years ago, battered down now to resemble a poor man's shanty. The day was as dark as midnight, and the wind cold and sharp—Gabriel pushed Jeffrey against one of the many swaying trees lining the road and kissed him hard on the lips, on the neck. He moved back and they walked again, kept on walking until they reached the stone steps carved against the incline. The steps led to the small, one-bedroom house.

The corners of the house were filled with hollow blocks.

Gabriel didn't know where they came from and thought they were probably left by some gang of kids or a construction crew years ago. The blocks could come in handy but inside his jacket were a coil of rope, two black plastic bags, a condom, a clean piece of cloth, and a foldable knife. Gabriel thought his own items were enough.

The inside of the house was pitch-black. Jeffrey was Gabriel's age, early twenties, but Gabriel was stronger, faster. Jeffrey fell to the floor the moment they entered the house, and Gabriel pulled his fist back, studying him. After a while, he leaned Jeffrey's unconscious body against the wall near the window so that Gabriel's back was to the door and tied Jeffrey's hands with the rope, lashing the rope around the rusty window grille. He put the black plastic bag over Jeffrey's head and placed the same coil of rope around his neck and held on to the end of it tightly. When Jeffrey stirred to consciousness again, Gabriel pressed his body against his and pulled the end of the rope. He thrust against Jeffrey, still fully clothed, and savored the way Jeffrey writhed against the ropes, trying to claw at his throat, trying to gasp for air. *Yes.* Then Jeffrey stopped moving and Gabriel unzipped both of their pants, feeling feverish, ripped open the condom with his teeth, readied himself.

After he was done, Gabriel pulled away, cleaned himself up, placed the used condom, the now soiled cloth, and the spare rope into the plastic bag left inside his jacket pocket.

"He's not dead yet."

Gabriel nearly jumped.

The little girl stood behind him, dead center in the doorway. She was wearing a long coat with huge black buttons, the coat belted at her waist. She held a black umbrella in one hand. She had white barrettes in her hair. The barrettes intrigued Gabriel—she looked so young he was amazed she could actually talk.

Gabriel stood up and brushed the dust off his jeans, not taking his eyes off her.

"How long have you been standing there?" he said, taking

out his foldable knife and flicking it at his side, showing her the blade.

The girl blinked once, twice, staring at his face as though reading him. Then she took a step toward him, the floor creaking beneath her like a gangplank over an ocean. She walked closer, inspecting Jeffrey by sight, even brushing against Gabriel's right arm, the one holding the knife. One quick thrust and—

"He's still alive," the girl said and raised her face to the hollow blocks above Jeffrey's head.

Gabriel hadn't noticed them before. They were arranged on top of what could have been a bookshelf, nailed to the wall. The girl raised her umbrella and hit the wooden supports beneath the shelf. *Whap.*

Gabriel reared back in surprise. "Stop that!"

The girl hit them again. *Whap.* The wood crumbled immediately, allowing the blocks to drop on Jeffrey's head and chest. One of his legs twitched, then became still. The girl was right.

Gabriel stared at this and groaned. "Oh, good," he said, pocketing his knife again. "Now how am I supposed to drag his body out of here?"

"Someone else can do it," the girl said. "I'll give the police a phone call, tell them I heard something crash inside the old house out by the lake."

At that moment, the skies rumbled and opened. Rain fell thickly, the sound it made on the roof deafening. The girl jerked her head and stepped back. She wiped away rainwater from her face, and not with an open palm, Gabriel noticed, but with the back of one of her hands. Like a child.

"The ceiling's dripping," she said and frowned at him as if it were his fault.

"It is," Gabriel said and glanced at the open door. "Do you think the police would believe that you just happened to pass by this house?"

"I take walks around this place often," the girl said. "This estate belongs to my family."

Gabriel did not know that.

"What's your name?" he asked.

"December," the girl said. "The kids at school call me Dee, but I don't like it. How about you? What's your name?"

"Gabriel."

A strong gust blew and Gabriel thought he felt the house sway.

"We need to get out of here," he said.

"We can share my umbrella," December said.

Gabriel refused the umbrella and just put his jacket's hood over his head and eyes. They walked along the edge of the lake and came to a well-worn path, the tree branches over their heads considerably shielding them from the rain.

"Do you do that often?" December said as they walked, Gabriel beside her.

"Do what?"

December glanced up at him and said nothing. Gabriel found himself telling her, "Sometimes I drive out of town. In the city, I leave them in the motel rooms."

December nodded.

"And I don't kill them all."

The girl nodded again.

Mud and foliage oozed around their shoes as they walked.

"This is an isolated spot," Gabriel said. December held her hand beyond her umbrella, gathering rainwater in her palm.

"Yes," December said.

Gabriel followed her, took out his knife again, flicked it again, and held the blade to the girl's back. "I can kill you right now," he said. "Leave your body here or throw it into the lake."

December glanced back. Again that look, like a scholar browsing through a difficult text. Gabriel thought the girl looked hurt for a while, then the pained expression was replaced by brightness. "You won't do that, though," she said, glowing with this epiphany.

She was right. Again. Confused, Gabriel folded his knife

and placed it in his pocket.

"This way," December said, holding out a hand for his hand. Gabriel found himself giving it to her.

They must have walked for ages. Gabriel felt like they were walking in a dream filled with wet wind and falling branches; perhaps he had fallen asleep inside the house by the lake on top of Jeffrey after he came. That sometimes happened, when he's too comfortable. Usually he'd stay up while his partner slept, and in his head, he'd say things like, *If he twitches his toe before I can count to ten, I'll kill him*, or, *If she kicks away that pillow with the blue stripes before the hour strikes, I'll get dressed and leave.*

But they soon reached December's house, which Gabriel hadn't seen before. It was in a sort of cul-de-sac, the mansion completely surrounded with trees swaying with the storm. Gabriel relinquished December's hand and wrapped his fingers around the bars of the estate's enormous gate. There was no guard but there was a white panel on the brick wall where the gate was connected. A little red button on the panel was blinking above a rubber pad.

December pressed the rubber pad.

"Yes?" a voice said, squawking from the panel.

"It's me," December said.

December held onto her umbrella. They waited. The front door of the house, which was at the end of a long driveway, opened, and out came a woman with gray hair and a black umbrella.

"Is that your mother?" Gabriel asked. December looked at him and frowned.

Gabriel stepped back from the gate.

"Where are your parents, then?" he asked.

"Not here," December said. "They travel. Do you live with your parents?"

"No," Gabriel said. "They're dead."

The woman reached the gate. She reached toward the brick wall—probably toward another panel—and the gates hissed and pulled apart.

"Come in," December told Gabriel.

"No, I'd rather go."

"No, come in. I need to make a call, remember?"

The girl could have winked. Gabriel sighed, exasperated. He greeted the old woman, who gave him a curt nod.

"Come *on,*" December said, took his hand again.

It was a house of bounty. Wall-to-wall carpeting, paintings on the wall, high ceilings, vases the color of opal and no plants in them. There didn't seem to be a lot of helpers around, however, which surprised Gabriel, but perhaps the parents had whisked them all away.

"Would you like to have your snack, miss?" a woman in a maid's uniform said, this one younger than the woman who had opened the gate for them.

"Sandwiches," December said. "Do you drink milk?"

Gabriel shrugged.

"Milk for two," December said. She said all this unsmilingly, almost rudely. But Gabriel didn't think she meant to be rude or to offend. She was *dismissive* of the maids, like they were boring wallpaper. She wouldn't even look them in the eye as she handed over her umbrella, as she gave her orders.

"We'll be upstairs," December said. "Come on, Gabriel."

Gabriel also noted that December did not even introduce him to the helpers. *He's my classmate's older brother. He's my piano teacher.* He saw the maids shoot him a suspicious look.

To get to December's bedroom, they walked on a darkened hallway, passing several closed doors. If the hallway were an alley, December's bedroom door would be the dead end. Another cul-de-sac.

December's bedroom was big enough to have an anteroom. In the anteroom were a TV/DVD set, a couch, a tiny table with a white doily on it. Behind the couch was a shelf filled with china dolls, none of which looked new or cared for. Gabriel spotted one with blonde curls dressed in a tattered orange dress. The bedroom proper had a bed, the sheets white, the blanket plaid, with a violin sitting on top of it. The walls were oak-paneled and bare. Gabriel realized that nothing in the room suggested that the occupant was a girl save for the dolls.

December flicked a switch. White light filled the anteroom, yellow light glowed inside the bedroom proper. Gabriel loved the yellow light, the muted effect of it. "You're a violin player?" he asked.

"I go to the music school." There was only one music school in town; everyone called it *the* music school.

Gabriel peeled off his drenched jacket and placed it on a chair by the door. The younger maid was standing in the doorway, holding a tray.

"Just put it on the chair there," December said, unbuttoning her coat. She was wearing a white, long-sleeved dress beneath it. The maid did as she was told, then left after shooting Gabriel another look.

December walked over to the tray, took a triangle of sandwich, handed one to him. They sat on the edge of the bed, eating their sandwiches and drinking their milk.

"So did you kill them?" December said.

"Who."

"Your parents," December said around a bite. "Did you kill them."

Gabriel looked at her.

"This isn't a melodramatic question," she said. "I'm not asking if you'd *driven* them to their deaths. I'm asking did you kill them?"

"I did not kill them."

December swallowed some milk.

"That's their house, the one you live in now?"

"No, it's all mine. I bought it with the inheritance money."

"So you weren't from around here?"

"I was born here. Then I studied in the city. College. Then I came back."

"Why?"

"Because the city moves too fast," Gabriel said. "Because you can't even stand in one corner and observe people without someone bumping into you."

December considered this answer for a moment. Then: "How do you earn money?"

"I paint."

December's eyes widened. "Oh, how *cool.*"

"Well, it's not what you think," Gabriel said, laughing. "I paint signboards. Hand-painted banners, like when a student graduates *cum laude* or if the mayor wins an award or gives funds to a new project. Graduations and the election period keep me busy every year." He smiled to himself. "It's the kind of job that would have driven an artist to suicide."

"But you *can* do portraits?"

"I suppose. And I play the piano."

"See?" December said, delighted. Gabriel laughed. "You're not *that* pathetic." A pause. "You play the piano?"

"Yes."

"I know how, too, but I'd rather play the violin."

Gabriel couldn't finish his glass of milk, so December offered to take it. She was holding his glass when she lifted the phone receiver and dialed.

"Yes," she said. "Hi. This is December from the big house? Yes. I was taking a walk and I think I heard something crash inside the shanty out by the lake. No. No, this is before the rain fell. Well, it *is* windy, but … of course. All right. Thank you. Yes, yes, thank you very much."

December sat down again and drank from his glass. "They said they'll check it out, but I seriously doubt they'd do that. The woman who answered the phone sounded lazy."

"It *is* stormy outside."

"But they're *the police,*" December said. "Isn't that their *job?*"

Gabriel didn't know what to make of that statement until December laughed. Gabriel joined her belatedly.

"Would you like another sandwich?" she asked.

"I really should go."

December smiled as he stood up. "Nice talking to you, Gabriel."

"Is December really your name?" Gabriel said as he shrugged into his jacket. "You're not pulling my leg?"

December frowned. "Well, that's just *insulting*."

They burst out laughing.

"We can meet by the lake again," the girl said. "Tomorrow. I'll bring more sandwiches."

"Wouldn't that be dangerous?" Gabriel said. "To meet by the lake, I mean."

"They *won't* check it," she said. "They all think I'm not right in the head."

Gabriel regarded her for a moment. Then: "What time?"

At nine the next morning, it wasn't raining anymore, but it was still very dark, and the wind seemed unable to make up its mind, increasing then suddenly dropping its speed every fifteen minutes or so like a child playing a game, trying to compensate for the absence of rain. Gabriel wore another jacket over his first because the moment he stepped outside his door, a breeze blew and froze him to the bone. He wondered if December was wearing the same belted coat again. It was stylish but didn't seem to be made of thick material. He wondered why he was wondering this.

The first thing he saw when he got to their meeting place from the road was a figure floundering in the middle of the lake. He saw a flash of long black hair and immediately ran to the water, not thinking, just stopping long enough to shed his outer jacket. He dove in and swam as fast as he could. The lake was deep enough to drown even a grown man. "December!" he shouted every time his mouth broke surface.

Then December turned her head and something in her stare made Gabriel freeze in mid-swim. She raised her hands from the water, and something her size bundled in peach-colored clothing floated to the surface.

It was another girl, now floating facedown on the surface of the lake, her dress ballooning around her body, her hair fanning out. Gabriel understood that the floundering thing he saw earlier was *this* girl, not December, who in fact had now turned to face him, treading water, gracefully, seemingly without much effort.

They stared at each other.

"You scared the life out of me," Gabriel said.

"I *can* swim," December said, looking indignant.

"I didn't know that. And anyway, what if you had a leg cramp?"

December sighed. "Yes, that is possible."

Gabriel refused to ask who the girl was.

"What will you do now?" he said.

"I'm thinking maybe I could ask you to carry her and leave her somewhere around the estate."

"You want to make the police to believe she drowned. Leaving her near some trees wouldn't make that believable."

"That's not what I was planning at all," December said. "I just wanted her out of my sight."

"Death by drowning is a practical alibi."

"Maybe we can tie a rock at the end of a rope and let it drag her down with it."

Gabriel sighed. "December, we don't have a—"

December was staring at the shanty, still miraculously erect despite the savage wind.

The inside of the house smelled awful; it would only be a matter of time before the wind carried Jeffrey's decaying smell and slammed it against the police station. Removing the cord around Jeffrey's neck was next to impossible, so Gabriel just untied the rope around Jeffrey's hands. It took him a fairly long time.

"I thought you had died in there," December said, who had left the water. Gabriel made her wear the jacket he had taken off earlier.

The task turned out to be harder in practice than in theory, but after several tries, Gabriel successfully secured the rope around the dead girl's waist. He held his breath and guided the body down to the bottom of the lake and placed more rocks on her back. The dead girl remained where she was, facing the sandy bottom.

Gabriel swam back up and took slow, deep breaths, running his hand across his face. December was standing on the edge, waiting for him. She was now carrying a picnic basket.

"I told you I'd bring sandwiches," she said.

Gabriel walked up to her, dripping wet.

"Oh," December said, staring at the ground, "you jumped in with your shoes."

"I thought you were drowning," Gabriel said, a bit peeved. "Of course I jumped in with my shoes."

December was silent.

"We could go back to our house," she said. "You could change into my father's clothes."

"No, your maids would ask too many questions."

December looked at him with a puzzled look, as though the idea was inconceivable to her.

"We could tell them I had leg cramps and you jumped in to save me."

Gabriel had to smile. He took the picnic basket from her. "It would be best if nobody knew we were at the lake today," he said. "Do you mind walking?"

"No, I love walking."

Gabriel nodded. "If you're for it, we could walk to my house. There aren't a lot of people around."

"You'd let me into your house?" December said, bouncing a little. Gabriel shifted his gaze to look at her.

She stopped, seeing him looking. "Okay," she said.

The wind must have scared everyone else in town, shoved them indoors. Gabriel and December, shivering now, met only two people on the road, an old man and an old woman, who walked with shuffling steps, their eyes trained on the ground.

Gabriel's house had only one floor but a lot of space. He had bought it from an old man who decided to move in with one of his kids in the city. The front porch led to the front door, which led to the combined living room and dining room, which led to the kitchen, which led to the kitchen door, which led to the back porch, the yard ending in a tall cement wall. On the wall in the living room/dining room were two doors, one leading to Gabriel's room, the other to a guest room, which he used as a studio/work area.

On the wall space between the doors hung framed charcoal and watercolor sketches of people in profile, people hunched over a book or a piece of bread, people sitting down, people laughing at something, people looking everywhere but at the artist. December, having dried off and changed into one of Gabriel's big college sweatshirts, stood in front of these sketches and studied them.

"Here," Gabriel said. He had wrung their clothes as best as he could and hung them in the bathroom; later he'd push them into the dryer. He was shaking two orange pills onto December's open palm.

"What's this?"

"Vitamin C."

December raised her eyebrows. Gabriel smiled and shoved the bottle's label at her face.

"Okay, okay," she said and crunched the pills in her mouth.

They unloaded the picnic basket on the couch, settling it between them. "I brought coffee," December said, handing him a padded thermos. "I noticed you didn't like milk that much."

"That's thoughtful," Gabriel said and screwed open the thermos. "What are you looking at?"

December was looking at the sketches.

"They wanted to be drawn like this?" she said.

"No," Gabriel said. "They didn't pay me for these. They didn't even know I was sketching them. They're just people I found sitting in parks, outside their homes. I don't get any money from doing this, but at least it keeps me occupied."

"To keep you from—"

December stopped. They sat unmoving for a second, the understanding passing between them.

"You know," Gabriel said, handing her a sandwich, "I've never thought of *that* since yesterday."

"Is that a good thing?" December asked.

He couldn't paint. Every single one of the sketches represented a successful kill, and after the encounter with Jeffrey, he tried painting an imagined field, a blue-black sky, but he couldn't finish it. He threw it away and was surprised to discover that he didn't see it as too much of a loss.

Gabriel took a sip of coffee. "I'm not sure yet."

"Maybe someday you can sketch me."

He sighed and stared into the open thermos.

"I won't look at you, if that's what you want," December said, pressing now. But Gabriel just laughed.

"Come on," December said after they'd eaten. "Well if you won't sketch me now, at least show me your piano."

Gabriel's room was considerably smaller than December's room, maybe even smaller than her anteroom. The curtains were drawn but they were thin enough to filter in a square of weak, gray light. To the left from the door, a study table, a wall of books.

Squatting near the windows, gleaming in the semi-dark, was the piano.

Gabriel sat in front of it, thought for a second, and moved over to give room for December. She sat beside him, her hands on her lap. "Play something," she said.

Gabriel placed his fingers over the keys and began Beethoven's "Rage Over A Lost Penny."

"Oh, *please*," December groaned, sending the rondo to a quick halt.

Gabriel looked at her, bit his lip, thinking, then began playing in almost tentative strokes, "Moonlight Sonata."

He played the sonata's First Movement, December looking on, hushed by the music, her hands on her lap.

There was silence after. "My parents are dead," December said. "They died last year in a car crash. I live alone in the house now with the help. Sometimes my father's siblings drop by to check on me, but I don't like them. The lawyers handle everything else."

Gabriel launched into Rachmaninoff's "Etude-Tableau Op. 39 No. 6," stopped, then settled with "Fur Elise."

"You remind me so much of myself when I was your age," Gabriel said as he played.

"Oh, you mean you wore dresses, too?"

Gabriel did not laugh, did not comment. He wanted to tell her to stop—*but stop what?*—and that she deserved something more—*but what does that mean exactly, to say that someone deserves something more?* This had never happened before, this frustration born of not being able to put what he wanted to say into words. His fingers, free of this burden, glided across the piano keys without effort.

December leaned toward him, resting her right temple against his arm. Gabriel let her.

* * *

December had string quartet practice in school the next day, so she asked Gabriel if perhaps he could accompany her. Gabriel readily said yes, meeting her at the mansion and offering to carry her violin. He wanted to see her play. Once out of the car and in front of the music school, Gabriel surprised himself by holding out his hand to hold hers.

The music school was a group of three whitewashed buildings sitting together—one facing the street, the two facing each other—on an enclosed property. The name of the school arched across the gate, loomed over Gabriel, the gray sky and swaying trees as its backdrop.

They entered the main building, the one facing the street. Walking past the lobby, Gabriel overheard scraps of conversation from a group of parents standing in a circle on the marble floor. One of the men waved at December. December gave him a small smile.

They entered a room with wooden floors and a high ceiling. There were three kids—two boys and another girl—already inside, fixing their instruments. They all looked older than December. "Hello, Dee," they said, and December glanced up at Gabriel as if to say, *Did you just hear that?*

December wasn't the only one with a companion, but the other people assisting the kids looked more like the house help than close relatives. Perhaps these were the kids of the parents laughing up a storm in the lobby Gabriel thought, settling on a seat in the front row.

"As I was saying," Violin Two, a boy, said. December had mentioned to Gabriel on the way over that she was Violin One. "It's the reason people are so unsatisfied and unhappy."

"What is?" December said, studying her music sheets.

"The belief that life has a purpose," Violin Two said.

December gave him a blank stare.

"Suicide bombers think life has a purpose and that that purpose is sacrifice and blowing up other people," Violin Two continued. "If they think life has no purpose, they'll be so depressed that instead of strapping themselves with dynamite, they'll be listening to My Chemical Romance or reading Camus."

"The MCR reference sort of threw me off," Viola said, another boy. Cello, a girl, snorted, hiding her laughter.

"Or they can ask themselves if they really exist," Violin Two said. "*That* can keep them busy for a lifetime. Crisis averted."

"You know what makes *me* unsatisfied and unhappy?" Viola said. "The fact that Veronica's still not here."

Gabriel noticed Cello looking at him. She quickly looked away, leaned toward December, and said something in a very soft voice. December nodded, said something back. Cello looked up again, saw him looking, and very nearly smiled.

Children to the Pied Piper Gabriel reflected but for some reason didn't pursue the thought.

"Where *is* Veronica?" Cello asked suddenly, looking back at the piano behind them.

"I've strangled her," December said, putting her violin to her chin. "Dropped her to the bottom of the lake."

A silence, then the kids started laughing.

"You wish," Viola said.

"Dee hates Veronica with a passion," Cello told Violin

Two, who apparently didn't know who they were talking about.

"Veronica's a decent pianist but she's a show-off," Viola said.

"Everyone in this school's a show-off," Cello said, and Viola laughed.

"Wait, was Veronica the girl you were talking to last Friday?" Violin Two asked Viola.

"She was talking *at* me, but yes."

"I think my mother just spoke to her mom yesterday. She didn't arrive home last night."

Cello and Viola stared at him, then at December, uneasy now, realizing how tasteless her earlier joke ("joke"—Gabriel added the quotation marks in his head) had suddenly become in light of the news.

"And?" Cello said.

"Well, I think they called the police," Violin Two said and shrugged, rapidly losing interest in his own story. "We're practicing 'Harp' today, right?"

They played the first movement, and Gabriel, the only person wide awake and intently listening among the quartet's small audience, began to realize that December's face had never before shown so much emotion as when she played the violin. She seemed too open and it overwhelmed him, as though she were a door that was supposed to be locked. He almost felt the need to look away.

The other people inside the classroom clapped after they were done playing. Gabriel followed suit. December caught his eye and they briefly smiled at each other.

"Now what," Cello said.

"I can play the piano for you, I suppose," Viola said to December, placing his instrument on his lap while studying the music sheets. "But I haven't practiced this sonata."

"Gabriel can play the piano," December said.

Gabriel wasn't surprised by this suggestion. "What piece were you supposed to practice today?"

"'Violin Sonata No. 9, Movement III.'"

Gabriel glanced at his shoes and smiled. "Do you know that there are actually other composers besides Beethoven?" he said, looking up.

This got a laugh from the quartet. Even December offered him a giggle.

"So will you play the piano for me?" December said, standing up, lifting her violin.

Gabriel felt forlorn, like December just asked him if he would lie across the train tracks to save her life. "Of course," Gabriel said.

"I think you're the boy who did the banner for my niece."

The man who had waved at December earlier was talking to him. Gabriel was already outside the building, waiting for December in the parking lot. The man was standing beside his car. Inside the car, on the driver's seat, was a big, muscular man with a shaved head.

"Did she graduate valedictorian?" Gabriel asked, intrigued by the man's driver.

"Salutatorian."

"Yes, then that's probably me. I sign my banners with my name, all letters in lowercase."

"I don't exactly remember seeing that but I recall the fine lettering."

Gabriel smiled and looked away.

"Gabriel, is it?" the man said.

"That's right, sir."

"I snuck in toward the end of the practice session. You play good piano."

"Thank you."

"How do you know December?"

The lie came easily enough. "I was walking by the estate during the storm. She was taking a walk and her umbrella got stuck. I just helped her. She said she loves taking walks."

"Oh, that's true," the man said. "So you just met?"

Gabriel sized him up and nodded cautiously.

"You seem very close." The man sighed and didn't meet

Gabriel's eye when he said, "Unnaturally so."

Gabriel was amused.

"She's a good kid, sir. She's like a little sister to me."

The man did not mirror Gabriel's smile. "Well, that better be the case."

When the kids came out, Gabriel saw that the man was Cello's father. Cello gave him another smile before boarding the car.

In time, only Gabriel and December were left in the parking lot.

"We'll just wait for the driver," she said, sitting on the curb.

"Who was that guy you greeted in the lobby?"

December cupped her face with both hands and frowned, thinking. "Oh, that's Bob. One of my parents' lawyers."

"No wonder he had a thug." Gabriel grinned. "He thinks I'm a pedophile."

December burst out laughing. "You should have told him you kill people, too."

Gabriel lost his smile. "Did you," he began, but someone passed by the parking lot, a man with a briefcase, perhaps a teacher. Gabriel waited for him to pass by, get out of earshot. The seconds ticked undisturbed.

Gabriel tried again. "Did you do that so I would play the piano for you?"

"Do what?"

Gabriel glanced at the sky, at the ground.

"I told you," December said and jumped to her feet, walking across the painted line on the ground separating the parking spaces, arms outstretched like a tightrope walker. "She annoys me."

Gabriel felt something heavy weigh on his chest. "December, you can't—"

December stopped, lowered her arms. She turned around slowly. "Can't what."

Gabriel looked away. "Can't what," December demanded.

"You can't just—" Gabriel's heart was racing. He didn't

know why he was saying what he was saying. He didn't know what he wanted to say.

"*What,*" December said.

Gabriel hung his head. "Nothing. Nothing."

"You think I drowned her *for* you?" December said. "Who do you think you are? You think you're *special* to me?"

"You can't," Gabriel said. "You can't do that."

"Do what?" December moved closer to him. "Kill? *You're* telling me this?"

Gabriel stared at her, his eyes weary. "It's not that simple."

December glared at him. "I can march up to the police right now and tell them what I saw that morning."

Gabriel said nothing.

"You can walk from here, right?" she said, turning away now, dismissing him.

Gabriel sighed. "I suppose so," he said. "Will you be all right, December?"

She didn't reply. Gabriel put his hands in his pockets and walked away.

* * *

Gabriel forgot that December had school the next day, so when he came over to the mansion that late afternoon to bring his peace offering, only the old woman, who was perhaps the *mayordoma,* met him at the gate. That's when he saw the tarpaulin-covered form in the yard. He didn't notice it before.

"Is that a boat?" Gabriel asked.

"Yes," the old woman said. "We were taking it out to clean it."

So that was why when December got home, she received a hand-written note from Gabriel telling her to meet him at the lake. Gabriel smiled and waved from the boat when she arrived.

He paddled over to her. "Hello," he said.

"My maids are scared of you," December said. "They said they helped you bring the boat here because they were afraid you'd strangle them."

"And yet they let you come here alone."

"They couldn't make me *not* do anything," December said. In a softer voice she added: "Besides they don't really care."

"Your maids said you haven't been on this boat in a long while."

December frowned. "My maids talk too much."

For a moment there was only the sound of water gently hitting the side of the boat.

Gabriel stood up carefully and reached out his hand. "Come on."

December looked at him. Ten seconds later she gave him her hand, and Gabriel was relieved.

He paddled to the middle of the lake, December facing him, hugging her knees to her chest.

Gabriel gestured back at the house behind him. "So the police haven't—"

December shook her head. "Is he an important guy?"

Gabriel shrugged. "Store helper. The previous helper was a girl and she ran away with some money months ago. I suppose the storeowner was just relieved this one disappeared without taking anything from him."

"Herbert said the police have been asking for Veronica," December said.

"Who's Herbert?"

"You've met him at the school. He plays second violin."

"Oh."

"They have no reason to look for her here."

"So you," Gabriel said, "you didn't invite her here, or something like that?"

"No, she was just walking on the road up there."

The sky was already starting to turn a deep orange. For a split-second, Gabriel realized that if December was serious about running to the police about Jeffrey, he could just raise one of the paddles at this very instant and hit December across the face, let another rock drag her to the lake's depths. But the maids would know; he would have to kill the maids, too.

For the first time in his life, Gabriel hated himself for thinking this way.

"I won't tell, I was just bluffing," December suddenly said. "You don't have to drown me here."

Gabriel was rattled, then hurt.

"What?" he said.

"I won't tell them about that guy in that house, I said. You don't have to kill me."

"Why would I do that?"

"Wasn't that your plan?"

"Jesus, December, *of course not.*"

"You're telling me it never crossed your mind *at all.*"

Gabriel sighed. "Let's not fight, okay."

They stayed in the boat for five more minutes, silent.

"I have a gift for you," Gabriel said. "It's in your room."

The old woman had placed it on December's bed. She squealed when she saw it.

It was a charcoal sketch of her, drawn as to make it look like she was facing the artist. Since it was sketched in charcoal, it was black-and-white, but Gabriel, at the last instant, decided to color her eyes with pastel, mixing brown and orange, the eyes dancing with light.

December lifted the sketch and gazed at it for a long while.

She was smiling brightly when she finally turned to him. "Thank you," she said and put her arms around his waist. The gesture surprised Gabriel but he was surprised more by what it made him feel. He felt his throat constricting. He placed one hand on December's shoulder and one on top of her head, pulling her closer to him. "I'm glad you liked it," Gabriel said and hardly recognized his own voice.

From somewhere inside the room came the buzz of the intercom. "Attorney Melendez is here, Miss," one of the maids said.

"That's Bob," December said and approached a box on the wall above the headboard. "Let him in."

"I should go," Gabriel said.

December sat on the edge of her bed. "Maybe he just wants me to read something. All these lawyers make me read so many papers, but I don't really understand any of them. They should just call my aunts."

Gabriel glanced at the door. "You know what he'd think when he finds me here?" he said, and December laughed.

Bob, in a white polo shirt this time, arrived minutes later with his driver (*Thug*, Gabriel thought). "Oh," he said when he saw Gabriel. December could hardly suppress her laughter.

But when she finally looked at her parents' lawyer, she saw something in his face that she didn't like. "And I even prepared a little speech to ease you into it," Bob said. "Grab him."

The order was directed at the driver, who lunged at Gabriel. Gabriel was too surprised to evade the attack. The driver whirled him around easily, pinned his hands behind his back, and pushed him facedown onto the bed, his knees hitting the floor. December shrieked. Gabriel turned his head to the side so he could breathe. He heard the lawyer lock the door. December grabbed her bedside lamp and made to hurl it at the driver, but he was quick, and he seemed used to this kind of situation. The driver reached out and slapped December across the face, flattening her against the bed. The lamp fell with a dull thud to the carpeted floor. Gabriel yelled when she was hit and felt that one of his hands was momentarily free of the driver's grip. But the driver saw this and he jabbed his fingers into Gabriel's side.

Gabriel screamed as the pain shot up his rib cage.

December began to shout his name but Bob was on her, covering her, gagging her with his right hand, his left hand pinning her right hand to the bed. He, still fully-clothed, humped against her, growled a bit, and dove into the skin of her neck. December tried to scream behind the hand on her mouth but only produced a long, disgusted moan.

"No!" Gabriel screamed, starting to cry, his tears seeping

into December's sheets. "No! No! Stop it!"

"You know," Bob said to him, "when I saw you at the school, I thought you've already gotten to her first."

"You bastard!" Gabriel shouted.

"There's one way to find out," Bob said, placing December's right hand on her chest, sandwiching it between their bodies. Bob pushed her up higher, so that Gabriel now faced their thighs. Bob's left hand, now free, moved beneath December's skirt, between her thighs. He grunted, his hand moving, moving. December struggled to move from beneath Bob's weight, uttered that muffled scream again.

Gabriel sobbed into the bed.

"Yes," Bob whispered into December's hair, and December suddenly jerked her right leg.

The sudden movement distracted Bob's driver, and Gabriel found that his right hand was free again. This time he was furious enough to ram his elbow into the driver's ribs, furious enough to lift the fallen lamp from the floor and hit the driver on the head with it. Gabriel whirled, lifted Bob by his collar off of December, and hit him, and continued hitting him even as he lay on the floor, as though Bob's face were a bright light against the carpet he couldn't turn off no matter how hard he tried. He wanted to hit him again and again and again, but December had sat up on the bed and shouted, "Gabriel!" And so he dropped the lamp on Bob's chest and came to her, gathering her in his arms.

They called the police. Gabriel hadn't killed the men, merely sent them to sleep, and so calling the police appeared to be the safest thing to do. They walked around December's room, photographing things, taking notes. The blood on Bob's fingers and December's underwear, and the streaks on her thighs, pretty much said it all. The police talked in gentle, apologetic tones to Gabriel and December, careful not to look too closely, as though they themselves had committed the crime and were ashamed.

While the police questioned the maids, Gabriel and

December sat at the bottom of the staircase, facing the wide open door. December, who had changed her clothes, rested her head against Gabriel's arm. At least two police cars were parked outside, along with an ambulance. They watched the sky change color.

"Gabriel," December said.

"Hm."

"Doesn't it get lonely in your house? You know, you're alone and all."

"I've never thought about it."

"Think about it now then."

"Yes," Gabriel said. "Yes, I suppose it does."

"You can live here. We have lots of rooms."

"Hm."

"The sky is pretty, isn't it?"

"It is."

"Have you ever tried painting the sky, Gabriel?"

"We did some exercises in college."

"I mean, for *yourself.* Have you ever tried painting the sky for *yourself.*"

"I," Gabriel said, suddenly weary. He could hear the maids crying in one of the rooms, the policemen asking questions, and moments later, he felt December pull back and stare at him, surprised, worried, because he was trembling, because he was crying, now, crying harder than the maids.

"I haven't," he said, and December told him that it's all right, Gabriel. It's all right.

Why the World Is Not my Oyster
Remy Braun

I can't remember if I need Romaine or Iceberg. Not like I even notice the difference between the two, because come on, lettuce is lettuce, but if I went home with Iceberg instead of Romaine, Robert would just lose it. Oh! So it was Romaine! Or was it? And so I'm standing in front of the produce section, talking to the heads of lettuce, hoping that one of them will just jump out of its Styrofoam cradle and into my shopping cart so that I can move on to the mustards, which we've run out of, as Robert has "reminded" me seven times. Per day.

I finish up in the condiment aisle, pass by the breads because I'm on this new no-carb diet that isn't the Atkins diet but still bans potato bread from my toaster, but linger in the cereal section, whisper a few sweet words, and continue on my supermarket journey. I stop to visit my dearest comrade, the butcher guy, and I ask him how the chops are today. He says they're not as good as mine. I order the same two pieces of boneless, skinless, white chicken as always and only wonder for a minute what it would be like to let this butcher handle me in his meat covered hands. Walking away with my plastic-wrapped dinner for two, I can't help but smell filet mignon on my clothes.

In line for the cashier, I flip through the tabloids, eyeing the Hershey bars (with almonds) lined up in a perfect, chocolaty row, but firmly shake my head and try to focus on which new starlet has an eating disorder today. As I break down and reach for a Hershey bar (with almonds), I see a green apron rushing towards me and question whether it's actually possible for my nutritionist to have a spy in the supermarket. His nametag, "Steve," doesn't really suggest covert operator. I grab the chocolate bar.

"Excuse me, ma'am, but is this your ring?" His open palm displays the sparkling, princess-cut, 2-karat diamond that Robert presented me with eight years, three apartments, and two miscarriages ago. I look down at the fourth finger on my left hand, bare, but not quite naked ...

"No."

He looked down at the ring, back at my face, and down at the ring again. I watch him walk away, clutching my ring in his sweaty fingers. Shaking my head, I try to understand what just happened and unwrap the chocolate bar, hoping that 270 calories will help me figure out why I just let some pimply stock boy with greasy hair put my wedding ring in the Food Emporium's lost and found bin. I push my shopping cart forward and concentrate on chewing as the cashier scans my Romaine lettuce and chicken cutlets. I chew until there's nothing separating my teeth but the thin skin I learned about in high school Biology, hand over my (Robert's) credit card, and sign my (Robert's) name on the receipt.

As I load my double-bagged groceries into the trunk of the SUV Robert just leased for me, I realize that what I just did isn't exactly okay. I slam the trunk door, push my shopping cart far away enough so that I won't hit it but the car next to me might, and get into the driver's seat. I just gave my wedding ring away. I turn the key in the ignition and put the car in reverse. I just gave my *wedding ring* away. I check my mirrors and look over my shoulder as I back the car out and head for the exit. *Who* gives her *wedding ring* away?! I slam on the brakes and imagine the screeching sound my tires would have made had Robert not been the type of person to walk around every night with a pressure-checker. I can't just leave my ring here, but what do I do? I can't go back in there and say, "Oh, hey, it actually *is* my wedding ring, I just forgot." Just because Steve probably goes to community college doesn't mean he can't figure out that that doesn't sound right. And then he'll think I'm trying to steal the ring, and he'll call the police, and I'll end up in a jail cell for the night, or two nights, or three, and I'll have to shower with other women (which I don't even consent to when I'm at the gym), and someone will try to make me their girlfriend, and I get hives just from thinking that women in the communal dressing room at Loehmann's can see me in my underwear. But I also can't go home to Robert without my wedding ring. What am I supposed to say to him? "Oh, hey Robert, I dropped my ring at the supermarket, and when the stock boy tried to give it back to me, I said it wasn't mine, please pass the salad with Romaine lettuce."

A honk brings me back to reality before I can begin to speculate just how Robert would react. Looking in my rearview mirror, I see a line of angry women in their SUVs and minivans, pissed off that I'm keeping them from their ovens and Pilates tapes. Eager, almost, to begin making dinner, squeezing in a precious twenty minutes of Jazzercise before devoting even more of their day to making their families happy and fed. I gag and put the car in drive.

An hour and fifteen minutes later, my cell phone's faux-Mozart ring tone blares heartily. Lying in my fully reclined driver's seat, covered in burger wrappers and ketchup packets, I remember vaguely something about diamond-covered vegetables. The phone rings again and I jump up, noticing that there is no ring on my finger, my husband has been trying to call me five times, and I have been napping for forty-five minutes in the McDonald's parking lot. And of course, I was parked in a handicapped spot. Maybe if I give Robert the ticket first, he won't be as angry about the case of the missing(ish) ring. The phone is still ringing. If I don't pick up, what will happen? Is his left arm tingling right now? Is it possible that he will actually have a heart attack? The phone stops ringing. I hold my breath. It rings again, I slowly exhale, and I press the talk button.

"Where have you been I've been trying to call you for the past thirteen minutes and I was so nervous that something had happened to you—"

I let him continue.

"And I thought that maybe you were hurt and I was worried because I haven't checked the airbags in your car yet this week and I didn't know if maybe you crashed into a church or something and the airbag didn't deploy so I didn't know whether or not I should start calling the hospitals to look for you ..."

I put the phone down and finished off my Oreo McFlurry, which had turned into that melty-gooey-liquid ice cream that always gets all over my clothes. Robert was still ranting into the phone as I licked renegade globs of ice cream from my cashmere sweater. Picking up the phone, I cut in.

"And I was thinking that maybe a tracking device—"

"Robert, that seems far too intense, why don't we just try using a leash first?"

"What? What does that mean, I don't understand—"

"Oh Robert, I can't hear you, I'm entering a no service ..."

I hang up the phone and close my eyes, reach down, and return my seat back to its full and upright position. I roll down the window and dump all of my trash and half-eaten food onto the ground and start driving back towards the supermarket, the parking ticket still flailing underneath my windshield wiper. I park in front of a jewelry store and bypass the parking meter but remember to lock my car twice. The very beautifully dressed man at the counter is staring at my head, so I pick the stray fries from my hair and stick them in my pocketbook. It's a good thing I don't need replacement diamonds more often. He smiles at me but apparently hasn't yet mastered the skill of hiding disgust in his eyebrows, as they are raised at least a mile high.

"Are you sure you're in the right place?" Handsome McMansome asks me as politely as he can without burning sage in my face.

"I want a 2-karat princess cut diamond on a platinum band with two small trilliant diamonds on either side. Size 7."

"That's impossible."

He leads me over to the case of rings, and I look at all of them but cannot find a single one that could pass for the ring I just polished that morning. "Can't you just take the two trilliants off of that ring and the princess off of that one and combine the three on a platinum setting in the next 10 minutes because I'm kind of in a hurry and would really appreciate it if you could cooperate with me just a little?"

I watch as he tries to maintain that glowing smile with the tricks they must have taught him in etiquette school, and as he's pretending to be wrapped in percale sheets with a man who has great hair and a gym membership, I watch him compose himself like the gentleman he thinks he is. "I already told you, that's impossible. Maybe you should go check out the selection at Wal-Mart."

I definitely hear Handsome McMansome let out the sigh of all sighs as he hears the little bell tinkle on my way out of the door to his evil jeweled kingdom. I hope he's as excited as I am when he finds the French fries I hid in his display case. On top of the diamond tennis bracelets.

I run into the toy shop next door and buy the first cowboys-'n-Indians plastic pistol I see. I then go and buy a can of black spray paint from the art supply store across the street. I go into the little alley between the art store and the deli and spray paint my gun on top of a dumpster. I run into the deli for a chocolate chip cookie as I'm waiting for the gun to dry. I buy another one to go. I drive back to the supermarket, and since the ticket has miraculously managed to remain intact and in place the whole time, I take it as a sign to park in the handicapped spot again. I grab my slightly sticky plastic gun, straighten my skirt, and leave the keys in the car this time. Walking through the automatic doors, I point the gun at Steve. He stares at me. I look at the gun. He looks at the gun. "Give me the ring," I said. He does. I leave.

When I pull up to the front of the house, I throw the toy gun into the trunk. I grab the ticket from the windshield and throw it back there, too. As I walk through the front door, I slip my ring over my finger. "Robert," I announce, "it's time to move again."

Into the Frying Pan
Tiffany Hawk

The last three flights I boarded tonight canceled. Unfortunately, they weren't called off before we filled every seat, served plastic trays of chicken and beef, poured umpteen cups of tap water passed off as bottled, and screened tonight's movie, *Chicken Run,* twice in order to calm the hundreds of people United is holding hostage.

Now, I'm resting my head against the window of a 727 parked at gate eighty three. They're deadheading me, or sending me as a passenger, to Denver, where they're short on crew. I'll find out what happens next when we get to Denver. *If* we get to Denver. The pilots are conducting something they refuse to call a slow down. As long as United management won't negotiate with their union, they won't pick up overtime, and they will demand every maintenance write-up be fixed, even those that could safely be deferred, such as the captain's automated seat adjuster. We've canceled 6,000 flights in the last month.

I close my eyes and hope for a moment of sleep.

Someone bumps me and I jerk upright. My contacts stick to my eyelids as I blink awake. I take that to mean I got a minute or two of sleep. I used to wonder if it was smarter to stay up all night rather than get only a few hours of sleep. Now, I know exactly how half an hour of sleep feels—significantly less painful than fifteen minutes and immeasurably less than one minute. But one minute, one glorious minute, can make all the difference. Nothing hurts as much as zero. God, I hope my mouth wasn't open.

It's a pilot. He looks about ten years older than I am, somewhere in his early thirties. He steps into my row, stooping so he doesn't hit his head on the overhead bins.

He looks down at me and smiles. I sit up a little straighter. He introduces himself as Rick and lets his hand linger as he shakes mine.

"Emily," I say without smiling back. If I've learned anything in my first few weeks on the job, it's that flight attendants don't flirt with pilots. Like crossing a picket line, it's just not done. There's a joke that demonstrates our party-line position on cockpit crew:

How many pilots does it take to screw in a light bulb? One.

He holds it up in the air and the world revolves around him.

"Emily what?" asks pilot Rick, who inevitably knows a half-dozen Emilies of both the "y" and more playful "ee" varieties.

I hesitate and then reluctantly, I say "Cavenaugh." The name has been attached to me for two years, but I'd like to step under a power washer and blast it off.

Rick pulls a small stack of clothes from his bag before stowing it in the overhead. "I'm gonna slip into something more comfortable." He laughs at this lame attempt at humor. "I'm commuting home."

As he enters the lav, I curl back into dozing position, hoping the reduced oxygen level on takeoff will help me sleep.

My recent insomnia isn't just the fear of missing a check in when the clock radio, wakeup call, *and* cell phone alarm fail. It's knowing that as a new flight attendant, one slip up will get you fired. Our constant fear of termination is not about the money. If you're the kind of person who can relocate anywhere, they tell you to, then spend twenty nights a month in twenty different hotels, you're not just earning a paycheck, you're running away.

Sometime later, Rick nudges me. I rouse and see the purser standing in the aisle with a pen and pencil.

"What would you like for dinner this evening Ms. Cavenaugh? The chicken parmesan or the salmon with lemon and capers."

It's my first time riding in first class and I'm excited, but still I say "I'll have whatever is left over."

The purser winks at me as if to say right on. I won't be the kind of flight attendant who morphs into a self-important corporate type when I'm sitting in first class—for free. When she reaches the last row and I hear what must be the tenth request for chicken, I know I'm having salmon.

"So where are you based?" asks the pilot who is now wearing a white green golf shirt and khakis.

"San Francisco."

"Ah, me too," he says. "But I commute to Denver. At least for the moment. Do you like San Francisco?"

I nod and don't tell him that I put in for a transfer to L.A. That I promised my husband I'd quit this job if I didn't get my transfer within my first six weeks. We hit six weeks a few days ago, and yesterday I slipped down the list from one-hundred and six to two hundred forty. When I saw Carl today, I lied and said my transfer was almost up. Still, he said, "Almost won't cut it." I'm not sure it matters now anyway.

The purser leans over to offer me a hot towel and twists to face Rick, placing her cleavage square in his face.

I feel the chocks release and the plane eases away from the jetbridge. Finally, I'm going somewhere.

After the purser carefully blows into the tubes of the demonstration life vest, she puts her hand on the Rick's shoulder and asks him to put his seat in the upright position. She once again leans across him, this time to pick up his pre-departure mimosa. She must be what they call a cockpit queen. I've heard of the type.

The plane creeps along the taxiway, repeatedly turning and rhythmically smacking the same pothole every few minutes.

"Recognize this box pattern?" asks Rick.

I don't, so I shake my head.

"We're going to be here a while."

His arm bumps against mine on the wide first-class armrest between us. I can feel its warmth and I am caught off guard by how soothing I find it. I have an urge to press my arm fully against his. Immediately, I want to pull it away, but that too would seem oddly deliberate. I sit straight forward, frozen in position. I slide my eyes to the left to see my hand next to his, my ring finger ringless for the first time in years. I slipped it into my purse this afternoon as I walked away from Carl in the parking structure outside the therapist's office. It's just an experiment to see what my hand feels like without its weight.

"When the ground controllers don't have room for another jet in the takeoff line, they keep us moving. They have a motto," says Rick. "A moving airplane is a happy airplane."

I laugh and shift in my seat, thankful for an excuse to let my arm drop. I look up at him. His blonde hair is thinning and has turned gray around his temples, but when he smiles, his dimples make him look like a sixteen year-old boy, innocent and kind. He is watching the purser who is standing in the galley repeatedly plunging a bag of tea into a Styrofoam cup.

"So how long have you been flying?" he asks me.

"Six and a half weeks," I say.

He looks me up and down, nodding. "I thought so. You're so regulation."

I widen my eyes to convey shock. "What do you mean by that?"

He leans across the armrest and says into my ear, "Maybe someday we can get you to let your hair down."

"But if it's below our chin we have to have it pinned up," I say and touch my tightly-formed French twist. Then I hear my cell phone ring from inside my purse. "Crap," I say, Carl again. This is the eighth time he's called tonight. I turn the phone off and stuff my purse back under the seat in front of me.

Eventually the box pattern becomes a straight line.

"Finally," says Rick.

A voice over the P.A. says, "Flight attendants prepare for takeoff." As if I were on the jumpseat, I shift into brace position for takeoff, legs together in front of the seat, hands tucked at my sides, head facing forward. We move into position at the end of the runway. I hear the engines spool up and begin my silent review. No matter how routine this job gets, we still rehearse for an evacuation with every takeoff and landing.

We race down the runway, gathering speed. Rick pulls the *Hemispheres* magazine out of his seatpocket as I mentally review throwing open doors and rushing people down slides. The plane hums louder and louder as we get ready to slingshot into the air. We're about to lift off and BANG. The noise is so loud it's as if we fired a missile from our right wing. I'm thrown forward, pressing into my seatbelt. The brakes scream and the whole plane slides from side to side.

"Holy Shit!" yells Rick. "Our gear collapsed."

The forward force is so powerful I have to press against the armrests to hold myself back in the seat.

Rick looks at me as he yells "We're full of fuel. We'll catch on fire!"

He has the entire first class cabin's attention. A man across the aisle unbuckles his seatbelt and the woman next to him screams at him to put it back on.

We continue to whip from left to right as we screech down the runway. I'm thrown back against my seat when we finally slam to a halt.

Just as I'm about to shout first command— "Release your seatbelts and get out" —a voice booms over the PA, slow and clear.

"Ladies and Gentlemen. This is your captain speaking. There's nothing to be alarmed about. We just experienced what we call a compressor stall. We'll pull off the runway for a few minutes so maintenance can inspect our engine."

In time with the passengers seated around me, I whip my

head around to look at Rick.

"Sorry," he whispers, "I guess it wasn't our gear." Thank God he wasn't in uniform or one hundred and sixty three passengers would have been rushing the doors and scrambling out window exits.

"What was it?" I ask still pressing into my seat.

"Just an engine failure."

I look at him and raise my eyebrows.

"There are two kinds of pilots," he says. "Those who have had an engine failure on takeoff. And those who will."

I give a sarcastic half laugh.

"I'm hoping that was my one and only," he says.

I hope so too. I wouldn't have wanted Mr. Cool Under Pressure in the cockpit for that one.

As if reading my mind, he says "Sorry about that. I'm kind of on edge right now." He shrugs his shoulders and says, "Personal stuff."

I offer an "ah," intended to let him off the hook without an explanation.

"My wife wants a divorce," he says shaking his head. "Fuck."

I think Whoa and Oh my God and Why are you telling me this. None of which seem appropriate, so I sit there staring at him, which is probably worse. I thought jumpseat therapy was just for flight attendants. I've found that a few minutes after meeting in briefing, my co-workers routinely confess the dirtiest details of their lives. I guess when you spend three out of four nights on the road, your latest flying partner is as close a connection as you've got.

He snaps his fingers and points his index finger out like a gun meant to say gotcha. "Too much information. I know. I'll shut up."

"Is it because of the job?" I ask. Before I accepted the job, someone told me that it would either make my relationship stronger or end it faster than I could imagine. I promised Carl it would make us rock solid, but now I wonder if I was hoping for the alternative.

Rick shrugs his shoulders.

He seems nice to me, but people would say that about Carl too. I can't imagine the pilot sitting next to me would ever take a book out of his wife's hands and throw it away because it was monopolizing her attention. I doubt he would make his wife read out loud to him so they could do everything together. There is no way he would kick his wife out of the car and leave her on the side of the road late at night just for reminding him to turn on his headlights. Or push her down onto the floor of the kitchen so hard she bruised her head on the cabinets. There is no way that his wife flew into town to meet with a marriage counselor today and heard him say, straight to her face, that physical aggression is an appropriate way to express anger. If the counselor asked for his ideas on a solution going forward, he certainly wouldn't say "If she just acts like a good wife, then none of this would have to happen."

Rick says "Let's change the subject. How about you? Do you commute?"

"No." I only got my flight benefits two days ago. A few weeks ago, I promised I'd start flying home for every day off as soon as they kicked in.

"Must be nice being young and single with no responsibilities."

"Yeah," I laugh.

"How old are you?"

"Twenty three."

"Ah, the good old days."

He reminisces about pilot training in the Navy, spending his days studying and his nights partying in Pensacola bars with groupie chicks who were looking for Maverick from *Top Gun.*

I nod along as if he's describing my life. In reality I'm so straight that I didn't even drink until I'd finished college. The first time I ever caught a buzz was right before graduation when I climbed into UCLA's Inverted Fountain, as called for by Bruin tradition, and popped Champagne with the other celebrating seniors. We were so pleased with ourselves. Years of all night studying and pre-test diarrhea had made us so much better than all the "losers" at lower-rank schools. No one mentioned the fact that every last one of us was really there because we'd been rejected from Berkeley or Stanford. Or how no one had any idea what to do next. I know I didn't. I guess that's why I moved home and married my high school sweetheart two weeks later.

"You must be living it up, flexing the flight benefits, flirting with passengers, flitting around the world all carefree. Drinking cosmos in Manhattan and absinthe in Paris with men in berets."

I haven't actually been called up for an international yet, but my training flight to London was enough to show me that if something in my life had to go, it wouldn't be the job. We hadn't even landed yet and I knew. About five hours after we left Chicago, the captain called me and LaWanda, the other trainee, up to the cockpit.

"I want to show you something," he said as he sprayed two pumps of Binaca in his mouth and turned off the lights. Then he told us to kneel and look outside. Thirty-seven thousand feet over Greenland, we pressed our faces against the 777 cockpit windows and watched the Northern Lights shoot miles above and below us, rising and falling, bursting and disappearing as abruptly as the equalizer bars on a stereo. It was several minutes before a radio call from Reykjavic Air Traffic Control broke the silence and we were sent back into the cabin to refill gin and tonics.

No matter how early in the morning or late at night when I put on my uniform, I can feel that moment's exhilaration. I can see the rest of the world every time I glance at a departure board. I can taste my freedom every time I glide, rollaboard in tow, through the neon tunnel at O'Hare while hidden speakers play Rhapsody in Blue, United's theme song.

Rick turns and looks straight at me and says "Don't ever

get married."

"I won't," I say.

He says his wife, a nurse, is fucking a doctor at her hospital. I don't know what to say, so I press my face to the glass and look back toward the tail of the plane. I can see a truck parked out there but no mechanic. We were on the runway for God's sake, we better not cancel.

He apologizes again for unloading all of this on me. I know it's really a request to continue, so I ask him if he suspected anything. For the last year, I've been imagining the signs that Carl was cheating, wishing he would cheat, so I would be off the hook. Besides, a girl on the side could have bought me some breathing room. He could ask *her* why the laundry wasn't done by 10 a.m., ask *her* to take back the fourteen dollars worth of fabric she'd bought because he hadn't been there to help pick it out, ask *her* why the hospital corners weren't flush with the edge of the mattress, ask *her* to wear turtlenecks and baggy sweaters so men don't check her out.

Rick did suspect, but he hoped it would pass, until he opened the door to his crash pad this morning and a process server threw a manila folder at him and ran down the stairs.

"You know what they say we carry in these, right," he says, kicking the black boxy flight bag stowed under the seat.

"Your divorce papers," I say and laugh, proud of myself for knowing the joke. I catch the rudeness of this response. "I'm sorry."

"An anonymous process server? What did she think? That I was going to hurt her or force her to stay with me or pull out a gun and shoot her and then myself?"

"Maybe."

"What do you mean by maybe?"

"Nothing," I say and wave my hand as if to brush the comment away. But it is interesting to know she didn't have to confront him with a divorce herself.

He starts flipping through the *Hemispheres* magazine on his lap. He doesn't stop on any page long enough to read more than the title.

I wonder if he had a big wedding, if hundreds of family members came out to support his vows, promising to help them stay together for better or worse. His wife probably doesn't care what other people think. I wish I didn't.

"Are you afraid to be on your own?" I ask.

"Me, fuck no. I'm not afraid of anything."

I've been afraid of everything. I was afraid to buy the wrong brand of Raisin Bran. I was afraid to get stuck in line at the checkout and get home five minutes late. I was afraid of leaving a water ring on the coffee table, of not getting the vacuum lines straight, I was afraid of accidentally looking in the direction of another man, a man I didn't even see.

Anything but death. I found out I wasn't afraid to die.

Last year, we were driving to see a friend of Carl's when a lowered Acura Prelude with after-market exhaust pipes pulled in front of us, admittedly too close.

"He cut me off," said Carl as he threw engine down a gear, whipped to the right and with the RPMs red-lining, passed the Prelude, pulled in front of it, and slammed on his brakes.

Miraculously the Prelude skidded into the next lane without hitting us. Moments later a traffic light turned yellow and the car moved in front of us, but instead of hitting the gas, he pressed the brakes and stopped at the light. The driver door opened. An enormous hulk of a body builder in a skin-tight, wife-beater tank top walked toward us. I don't know why but he came up to my side of the car, stood at the window looking down at me. I looked right back at him, surprised at my calm. He then began kicking my door so hard the car rocked back and forth. Four kicks later, he slowly walked back to his car and drove away.

Carl had his hands on the steering wheel, his knuckles white. "I nearly shit my pants," he said. "He could have killed us."

I thought: That's interesting. He really could have. It was as if I was on Valium. I couldn't get my heart rate up.

I couldn't get that near-death rush. I realized that I wasn't afraid to die because I was already dead.

Rick waves at me, and when I look up he says "Thought I lost you there."

I turn toward him. His eyes are a gentle blue. They look safe. I'm tempted to tell him everything.

"So. On to a happier subject," he says. "Are you seeing anyone?"

I shake my head. I don't have the energy to see anyone. If you ask Carl, I never did. No matter how I tried, I didn't have the strength, the focus, the amount of love it took to be the wife he needed. At first, I was legitimately devoted to him, and then I was even more deeply devoted to avoiding a blowout, but I couldn't get it right. I picked up a book, I got stuck in traffic, I answered the phone.

Just weeks ago, I answered the phone. It was my mom. Carl held up his hand up to demonstrate the number five—as in I'd better be off the phone in five minutes. But I pushed it. Ten minutes later, I still had the receiver pinched between my head and shoulder. I could hear him in the kitchen slamming cabinets. I'm not sure if he was looking for something or just trying to get my attention.

When I hung up, he said "You've been on the phone for more than twenty minutes."

"I'm sorry."

He grabbed a Calphalon frying pan and held it over his head.

"Who the fuck," he said as he slammed the pan into the top of the stove, "do you think you are?"

I saw an inch-deep dent on the edge of the stove and the frying pan was no longer round— he had completely flattened one side. I started to back away, but he ran past me and stood in the doorway with his arms out, blocking the exit from the kitchen.

I tried to squeeze by but he grabbed me by the shoulders.

I squirmed against the hands that were pressing into my

shoulders and shaking me.

He pushed with all his strength. I flew back and crashed into the floor and cabinets. The physical pain hit immediately—the back of my head throbbed, my left elbow burned, my wrists ached. I lay on the floor looking up at him. He stared down at me, both of us expressionless with shock.

I felt a burning in my throat and knew I was about to cry. But before my tears could form, his did. He dropped to his knees, shaking, sobbing, apologizing.

But I didn't move. I lay crumpled against the cabinet and watched the last ounce of respect I had been reserving drain from the man in front of me. It was so after-school special that I could almost see the camera on him as he ran through his lines.

"I'm sorry, I'm sorry, I'm sorry," he repeated.

My fear evaporated and the prisoner I had become floated off with it. I was filled with an enormous sense of relief.

I said, "It's okay." And what I meant was that I would be okay. By escalating from throwing things to throwing me, he had given me a gift. I could hardly suppress a smile.

I had to go to work that night, but I promised I'd come home to see a counselor, which he had offered to do. Before I drove back to my crash pad in San Francisco, I furtively packed the few photos and mementos that mattered to me. At the last minute, when he wasn't there to see, I took the frying pan too.

"Ladies and Gentlemen, your captain here again. Maintenance has given us the all clear, and we're going to attempt another take-off."

"Attempt?" I say to Rick.

He smiles and winks.

I feel the parking brake release, and once again, we are moving.

We turn toward the runway. Outside the window, I see a blinking trail of commercial jets from twenty-seat props to the double-decker 747s. We take our place in line and inch our way forward.

I look around at the silent cabin. We could probably hear each other breathe if it wasn't for the hum of the air conditioning. I've heard that when a flight suddenly becomes "eventful," you won't see the chaos of a scene from *Airplane!* You'll see quiet passengers squeezing their armrests and facing forward as if turned to stone. Well, unless you're seated next to Pilot Rick.

"Flight Attendants, prepare for takeoff."

I hold my breath and grip my armrests, surprised at the nervous energy jolting through my body. I want to sing with joy that I'm afraid, I'm afraid to die.

The airplane trembles as it builds up power, a windup toy about to be released, and we're screaming down the runway again.

No bang, no brakes, we lift off into smooth, quiet air.

I'm alive.

Confessions of a Teenage Cheerleading Ninja Wheelchairnapper
Eileen Mullane

By the time I reached high school, I was sick of hanging out with Colette. We'd been friends since 6th grade, but I'd outgrown her. She sits in this wheelchair all day and rolls down the hallways when everyone else is walking, and she never lets me try it. Ever. A real friend would just hang out on the ground or in a normal chair for five seconds while I wheeled around. But no! Even though I offered to pick her up and place her somewhere comfortable, she won't have it. To me, that is unreasonable.

Colette was run over by her stepdad in her own driveway as a toddler. It's not like she has some increasingly debilitating disease or anything. The worst is over. And it was actually kind of a good thing because, turns out said stepdad was molesting her twelve-year-old neighbor. If she'd had a working lower half, the probability of Colette being raped out would have increased like a million percent. So, even though when Colette's stepdad went to jail, her mom took off with a Hell's Angel and dumped Colette with her grandma, she is a lucky girl.

I guess it makes sense that it was Colette's serendipitous wheelchair that attracted me to her in the first place. Being in a wheelchair at Belmonte Middle School meant that you got to ride the elevator. And if you were the best friend of a person in a wheelchair, you got to be their "buddy" and accompany them on the elevator, which none of the other students were allowed to go near. Those sad losers had to use the stairs.

But now I was in high school, where the handicapped were deemed perfectly capable of carrying themselves all over solo. And even if Watertown High did allow the crippled their "buddy", it wouldn't be worth it. In middle school, people would stair at us walking down the hall. We were exotic—the girl in the wheelchair and her saintly friend. Now people just averted their eyes. Dog forbid anyone should stare at a girl in a wheelchair! Or in her vicinity, at me! It's not a crime to stare. She's unusual. That's a fact. More than 99 percent of high schoolers do not use wheelchairs. It's actually more insulting not to stare. If you're not staring, you're rude.

I had been planning to go out for cheerleader for years. It was my dream that I indulged Colette to share. Imagine my shock and horror when, due to Watertown High's bullshit diversity initiative, she actually made the squad! What a farce. Of course I did too. Of course! But say her PC mercy squad spot wasn't totally a mockery of the art of cheer—to have someone that can't use their bottom half there, when actually you need to be able to do at least five back hand springs in a row—better make it eight if you even want a chance to get on. Well, that must have made Colette feel like as big an asshole as she looked. Real nice, Watertown High Diversity Committee. Real, real nice.

And do you have any idea how much attention a girl in a wheelchair gets on a cheerleading squad? It was as if everyone was there just to cheer on Colette and not even for the football! Cheering for a cheerleader? How fucked up is that? Fuck if I was going to let some bitch on wheels desecrate my life's work. So I stole her wheelchair.

Plus, stealing someone's wheelchair is hilarious! Especially if your family is like Colette's and it's just her and her grandmother who is, get this, also in a wheelchair! Stealing the wheelchair was easy. All I had to do was tell her that I'd changed my mind about going for a run that night. To bust her balls, whenever Colette asked me to hang out, I always told her, "No, I'm going for a run," then she'd usually invite me to sleepover after. "Then just sleep over after. I just want to hang out with you." And I'd say, "Are you deaf or crippled? You can't be both." Even though you actually can.

So, I just told her I wasn't going for a run after all, and as long as she had a six-pack of Zima for me hiding in her bedroom, I would sleepover. As soon as I got to her house, I gave her an Ambien disguised as an Ativan, and when she passed, out I stole her wheelchair. Easy breezy. But not before drunk wheeling around her driveway for a minute. Turns out wheelchairs are not as fun as I thought they were. About sixteen seconds in, the novelty wore off; I folded up the chair and shoved it under the porch.

Okay: stealing someone's wheelchair is hilarious. But because Colette and her Grandmother were so poor they couldn't afford to buy a new one and had to choose, every morning, which one of them would be able to get out of bed for the day—this was ultra hilarious! I had planned on returning the chair that next night, mysteriously, like it was just back from nowhere. I even thought of leaving a note on it that said "Sorry, Colette. Needed a vacation. Sick to death of carting you around. –Chair". Oh my God, Hilarious! But I couldn't. By the time I woke up that morning, Colette had told her sob story to the police, and everyone in town knew.

By late afternoon, I was running a raffle to raise money for a new wheelchair, as well as running the phones for the anonymous tip hotline I'd set up on leads to the chair's whereabouts. I was so not going to just sit back while Colette got all the glory. My plan now was to return the chair and split the raffle profit with Colette and her grandmother 50/50 so they could buy food and I could get a new two-way pager.

But I got scared. I waited till dark, shoved the hunk of metal into my Audi, took it to my parent's yacht club, and chucked it into the Atlantic. That felt pretty good.

To add insult to injury, all the raffle money ended up going towards Colette's new electric scooter. I'm thinking of going into politics just so I can propose legislation to make her wear a helmet all the time. That would be hilarious! But at least it almost made sense now, having her on the squad. I could just pile all my cheer gear on top of her when we had to walk from school to the field. She doesn't feel weight, the motor does. I need to save my energy for the football games.

The Cat Lady's Kiss
Jerome Charyn

She'd never been kissed by a man, never even fumbled around on the dunes of Orchard Beach. She lost her cherry to Queen Donadio, the head cashier at the Italian market on Arthur Avenue. It wasn't love or anything like that. Angela must have been fifteen and the cashier kept eyeballing her one afternoon until she felt hypnotized, so she followed Queenie into the storage room. Angela didn't have to do a thing. Queenie plucked off Angela's clothes and, without a word of warning, began to nibble between her legs. Most of Queenie's scalp had vanished and Angela didn't know whether to laugh or cry. It was like having a wet tickle. And then she started to moan in rhythm to the maniacal wanderings of Queenie's tongue, and she let out a cry that was like the mooing of a cow robbed of all her milk.

Queenie dropped her after that, didn't even say one word of hello, and it wouldn't have mattered, because Angela got into trouble. Her mother was away in a mental hospital, and her father never worked; he kept sniffing around whenever Angela had her period. She didn't have the heart to punish her own Papi. They were starving and Angela began to steal—at first it was bread and apples to keep them alive, and then she became a bandit in the Bronx, stealing purses from old ladies. One of the old ladies yelled too loud, and Angela beat her over the head to stop all the yelling. The woman started to cackle and had a stroke.

Angela sat in a juvenile facility and was sent off in shackles to a prison farm the minute she turned seventeen. She had to punk for the trustees and older inmates who looked after her and saw to Angela's education. She even finished high school at the farm. Part of her education was a floating film club: an unfrocked professor would wander from prison farm to prison farm with a DVD player and a whole bag of films out of the 1940s. The one Angela liked best was about a woman who turned into a ferocious cat whenever a man tried to kiss her; even her husband couldn't kiss this cat lady, who might have torn him to ribbons, fond of him as she was.

The older inmates would laugh and say, "Yeah, she would have loved him to death." And they began to call Angela the cat lady who'd never been kissed by a man.

She was twenty-one when she left the farm. She returned to the Bronx with an institutional grey complexion. She went to work at the market on Arthur Avenue. The new head cashier was a man named Robertson. He was a jailbird, like Angela, with his own grey pall. He must have been forty. He had big ears and hands as soft and smooth as a girl's. He wouldn't leave off looking at Angela.

Robertson was quite clever with his hands. He would construct figures out of stray pieces of wire, twist that wire into walruses and lithe, prowling cats. And when he gave these wire figures to Angela, his fingers trembled. He never leered at her once or touched her behind. He was like a strange, balding knight with big ears.

Angela didn't know what to do about Robertson. She felt a slight tug in her loins, but it frightened her. "Miss Angela," he said after six months of silent, stubborn courtship. "I sure as hell would like it if we could make love."

"Where?" she asked, already imagining him ripped to shreds.

"Where else? In the storage room."

"Mr. Robertson, it would have to be at your own risk."

But her balding knight walked her into the storage room and bolted the door from inside. He touched her face. She began to purr, but it quickly became a growl.

"Mr. Robertson, do what you want with me. But we can't kiss. I'm the cat lady. And loving me might mean your own death."

He undressed her with his beautiful, soft hands.

"I wish," he said, "I wish I could shape you out of wire."

"Mr. Robertson, you already did. I'm that prowling wire cat."

He stroked her flanks, ran his fingers across her breasts until her nipples were taut and fierce as knives.

"Mr. Robertson, you'll have to make me wet. I've never been with a man."

He wouldn't stoop between her legs. He kept stroking Angela with his soft hands until her whole body quaked. But the more he aroused her, the more she felt her whiskers grow. He hovered near her mouth. Her thighs tingled, tingled with dread.

She thought of her father, who had tried to rape her with his wrinkled prick. Perhaps she was the cat lady long before she'd gone to the prison farm, waiting for her father to kiss her, so she could rip out his throat and claw him blind. Poor Papi, she sang to herself, as her own storage-room magician kept fondling her with his soft hands.

And now she knew why this balding knight appealed to her. He had Papi's big ears and famished look. Her mother had been out of her mind ever since Angela was a child, trying to stick her own head into the oven, hovering on the fire escape in her nightgown, and being led off to the asylum.

"Angela," she had wept, "your father stopped fucking me five minutes after you were born. You're his new bride."

And little Angela would walk to kindergarten pretending to wear a bride's veil. But it made no sense being married to Papi, who snored all the time and smelled like a goat. And she tore her own pretended veil.

And now she was in the same storage room where Queenie had licked her to the edge of madness seven years ago. But she didn't miss Queenie. She had Robertson, the jailbird, who began to hum under his breath, and her body stirred to that whispering music. He was shaping her with his hands, turning her into a wire creature.

She growled once, but it was no less a song than

Robertson's.

His lips grazed hers. Her mouth opened into a sweet well. His tongue tasted of cinnamon cloves and cherries on a tree. She ripped at him, but her paws didn't leave a mark. His tongue went deep. Robertson had learned how to survive a cat lady's kiss.

He grew morose within a week. And Angela wondered if he was as fickle as Queenie. But it wasn't that. A hopeless gambler, he had lost a bundle to the Albanians, who had come to Arthur Avenue with their own "caravans"—rag shops and rinky dink cafés and social clubs that the Italians tolerated because these donkeys from Albania kept Latinos from overwhelming Arthur Avenue and turning it into a second South Bronx.

The Albanians never bought property. They rented from Italian landlords and didn't interfere with the local mob bosses. These donkeys had become the enforcers of the Neapolitan social club, which had dominion over Arthur Avenue and the Belmont section of the Bronx. But Belmont was a landlocked island surrounded by the Latino wild men of Tremont and Fordham Road. It was the natural barriers of the Bronx Zoo and Quarry Road that kept the wild men away from Belmont—Arthur Avenue was hard to find— and also the Albanians, who had their own wild men. Their chieftain was Lord Lekë and he held sway over Bathgate Avenue at the ragged edge of the old Italian neighborhood.

It was this Albanian wild man who coveted Angela, had seen her in the market, had thought of kidnapping her, but didn't want to bring an earthquake to Arthur Avenue. So he sent out his spies on a reconnaissance mission. They discovered her with that jailbird, Robertson, who was a complete outsider, having grown up in Montana or some other place that didn't really exist in the minds of the Albanians. Lord Lekë and his clan sucked him deeper and deeper into their gambling dens, offered him access to their own harem of whores, and then put the screws on him. Either Robertson signed Angela over to his clan, or Lekë would send him to live with the snow leopards in the Bronx Zoo.

"But Miss Angela is not a cow," the jailbird tried to reason. "And I cannot sign her over to you, Lord Lekë."

"But you could persuade her about my charms … she doesn't have to live on Bathgate Avenue. All she has to do is visit me once, and I will cancel your debt."

Despite his fears, Robertson couldn't present such a proposal to Angela. All he could do was twist his pieces of wire into some miniature of Lekë's long nose and winter cape. And Angela, who'd been through the medieval rites and rituals of prison life, understood right away.

"That Albanian bastard thinks your markers are also mine and that he can paw me whenever he wants."

Robertson didn't say a word. His eyes practically disappeared inside his skull, and Angela knew that he would either fall into his own mad oblivion or run away. But he didn't run. And one morning, he failed to show up at work. Angela found him across Quarry Road at St. Barnabas. His face was a mask of bruises. And Angela couldn't see much else under his hospital gown.

She started to cry. "Why didn't you run home to Montana?"

"My home is in the Bronx," he said, "with you."

He'd continued his wire menagerie on the night table near his bed. Leopards and rhinos, ostriches and giraffes, like the inhabitants of some new Noah's ark. She visited him every evening after work, sat beside him, and after having sworn to herself that she'd never knit, sew, or cook for a man, she knit her balding knight a sweater. But St. Barnabas couldn't hold him forever.

So Angela did what she had to do. She couldn't have gone to the Neapolitans at their club, because she was a Latina and a little freak who liked women as much as men. She'd never been to Bathgate Avenue before, though it was five minutes from the market where she worked. She'd seen the Albanians at Dominick's; they always occupied the last two tables, always ate alone; they brought their own cotton napkins, their own knives and forks, and if one of the Neapolitan lords entered the restaurant, they would salute him with their wines glasses and return to their incredible gluttony. Dominick's had no menus, only markers on the wall. But each Albanian went through Dominick's secret repertoire of pasta dishes, each had a salad meant for five, and five espressos served in little glasses. They were never boisterous and they never asked for the bill. They would bow to the waiter and hand him an envelope stuffed with cash.

Angela knew the Albanians were taking their own time. They would swallow up Arthur Avenue in ten or twenty years, imprison the Neapolitans inside their own club without ever declaring a state of war. She recognized how shrewd their chieftain was, Lekë with his long nose, his brutal blond looks, his thick hands, and the winter cape he wore no matter what the season. He'd seen Angela across the dining room with its row after row of communal tables, had sent her a flower and a glass of coffee, which she realized must have been some kind of Albanian ritual. But she wouldn't respond. She never did, no matter how many times the coffees came in their little glasses. And now she had to prevent her bald knight from being beaten to death.

The Albanians of Bathgate Avenue had no church. They were agnostics who might have preserved a few Muslim, Christian, and Jewish signs. Albanian farmers and bandits had protected the Jews during the German occupation of their country. Not one Jew was delivered to the Gestapo and the SS. Some of the bandits began wearing skullcaps as a mark of respect; they never violated Jewish women. Stars of David and Jewish candelabra remained in Albanian homes long after the war.

And that's what Angela found in the windows of Bathgate Avenue; Jewish stars and candelabra mingled with crosses and paintings of Jesus. She didn't waver for a minute. She walked into Lekë's social club, even though the door had been painted black and there was a sign that said *CATS*

AND STRANGERS NOT ALLOWED. She'd entered a
cavern where money flew like feathers; she'd never seen such
an enterprise. Men wagered over bundles of sticks, threw
chess pieces into the air like lucky coins, and mutilated deck
after deck as they tore up cards they didn't happen to like.
There were women at the tables wearing headscarves; they
gambled with the men. They were obedient and insolent in
the same breath, bowing to Lekë and his lieutenants, who
sat on enormous pillows, and taunting them with their eyes.

They seemed frightened of Angela, who wore no scarf
and did not bow to any of the gamblers. Lekë stared at
her from his pasha's pillow—a blue-eyed Albanian. Angela
navigated among the horde of gamblers, propelled by her
love for that balding knight at St. Barnabas, and paused near
the pasha's cowboy boots. The social club was silent as a
mouse.

"Lord Lekë, we have things to discuss."

He laughed. "Have you come to seek employment, my
little cashier?"

The Albanians chortled and clapped their hands. "Lord,"
one of his lieutenants shouted, "put her to work on her back."

And the women laughed louder than the men, causing
their headscarves to ripple.

"Quiet," Lekë said. "Show the lady some respect … I have
no secrets from my men, Miss Angela. We are a family—
Michael, make her some tea!"

Lekë's minions served Angela tea in a glass that was
much too hot to hold, but she held it anyhow, drank the
bittersweet water. They served her little cakes—almond
tarts with raspberry cream at the bottom. But no one asked
her to sit, and all of a sudden, she was the only one in this
dark den who was still standing. It was a cave in the middle
of the Bronx, with images of some medieval prince on the
wall. He had a handlebar mustache, bushy eyebrows, and long
curly hair; he wore a kind of skullcap, an embroidered jacket,
and sticking out of his cummerbund was a knife encrusted
with jewels. He was, she would learn, Lekë Dukagjini, a

fifteenth-century mountain prince who fought against the Turks and instituted his own highland code that governed tribal warfare; in this code, women could govern as well as men, and there were many "virgin warriors" among the Dukagjinis, women who fought and dressed as mountain men. A popular myth was that all Albanians were descended from this one warrior-prince, who watered the highland lakes and many a mountain woman with his sperm and his blood; he lost his limbs in battle, dispatched ten thousand Turks. And the current prince of Bathgate Avenue was named after this ferocious man, as one of his lieutenants explained while she sipped her tea.

Lord Lekë was responsible for the welfare of every single Albanian in the Bronx. Daughters could not be married without his consent. Old men would come to him at any hour in fits of depression. Their lord would heal them with a bear hug and a hot glass of tea. He would appear at births and deaths, but he himself had fathered no one, did not have a child. And that is why his minions were so curious about the woman next to his cowboy boots. Was their *baba* in love?

She bowed to him. "You must not harm my fiancé. How has he wronged you?"

"He exists," said Lord Lekë. "That is enough of a wound. He blocks my avenue, Mamzelle."

"And what avenue could that be?" Angela asked like a counselor-at-law.

"My avenue from me to you."

But she outsmarted this Bronx mountain bandit. She meant to murder him in front of all his minions—with a cat lady's kiss.

"You are mistaken, my lord. He hasn't blocked this avenue at all. Haven't I come to your club?"

"To plead for his life."

"Not at all," she said, and she could feel her whiskers growing. "Would my lord care for a kiss?"

But she didn't understand Bronx mountain lore. No woman, descended from the Dukagjinis or not, could demand a kiss from Lord Lekë, the *baba* of the Bronx. It was Lekë's right to appear in a woman's bedroom and ravish her, even with a husband at her side—it brought luck and long life to copulate with their lord, and husbands often delivered their own wives to Lord Lekë, but he wouldn't ravish them. He kissed them on the forehead and sent them home.

The lord's minions surrounded Angela with a menacing air. Lekë rose off his pillow to rant at them.

"Brothers, you will insult your king if you hurt this lady. She is a Latina. She does not understand our ways … you must escort her home."

He collapsed onto his pillow and closed his eyes. Meanwhile, a horde of men and women accompanied her to Arthur Avenue like some miraculous honor guard.

***

She couldn't even find her balding knight. He vanished from St. Barnabas, left a note, and a thousand dollars in crisp new bills.

Angela, I have a very small future here.
Your loving friend, Robertson

She wouldn't return to that madcap social club with all its riddles. She waited until Lord Lekë appeared at Dominick's with his clan. And while he sampled the pasta dishes with a look of ravishment, she went up to him and tossed the thousand dollars into his eyes. The rapture was gone, but he would allow none of his minions to rise from the table.

"What is my crime, Miss Angela?"

"You sent my man away and had him throw silver into my eyes—a thousand dollars."

"I did no such thing," said this lord of the Albanians. "I invited your fiancé to leave. I paid him, yes, but it wasn't blood money or a bribe. And it was much, much more than a thousand. He swindled you, I think. Mine was an honest proposal. I could break his leg, or he could have a monthly stipend from me. He took the stipend. Sit down. Join us at the table and my men will worship you forever. You'll be our queen."

Angela was trembling now. "Keep away from me or I'll rip your heart out."

Lord Lekë began to laugh. "Children, she has fire … don't bring me heiresses or lady bankers. My heart is locked. I will have no one but her as my bride, or I'll never marry."

She had never seen such imbecilic stubbornness, except in her father. She considered moving away from Arthur Avenue, abandoning the Bronx. This lord wouldn't have much sway outside the borough. Manhattan wasn't so fond of Albanians, who couldn't seem to flourish without the hills and highlands of the Bronx. But why should she run away? She'd lived here all her life, except for her own hard time in the prison farm. Her mother had been the janitor at an apartment house on Crescent Avenue before she went mad. The landlord had given them a ground-floor apartment in that building. The neighborhood had adopted little Angela. She'd worked behind the provolone stand at the Arthur Avenue indoor market when she was twelve, loved to watch the cigar makers, the widows with their littler stash of stationery or their pots and pans. She remembered the chicken slaughterer who used to be at the end of the block with feathers and squirts of blood in the window. Her Papi would earn a few dollars wringing the chickens' necks. And he could never rid himself of the chicken scales on his hands, or that horrendous smell of death.

He still had that smell, years after the chicken slaughterer vanished from Arthur Avenue. He sat in their small apartment like a man whose own madness had set him on fire but who didn't have enough substance to really burn—one day, he would shrivel up and shrink into the atmosphere, shoes and all. But when she returned home after her trip to Bathgate Avenue, Papi wasn't there. Neither was the furniture, nor Angela's narrow bed. The apartment could have been swept clean by locusts.

Had the landlord reclaimed the apartment after all these

years? But where the hell was Papi? And then the landlord appeared with a nervous grin. He couldn't even look into Angela's eyes. He'd rented the apartment to a plumber and moved Angela upstairs to the fifth floor. He wouldn't even raise her rent.

So she climbed to the fifth floor, and there was Papi sitting like a potentate. The new apartment looked out onto the red behemoth of St. Barnabas and the jagged landscape of the Bronx, cut in half by an expressway, which had turned everything around it into a vast moonscape of flattened warehouses and empty lots. She had been born after the expressway was built, and that's why she clung to the little oasis of Arthur Avenue, which was just beyond that moonscape and did not preside over its ruin.

But Angela wasn't a Bronx moocow. She was clever enough to know who the landlord's "plumber" was—Lord Lekë. He hadn't bought the apartment house, which belonged to the little kingdom of Arthur Avenue. He'd finessed the Italian chieftains by renting Angela's apartment at a million times what it was worth, she imagined, and thus allowing the landlord to "lend" his prize apartment near the roof to a scruffy old man with his dyke of a daughter.

She couldn't ask the landlord to give her back the apartment on the ground floor. She'd never even had a lease. Angela was caught in some kind of crazy wind. It was like the chess pieces that the Albanians tossed into the air. No one knew where the pawns and knights would land.

The wild man left begonias outside her door—begonias, bracelets, and diamond rings. She couldn't accept such gifts. It would have meant that she belonged to Lekë, even if he hadn't come to claim her. She didn't have the slightest desire to return to Little Albania. So she scribbled a note to Lord Lekë and left it on his table at Dominick's.

My Lord, you must take back your presents.
I am not in love with you and never will be.

It didn't take long for the wild man to respond. Several

of the clan's wives appeared in headscarves, took Angela by the hand, and accompanied her to Lekë's stronghold, which wasn't even in Little Albania, but was on the Grand Concourse, near Fordham Road, in Latino territory. The cops held no sway here. The neighborhood was called Paradise Road, in honor of a nearby movie palace that had once been the crown jewel of the West Bronx, with an "atmospheric" indoor sky, filled with stars and wandering clouds. Angela was born a little too late, after the Loew's Paradise had been chopped into pieces, its ornate statues and staircases removed, and its immortal sky went dark, while Paradise Road itself was embroiled in a drug war. But the Albanians had pushed the drug lords aside, and even if Paradise Road wasn't part of Lekë's kingdom, the Latino warlords left him alone.

He occupied the penthouse of an Art Deco palace that local architects and builders had put up eighty years ago, when the Grand Concourse was the Bronx's own Jewish boulevard. A Concourse millionaire had lived in the penthouse. Lekë moved in after the millionaire fled to Palm Beach, and the Concourse grew into a wild land. Paradise Road had sharpshooters reigning from the roofs. The drug lords had put them there. But after a while the sharpshooters were bored to death and would pick off children and old men … until Lekë had them hurled off the roofs.

The building had an Albanian doorman, who signaled with his cell that Angela had arrived and rode upstairs with her in an elevator that had a silver ceiling. She was startled by the penthouse. It didn't have one image of Lekë's ancestors on the walls, no Dukagjini in fierce tribal dress with battleaxes and rivers of blood. Lekë himself didn't seem so fierce away from his clan. He greeted Angela in a silken robe.

"Lord, you must not send me diamond rings."

"And why not?" he asked in a softer voice, without so much gravel. "You're the one I intend to marry."

"I'll never marry you, sire, even if you have my father

thrown into the street."

"Ah," he said, "now I'll have that kiss you promised me in our gambling hall."

Her whiskers were sprouting again, but she felt sorry for this warrior-king who kept sending her diamonds, and she was in no mood to maul him.

"Sire, my kisses could be fatal."

He pulled her close to him. She could smell the wild man's perfume. Angela herself began to feel strange and confused, even a little dizzy. She could hear Lekë's heart beat under his silk robe. She started to growl. The wild man rubbed against her. Her tongue darted into his mouth. His robe loosened. The lord of all the Albanians in the Bronx had a clit.

* * *

They were married within a month, not at a chapel, but in the cave on Bathgate Avenue. Angela's Papi was there, and so were members of the Neapolitan social club and the Latino lord of Paradise Road. Angela was dressed in white. She'd invited a few of her sisters from the farm who had come to the wedding on a weekend pass. These sisters were startled to see *their* cat lady as a bride. How could they have known that this blond assassin and warlord was sometimes a lady and sometimes a man? He'd been wearing men's clothes ever since he was five. Lekë had come to America at fifteen, took over Little Albania before he was twenty. None of his subjects suspected he wasn't always a man, though Albania had a long history of hunters and kings who went into battle smeared with their own menstrual blood.

Lekë was often filled with gloom. That's why he gravitated to the Grand Concourse. He could sport around as a woman or a man in his penthouse along Paradise Road. And he could also sport with his bride. He'd been in love with Angela from the moment he saw her in the Italian market with that sad, beautiful face and lithe body of a jailbird, and he would have destroyed a whole army of Robertsons to have her.

She couldn't always tell whether she was making love to a woman or a man—Lord Lekë was both. He wasn't like Angela's muscle-bound sisters at the farm, whose lust was limited to conquering all the new "chickens." Lekë was always gentle with her, and it was the gentleness of a man. Angela was now queen of all the Dukagjinis, who doted on her and waited for a male heir.

She'd never been happy, not once in her life, until the king claimed her as his bride. But it was Lekë who seemed forlorn.

"I'd like to throw it over," he said. "This pathetic charade of kingliness ... all my little lords with their male jokes. I'd love to crush their skulls. I promise you I'll go to my next meet wearing a dress."

"Lekë darling, you've never worn a dress in your life."

He came down off his hill one afternoon and was seen wearing lipstick and a scowl while he sat with his lieutenants. What could he have said to these young, ambitious hunters of his clan? Did he have to remind them that the Dukagjinis had had other women warriors? Did they all laugh and toss little wooden knights into the air?

He survived until the next afternoon. While Angela was out walking with a bodyguard, his own hunters threw him off the terrace. They buried him at Woodlawn, traveling in a long procession to their own family plot, but without Angela, who was no longer recognized as their queen. They removed all her clothes from the penthouse. She returned to Papi's fifth-floor apartment on Crescent Avenue. He didn't even say a word, just looked at her with his bloodshot eyes and howled once. It could have been the sound of her own heart. Her cash ran out after a month and she had to go back to work at the Italian market. It was almost as if she'd never been gone, as if she'd dreamt of that warrior-king from Little Albania, so near to Arthur Avenue and so far away.

The Cat Lady's Kiss

On Comedy
Gerald Stern

I've been thinking about comedy, and comics, for years now, partly for their own sake and partly for the connection there is with "tragedy," and partly the connection, or the *presence*, in the artist, of course, particularly in poetry. Gilbert hates poems that are "funny," yet there's a comic element in his poetry, maybe or maybe not intentional, and my friend Collins, who writes comic, even funny, poems doesn't make me guffaw too much: it's the wistful melancholic and lonely I like in his poetry. There are some standard texts on the subject, beginning with a Neanderthal joke that made the Cro-Magnons pull their long hair and moan, and there's Aristotle and a few others. Naturally, it's got to do with anger and bitterness. And in my case, how I went almost unthinking, plunging ahead into any thorns and brambles that lay in my way. And of course sometimes bled sometimes. And didn't *prepare*. And didn't *care*. Though I was overly sensitive really—and subject to hurt feelings. And did this truly from the very beginning; until it became such a habit—more than a habit, a way of being, call it loose, improvisational, tentative, capricious, stubborn, attentive, secret, or very secret. And how you take up comedy or the comic, as a way of getting even—at least sometimes. And how you're getting even with yourself, at least at first, for being a prig; for not having the courage; for being Matthew Arnold; for not being Thomas Hardy; for having a tight pen: for being too interested in beauty: and then later for choking on a fish bone: for changing partners while dancing; for lining your dresser drawers with envy; for reading the 1950s newspapers; for not forgiving; for one foot being longer than the other; for letting people die; for letting them die too soon;

for being silent for twelve years; for not reading fourteen books; for not reading them over and over.

For the comic is a way of sticking your hand in someone's mouth, or pulling your own teeth with pliers. Or being merciless, or keeping your distance and getting even. Tit for tit. Being bewildered. Being low-down. Bullying back. Cruelty really. Lack of respect. For every day is Karneval, and every wife is exhausted. And Karneval is such that you can spit in anyone's eye, you can break a window—or open it in the snow—or jump on top of a car roof, or shoot an arrow into the sofa, or bark at a dog or kiss the cleaning woman or kiss the bus driver or sing in Yiddish, for example, in a French restaurant, or imitate a cripple, you who are now one of them.

Spit is important here. Though spitting in a king's eye is really a metaphor. No one spits in a king's eye. For one thing an eye is hard to find, and spit is mostly not a clear stream. Just throwing a shoe gets you beat half to death. Karneval is a temporary disruption of the rules, behavior that would get you thrown into jail or drowned, say, or starved or beaten with nail-studded clubs, preferably 2 by 4s. For subversion is only temporary and may be just a letting off of steam. And the police are watching, and they are looking at their clocks. And either Karneval (A) helps to create a kind of permanent farcical and rebellious attitude among the less powerful and the powerless or (B) it is a way of reconciling people to their more typical roles, and letting them go back to the office or factory more content, even happier, because of those small moments. Maybe even too obvious to have to say. And, of course, sexual freedom, subversion, masks, liberties, reminiscent of the one or two days or weeks—of freedom and choice—for women in earlier cultures, where horns were tolerated, nay, encouraged, and the husband smiled blandly and slept a little on the train ride home holding his wild wife's hand.

Though I'm moving to the left—(A)—even as I unite, for I do think the subversion—and the inversion—and the spit in the eye may be worth something more permanent, may have a lasting and substantial effect, may help build up true resistance almost to the point that the corporations and the governments and the churches, of whatever color, may begin to feel uneasy and may finally openly limit freedoms and privileges if there is too much orneriness and horniness displayed. I may have to read Rabelais again—I *will* read him, but my main point is that the comic, the comedian, is at, is in, a permanent Karneval, a disruptive, disastrous state at least in his mind and his heart if not also in his appurtenances, his clothes, his nose, his rose.

My father was the absolute embodiment of obedience. He got a haircut every ten days, he put on a different suit and a fresh starched shirt every morning and in forty-five years, he never missed one day of work. But one Sunday he, my mother, and I went to a cousin's wedding—at the Schenley Hotel—and he drank a bit there and on the way home, backing out of a parking space, he hit a pole behind us and then a fire-plug in front and, rather liking it, went back and forth, from pole to plug, deliberately smashing up his shiny Pontiac, my mother screaming "Harry, Harry," my father laughing like a mad man. When he got home, he dropped his pants and fell into bed. He was wild, subversive, for one hour—and it cost him hundreds. He lived with his older sisters as a boy and was a kind of orphan who had to be good. He was a loving man, embarrassed by "misbehavior." And long hair.

The comedian doesn't seem to get embarrassed. But who knows what his sleep is like—or his dreams. His *going* to sleep. The brim of his hat is always too small and his pants too large. His shoes are a crazy color. If his culture, his country, is terrified of sex, he makes sexual jokes; if it is terrified of government, he makes political jokes. He—she—corrects our lies, our self-deceit. She forces us to laugh at our false behavior. She constantly reminds us that we are animals and have animal functions, which we constantly deny.

I am in Leipzig, Johann Sebastian Bach's city, for the

Leipzig Book Fair. It is the 325th year of his birth, so they're certainly going to do something special to celebrate the occasion. I remember his 300th and how we celebrated it in Philadelphia in 1985. In a restaurant last night after my reading, there were little white clay busts of Bach in a display case, but I didn't see anyone buying them. The restaurant was folk-style—the waitresses were dressed in colorful Bavarian costumes, but the mood wasn't festive since it was late and they were tired. We ate, I'm ashamed to say, Sauerbraten, some kind of potato dumpling, and some tasteless skinny carrots. I thought of apfel strudel, but I resisted. The "country bread" was good though. A few meters away was the bronze bust of the founder of the restaurant. I remember he was born in 1853 and died in 1927. There wasn't a small sledge hammer around to wound him or change his shape. Before my reading—German and English, with my translator Thomas Pletzinger and my editor Hans Koch—I talked to the audience and asked them about the comic auf Deutschland, but they were loath to speak or embarrassed or just stupid. It reminded me of classes I had in my early years, pulling teeth, as we say in Lenni Lenape. I talked about Jewish comedians and African American and Irish. I was interested in the German but they didn't have one word to say. Hans suggested that *Schadenfreude* was the typical German humor, a sort of laughing at someone else's pain, and he gave me, as an example, German soldaten making Jews use tooth brushes dipped in soapy water to clean sidewalks and streets. Laughing. Hans is eternally furious at the fucking Nazis. I remember some German films from the Weimar, and I think the comedians were good, anti-pompous, Germanicus-reversus. Satire a la Jon Stewart seems to be in now, but the audience is small. A lovely, brilliant, debut novelist who had been sitting at a nearby table and came over to talk to me had some interesting things to say about the confluence of comedy and tragedy with references to Carol Burnett—but I may have had too much wine.

I read "Roses" at my reading and told the audience—as

I always do when I read that poem—how roses are named after famous people, artists, movie-stars, millionaires, and I don't know any longer which of the ones I made up, and when I talked about rose bushes, I naturally recalled a certain prick and liar who inhabited the White House for eight ridiculous years and how you should piss on Bushes and how unfortunate it is that women can't, given the nature of the genitals, though a young woman from the U. S. Embassy later told me she *had* pissed on rose bushes and how that laden stream was actually good for the Bush. When I talked about Chancellor Merkel pissing, no-one seemed to object, but I was kind to the Nazi Pope and didn't talk about the dress he wears—or how *he* pisses. I gave five readings over a period of ten days in Berlin, Hamburg, Köln, and Leipzig. I had amazing audiences, intelligent, attentive, and sympathetic. Leipzig was a slight exception. In one place, Köln, they hired an actor to read my poems in German. This made me nervous, but he turned out to be a terrific guy—and he looked like Larry David, speaking of funny. We went late at night to the chocolate factory overlooking the Rhine to eat and drink. I sang Heine's song there—to universal applause. (Ruhig fliesset der Rhine.) (In abend Sonnenschein.) My only objection—reservation—about Deutschland is that they treated me with too much respect, even reverence. Partly because of my age, partly because I was a Jew, partly because of the poems. I don't think I was ever applauded as long as I was in both Hamburg and Köln. I was embarrassed. And in Köln, they lined up all the way to the door to buy books and talk to me. What if the dumb French and British would have stopped Hitler's army, carrying wooden guns, in 1936 in the Ruhr? What if *that* were the Final Solution? And Chamberlain—let it rain boiling water on him and his umbrella forever, the wet street he lives on in Hell! Can there be no comedy after the Holocaust? There can *only* be comedy. Chaplin was a bit sentimental in *The Great Dictator*, but he knew where—and how—to focus. He and Jack Oakie. Though he ended up preaching, didn't he? What could he do after the Kamps were discovered? Preaching is always the secret problem for comics. Thank God they only hurl *numbers* at each other—and check their bibles at the door. Depending on how it was told, certain numbers kill them. They scream with joy over no. 17.

It's too exhausting, let alone meaningless, to compare the two kinds of Mongolian humor and how the political border between them did and did not matter or to compare Averroes with Avicenna. And Bob Hope with the Marx Brothers. Kant himself listened to frog song and condemned the cutting up of pouches, not to mention Henri Bergson and Arthur Koestler, a champion of collision. The Buddha laughs mostly at himself, as Yahweh must, who lost his footing. The historically powerless, including peasants, Kurds, blacks, women, poor people, and immigrant Jews have a lot to say—a lot of it ironic—when they are allowed to say it. The low-residency MFA program in comedy teaches surprise, scatology, ridicule, slapstick, incongruity, conflict, repetitiveness, sudden glory, the unexpected, satire, hat attire, parody, paradox, as well as screwball, blueball, and taboo. Love is called tripping on the mons and ends up with both of them soaking their feet in hot water. In a shiksel, as my grandmother used to say as she rubbed the welts. In the South, there was race humor. Also in the North. The Odyssey is a Comedy.

Just think of Tiger Woods. It wouldn't be quite so funny if there wasn't a Bill Clinton before. One is a parody of the other. The fall of two giants is not a tragedy because of what they bumped into. A blow job and a car window broken by a golf club are just not tragic. Among other things, it's the boring sport itself, especially the holes. I'm not sure what a birdie is, but Woods is. Hèlas, Gatorade will probably drop him. Maybe he can endorse Trojans. The best idea since turning ketchup bottles upside down. Corporate America, be brave! Ah, Monica.

Some expert on the subject will theorize on burlesque, clowns, and the like. I like to think about American humor and how it was—is—embodied in the culture. Twain is obvious, but Melville—in his later self-conscious work, is a comedian. *Moby Dick* is itself a comedy, but the *Confidence Man* is supreme comedy on many levels, except perhaps the ending. Although he didn't know that it would later be McCarthy the drunk and Palin the idiot in the hold of the ship, not Uncle Sam—or whatever his name was at the time. Brother Jonathan. In one sly way or other American humor is "truth-telling," though I guess all humor finally is. God, we live so much on falsehood that humor—for us—is supreme relief. But it's fractured here and multi-faced; who can believe that the same country that invented the reticent sly Yankee also would produce the Three Stooges? And Bert Williams. There is a deep connection between the grand rupture of the second decade of the 20th —including film, radio, automobiles, and urbanization—and the entrance of European, especially Jewish, comedy. (How you gonna keep them down on the farm ...)

I'm so interested in this because I see comedy as the most human of all enterprises and because of its unexpected, almost magical nature. I want to even say mystical, but that's a weird word to use for the Marx Brothers, those priests of the 1930s. Also because I'm a kind of comedian in my life and because I celebrate, well, *activate*—the comic in my work, my writing. I'm interested, in particular, how my "later" poems are more comic than my "early." And I'm not speaking of funny poems or light verse, or wit or cuteness or puns as such, though those things may be used. Norton is about to publish my *Early Collected*, and I'm delighted by how those poems—from 1965 to 1992—hold up. But by and large they were not comic in the sense I'm using the word. *I* was comic, but my poems generally weren't. Unless the whole mad act of writing poetry, organizing words rhythmically on the page and scratching your head with a pencil, is itself comic. Chaucer is comic and Burns and early Donne and Byron. And Blake, Nietzsche, Balzac, Rimbaud, Auden, Cervantes, Villon, and Rabelais. I should probably say comedic. Dante of course called his great work a 'comedy,' but that's something else. I believe what we call comic and what we call 'tragic' have the exact same roots, no matter what Aristotle says. So do others. It is possible that what we do now, for various reasons, can *only* be comic. Some writers are salted such that every word is comic, every effort. Now we are at last talking about Kafka as comic. Maybe he was so in even a narrow sense. When he read the *Metamorphosis* to Max Brod, they both fell off their chairs laughing. Hans Koch (my German editor) used to visit Brod's widow every summer in Tel Aviv, and she had stories about K. Though God, I'm serious when I'm comic. And, truthfully, I don't even smile when I scratch around in my notebooks. And if there is one thing I *hate*, it's when someone, after a reading, tells me I'm a stand-up comedian. Yes, it's true—I'm a great performer. But look at the God-damned poems and understand the *package*. Nor is it only tourettes, which every clown, comedian, slack-rope walker and baseball player has. Nor is it only fear—or anger. You know what it is? Clarity. Clarity on the highest level. *Klarheit*. Musicians and painters understand it more than poets. My examples? "The Shirt Poem," "Soap," "God of Rain, God of Water," from *Early*. "Lilies," "Roses," "Standing Up," "Spanglish," "Fleur," "Dumbbells," "Mars," "My Dear" from *Later* (no single book yet). "The Preacher," written in 2007, a 27 page "take-off" on *Ecclesiastes*, is a comic (and deadly serious) celebration of the hole in the universe, whatever that is; and "I," only just published on-line, is a 35-page version and a weeping mockery of *Isaiah*, or "The Isaiahs," as seen across the street from an abandoned synagogue on 30th Street (in NY) inside a Greek diner. The poems are on two levels. One, they are actually *humorous*—at least in part—as the result of language, subject, pacing, or rhyme; and two, they are deeply serious yet comedic at the same time, as the result of language and emotion. The interconnection.

Jewish comedians I love and hate. Lenny Bruce, of course, but I'm mostly irritated now by Woody Allen. I love Mel Brooks, his heart, his mind. I'm not very fond of the Nouveau Assimilated, but I deeply admire Jon Stewart's intelligence and humanity (though for a stand-up, he mostly sits down) and—I'm sorry—I like Lewis Black, his mayhem, his nervous patter, his loud voice, his tough social observation, his craziness. I think it is good news—and healthy—that Jewish humor still persists; we haven't lost our memory altogether. I haven't kept up with Jewish comedy in Holland and Switzerland. I *do* like the idea of a Norwegian Jew talking to polar bears. Before he's eaten.

As grace would have it, I turned on the television last night to a Marx Brothers extravaganza—a better word—for them—than "festival." There were four films—I could have watched till 3 am, but I got tired. Everything in the way of irreverence, mockery, bathos, the ridiculing of institutions, word-play, hi-jinks, disrespect, craziness, anti-authoritarianism, and affection was there. But it was, to my eyes, gentle. There must be some connection with Talmud and Midrash, the passion for words—for talk—(though Harpo, if noisy, is silent); and there is pride, revenge, and absurdity, shtetl staples; and there is brilliance—much respected—and irony; and victory. It's called "over-the-top" now, isn't it? Is that a term from trench warfare? Does trench warfare account for earthiness (of course), one-liners, extravagance, and speed? (I could prove it!) The Jewish comedians helped Jews assimilate, but they didn't prevent FDR from turning the half-dead away. Speaking of trench warfare, I'll tell a joke from World War I—in English. Two short guys heed Uncle Sam's plea, join up, go through basic, take a train to New York, board a ship (amidst waving handkerchiefs), arrive in France (more hankies), are sent to the front, a whistle blows, they climb up the ladder and start to charge towards the Germans; bombs are bursting, people are falling, and one of them turns around and runs back. "Where you going, Jake?" "You can get killed here," he says. (Terrible in Hebrew.)

There is nothing more clear than convoluted reasoning.

The Babylonians, who spoke Aramaic, called it *pilpul*. It originally meant to spice or season, but came to mean "to dispute violently." The Babylonian comedians actually fought each other on the stage with sticks. Only later did they resort to words, which were more violent and hurt more. Ragos' Auction House here in Lambertville has some Babylonian items in its catalog, and among them are "comedian's sticks" with a number, a proposed price, and, of course, an image. If the bid is not too high, I'll buy them and put them in my umbrella stand next to my basket of softballs and my plaster-of-Paris pig. I'll either beat Billy Collins or Tony Hoagland, whoever comes first to visit.

I got a book in the mail today—for everything comes on time, as Rambam says—called *Seriously Funny*, an anthology that contains my poem, "Grapefruit," written in 1985 or 6. It's, as it says, a book of poems that are funny. Yet *serious*. I'm happy to be in the book and I'm grateful to the editors, but I never thought of "Grapefruit" as a comic poem, though when I read it now—from a stranger's point of view—I see that it truly is, full as it is of mockery, false holiness, bluntness, earthiness, and weird presence. But I never *presented* it as "funny"; it's as if the subject—and the language—came from the lips of a possessed one who had no idea people might be amused—or shocked. I have other poems whose intent was comic, but that's different. And, I say to the dear editors, one of whom I smoked pot with in Dublin a few years ago—under a tree—that he, that they, should have included at least nine other poems of mine along with their own "favorites." Love to them both. The real secret of comedy—not only Jewish—is higher and lower co-mingling, co-mocking, confusion, man and God, Yiddish and Hebrew, Alabama and Harlem, light and heavy, the exalted, the workaday. Literature, the higher art, can have a comic impulse, but the stakes are different. It's interesting that Samuel Clemens was a lecturer, a stand-up, as well as an exquisite writer. Maybe the poets, some of the poets, can have sticky feet on both branches. Maybe it's mostly my own feet I'm writing about, trying to stay upright in the branches. Being very close and very far away at the same time.

This is what happened on the 300th anniversary of J. S. Bach's birthday—in Philadelphia. I was living in Iowa City, Iowa, and had a house in Easton, P. A. I was sitting in my office when I got a phone call from Steve Berg, the editor of *APR*. I would be getting a call (he said) in a minute from a retired banker (in charge of culture at the Mellon Bank) asking me to write a poem about Bach and read it— in Philadelphia at an Episcopalian church. The price was a thousand, Steve said. When the banker called I squeezed another thou' out of him—for the reading itself—plus expenses. It was 1985. I labored at the dumb poem for weeks, trying to tone it down, calling Berg endlessly for advice. When I was through, I hated it, and as fury would have it, when Diane Freund and I drove down the river from Easton (where I had a house) to Philadelphia and stopped in Frenchtown, New Jersey, for breakfast, there was my poem on the front page of the *Philadelphia Inquirer*. I helped re-name an alley Johann Sebastian Bach Way, we had lunch with the cultured banker, I read the poem that evening, along with some organ music, and I was interviewed the next day by Terri Gross on *Fresh Air*.

She wanted to talk about Bach, but I preferred talking about the bombing of the MOVE Compound—a weird African American urban cult—and Mayer Goode's role— getting a "device" from the F.B.I., confronting MOVE leaders, etc. Goode was a technocrat and thought the world was mathematical. I called him Mayer Bad, to Terry Gross's horror (since money for the station came from the city of Philadelphia), and talked about how information was handled in America and what *our* forms of censorship were, (partial, almost hidden). Terry was upset, for poor Bach was being ignored, but I thought it was more important to discuss the official view of a crazy, quasi-religious, school-denying, garbage flinging cult, everyone with the last name of "Africa" who were called "terrorists" and murdered, because they were noisy and disobedient; and because of the horde of weapons they supposedly had, that turned out to be one revolver and one shotgun. Hardly enough for one ten-year old truck in southern Georgia. Nor did the *Inquirer* print this information, but a small group Mayor Bad had appointed—priests, social workers, and the like—wrote a report which you had to go to an obscure vault in the main library to obtain. I have a copy of the report; the Philadelphia Library probably hasn't destroyed all the copies. Six children died. And I have never been invited back to *Fresh Air*.

It's bizarre, except for the murders. I called Goode Nero and said he fiddled while Philadelphia burned. The compound actually *did* burn as a result of the "device." My question—of myself—is why I did it, why I did my radio act and what was I doing. Certainly, it's for clarity and justice, *that* vengeance. But it's also for the shock, the victory, the last laugh, the last word, the power, the revelation. I'm not altogether happy about it. I don't like balancing in the foliage on my two sticky limbs singing songs of righteousness. I don't know if the beautiful note, the *vibration*, is not itself too much of a motive or cause. One that Aristotle missed. I organized the biggest march in Pennsylvania (in Indiana, P. A.) to mourn the ungodly death of the three civil rights workers (The Mississippi Three) on a certain Monday, but I did it off-handedly and for my friend Mary Vowels, who was blocked by her evasive, high-class Presbyterian priest, by manipulating the state police, the University authorities, the radio stations, and the fundamentalist churches. Easy work; culminating in a crowd of maybe 15,000 in front of the county court house (second telling), the provost, the deans, the professors, the mayor, the students, the townspeople, a microphone, prayers, speeches and a lovely African-American contralto singing, on the courthouse steps, and a banner headline in the *Indiana Gazette* stating "We Shall Overcome: A New Song for Indiana," in a de-facto segregated city. But if I believed—fervently—my feet were still sticky. And I roared in private. For I was doing two things.

And so it was the two times I was almost denied tenure and refused to be noble, or a gentleman, and "organized" the students—successfully—especially in one institution where the entire student body assembled in the parking lot (1970-71) until the president of the college, rosy-cheeked and starched, sent his assistant out to invite me into his office and gave me my letter of intent. And so it was at the table where I fought for the faculty, sang songs in French and Yiddish and signed agreements, once on a paper napkin at the counter of a diner, once at the Marlboro-Blenheim in Atlantic City before it was blown up, for Trump's sake, outmaneuvering the college negotiators who were later fired; once in secret—playing pool and eating steak at the home of the administration's new negotiator; and so it was when I helped integrate a swimming pool and was the only (white) man permanently barred from the pool. Sticky-footed and roaring. Nothing to brag about. I was more clown than statesman. I was my own kind of Yippee. A minor unknown yippee.

My question is, does it connect with the poetry in anyway? My answer is I am laboring excessively. But as both God and Popeye said: "I yam what I yam." When I started, I was an aesthete—I separated poetry from the rest; but I came finally to include every wart and pimple, or at least most of the warts and pimples. That's what poetry should do—as it does other things. Though so doing (warts and pimples) is not itself what poetry is about. And anyhow, who knows? For one thing, you're different when you're older than you were when you weren't older, and anyhow, mankind cannot bear very much reality, as Sarah Silverman says, or said. Which reminds me somehow of the gathering of Jewish poets in Boston a couple of decades ago. We were standing in an anteroom, and the rabbi in charge, after lecturing us, asked us if we had any questions. I said, "When do we get paid?" And he accused me of anti-Semitism. We were all staying at the Worst-Western or a Qualityless Inn, which featured a large mirror against the wall, beside the bed, which more or less doubled the size of the room. At the time, I couldn't see too well, though now I have 20-20. I woke up in the half dark and had the uneasy feeling that someone else was in the bed with me, but I couldn't remember where or when. I looked at him—it was a him—waved and said, "How ya doin'?" He waved at the very same time and said the very same thing, but it took me a long 20 or 30 seconds to figure it out. After that, I must admit, I spent a good half hour exchanging pleasantries. I must confess I kissed him—or he kissed me. That shadow.

But it's 2010 now and stand-up has become a plague. Idiots of every stripe performing on "Comedy Stupid." Expressing their deep feelings—about tooth paste; or someone has written a piece for them about mouthwash or erectile lochson. And, of course, it's disgusting. *De rigueur.* And the audience is laughing and clapping and enlightened beyond measure. It's trivial humor, of no social or any other significance. Flippant, narcissistic, not funny. Both embarrassing and useless. Cognate, in part, with the other arts, but lacking even their attempts at the New Vulgar, without purpose, connected to nothing. One fool went on for 12 minutes—I timed him—about the weirdness of bathrobes. It could be a good subject, but he knew nothing about those robes and their history and how class was involved, and pretension, and central heating. He ended up making toilet jokes, what the idiots call "potty humor," something about the belt caught in the commode—but it was a one-liner—he couldn't *build* on it. If I were more Zen, I would have slapped him, but I didn't want to hurt Anne Marie's TV. I have enough trouble just turning it on.

Richard Pryor is perhaps the best comedian of the twentieth century. With due respect.

I think so, now that Zharkov has appeared, 490 years before his time. The key to Pryor's humor is that he speaks to black issues, and as a black man, but it—finally—is a *human* issue he's speaking to, so that white audiences as well as black can be moved by him; and, further, in so doing, the particulars of African American life, the *particulars*, become more and more familiar to the overriding white audience, nor does he have to drive the point home that we're "all one," he doesn't have to lecture, for that point, so to speak, takes care of itself. It turned out not to be so huge and overwhelming a problem as we might have thought it would be. Italian life, Jewish life have their particulars—language, culture, custom—but it is not appreciated only, or merely, by Italians and Jews. Even WASPs discovered that they had particulars and that they were WASP particulars, not the universal by which everything else is judged. And it was Pryor's own humanity, his life, his understanding, finally his huge heart, that made this possible. He went from short fuse in the beginning, to a kind of untransformed and raw tenderness at the end. He allowed pain, confusion, and suffering—his and everyone's—to be rendered literally (filtered, accompanied, by his comic genius). It's as if nobody had thought of it before. He was irreverent and emotional, a kind of expressionistic artist.

If he was shocking at first—even revolutionary—he was quickly accepted and, finally, revered. It was black street humor and satire; it was blasphemy; but it was always *personal* and absolutely honest. And it was hilarious. Nor was he the first to let the words just take over. Lenny Bruce—and others—had done it before, but not so completely. He himself was the character he created. There was no distinction. Style and substance integrated. He was difficult and disturbed, but what comic isn't—more than this one, less than that one.

What is amazing is that African American humor became mainstream. "Pride, self-mockery, blunt confrontation of reality, double-edged irony, satiric wit, assertive defiance, poetic obscenity, and verbal acuity"—Mel Watkin's words. In Pryor's case it was—in the end—deep sanity, and humanity. The comedian's gift. He will be remembered for that.

Bert Williams, Charlie Chaplin, Mel Brooks, W. C. Fields, Lenny Bruce, Groucho Marx, Harpo Marx, Buster Keaton, Stan Laurel, George Carlin, Jack Benny, Fred Allen, Richard Pryor, Chris Rock.

Roses

There was a rose called Guy de Maupassant,
a carmine pink that smelled like a Granny Smith
and there was another from the seventeenth century
that wept too much and wilted when you looked;
and one that caused tuberculosis, doctors
dug them up, they wore white masks and posted
warnings in the windows. One wet day
it started to hail and pellets the size of snowballs
fell on the roses. It's hard for me to look at
a Duchess of Windsor, it was worn by Franco
and Mussolini, it stabbed Jews; yesterday I bought
six roses from a Haitian on Lower Broadway;
he wrapped them in blue tissue paper, it was
starting to snow and both of us had on the wrong shoes,
though it was wind, he said, not snow that ruined
roses and all you had to do was hold them
against your chest. He had a ring on his pinky
the size of a grape and half his teeth were gone.
So I loved him and spoke to him in false Creole
for which he hugged me and enveloped me
in his camel hair coat with most of the buttons missing,
and we were brothers for life, we swore it in French.

—G. Stern

Grapefruit

I'm eating breakfast even if it means standing
in front of the sink and tearing at the grapefruit,
even if I'm leaning over to keep the juices
away from my chest and stomach and even if a spider
is hanging from my ear and a wild flea
is crawling down my leg. My window is wavy
and dirty. There is a wavy tree outside
with pitiful leaves in front of the rusty fence
and there is a patch of useless rhubarb, the leaves
bent over, the stalks too large and bitter for eating,
and there is some lettuce and spinach too old for picking
beside the rhubarb. This is the way the saints
ate, only they dug for thistles, the feel
of thorns in the throat it was a blessing, my pity
it knows no bounds. There is a thin tomato plant
inside a rolled-up piece of wire, the worms
are already there, the birds are bored. In time
I'll stand beside the rolled-up fence with tears
of gratitude in my eyes. I'll hold a puny
pinched tomato in my open hand,
I'll hold it to my lips. Blessed art Thou,
King of tomatoes, King of grapefruit. The thistle
must have juices, there must be a trick. I hate
to say it but I'm thinking if there is a saint
in our time what will he be, and what will he eat?
I hated rhubarb, all that stringy sweetness--
a fake applesauce--I hated spinach,
always with egg and vinegar, I hated
oranges when they were quartered, that was the signal
for castor oil--aside from the peeled navel
I love the Florida cut in two. I bend
my head forward, my chin is in the air,
I hold my right hand off to the side, the pinkie
is waving; I am back again at the sink;
oh loneliness, I stand at the sink, my garden

is dry and blooming, I love my lettuce, I love
my cornflowers, the sun is doing it all,
the sun and a little dirt and a little water.
I lie on the ground out there, there is one yard
between the house and the tree; I am more calm there
looking back at this window, looking up
a little at the sky, a blue passageway
with smears of white--and gray--a bird crossing
from berm to berm, from ditch to ditch, another one,
a wild highway, a wild skyway, a flock
of little ones to make me feel gay, they fly
down the thruway, I move my eyes back and forth
to see them appear and disappear, I stretch
my neck, a kind of exercise. Ah sky,
my breakfast is over, my lunch is over, the wind
has stopped, it is the hour of deepest thought.
Now I brood, I grimace, how quickly the day goes,
how full it is of sunshine, and wind, how many
smells there are, how gorgeous is the distant
sound of dogs, and engines--Blessed art Thou
Lord of the falling leaf, Lord of the rhubarb,
Lord of the roving cat, Lord of the cloud.
Blessed art Thou oh grapefruit King of the universe,
Blessed art Thou my sink, oh Blessed art Thou
Thou milkweed Queen of the sky, burster of seeds,
Who bringeth forth juice from the earth.

—G. Stern

Contributors to StoryQuarterly 44

Remy Braun lives in New York City, where she is pursuing a BA in storytelling.

Jerome Charyn lives in New York and Paris. His most recent novel is *The Secret Life of Emily Dickinson*. He is currently working on a novel about Abraham Lincoln. His study of Joe DiMaggio, *Joe DiMaggio: The Long Vigil*, will be published by Yale University Press in April 2011 in its American Icon series.

Kelly Cherry's most recent publications are *Girl in a Library: On Women Writers & the Writing Life* (BkMk) and *The Retreats of Thought: Poems* (L.S.U.). Boson Books will bring out her collection *The Woman Who: Stories* in 2010.

Moira Crone is the author of four books of fiction, most recently the collection *What Gets Into Us* (2007). Her works have appeared in over forty journals including *The New Yorker, Image, Mademoiselle*, and *Oxford American*. In 2009, she won the Robert Penn Warren Award for Fiction from the Southern Fellowship of Writers. She lives in New Orleans and "Do Over" is part of collection in progress, working title, *Reconstruction*, about the reconstitution of New Orleanians and their city since 2005. For many years, she directed the writing program at Louisiana State University

Frank Dineen has been a self-employed writer nearly all his working life, turning recently to fiction. His stories have been shortlisted for the UK-based Bridport Prize in 2008 and 2009, and longlisted for the Ireland's Fish Prize in 2010. He's also the author of a novel, *Immortal Longings*, and wrote and composed three produced musicals. In 2008, his song lyrics were featured at the Los Angeles Festival of New American Musicals. He holds an MS in Journalism from Northwestern University's Medill School.

Denise Gess was the author of two novels, *Good Deeds* and *Red Whiskey Blues* (both Crown) and co-author, with William Lutz, of the non-fiction book *Firestorm at Peshtigo* (Henry Holt, 2002). An essayist and short story writer, Denise was a contributing editor to *StoryQuarterly* and *Philadelphia Stories.* She taught at Rutgers University and was an Associate Professor of English at Rowan University. She lived in Philadelphia, Pennsylvania, until her death on August 22, 2009.

Mathew Goldberg's fiction has appeared in *Shenandoah, the Mississippi Review,* and *American Short Fiction,* among other journals. He earned an engineering degree from Duke University and an MFA from the University of Arkansas. He is currently a member of the English faculty at Missouri University of Science and Technology.

Tiffany Hawk is a former flight attendant and a writer whose essays have appeared in such publications as *The New York Times,* the *Los Angeles Times,* and *The Potomac Review.*

John Oliver Hodges lives in Flushing, New York. His short stories have appeared or will be appearing in *Cream City Review, Echo Ink Review, The Literary Review, Redivider,* and elsewhere.

Jane Hoppen currently resides in Brooklyn, NY, and has published fiction in various literary magazines, including *The Dirty Goat, PANK, Western Humanities Review, Forge Journal, Superstition Review, Room of One's Own,* and *Cantaraville.*

Kyle Lang is a native Oregonian who has written poetry,

fiction, and nonfiction. His work has appeared in *M Review* and *Going Down Swinging*.

Bill Lawrence is the author of the plays *Feed My Sheep*, *The Gatekeeper*, and *The Marmot Speaks*, which were produced regionally in Colorado and Los Angeles. His most recent play, *The Fighting Jardiniers*, was commissioned by St. Mary's College of Notre Dame, Indiana, and was produced at The Moreau Center for the Arts to celebrate the Feast Day of Father Basil Moreau. An original member of The Foundry Theatre Works-LA, he has had short work published in the *Creede Magazine* and *Static Movement*. He participated in workshopping Frank Pierson's *Ain't that America*, for the Sundance Screenwriters Lab and has been a guest artist for Pam Houston's summer writing workshops. He currently lives in Santa Monica, California.

Paul Lisicky is author of *Lawnboy, Famous Builder*, and two forthcoming books, *The Burning House* (2011) and *Unbuilt Projects* (2012). His work has appeared in *Ploughshares*, *The Iowa Review, Black Warrior Review, Gulf Coast, The Seattle Review, Prairie Schooner*, and many other magazines and anthologies. He has taught in the graduate writing programs at Cornell University, Rutgers - Newark, and Sarah Lawrence College. He currently teaches at NYU and in the low residency MFA Program at Fairfield University, and serves on the Writing Committee of the Fine Arts Work Center in Provincetown.

William Lutz is Emeritus Professor of English at Rutgers University. He was married to Denise Gess.

James Marcus is the author of *Amazonia: Five Years at the Epicenter of the Dot-Com Juggernaut* and six translations from the Italian, including works by Leonardo Sciscia, Goffredo Parise, and Oriana Fallaci. He has contributed to *The Atlantic Monthly, The Los Angeles Times Book Review, Salon, Newsday,*

The Atlantic Monthly, Lingua Franca, The Nation, and many other publications.

Staci Stokes Morgan teaches writing and literature at an international school in China and previously taught in New Orleans and Hawaii. She is at work on her first novel.

Eileen Mullane co-wrote and starred Off-Broadway in *Fess Up and Mull it Over* and has read and performed her stories, plays, and essays at such theaters as The Magnet and UCB in NYC, and The Groundlings Theater in Los Angeles. She recently completed her first screenplay, *Snake VS. Hawk,* and is at work on a book about parties (as in social gatherings). She lives in Topanga, California.

Bonnie Nadzam has published fiction and poetry in several journals. Her first novel, *Lamb,* is forthcoming from The Other Press.

David Naimon is a writer, naturopathic physician, acupuncturist, and host of the radio show Healthwatch in Portland, Oregon. His story, "The Golem of Orla Shalom," appeared in issue 84 of *ZYZZYVA.*

Kirk Nesset is author of two books of fiction, *Mr. Agreeable* and *Paradise Road,* as well as *The Stories of Raymond Carver* (nonfiction), *Saint X* (poems, forthcoming), and *Alphabet of the World: Selected Works by Eugenio Montejo* (translations, forthcoming). He was awarded the Drue Heinz Literature Prize in 2007 and has received a Pushcart Prize and grants from the Pennsylvania Council on the Arts. His work has appeared in *The Paris Review, Kenyon Review, Southern Review, American Poetry Review, Gettysburg Review, Ploughshares, Prairie Schooner,* and elsewhere. He teaches at Allegheny College.

Nicole Pearce holds an MFA from Vermont College of

Fine Arts. While there, her work was selected to represent the school in both the AWP Intro Journal Awards and the Best New American Voices for 2009. Her short fiction has also earned finalist status in three *Glimmer Train* fiction competitions. Most recently, her story, "Falling from Trees," made the top 25 in *Glimmer Train's* Very Short Fiction Award (February 2009). "Contents May Have Shifted" will be her first published story.

Adam Peterson lives in Houston where he co-edits The Cupboard, a prose chapbook series. His series of short-shorts, *My Untimely Death*, is available from Subito Press at the University of Colorado, and his fiction has recently appeared in *Alaska Quarterly Review, Cincinnati Review*, and *Indiana Review* among other journals.

Bethany R. Reece recently received her M.F.A. from Washington University in St. Louis. She was awarded a third year fellowship there, as well as having received several other fellowships for her writing over the years. She is currently (happily) mired in the production of several larger composite pieces and is employed at an elder and disability law firm in Denver, Colorado.

Kendra Langford Shaw grew up on an Alaskan island and a Montana ranch. She has a B.A. in creative writing from the University of Montana, and her fiction has previously appeared in *The Antioch Review*. She and her husband Johnathan live in Montana where Kendra is at work on a collection of short stories and a memoir about two years spent teaching English in Japan.

Vic Sizemore is a 2009 graduate of the MFA program in fiction at Seattle Pacific University. He has fiction published or forthcoming in *Connecticut Review, Southern Humanities Review, Portland Review* and elsewhere. He won the summer 2009 *New Millennium Writings* Award for fiction and was a finalist for the 2008-2009 Sherwood Anderson Award. He lives in Lynchburg, Virginia, with his wife and three children. He teaches writing at Central Virginia Community College. Sizemore is a former Marine who served in Operation Desert Shield/Desert Storm.

Gerald Stern is the author of 15 books of poetry, including, most recently, *Save the Last Dance* (Norton, 2008) and *Everything is Burning* (Norton, 2005), as well as *This Time: New and Selected Poems*, which won the 1998 National Book Award. The paperback of his personal essays titled *What I Can't Bear Losing* was published in the fall of 2009 by Trinity University Press. He was awarded the 2005 Wallace Stevens Award by the Academy of American Poets and is currently a Chancellor of the Academy of American Poets. He is retired from the University of Iowa Writers' Workshop. *Early Collected: Poems from 1965-1992* was published by W. W. Norton in the spring of 2010. "Comedy" is part twenty-one of his new manuscript in prose, titled *The Stillness After.*

Laura L. Sullivan has an English degree from Cornell University. Her novel *Under the Green Hill* will be published in Fall 2010 by Henry Holt Books for Young Readers with the sequel, *Guardian of the Green Hill*, following in 2011.

Frank Tavares is a writer and Professor of Communication at Southern Connecticut State University. His work has appeared in a variety of literary journals, including *Louisiana Literature, The Connecticut Review, GW Review*, and others. Listeners to NPR recognize his as the "Support-For-NPR-Comes-From-NPR-Member-Stations" voice heard at the end of national network news and information programs. Tavares also writes and consults about public broadcasting issues and is one of the founding editors of *The Journal of Radio and Audio Media.*

Eliza Victoria was born in 1986. Her fiction and poetry

has appeared or is forthcoming in various publications based in her native Philippines and abroad, including the *Philippines Graphic, Philippines Free Press, Philippine Speculative Fiction IV* and *V, Expanded Horizons, Cantaraville, elimae,* and *The Houston Literary Review.* In 2009, she received an award for her poetry collection *Reportage* from the Carlos Palanca Memorial Awards for Literature—considered the Philippines' most prestigious literary contest.

Jesse Waters was a winner of the 2001 River Styx International Poetry Contest. His fiction, poetry, and non-fiction work has appeared in such journals as *88: A Journal of Contemporary Poetry, The Adirondack Review, Coal Hill Review, The Cortland Review, Cimarron Review, Concrete Wolf, Iowa Review, Plainsongs, Magma, River Styx, Slide, Sycamore Review,* and others.

Marc Watkins is finishing his last semester at Texas State University's MFA Program, where he holds the W. Morgan and Lou Claire Rose Fellowship in Fiction. He has published several stories and won *Boulevard'*s "Short Fiction Contest for Emerging Writers." His first book, a novel set in the Ozarks, is nearing completion.